P9-DBL-781

The Lioness

Also by Chris Bohjalian

NOVELS

Hour of the Witch
The Red Lotus
The Flight Attendant
The Sleepwalker
The Guest Room
Close Your Eyes, Hold Hands
The Light in the Ruins
The Sandcastle Girls
The Night Strangers
Secrets of Eden
Skeletons at the Feast
The Double Bind
Before You Know Kindness
The Buffalo Soldier
Trans-Sister Radio
The Law of Similars
Midwives
Water Witches
Past the Bleachers
Hangman
A Killing in the Real World

ESSAY COLLECTIONS

Idyll Banter

STAGE PLAYS

Midwives
Wingspan (originally produced as *Grounded*)

Chris
Bohjalian

DOUBLEDAY   *New York*

THE
LIONESS

This is a work of fiction.
Names, characters, places, and incidents either are the product of
the author's imagination or are used fictitiously. Any resemblance to actual
persons, living or dead, events, or locales is entirely coincidental.

Copyright © 2022 by Quaker Village Books LLC

All rights reserved. Published in the United States by Doubleday,
a division of Penguin Random House LLC, New York, and distributed in
Canada by Penguin Random House Canada Limited, Toronto.

www.doubleday.com

DOUBLEDAY and the portrayal of an anchor with a dolphin are registered
trademarks of Penguin Random House LLC.

Book design by Maria Carella
Front-of-jacket photograph © Horst P. Horst/Condé Nast;
scratches © Garder Elena / Shutterstock; lion © Vasya Kobelev / Shutterstock
Jacket design by John Fontana

Library of Congress Cataloging-in-Publication Data
Names: Bohjalian, Chris, author.
Title: The lioness / Chris Bohjalian.
Description: First Edition. | New York : Doubleday, [2022]
Identifiers: LCCN 2021026598 (print) | LCCN 2021026599 (ebook) |
ISBN 9780385544825 (hardcover) | ISBN 9780525565970 (paperback) |
ISBN 9780385544832 (ebook)
Subjects: GSAFD: Suspense fiction. | Historical fiction.
Classification: LCC PS3552.O495 L56 2022 (print) | LCC PS3552.O495 (ebook) |
DDC 813/.54—dc23
LC record available at https://lccn.loc.gov/2021026598
LC ebook record available at https://lccn.loc.gov/2021026599

MANUFACTURED IN THE UNITED STATES OF AMERICA

1 3 5 7 9 10 8 6 4 2

First Edition

For my pod, literal and metaphoric, from 2020, the Year That
Satan Spawned, and the first half of 2021.

When I was hanging on by my fingernails, you gave me your hand.
You are my safari.

Grace Experience Blewer
Victoria Blewer
Julia Cox
Robert Cox
Todd Doughty
Andrew Furtsch
Joan Heaton
Jenny Jackson
Stephen Kiernan
Gerd Krahn
Laura Krahn
Brian Lipson
Khatchig Mouradian
Hawk Ostby
Monica Ostby
Lisa Goodyear-Prescott
Reed Prescott
Deborah Schneider
John Searles
Stephen Shore
Adam Turteltaub
and (yes)
Horton and Jesse

Everything I learned, I learned from the movies.

—AUDREY HEPBURN

If you want a happy ending, that depends, of course, on where you stop your story.

—ORSON WELLES

Registered Guest List

MARRIED COUPLES

David Hill: gallerist
Katie Barstow: actress

Billy Stepanov: psychologist and Katie Barstow's older
    brother
Margie Stepanov: homemaker

Felix Demeter: screenwriter
Carmen Tedesco: actress

SINGLE GUESTS

Terrance Dutton: actor
Reggie Stout: Katie Barstow's publicist
Peter Merrick: Katie Barstow's agent

Team Leaders

Charlie Patton: owner of Charles Patton Safari
    Adventures
Juma Sykes: head guide
Muema Kambona: second guide
Benjamin Kikwete: porter and guest liaison

The Lioness

Prologue

Oh, I can't speak for the dead. And I won't speak for the missing. I can only tell you what I think happened. Others—the dead and the missing—would probably have their own versions. Blame, I can tell you firsthand, is every bit as subjective as truth.

Of course, I am also confident that the missing will never be found: the Serengeti is vast and it's been years. Years. But Africa is changing. One never knows. Someday it's possible that some of their bones—a femur that is recognizably human or a skull that was clearly a woman's or a man's—will be spotted beside a dirt road where a jackal or hyena or magnificent lappet-faced vulture decades ago finished off what a leopard or lion didn't. Just think for a moment of the age of the fossils and remnants of ancient man that have been found a little south of where we were in the Olduvai Gorge. Mary Leakey began piecing together the Nutcracker Man only five years before we were there when she saw what looked like two teeth in a jaw. Nutcracker Man lived two million years ago. We went there and (most of us, anyway) died there in 1964.

So, perhaps a ranger will discover the bones while tracking a poacher. It could be just that ordinary.

But let's be clear. This story was never about Western, privileged tourists or local Maasai or Tanzanians. It was never about rich or poor, Americans or Africans. We were all just people, and most of us had no idea what was happening. We had no idea what to do. We made the best decisions we could, but think of who we were and where we were. The mantra for most of us? Just stay alive. See if, somehow, we might see the sun rise one more time.

Safari

Katie Barstow

Hollywood royalty gathered Saturday night at the Beverly Wilshire Hotel, where Katie Barstow wed Rodeo Drive gallerist David Hill. The two of them left afterward for Paris and then the wilds of Africa on a "safari." Rumor has it that the actress is bringing along an entourage into the jungle that will include her brother and sister-in-law, Billy and Margie Stepanov; her agent, Peter Merrick; her publicist, Reggie Stout; actress Carmen Tedesco and her husband, Felix Demeter; and Katie's friend and co-star in the still controversial Tender Madness, *Terrance Dutton. The little group has nicknamed themselves the Lions of Hollywood—though anyone who knows Katie Barstow or has seen her on the screen understands that she is the lioness in charge of this pride.*

—The Hollywood Reporter, NOVEMBER 9, 1964

She was watching the giraffes at the watering hole after breakfast, no longer as awed by their presence as she'd been even four days ago, when she'd first seen a great herd of them eating leaves from a copse of tall umbrella acacia, their heads occasionally bobbing up to stare back, unfazed and not especially alarmed by the humans. Their eyes were sweet. Their horns were the antennae on a child's extraterrestrial Halloween mask. The inscrutable creatures were wary of these humans, but they felt no need to flee.

They'd just finished breakfast and were still at their camp.

Her husband, David, was on her left, and her brother, Billy, was on her right. Both had their cameras out. Terrance was sitting nearby with his notebook on his knees, sketching the creatures. Katie had known that Terrance was as talented a visual artist as he was an actor—her husband loved his paintings—but she was still stunned by how quickly and how remarkably he was drawing the animals they saw. The eyes of his elephant had broken her heart. Earlier that autumn, when they were still in L.A., David had said it was only a matter of time before he could risk giving the man a show. ("He's a movie star," she told David when she heard the hesitation in his voice. "He's a Black movie star," David had reminded her, and while he was only acknowledging the backlash he might face from some quarters, she had still felt the need to remind him it was 1964, not 1864. His gallery's fiscal foundation couldn't possibly be so weak that it couldn't withstand blowback from racist critics and so-called connoisseurs.)

The group, all nine of them and their guides, were about to climb into the Land Rovers and start the drive to the next camp, a journey through the savanna that would take three hours if they didn't stop, but would, in fact, take seven or eight because they expected to pause often for the Serengeti's great menagerie of animals. You just never knew what you would see and where you might detour. Yesterday, they had been particularly lucky. They had witnessed the great wildebeest crossing at the Mara River: thousands of wildebeest and zebras storming down the sandy banks into the water and attempting to reach the grass on the other side.

There were five giraffes this morning, three with their legs splayed awkwardly as they stretched their long necks down to the water to drink. She felt a small pang of guilt that she was taking for granted her witness to their presence, animals over fifteen feet tall—their legs alone were taller than she was—with their cream-colored coats and those iconic tawny spots. She wondered at the way her mind was wandering instead to the differences between coincidence and synchronicity. Her brother, a psychologist, had been expounding on the two words over breakfast in the meal tent.

A coincidence, he had said, was the fact that there were nine Americans on this photo safari, and last month two had been caught in the same end-of-the-world traffic jam that brought freeway traffic to a standstill before the Beatles' appearance at the Hollywood Bowl: Katie's husband and Katie's agent. Though David Hill was nearly thirty years younger than Peter Merrick, the idea that they had turned off their engines and stood smoking Lucky Strikes on the highway beside their cars at almost exactly the same moment near almost exactly the same exit had still been fascinating enough that it had broken the ice their first night in the Serengeti, and led David and Peter to bond in ways that transcended the generation and a half that separated them. (It also gave them something less awkward to discuss than the reality that Katie Barstow, their more obvious commonality, made dramatically more money than either of them, or that they were two big, strapping men who depended upon the earning power of a one-hundred-pound woman with a childhood more freakish than fairy tale who was barely five feet tall.)

Synchronicity was something more profound, a connection that suggested a higher power was at work. In this case—on this safari—it was the idea that on their second afternoon in the savanna, one of their guides overheard two of the guests discussing Katie's latest film and the MGM lion that was the first thing a person saw in the theater, and on a hunch drove the Land Rover to the far side of a tremendous outcropping of boulders, one of the kopjes not far from their camp, and there they were: a female lion and four of her cubs. Regal and proud, the cubs content, all of them lounging in the grass beneath the trees that grew beside the rocks. Even when the second vehicle had roared up behind the first so that everyone could see the animals and snap their photos, the mother lion had done little more than yawn. The cubs looked on a bit more intently, slightly more curious, but since their mother wasn't alarmed, they merely rolled over, stretched their small legs with deceptively large paws, and found more comfortable positions in the grass. The two Land Rovers were barely a dozen yards from the lioness.

"Katie?"

She turned now toward David.

"I think we need to bring a few home," her husband said, motioning at the giraffes at the watering hole. "And a couple of zebras. We'd never need a lawn service."

"The zebras would certainly help. But giraffes don't eat grass," she reminded him. They'd just bought a ranch. Or, to be precise, she had just bought a ranch. Thirty acres. It was near Santa Clarita, north of the valley. She'd considered buying something in Malibu, but she'd grown up on Manhattan's Upper West Side, a theater kid born to theater parents, and now that she was—and the words simultaneously made her bask and cringe—a movie star, she wanted to steer clear of the mod world that these days marked the sands: the beach houses with their massive windows, circular fireplaces, and Peter Max paintings against the crisp, white walls. She imagined someday she might have a horse. Or horses. One would be lonely. She'd ridden horses in two different movies and enjoyed the experience. She'd felt horrible when she'd watched her stunt double put the animal through some terrifying gallops and then send it to its knees after the creature was, supposedly, shot.

"Point noted," David agreed.

Beside them, Billy was photographing the giraffes with a camera that had a lens so stout it looked to Katie like a club, and his wife, Margie, was staring at the giraffes through binoculars so delicate they reminded Katie of opera glasses. Billy was thirty-five, David's age and five years her senior, and Margie was thirty-three. Margie had found out she was pregnant in August, and her doctor had thought morning sickness alone was a reason why she shouldn't go on the safari, but she was game. Said she wouldn't miss it. This was both her brother's and Margie's second marriage. Billy had a four-year-old son at home from his first, but Margie had left no children in her wake when her previous marriage had imploded. Katie knew that she was supposed to want children, and speculated sometimes what it meant that she didn't. Perhaps she was too ambitious. Or immature. Or selfish. Perhaps it was her hatred of her own parents, who had made her career possible, and yet had also been mercenary and mean and fake. And, yes, cruel. They had not been cruel to each other, which in hindsight was rather surprising, but they had been cruel to Billy and her. (Billy, however, had borne the brunt of the abuse. Most of the real horrors had been inflicted upon him, and it was their mother who was behind the lion's share of that carnage. How Billy had become who he was, rather than whoever was strangling all those women in Boston, was a mystery to her. But, thank God, he had grown into a pretty gentle therapist instead of a pretty violent monster.)

Katie's team at the studio, her publicist, and her agent all expected that someday soon she and David would have a baby. And most of them had mixed emotions about that. On the one hand, at thirty she was already outgrowing "starlet": how many more times could she play the ingenue? Besides, now that she was married, it would be unnatural not to have a baby. What would her fans think? On the other hand, most of her entourage disliked the idea of her taking time off, given the box office bullion of everything she touched. Even *Tender Madness,* her movie with Terrance, had done well, despite the inference in one of the scenes at the mental hospital that the pair had kissed after the cut. (They had, though the moment had wound up on the cutting room floor.)

Reggie Stout was the lone exception: he honestly seemed to want only what she wanted. He was far more to her than a publicist and she put considerably more stock in his counsel than she did in even her agent's—and she trusted Peter Merrick a very great deal. Reggie seemed as invested in her future and her happiness as a real father might be, though this was supposition since some days she hoped desperately that Roman Stepanov was not her real father. Even now, she and Billy joked that both of them were babies who had been swapped out at birth, and they weren't really related to the two grown-ups who had pretended to be their parents. She had chosen Billy to walk her down the aisle the week before last, since her own father had died last year within days of Jack Kennedy, though in far less dramatic circumstances. He'd had a heart attack in a cab on the way home from the theater. The cabbie, at her mother's direction, had turned around and raced to St. Luke's, but her father was dead by the time he was wheeled into the emergency room.

The New York papers would have devoted more space than they did to the Broadway icon's death, but the president took precedent. Katie was grateful, because the last thing she would have wanted that horrible week was to do press with her mother and have to feign grief. She was a good actress—but not that good. Billy was convinced she had chosen movies over the stage, which was the family business, because it meant that she was usually at least three time zones away from their mother, a woman he once called "a singular rarity: a cold-blooded mammal." Both siblings detested her. They had disliked their father, with reason, but they had loathed their mother—though, arguably, Billy had greater cause than Katie.

"This is when the giraffe is most vulnerable," Juma, their African guide, was saying, his accent sounding both British and Maasai to Katie. "How much does a giraffe's neck weigh?" he asked good-naturedly. He was easily seventy, and he was like a schoolteacher with these Americans. He didn't merely want them to see the Serengeti: he wanted them to understand it. It was a world that he loved and a world he loved sharing.

"Easily six hundred pounds," Katie answered. She was the only one of the nine guests who'd never been to college, and she understood it was a little pathetic the way she always had to be first with the correct answer. But she did. She needed Juma's approval.

Carmen was like that, too, though she had been to college. In her case, Katie supposed, it was because Carmen always played supporting roles: she was usually the leading lady's best friend or sister, the gal with a couple of memorable wisecracks but never the sort of scene that allowed her to show off real acting chops. Being the smartest woman in the room was her way of compensating.

"Good, good," Juma was reassuring her. "It takes time to look up and look around. That's why they don't all drink at once."

"And their legs," Katie said. "They're in no position to run."

"No," Juma agreed. "Excellent."

David put his arm around her shoulders and pulled her into him. He whispered into her ear, "Thank you."

She turned from the giraffes to her husband. They'd now been married thirteen days. They'd honeymooned alone—in style and civilization—in Paris, before meeting the other seven guests she was bringing on safari at the airport outside Paris and flying to Nairobi. Now they were still traveling in style and in a most civilized fashion—the kerosene-powered ice maker the excursion company provided awed her, because, of course, you had to have a proper gin and tonic at the end of a long day on safari—though the civilization was provided by an entourage of seventeen Kenyans and Tanzanians (including two armed rangers), sixteen of whom were Black. The exception was Charlie Patton, no relation, he pointedly told everyone as soon as he was introduced, to the American general. Patton had once been one of the great white hunters, born to colonials at the very end of the nineteenth century—he still had the sort of handlebar moustache she associated with cavalry officers from another era—but he had figured out the real money now was with the likes of movie stars such as Katie Barstow. People who wanted to photograph elephants, not shoot them. People who might want a zebra rug or a zebra purse but didn't want to see the damn thing actually killed.

"Thank you for what?" she asked David, turning from the

guide to her husband. She spoke softly in response to his whisper. The camera loved it when she spoke quietly, and directors had often told her that her voice, when she murmured, was gold.

"For this," he said. "For bringing me here. For bringing us here."

She took his fingers that were on her shoulder and brought them to her lips. She kissed them. Though David was her first husband, three years ago she had been briefly engaged. That fellow—that actor—had been threatened by her bank account. Not by her, but by her box office grosses. She had broken it off when he disappeared, drunk, the night of the *Wild Girl* premiere. He ended up going to Italy to lick his wounds and be the bad guy in bad films: *Gunfight in Bloody Sands* and *The Smoking Winchester.* Her brother the shrink had warned her that it would be difficult to find a man she might actually love who would ever be completely comfortable with her success, unless he were at least as successful. But men like that? They were rare. Grace Kelly had had to marry an honest-to-God prince. Elizabeth Taylor had just married her fifth husband, Richard Burton, an actor whose star was as bright as hers, even if the movies weren't the blockbusters that Liz's were.

But David was different. He was a gallerist: he owned a gallery in Beverly Hills. He'd grown up in Manhattan, too, in the same building as her own family, and had always been in her world because of his friendship with Billy. In some ways, he'd been like an older brother to her, too—albeit one she lost touch with until he moved west and opened a gallery on the corner of Rodeo and Brighton. Her brother was the one who'd suggested they get together, and so they had: he'd brought David to her house that first time and then had the two of them to his place for lunch. Their first date had been dinner at Taylor's Steakhouse.

"It is amazing, isn't it?" she said to him now. "More magic than I ever expected."

The giraffes that were drinking raised their gargantuan

necks and joined the two others that were staring at the five humans. They grew more attentive. Alert. She tried to imagine what one of them had done to interest the giraffes, but suddenly they were retreating, retreating fast, racing in that distinctive giraffe gait: what Juma called "pacing," the two right legs moving and then the two left. She smiled at their beauty, their grace, but then she heard the pops behind her, understood they were gunshots, and—more curious than alarmed—along with all of the people around her turned to look back at the camp.

CHAPTER TWO

David Hill

Rodeo Drive gallerist David Hill was spotted having a very intimate dinner with Katie Barstow. Sources tell us the pair are childhood friends from New York City, but the two of them looked like much more than mere childhood "chums."
—The Hollywood Reporter, FEBRUARY 13, 1964

He watched the white men appearing from nowhere with their guns. It wasn't what he expected—not that he really had expectations—but he sure as hell didn't anticipate that someone was going to die on this safari. He'd never before seen a human being shot. His camera slipped from his fingers, and he only understood that he was no longer holding it when he felt the sting of it hitting the bridge of his foot.

. . .

David had known Katie Barstow when she was a little girl named Katie Stepanov—since she was his pal Billy Stepanov's kid sister. The Stepanovs lived two floors above his family in the monolith on Central Park West, in a dark, sprawling apartment with beautiful views to the east and waterfalls of light in the morning, and then shadows the rest of the day. The boys joked the whole building was haunted, and there likely were ghosts in the Stepanovs' place. Sometimes the two of them went out of their way to frighten Katie by conjecturing what sorts of spirits lived there in the pall. In the maid's room, where no maid actually slept because the "Irish girls" who cleaned the apartment and did much of the cooking arrived in the morning and left after dinner, and so it was where both Stepanov siblings hid those nights when their parents, usually (but not always) drunk, were bickering in the master bedroom. In the supernaturally vast walk-in coat closet opposite the front door, where David knew Glenda Stepanov would lock her son when she wanted to punish him. In the study, with the framed posters from Broadway dramas and musicals, many signed by the very same actors and actresses who appeared, on occasion, in the living room and sipped bourbon or rye from cocktail glasses with unicorns cut into the glass. Katie was always the kid who sang at her parents' parties or recited poetry or simply smiled adorably and was, justifiably, adored. She drove her older brother crazy, in part because most younger sisters drive their older brothers crazy—the behavior was existent deep inside the genetic code in much the same way that birds knew to fly south and bears to hibernate—and in part because Katie was just so much more drawn to the family business. Or, to be precise, the family passion. Theater. Roman and Glenda Stepanov produced Broadway musicals, and it was only a matter of time before Katie would be in one. She was twelve when she was first cast. She was onstage for about three minutes in the first act and about six in the second, but that was enough for the critics, with cause, to fall in love with her.

It was also enough for her mother, who was never going to win a Tony for Warmest Parent and sometimes made Gypsy's mother, Mama Rose, look like an absolute slacker when it came to stage parenting, to stop allowing dessert or chocolate in the home. She began to obsess about her daughter's complexion and weight, and to start choosing all of her daughter's clothing. She hired a governess for the child, a statuesque thirty-something burlesque queen whom both Billy and David thought was beautiful and, yes, insane. She was ferocious, and the teenage boys felt bad when they watched the beauty and exercise regimes to which she subjected Katie, and the way food (often terrible food) became a reward. In theory, the woman had experience as both a stylist and nutritionist, but David and Billy were sure that her "training" had been at places like Minsky's. Makeup sat like spackle in the deeper lines and crevices of her face.

The two boys were seventeen when Katie's first show opened in 1946. The war had ended before they were needed, and, in hindsight, the two of them had been more focused on the fact that soon they would go to college and not, thank God, to Iwo Jima. David's father did something vague for the Office of Strategic Services and was constantly traveling to Washington, D.C., for meetings, but his precise responsibilities existed behind an opaque curtain of spy craft and bureaucracy, and that was as close as either David or Billy ever got to the war. But a kid like Katie? David had thought she was utterly oblivious to the veterans coming home without an arm or a leg, or the images that Eisenhower had filmed in color at Buchenwald. She was a sheltered child, and she had seemed too absorbed by what her mother referred to some mornings as her future and some afternoons as her career. It had seemed to him that, pure and simple, she was about as shallow and mercenary as Glenda Stepanov. Billy and he shared a lot, but Billy, back then, wasn't capable of revealing how miserable his sister was; Billy likely feared that he had already told him too much about how secretly horrible both of his parents were.

It was only when David met Katie again in California, years later, that he understood how mistaken he'd been and how profoundly he had underestimated her. She was a good actress at least in part because of the scars and wounds from her childhood, and because, yes, she had indeed seen those World War II veterans without arms and she had wept alone in her bedroom after she had watched the footage from the death camps in a newsreel at the cinema. She'd told him on their first date in Hollywood that her parents had distant cousins—third cousins, maybe even fourth, she really didn't understand the genealogical terminology for relatives that many persons removed—who had been killed by the Nazis in Russia. They were dining in a dim, candlelit corner of the restaurant. They had been brought there through the back alley and then through the kitchen. It was the only way that Katie Barstow could have even a semblance of privacy. The head chef and a chief waiter had bowed deferentially, despite the chaos in the kitchen, as the maître d' had escorted them through the madness. But still, Katie had warned him that their pictures would be snapped the moment they finished dinner and left the restaurant, returning to the alley, where David had surreptitiously been allowed to park. She prepared him to squint against what she called a galaxy of exploding suns: the flashbulbs.

"Why Barstow?" he asked her, after the sommelier had uncorked the second Chianti. The fellow smiled without opening his mouth as he poured, the grin all lips and no teeth. "Your parents were never blacklisted during the McCarthy hearings, despite all that hearty Russian blood coursing inside them. Inside you."

"No," she agreed. "They were lucky."

"My father thought it was madness, but he's always been very clear: don't underestimate the Russians. Not ever. The Soviets are much better at spying than we'll ever be. He says they're a far more insidious foe than the Nazis, who quite literally wore their horribleness on their sleeves."

"Really? They're that good?"

"According to my father," he said. He knew not to tell her any more. At least not yet. He supposed that he'd take some suspicions to his grave. "So, tell me: why?"

"Why did I change my name or why did I change it to Barstow?"

He shrugged. "Both, I guess."

"It was the studio's idea. When they signed me. They wanted a name that sounded more vanilla."

"More American."

"I suppose. And yes: less Russian. Not Russian."

"And they came up with Barstow?"

She sipped her wine and her lips curled ever so slightly—and there it was, the enigmatic smile that launched a thousand magazine covers. "I did. It's that little city on Route 66. We drove through it when we were coming to California. My mother and I."

"There are a lot of cities on Route 66."

"Ah, but only one with an ostrich farm."

"You went there?"

"To the ostrich farm? Yes! Wouldn't you?"

"I don't know."

"An ostrich has three stomachs and only two toes on each foot. They're seven feet tall and can run forty miles an hour."

"Why not Katie Ostrich?" He had been kidding, but she seemed to think about it.

"The phonetics are wrong. And it sounds fake."

But then she elaborated on how she loved movies in which there were exotic animals, and how even now she was a little jealous of Mia Farrow and Elsa Martinelli and Deborah Kerr because they had all filmed movies in Africa.

"*Hatari* is a terrible movie," he'd said, afraid the moment he had spoken that he had offended her because she might know someone in the cast or the crew. Hollywood was a surprisingly small community. God, for all he knew, her friend Terrance Dutton was in it.

But she had agreed with him. "In all fairness, I've made some real stinkers, too. But think about it: Elsa was on the set with hippos and lions and—don't laugh—ostriches. And the ostriches weren't on a fenced-in farm in a part of the world where they don't belong. They were in Africa, where they're supposed to be."

"You've never been to Africa?"

"No, have you?"

He hadn't. He wanted to suggest that it would be fun to take her there someday, but the gallery hadn't gotten off to a great start. It was barely holding its own, and the bank wasn't about to extend a penny more credit: not to the business and not to him. And his parents certainly weren't going to lend him the money: whatever the hell his father had done with the OSS and did now with the CIA—personnel, really?—it wasn't lucrative. Even if it was important, you didn't get rich beating the Nazis or trying to outwit the communists unless you were a defense contractor. His parents simply didn't have the kind of cash that he needed sitting around. The two of them had moved to Washington, D.C., in 1954 because his father's responsibilities demanded that he be there full-time, but he hoped to retire in three or four years. He was now, at least ostensibly, in personnel and training. Nothing clandestine, he'd insist, a lot of paper pushing. But David suspected there was more to it than that. Mind control. Brainwashing. He'd overheard a little one time when he'd visited his parents in Washington, and he'd seen the manila folder his father had tried to hide in a newspaper after breakfast. Regardless, one moment his old man would be talking about East Berlin or Vietnam, and the next his vision of a little place on a golf course in Sarasota, Florida, where he and his wife could live out their days, always with a brooding aside about how little money he had been able to squirrel away. Apparently, it was going to be a photo finish to see what happened first, after he retired: he and his wife died or they went broke.

"I haven't," David said finally. "Maybe someday. Africa. Imagine."

"I'll get there. Either because I'm making a picture or on my own."

"Do you worry about all the revolutions? Central Africa, East Africa. I can't keep the countries straight, but it all feels like insanity."

"No. I don't worry."

He couldn't decide whether she was brave or naive. The little he knew about Africa was what he'd read over the last few years in the newspapers, and he wasn't sure he'd finished any one of the articles. "Congo. Kenya. Tanganyika," he said. "They're all a blur."

"The Serengeti doesn't change. Wildebeest don't respect national boundaries. They don't care about borders."

"You've done your homework. I'm not sure I even know what a wildebeest looks like."

"Imagine a very wise, very slender American buffalo."

"Wise?"

"They have little beards that make them look like professors."

"I never had a professor with a beard."

"Well, I wouldn't know about that," she said, and he realized that he had inadvertently pressed upon a bruise: the fact that she had not gone to college. Her mother felt she had wasted too much time on the stage and was already desperately far behind the Natalie Woods of the world. College was never an option.

"I have a neighbor with children, so I expect they'll have an encyclopedia. I'll stop by and look up *wildebeest*," he told her, hoping to convey both that he had clear gaps in his education, too, and he was interested in the things that interested her.

"The wildebeest is less woolly and has much bigger horns than the buffalo."

"You do know your exotic animals."

"I do," she agreed. Then: "If your neighbor doesn't have an encyclopedia, I have the Pan Am guide to safaris, and it has some wonderful photographs."

"Thank you."

"I could bring it next time."

He nodded. He very much liked the idea that there would be a next time.

CHAPTER THREE

Billy Stepanov

"Katie lights up every room she's in—and always has," says her brother, Billy. Billy, though five years her senior, followed her to California, where today he is a therapist.
—*The Hollywood Reporter,* MARCH 14, 1964

Someone was shooting, and Billy's first assumption was that one of the rangers had spotted a lion and was firing into the air to scare it away. Or it was Peter Merrick, Katie's agent. The older guy had brought a gun to go hunting when the photo portion of this safari was behind them. Maybe he'd seen something. Billy already imagined the rangers berating the fellow for discharging his rifle here in the reserve.

But when he turned, he understood. Or, at least, he understood something. This wasn't harmless.

It was happening fast, and his wife, Margie, was screaming. There were at least three men, all white, and before Billy's eyes—before all of their eyes—one of them mowed down the Black ranger who tried to intervene. The porters were falling onto the dry grass, not dead, but terrified, obeying the men with the guns who wanted them on their bellies on the ground right now. Right. Now. One of the men was pointing a double-barreled rifle, the kind that Charlie Patton had said was used to drop elephants, at Muema, the second guide, and motioning for him to join the rest of the staff and lie down on his stomach.

It was the last thing Billy's mind registered before Juma was pushing Katie and Terrance toward the Land Rover and David was dropping his camera. Billy followed them, trying to shield Margie as he herded her inside the vehicle too, his own bulky camera lens bouncing against his chest like a cudgel.

.   .   .

Only days earlier, he'd been on an airplane. A big one.

He was, in his mind, once more snuffing out his cigarette in the ashtray in the armrest of his seat, flipping down its metal lid, and gazing out the window at the moon. It was nearly full. Soon they would begin their descent into Nairobi. It was roughly three years ago that Dag Hammarskjöld had died in a plane crash not far from here: somewhere in the Congo.

He glanced at Margie, and she was dozing in her seat, her sleep mask over her eyes. He adjusted her blanket, pulling it over her shoulders.

He liked the 707, though this one was a little long in the tooth. There was a stain on the aisle carpet, and the tray table pitched at an angle that had forced him to watch his scotch (and then his coffee) with care. This was their fourth clipper and their fourth leg, and the first where he hadn't bothered to eat. He looked at his watch, which was still set to California time. He was so tired that it took him a moment to calculate what time it was in Kenya and remember how long it had been since he and Margie had left L.A. Finally, he figured it out: twenty-seven hours. They had maybe one more hour to go. That was it. Not a minute more. Thank God.

The trip had been a hell of a lot easier for his kid sister and David. They'd spent almost a week in France after the wedding and joined their guests at the gate at the airport in Paris, so this was only their second flight. They were also in first class. Katie was generously paying for everyone's flights and everyone's safari, but the first-class cabin on the two legs linking France and Kenya didn't have enough seats for all of them, and so her other seven guests had only been in the front of the plane from Los Angeles to New York, and then New York to Paris.

"Billy?"

He looked over at Margie. She'd pulled her mask up to her forehead so she could look around the cabin.

"Good morning, sweetie," he said, and kissed her. There was still, even now, a trace of Arpège on her skin.

"It's not morning."

"No, it's not."

"What time is it?"

"In what country?"

She smiled. "I'll rephrase: how much longer 'til we land?"

"Forty-five minutes. Worst case."

She nodded and pulled the blind back over her eyes, and instantly he regretted saying to her, *worst case*. That wasn't the worst case. The worst case was that they crashed. Think Hammarskjöld. He hated flying, everything about it, though mostly he hated the fact he was five miles in the air. It was why he hadn't slept; it was why he couldn't sleep. He listened to every sound the engines made and felt every lurch when they plowed through a cloud. He had to. He knew it was irrational, the precise sort of craziness that he heard from his patients, but he honestly believed that the plane would only stay aloft if he remained awake. If he slept, he'd never wake up. Or he'd only wake up when he heard the this-plane-is-going-down cries or for the millisecond immediately after the front of the tube slammed into the top of a mountain. Kilimanjaro, maybe, if they were off course. Apparently, the new government in Tanganyika and Zanzibar had just opened an airport near Kilimanjaro, but Pan Am wouldn't use it. Thank God. A new airport with new air traffic controllers? Nope.

In all fairness, Tanganyika and Zanzibar seemed pretty damn stable. Or whatever the hell they had renamed the country last month. Tanzania. The Serengeti seemed perfectly safe—at least when it came to human predators. There must have been forty Americans and Europeans on this plane with Margie and him and the rest of Katie's retinue who were going on photo or hunting safaris in or near there. The new nation had experienced nothing like the bloodshed and civil war that were occurring next door in the Congo. Of course, the most catastrophic of the violence this summer, that whole Simba rebellion, was in the eastern Congo, and that bordered Tanganyika and Zanzibar. That kidnapping? Those nuns? Jesus Christ. But the travel agents and the safari outfit were clear: they'd be nowhere near the border with Congo or the secessionist province. They'd fly into Kenya and head south into the Serengeti. It was done all the time: it took more than political unrest in the nation next door—okay, a shooting war between rival political factions—to slow the growth of Serengeti tourism.

No one knew that Billy was afraid of flying, though he supposed that Margie suspected it. His first wife had. But he always insisted that he was awake through every minute of every flight because of his sinuses or his ears, or because he liked to get work done on the flights.

"What sort of work?" Margie had asked the first time they were packing to fly cross-country from Los Angeles to New York to visit his parents. They were in the bedroom, their suitcases open on the bed.

"Oh, you know. Read professional magazines. University studies. Look over patient notes."

He was pretty sure she hadn't bought a word of it: it wasn't like he read professional magazines or university studies all that often when they were on the ground.

He thought of his little boy at home in California. Marcus— who had grown into Marc, unless he or his ex-wife really needed to get the boy's attention or make a point, in which case that second syllable was everything—was four. He thought, too, of his ex-wife. On the other side of the world, right about now the two of them were probably walking home from the park with the swing sets and the massive slide a couple of blocks from their house. The house Billy himself had once lived in. The house with the little pool of its own. His new bungalow, the one he lived in with Margie, hadn't a pool, but he was only about a ten-minute drive to his sister Katie's, and she wouldn't have cared if he bought a water chaise and a case of beer and lived in her pool. Hers was a Hollywood classic: shaped like a kidney with a diving board at one end, where the water was five meters deep. God, his kid sister had a pool that was almost as big as the first floor of the bungalow where he lived now. She had as many bedrooms in her place as he had rooms in his.

He wondered if there was a word for sibling gigolo-hood. Sycophant? Minion? Hanger-on? Well, all eight of the guests on this safari, including Katie's husband, were, in a way, the movie star's hangers-on. None of them would be on this plane or this trip if it weren't for Katie. What was it that their mother had said to him at Katie's and David's wedding? Glenda Stepanov was at that stage where people who knew her would know she was drunk, but everyone else would assume she was just being Katie Barstow's eccentric, acerbic mom. *You knocked up Margie pretty damn quick. Who's going to pay for my new grandchild's college some-day? Me or your sister?* It was not an unreasonable question, given his alimony and child support, and the fact that already he had availed upon his mother for a little help with the down payment on the bungalow. Already he was stretched thin, no doubt about it, and a new baby was certainly going to exacerbate that. It was his mother's language and his mother's tone that was so hurtful. So typically hurtful.

Among the smaller disfigurements to his psyche, but one he contemplated often as a therapist himself, was that Halloween when he was eight and Katie was three. *The Haunting of Emily Dickinson* had just opened at the Beck, and there was a perfor-mance on the thirty-first: Halloween night. The show was an odd one for his father, Roman Stepanov, to produce: a ghost story that they all pretended had a literary pedigree. (It didn't.

No one really thought the poet was beleaguered by ghosts: not then, not now.) And the reviews had been, even when viewed charitably, mixed. Hence a redoubled effort with the social and gossip press. There was going to be a media reception before the performance and an appropriately themed cast party after the Halloween show, with yet more reporters and columnists invited. Their parents would be at the theater for both functions, and so the plan had been for the two children to go trick-or-treating throughout the apartment building with his friend David Hill and David's mom. In theory, it shouldn't have been a big deal. And yet it was. Or it became one. Glenda Stepanov decided on the thirtieth, the day before Halloween, that she herself should take Billy and Katie trick-or-treating that very moment. She made this decision after nine that night, when Roman was out and she was drunk. She had to wake Katie from a sound sleep. Billy recalled that he was in bed, too, though he hadn't dozed off yet. Roman was having costumes made for the kids by one of his show's costume designers: Katie was going to be a kitten and Billy was going to be a pirate. But the outfits weren't quite finished and were still at the Beck. And so when his mother pulled him, a little dazed, from the bed, she dressed him in his costume from the year before: cowboy chaps that now were too short, a flannel shirt so tight he barely could button it, and a cowboy hat, all of which stunk of mothballs. She put Katie into the same cotton-and-wool-stuffed pumpkin she had worn when she was two, and it still reeked of the diaper she had worn underneath it the year before. Katie was howling because she had been dragged from a deep sleep, and he was crying because it was the wrong night and he wanted to trick-or-treat with David, but Glenda was brooking no dissent. They were going that moment, even though it was nine thirty at night and it was the day before Halloween.

It was, predictably, a disaster. Half the apartments didn't have candy yet or hadn't baked treats. The half that did had to find them. And everyone could see that the two kids had been crying (or were crying). They could also see, despite Glenda's charm as she explained to the neighbors as they opened their doors that the children would be busy tomorrow night at the theater (a lie), that she was a toxic mixture of mania and gin. She was a farce. The other adults were in their dressing gowns and bathrobes, but she was the mess. And when she brought the kids home around ten thirty, after knocking on perhaps fifteen doors, she was furious at what she viewed as their misbehavior and the way they had embarrassed her. She made Katie sleep that night back in her crib instead of her bed, and she placed the heavy wooden extender to the dining room table across the top so she couldn't escape. She made Billy sleep on the floor of that terrifying coat closet. He was still awake when his father got home, but Roman knew not to rescue his children. Not when Glenda was in one of her moods.

The stewardess passed by Billy as they neared Nairobi, saw his eyes were open, and asked him if he would like anything. There was a slight whisper of French in her accent.

"All good," he said, which meant, inevitably, that the plane chose that moment to pitch abruptly, and the drink on the passenger's tray table across the aisle sloshed onto the white table linen. The other passengers who were awake craned their necks as one to stare out the windows. He was relieved that his glass was empty.

"Just a little turbulence," the stewardess said to him, and she smiled in a way that was knowing and kind. She was no more than twenty-five years old, but she saw through him like glass. An idea came to him: the kind of person who became a stewardess would make one hell of a good therapist.

.   .   .

Margie had stopped shrieking now that they were in the Land Rover and Katie hadn't said a word, at least not one that Billy had heard. David had said something about surrendering so no one got hurt, but Juma ignored him, ordering him into the vehicle. Now the guide was fumbling to get the car key into the slot, an uncharacteristic lack of competence, but the moment was brief. Billy looked around, unsure how they had wound up in the seats they were in because it had all happened so fast. But Katie was in the front seat, sharing it with the cooler and the toilet paper and the bags of nuts that Juma always stored there, David and Terrance were in the second row, and Billy and Margie were together in the third, Margie pressed against the right window. The engine started and they were fleeing. They were leaving behind, it seemed, Katie's agent and her publicist, and Carmen Tedesco—Katie's best friend in the world, the maid of honor at her wedding—and Carmen's husband, Felix. They were leaving behind that hunter, Charlie Patton, and his mammoth staff: all those porters who boiled them water for the baths they savored in those canvas tubs, and barbecued the guinea fowl and Thomson's gazelle that had been shot in some edge of the Serengeti where it was still legal to hunt, and brought to their tents their coffee and hot water first thing in the morning. They were running away like terrified zebras, racing like impalas that had spotted a lion.

And Billy didn't care, because—whether it was pious or pathetic—all he cared about that moment was getting his wife and his unborn child out of there.

"Poachers?" Terrance asked, but Juma ignored him.

Their guide had just eased the clutch into gear and started to accelerate when the back window and one of the side windows of the Land Rover exploded and Billy felt the glass shards raining upon Margie and him, and something sharp slicing into the back of his neck, just above his shirt collar. Once more, his wife was screaming, and before the vehicle had gone very far—maybe twenty yards, maybe thirty—he felt the back of it wobble like a plane flying through a patch of (a synonym he noticed more and more pilots and stewardesses using these days) rough air. He told Margie to duck, and he may have shouted the word, wrapping himself over her crouching body as if he were a blanket. Juma tried to gun the Land Rover, but it was evident that one of the tires had been shot and he was riding on a rim. He stopped.

"Do we get out and run?" Katie asked.

"Can you outrun a bullet?" Juma asked in return.

Billy held Margie as tight as he could, hoping to quiet her because she was sobbing. Over and over, she moaned, "I don't want to die, I don't want to die," her body timorous and small.

"They won't kill you," Juma reassured her. "Stay here."

Katie turned back to her guests in the second and third rows of seats, her eyes wide but unreadable: Billy couldn't tell how deep was his sister's terror, though on the surface she seemed a hell of a lot more stoic than Margie. The five of them watched as Juma climbed out the driver's-side door of the Land Rover, his hands up as if he were acting—surrendering—in one of Katie's movies. He was standing there, right beside the vehicle, when they all heard another shot and the glass window beside the door was awash in Juma's brains and blood, a Rorschach of red, gray, and black, and the body dropped like a shot topi or eland or any of the other beautiful antelopes they'd seen here in the Serengeti. And somehow Billy knew—he just knew, even as his wife started once more to howl—that the poor son of a bitch had been killed by that double-barreled rifle that was meant to bring down game much bigger than a topi or eland. Juma Sykes had been all but decapitated by a goddamn elephant gun.

CHAPTER FOUR

Benjamin Kikwete

The "honeymoon" safari will be led by the great white hunter, Charlie Patton, and his team. Patton and his staff used to cater to the likes of Ernest Hemingway, and Katie and her guests will be cared for by the sons of some of the very same men who would skin "Papa" Hemingway's trophies.
—*The Hollywood Reporter,* NOVEMBER 9, 1964

He was down in the dirt on his stomach beside Muema, the second guide, neither of them wounded, watching as the tallest of the intruders—a man so thin and lanky, his Adam's apple looked like a small jackfruit on his neck—shot out a couple of windows and one of the wheels of the Land Rover. He was an expert marksman. So far, Benjamin had counted seven men, all white, who'd appeared out of nowhere from the brush behind the dining tent, but he knew there were more. He tried to account for the guests, but it was happening quickly and he didn't know who was in the retreating Rover and who wasn't. He tried to find his boss, Charlie Patton, but he had no idea now where he was, either.

Benjamin respected Patton, but he didn't revere him the way his father did: his father had worked for the man, too, as a gun bearer when Patton was still running hunting safaris exclusively. Patton was almost four times Benjamin's age: Benjamin's father had told him the man was sixty-eight.

Now the porter put his head up, scanning the horror that was unfolding, raising up on his elbows to survey the whole of the camp, and instantly he felt Muema's hand on his back, pressing him back into the ground. They were beside a tire track: a groove. Benjamin noticed a dung beetle trying to roll a piece of elephant shit it had meticulously shaped into a marble up and out of the rut, but the rut was like a canal to the insect. Twice the beetle had almost pushed the excrement over the side and onto the flat dirt beyond, and each time the weight of the dung had been too much and it rolled back over the creature to the bottom of the track.

. . .

Earlier that week, Benjamin hadn't expected a movie star among the clients. When Patton was briefing his team and they were gathering in the street outside the hotel in Nairobi, he had known there would be nine wealthy Americans, six men and three women. There were three married couples and three single men, and six tents for the guests. That was all he was focused upon: the catering needs of nine people who had never before been to the Serengeti. He understood, more or less, the type and what to expect: he'd accompanied his father perhaps two dozen times since he'd been barely a teenager, and Patton's groups would arrive in Kenya and start south into Tanganyika. His father had watched as Patton transitioned his business from escorting hunters who wanted to bring home trophies to tourists who expected only to bring back photographs. Patton still carried himself with the bravado and élan of one of the great white hunters, but most of the times that Benjamin had been among Patton's porters, the groups had been photo safaris and his boss hadn't even bothered with gun bearers and skinners.

Or the gun bearers and the skinners, if they were able (and willing) to cook, would be along to prepare for the guests their grilled meats and vegetables and rice. But this work was too demeaning for some of the men. They already felt invisible among these white people from Europe and America. To be reduced from gun bearers to cooks? That sort of degradation made it feel even worse.

This was only the second time that Benjamin had joined Patton without his father, and when he was waiting outside the hotel that first morning and discovered that the woman leading the safari—and it *was* a woman leading the party, that was evident—was a movie star, he was disappointed that his father wasn't with him. His father would have loved to have been a part of this group. Moreover, one of the American actors with her was Black, another surprise that was at once a gift and a validation. Benjamin's father used to take his brothers and sisters and him to the cinema, one child at a time, on their birthdays once they turned eight, mature enough in his opinion to appreciate the experience. And now his father was missing precisely the sort of people who he might once have seen on the screen. Benjamin thought he had even heard of Katie Barstow, though he couldn't name one of her pictures off the top of his head and the odds that he had seen one were slim. Altogether, he had had six brothers and three sisters, four of whom were alive even now. They were a small, tightly knit band that had managed to survive the litany of illnesses that cratered so many families: the sleeping sickness carried by the tsetse flies and the malaria brought on by the mosquitoes and the malnutrition gifted East Africa by the endless cycles of drought and flood, and the way Europeans had wrested control long ago of the food chain. Each sibling saw exactly one movie a year.

The movie theater that he and his father would visit had about fifty folding chairs, and the ceiling was four meters above the floor. Originally it had been a brick factory on the outskirts of town, but it hadn't been one in years, and so an entrepreneur had painted a wall white and brought in a projector. One day Benjamin had peered inside the movie palace in the center of the city: the real theater. The Embassy. That cinema had a screen that had seemed, when he'd been a boy, as wide as the sky, and it boasted pillowed seats—easily two hundred of them—and red velvet drapes. Colonials attended the Embassy. White people. Unlike at the old brick factory, the floor at the Embassy was sloped so that the audience there wasn't constantly craning their necks to see around the heads in the rows ahead of them, the way that Benjamin and his father had to. When a movie had finished its run at the Embassy, the print would be brought to the old brick factory for a couple of days.

The movie theater where Benjamin and his father would go lacked a name. It simply had a wooden sign with the word MOVIES painted in garish red and yellow paint. It was a five-minute walk from the Catholic church, which had soaring windows, one of which was a stained-glass image of Jesus Christ being crucified, and a high, dark wooden ceiling. But it was the painting behind the altar that had fascinated Benjamin as a child. In it, Jesus was a little boy, and he was standing with Mary and a white man in full safari regalia: wide-brimmed hat, a jacket with bullet loops, pants with plenty of zippered pockets. The three of them were standing in a clearing in the jungle, and all around them African men and women and children were kneeling, their faces either adoring or awed. And in the distance, behind Jesus, Mary, and the hunter, there was an African witch doctor, complete with a feathered crown, running away, looking absolutely terrified as he gazed back over his shoulder.

After seeing the movie *Barabbas* a couple of years ago, Benjamin had gone directly from the movie theater to the church to compare the crucifixion he had just seen on film with its portrayal in the stained-glass window. He wanted to see how different artists, ones who made films versus ones who worked with glass, approached the death of his savior. He decided he preferred the Hollywood version. That eclipse had mesmerized him.

Now that he had spent a few days in the Serengeti with the actress's group, he'd concluded that Katie Barstow was not what he expected from a movie star. She was neither troublesome nor demanding, and he appreciated that. She was actually rather *undemanding.* This was the term his father and Patton used for the easiest clients. It was Patton's supreme compliment. Their first night at their first camp, she had requested that her bath be ready at six fifteen. He had been with the advance lorry and among the group that had unfurled the waterproof canvas bathtubs and set them on their stanchions, including the one that would be in the tent for the movie star and her husband. He'd been among the group boiling the water for the guests who wanted their baths before cocktails and had carried the great drums of scalding-hot water into Katie Barstow's tent for her bath. But the canvas had had a small tear (or tears), imperceptible to the naked eye unless you followed the leak, and so the water had seeped from the tub, both preventing the guest from having her bath and turning that section of her tent into a swamp.

Over the years, he had seen other clients who would have become enraged. They had been promised so much and were spending so much and came from such privilege that they managed to forget where they were: a world where a group of trained men created civilization in one small spot for a night and then tore it all down, leaving as the only remnants tire tracks, flattened grass, a fire pit (or two), and the bones of whatever game they had cooked. Benjamin had had women berate him because they chipped their nails and men castigate him because the dining tent lacked the right bourbon. Their behavior was always embarrassing and sometimes it was dangerous. It was perilous for Benjamin because a person could be fired for this sort of fiasco, and it was hazardous for the guests because, in the midst of their tantrums, they might stalk from the camp and wind up bitten by a snake or mauled by any one of a dozen different kinds of wild animals before a ranger or porter could bring them back to the safety of the tents. Benjamin himself had had to retrieve one American who had something to do with oil, and who, when they had run out of brandy after dinner—and the meal was a meat he complained was too gamy—had wandered off in a huff toward a candelabra tree. He was drunk, and it was evident that he was about to see if this particular euphorbia was as toxic as he had been told. Benjamin had grabbed him just before he'd attempted to snap one of the candle-like branches, which would inevitably have released the latex that would have burned him at best and blinded him at worst. The next morning, the American had grown sheepish when Benjamin had shown him the lion tracks on the far side of the tree. He would never know if the lion had been there at the same moment that he had been dragging the American against his will back to the camp, but the very idea caused his stomach to roll over.

When the movie star had learned that her bath would be delayed until after dinner and she and her husband would have to dine with the stink of bug dope on their clothes and the dust and dirt from the savanna on their skin, she'd shrugged and told Benjamin she was sorry that the porters would have to boil more water. He could see the great perspiration stains down her back and even on the seat of her trousers, because the plastic cushions they used in the Rovers grew so sticky and hot it almost seemed like you could cook on them. Then the actress had moved the luggage stand away from the swamp in that corner of the tent and said to her husband, "David, I've moved the rack. Be careful you don't walk into it if you get up in the night."

"Got it," her husband had said.

"A drink?" she'd asked him.

"I always supposed actresses were vain."

"Oh, we are. Trust me: we are. But you saw me when I was a three-year-old spilling my orange juice."

"It's true. I was a witness to that. I think I also saw you wet your pants in Central Park when you were four."

She motioned at her khakis and Benjamin would have preferred not to be present for this exchange, but the Americans didn't seem to care. "This is only sweat, I promise. And I think Kidogo will still mix me a gin and tonic, even if I am a bit grubby for the likes of your gallery."

"But not for the gallerist."

"Good."

She turned to him. "Thank you, Benjamin," she said.

Then the two of them left him alone to throw some sand on the mud and replace the bathtub. He was pleased that already this Katie Barstow knew both his and Kidogo's names. Yes, he was staff, but he was still a man. There would be guests in some groups who wouldn't bother to learn the names of anyone but Patton the entire time they were together with them in the Serengeti.

He liked most of these Americans, though he had a particular fondness for Katie because she was kind and for Terrance Dutton and Reggie Stout because they were competent. Dutton was one of only three Black men he'd ever had as a guest, the other two being London bankers. Stout was a movie publicist and, Benjamin had overheard, a war hero.

At one point he had seen Dutton alone at the end of the day, standing with a pair of binoculars at his eyes and a gin and tonic on the ground beside him. Benjamin had stood motionless because he didn't want to frighten away whatever bird or animal the actor was watching. But the man had sensed the porter behind him.

"It's okay," the actor said, and he brought the binoculars down from his eyes and leaned over for his drink. "I think that's a purple grenadier," he continued, pointing at a tree thirty meters from the camp.

Even without the binoculars, Benjamin could see that he was correct. "It is," he said.

"What a beautiful bird. That red beak. Red crown. The blue around the eyes."

"It's one of my favorites," said Benjamin.

"May I ask you something?" the actor asked, turning toward him.

Benjamin nodded.

"Does this ever get tiresome for you?"

"The Serengeti? It hasn't yet. It hasn't for my father."

"No. I don't suppose lions and rhinos and purple grenadiers ever do." He finished his drink. Quietly, his tone pensive, he continued, "But my mother cleaned bedrooms and bathrooms in a Memphis, Tennessee, hotel where she would never have been allowed to stay as a guest—or even eat. My father was a bartender in a restaurant two blocks away where he would have been fired on the spot if he had ever entered the establishment through the front door. I know there were days for them when the sheer indignity of it all exhausted them."

When he said the words *establishment* and *indignity,* the pronunciation was so distinctive that Benjamin realized suddenly that his father had taken him to a movie with Terrance Dutton. Dutton had played a minister who had been wrongly charged with murdering his wife, and his white lawyer wasn't much help in defending him. And so he had defended himself. He'd done a brilliant job with the evidence and clearly was innocent, but the court had nonetheless found him guilty and the poor guy had been sent to the electric chair.

"I've seen one of your movies," Benjamin said, carefully formulating his response. One of Charlie Patton's critical rules was that you never discussed African politics with a guest. You never discussed politics, period. "The one where you played the minister."

The actor rolled his eyes amiably. "Well intentioned. But it was trying too hard to capitalize on *To Kill a Mockingbird.* And I'm not Gregory Peck—or Sidney Poitier, for that matter. Now those two have acting chops."

"I liked it. My father liked it. I'm sure such things could happen here. Maybe they have. But we're our own country now," he said, still choosing his words with utmost care. "We're in charge."

"People, you mean, like you and me," said Dutton.

Benjamin nodded. Just then the purple grenadier lifted off from the branch and flew past them against a sky as pink as a bougainvillea. Together they watched it. "No, bwana," he told the actor definitively. "This could never grow tiresome."

Dutton was a tall man and he put his free arm, the one without the empty highball glass, around Benjamin's shoulders, and together they started back to the camp. "Fair enough," he said. "One thing."

Benjamin waited.

"Please, don't call me bwana."

"Would you prefer 'Mr. Dutton'?"

"God, no. Just call me Terrance."

Benjamin honestly wasn't sure that he could—and he certainly wouldn't in front of Charlie Patton. There were protocols. Just as you steered clear of politics with the guests, you never called them by their given names. Nevertheless, when the porter returned home, he knew that the very first thing he was going to do was tell his father that a Black Hollywood movie star had been on the safari and had asked Benjamin to call him by his first name.

.   .   .

Benjamin saw that the first person to emerge from the Land Rover with the shattered window and the flat tire was Juma, a guide from Arusha who was a decade older than Benjamin's father. He was easily seventy and a grandfather. But his eyesight was still astonishing, whether he was spotting a secretary bird as it pecked its way along the ground in the distance or announcing with confidence that the tiny black dot in the bottom of the Ngorongoro Crater was a rhino. He was growing a little wide in the belly, and sometimes the food on safari no longer agreed with him, but he had no plans to retire anytime soon. He was revered by the porters and perhaps even by Patton.

He shut the door to the jeep. He put his hands up high, and it seemed as if he was about to say something. Benjamin would never know. Because it was right then that the white marksman with the elephant gun brought it back up to his shoulder, stared through the sight, aiming, and quite literally blew apart the entire right side of the old guide's skull. Benjamin closed his eyes, horrified, but even with his eyes shut he kept seeing the older man's death. He had seen too much. He had a sense that the shooter had only filled one of the barrels with a bullet, but it didn't matter: Benjamin had witnessed a hunter take down a tree with a 1,600-grain bullet. The human head? It became porridge.

CHAPTER FIVE

Reggie Stout

"Sometimes a marriage lasts a lifetime. Sometimes it lasts five years. What is that great Oscar Wilde quote? 'The mystery of love is greater than the mystery of death.' I know that right now Marilyn is in a very vulnerable place," said Reggie Stout, the star's publicist.
—*Movie Star Confidential,* FEBRUARY 1961

Reggie Stout was on the ground, Carmen Tedesco to his right and the actress's husband, Felix, to his left. Carmen was just staring, her chin in the dry dirt, but Felix was whimpering, those haunted hazel eyes of his lost, at least for the moment, to his tears. It sounded to Reggie as if Felix was hyperventilating. He'd heard other young men make exactly that sort of noise on Okinawa in the spring of 1945, usually in the dark and always after a counterattack. When a new attack loomed, regardless of who was going to start it, the soldiers always were deathly quiet. (That was the adverb one sergeant used because he was superstitious and thought saying the word out loud would add an extra layer of protection.) When a soldier cried softly the way Felix was right now, it meant that he was wounded and, more likely than not, going to live. In Reggie's experience, the dying in the jungle mostly were silent.

Reggie wasn't sure where Peter Merrick was, but he hadn't heard any more shots—other, of course, than the final one that had taken off the head of that lovely grandfather Juma, who was

Charlie Patton's right-hand man—and the men who'd appeared out of nowhere like lions didn't seem to bother to kill people with a whole lot of stealth. No garroting or knives here; they were quite comfortable with the blast of a gun. He thought their accents very likely were Russian, but he wasn't positive.

He knew that he wasn't supposed to look back over his shoulder, but he allowed himself one furtive glance at the fellow who had ordered them to lie down where they were: it was one of the youngest of their attackers who was behind them. The kid was holding what Patton had told Reggie a couple of days ago was a Mannlicher, a pretty ancient rifle, and a name that the hunter pronounced in such a fashion that Reggie had thought it sounded more like a Bavarian dessert than a weapon: *munn-leesher*. Patton had one in his arsenal, and it was back on their first day in the Serengeti that he had given Reggie a tour of the guns because he had overheard his guests talking and realized that although this was a Hollywood crowd, one of the group was a veteran who had been involved in (the guide's words) "a real melee." Reggie himself would never have used that expression to describe Okinawa. Patton had brought the guns with him even though this was a photo safari and there were two armed rangers with them, because Katie's agent, Peter Merrick, was staying an extra week and going hunting with Patton after the other Americans had returned to California. It was, Reggie thought, an armory that was as ridiculous as it was impressive. The man kept the guns lined up in a rack in the back of one of the lorries, each weapon a spire in a wrought-iron fence, their muzzles—some with sights—the decorative finials.

Reggie wondered whether the men who had descended upon their camp had discovered that truck yet. For all he knew, they had already commandeered the weapons, and the Mannlicher in the kid's hands was Patton's. But if they hadn't found the hunter's arsenal? Reggie pondered whether he himself might be able to sneak to the lorry and, if he succeeded, grab one of the guns and some ammunition.

.   .   .

A safari. He'd been flattered that Katie had invited him, but also surprised. It was one thing to speak at her wedding and raise his glass in one of the very first toasts at the reception; it was another to be asked to be among the seven people whom she and her husband were bringing to Africa. He was only ten years older than she was, but sometimes he felt twice her age.

But, what the hell, when would he have another chance to see Africa? Why not tag along? He had offered to pay his share, but Katie Barstow had said no. Absolutely not. He was her guest.

Katie was among the few clients whom Reggie Stout managed directly these days, but his firm also represented Carmen Tedesco, who was here too. Carmen was Katie's age, but her star was nowhere near as high in the sky as Katie's and never would be. But that didn't matter to Reggie: he was still keeping a fatherly eye on her as well as on Katie here in the Serengeti. On the flights to Africa, he had probably spoken to Carmen more than he had in the four years she'd been a client of his firm.

Now Muema—the second guide—and a ranger with a gun were taking them on a nature hike along the perimeter of their first camp. Only Carmen and her husband, Felix, and he had gone on the stroll, the rest of the group choosing to bathe and drink before dinner. The guide was standing before a whistling thorn acacia that stood eight feet tall and explaining how the tree was spectacularly adept at protecting itself from being eaten by impalas and giraffes. It had barbed wire–like thorns scattered among the leaves, but it also had small black globes that were home to cocktail ants and gave the plant its name: the wind whistled as it breezed through the insect holes in those globes. Felix took a picture of it with one of those new Kodak Instamatics that used a cartridge with the film neatly tucked inside it. The camera was the shape of a cigarette box, and not that much bigger.

"Katie should plant some of those at the ranch she's bought in Santa Clarita," Carmen said to him.

"She's worried about impalas and giraffes?" he teased her in response.

"She's been told there are coyotes out there."

"Pretty sure coyotes eat meat. Rats, right? And squirrels. And cats and dogs."

"They do," she agreed, but then she surprised him by adding, "Technically, they're omnivores. Coyotes, that is. They eat plants, too. Not a lot. But some grasses and leaves. They also might be drawn to her place by the garbage."

"How in the world do you know that coyotes are omnivores?"

"You think I'm just a pretty face."

"Not true," he said, and was about to add more, but she cut him off.

"Yes, you do. And it's fine. It's better to have a pretty face than not. But I know lots of obscure facts. My brain seems to retain knowledge I don't need like one of those great big computers you hear about."

He smiled at her, a little taken aback by her confidence. In the space of thirty seconds, she had revealed that she thought she was pretty (which she was) and that she thought she was smart (which he hadn't known until this trip, but was becoming more and more aware of daily).

"That's a good talent to have when memorizing lines, I suppose."

"It's even more helpful when figuring out a character. I do a lot of homework. I have to."

"Why?" He knew that some actors did far more research than others. Some did absolutely none, other than learning lines. He had one client who had asked him two days before he was due on the set to play Aaron Burr whether he thought a duel in early America was even remotely possible and why the screenwriters had made up a character like Burr in the first place. He wanted to know whether Reggie thought it might be okay to suggest a better name than Burr.

They were starting to walk again, following their guide. He noticed that they were never so far from the camp that they couldn't see the tents and the lorries, but they were moving in the shape of a protractor, a great half moon. Muema was pointing out a few dozen wildebeest that were grazing, seven or eight zebras intermingled with them. Some of the animals looked up from the grass, but most were oblivious to the humans. They couldn't care less that these intrusive animals that walked on two legs were watching them dine.

"I want to be a smart actress," Carmen answered. "I have to be. Let's face it, I'm not Katie."

He nodded. He considered lying to her and saying something polite about how talented she was, because she was indeed an immensely gifted actress. But he also understood what she was getting at. Katie Barstow was who she was not simply because she could act and the camera loved her (though both were true), but because she had an indefinable but almost corporeal specialness, the quintessence of dreams: a quality that transcended her beauty and her brains. It was an aura: she was damaged. You could sense it, you could feel it, you could see it. She had always been the most interesting person on the stage—that one person in the crowd you had to watch—and now she was invariably the most interesting person on the screen.

"Katie is a once in a generation talent," he agreed. "But you—"

"I make a good living as pretty sidekicks and bookish things that happen to fill out a sweater nicely, thank you very much," she told him.

"And a corset," her husband, Felix, added, referring to her role as a Russian aristocrat in a 1962 film about the last Russian czar. He put his little camera back in his pants pocket.

"Precisely," she agreed. "But you know what?"

Reggie waited.

"I was also the only person on that set who could name all of Nicholas and Alexandra's children."

"I could name one: Anastasia."

"There were actors in the cast who couldn't have named even her."

"I probably represent some," he said, chuckling.

"Perhaps."

"I hope you know you're a gem, Carmen. You really are. You have so many fans in this world—and in my firm."

"I do know that. Thank you. And I appreciate all that all of you do for me. Jean Cummings is great."

Jean was Carmen's publicist. "She takes good care of you?"

"She does." The ranger with the gun suddenly was beside them, and instantly Carmen was looking around. Did the ranger suppose one of the wildebeest was about to charge? Did Carmen? There seemed no chance of that to Reggie. The ranger grinned: they weren't in danger. He simply happened to be walking near them right now. Reggie recalled that the fellow had said earlier that he was from Kilimanjaro.

"Have you ever climbed Kilimanjaro?" Reggie asked him. He presumed the answer would be yes. He was just making small talk.

"No. I tried, but I got sick at around eighteen thousand feet. Too much altitude," the young man said.

"Eighteen thousand feet? You were so close!" said the actress. "You were only thirteen hundred feet from the summit! That's heartbreaking!"

The ranger was tall and slender, and Reggie supposed he was even younger than he looked. He might not even be twenty. "Reaching the summit? Wasn't worth dying." He was smiling.

Reggie turned toward Carmen. "You know the height of Kilimanjaro?"

"I told you: I know lots of things I'll never need. You watch. By the end of this safari, you're going to think I'm wasting my time as an actress."

"Oh, I'd never think that."

"Well, you wouldn't be the first." Then she raised an eyebrow and said to the ranger beside her, "I think you showed excellent judgment. You are absolutely right, and I was absolutely wrong: tagging the top of a mountain isn't worth anyone's life. I'm not sure even Hemingway scaled Kilimanjaro, and he used its name in that short story of his."

The ranger nodded, and Muema joined them. "Hemingway," he murmured thoughtfully.

"Have you read him?" she asked.

"I have. Have you read Chinua Achebe?"

Reggie had heard of the African writer but knew nothing about him. Would Carmen surprise him yet again by having a paperback copy of one of the man's books with her on the safari?

"No," she said. "Should I?"

The guide shrugged good-naturedly. "Start with *Things Fall Apart*. It may give you a different appreciation for Africa. When I read Hemingway? I see only a . . . a foreigner's view of this land. I don't see the people I know. I see only the people who come here."

"White people?" Carmen asked.

There was a moment when everyone went quiet: Reggie knew Carmen had meant nothing audacious with her two-word question, but he could see how she had put the guide in an uncomfortable position. So, Reggie thought he would jump in and joke about the hubris of Western tourists to take the guide off the hook, but Muema said placidly, "Yes. The people who came here long ago and stayed and the people who come here now and visit. The thing I think you will enjoy about Achebe? You will see instead the people who have been here forever. You're meeting the animals on this safari. Oh, you're meeting me and Juma and Benjamin. But with Achebe? You'll meet lots of us. And you will meet us"—and here he grinned in a fashion that was almost mischievous—"when we aren't simply trying to keep our clients from getting eaten."

.   .   .

And now Carmen's husband, Felix, was no longer whimpering: he was vomiting. It was either the actual sight of a man's head all but shot from its body or the ramifications of what the guide's decapitation might mean for all of them, but Felix had now gone from simpering like a little boy to disgorging his breakfast onto the ground, his back rippling like a moving snake as he heaved. One of the men who had shouted at gunpoint to lie down put his foot on Felix's back to flatten it and pointed the rifle at his head. He was wearing what might have been military-grade hiking boots.

He shouted something about Felix to one of his associates, who laughed, and this time the language—not merely the accent—definitely sounded Russian. Reggie even thought he heard a word that he knew from Carmen's picture about the Romanovs: *mertv. Dead.* And so Reggie had every expectation that poor Felix was about to get killed too. But then that very ranger who hadn't made it to the top of Kilimanjaro, a young man who might still have been a teenager, appeared from behind the green dining tent, his own rifle at his shoulder, aiming. He might have shot one of their attackers; he might have shot the guy whose boot was pressing Felix's spine into the earth. But he was dropped first, when another of their assailants fired at him, ripping a line of holes through his uniform shirt from his collar to the buckle of his belt.

CHAPTER SIX

Carmen Tedesco

*Starlet Carmen Tedesco laughs about it now, but she admits that
when her sister cheerleaders trapped her in a locker in ninth grade
and called her "brainiac," she felt like an outsider. "It was just a
hazing initiation, a rite of passage," she says, sounding a wee bit
like a college professor, "but back then? I felt like a sardine that
nobody much cared for." Nevertheless, she credits the moment with
turning her from sports to the stage. She left the cheerleading squad
and auditioned for the school musical. "I wanted nothing to do with
cheerleaders and athletes after that," she told us. "Nothing at all."*
—The Hollywood Reporter, APRIL 14, 1960

It was a weird out-of-body feeling and a wildly inappropriate
reaction to the fact that she had just seen two men killed in
the space of thirty seconds and at any moment might herself be
ripped apart by one of those weapons built to stop a charging
rhino in its tracks. But this was the thought, and it didn't merely
pass through her mind, it lodged there like a tremendous rock
in a river: I am Margot Macomber, and I am thoroughly despicable. She wasn't thinking of Joan Bennett in the movie: she'd
seen the trailer, but never the actual film. She was recalling very
precisely the Hemingway short story about a woman on safari
who sees her husband, Francis, behave like a coward when he
runs from a lion, and then punishes him by cuckolding him and
sleeping with their hired hunter. Their hired gun. Later, after

her husband grows a backbone, she shoots him. Had she thought of Hemingway because she'd been discussing the writer with Muema just the other day? Perhaps. Didn't matter. He was in her head now.

Carmen had no desire to shoot Felix, but she couldn't believe that her husband was crying. She was shocked that he had thrown up into the dirt beside him. Beside her. This was a part of him she'd never seen, probably because she'd never before seen him in a situation where his death was possibly imminent. But so was hers and so was Reggie Stout's, and neither of them was sniveling in the dust and vomiting up breakfast. And she was a woman. And she knew what the gossips (and Felix) whispered about Reggie. Sure, he was a war hero. But still.

How was it possible, Carmen thought, and what did it say about her that right now—right now, facedown on the ground— she was thinking about how pathetic her husband was, and how glad she was that (thank God) she hadn't taken his name, since she was likely to divorce him when they returned to California?

Assuming, of course, that he or she or both of them didn't die here in East Africa on her best friend's honeymoon. Was it irony or destiny that she and Katie had met on the set of a movie called *Hanging Rock*?

.   .   .

Hanging Rock would have been a pretty good name for a movie if it had had anything at all to do with the former volcano in Australia that carried that moniker. It didn't. It was a Western, which left Carmen flummoxed: You could drop a rope from a branch and create a hanging tree, but who hung a noose from a rock? Or, for that matter, if you interpreted the two words a little differently, why would you dangle a rock from a rope at the end of a tree limb? Carmen had wanted to ask these questions from the moment she'd been cast, but she had the common sense to keep her disdain to herself. The film was about a corrupt sheriff in a corrupt cow town sometime in the late nineteenth century, and the decent, courageous cattleman who wants to avenge the unfair prairie justice—a hanging—that was meted out upon his older brother: Porter Rock. It came out in 1958, which was a good year for movies. Most of the film was terrible, and it never had a chance for any best-picture awards. But some people thought Katie should have gotten a Best Actress nomination over Anna Magnani for her work in *Wild Is the Wind* and Deborah Kerr for *Heaven Knows, Mr. Allison.* She was never going to beat Joanne Woodward for her performance that year in *The Three Faces of Eve,* but a lot of critics had what seemed a genuine love for Katie's portrayal of Porter Rock's kid sister.

Carmen had two scenes with Katie in that film and they were her only moments in the movie. (They'd filmed a third scene of her confronting the sheriff that she was proud of, but she discovered at the premiere that it had been cut.) Both of the remaining scenes were on an outdoor set in the backlot and involved horses, and so she and Katie had a lot of time to bond while the lighting was set and the animals were wrangled onto their marks. She hadn't realized until they'd started to chat that she'd seen Katie onstage when they'd both been teenagers, because back then Katie was using her family name: she was still Katie Stepanov. Carmen was never the type who went gaga over anyone or anything, but she'd nonetheless found herself, at first, uncharacteristically awed.

"It helped that my parents produced a lot of shows," Katie said. "I had a leg up on everyone else my age."

"But you also had—also have—a lot more talent than everyone else your age."

Katie shrugged. "Again: I was getting lessons and coaching from the time I was, I don't know, three years old."

They discovered they were the same age and both came from the East Coast, though Carmen had grown up in the Westchester suburbs of New York City and her father was an adman and her mother a homemaker. There was no Stepanov or Broadway

glamor to her childhood: she was the kid in a balcony seat at
the Nederlander, and Katie was the kid on the stage. But that
was, in its way, the template for their friendship. Carmen was a
lady in waiting to the first daughter from a family of East Coast
entertainment royalty that now, thanks to Katie, had a beach-
head on the West Coast. But Katie looked after Carmen, too,
making sure that Reggie's PR firm took her on and advocating
on Carmen's behalf when there was the right sort of role for her
friend: a role that had a great line or a great moment. A scene
that demanded a little nuance.

And that was fine. Most of the time, Carmen took great
pleasure in the reality that she was a Hollywood actress, even
if she was never going to have her own star on the Hollywood
Walk of Fame. She knew how fortunate she was. She knew the
breaks she'd had to get where she was and how easily it could
all disappear. Careers dissipated because of low grosses and bad
choices, and they disappeared beneath the pounds of pancake
and clown makeup they'd put on Bette Davis the year before last
for *What Ever Happened to Baby Jane?* She knew the euphemism:
aging out.

When she thought of her mother or her sister back in Westchester or got letters from them, she would breathe a sigh of
relief that she was here and not there. Neither worked. Neither
had ever worked. Her mother still mailed her magazine recipes
that she cut from *Women's Day* in which the ingredients were
canned pineapple, mayonnaise, and cream cheese. Her sister sent
her housekeeping articles from *Ladies' Home Journal* that supposed she cared so much about a polished floor that she'd spread
the wax evenly on the brush with a butter knife. Her sister was
married now and had a three-year-old son, and both her mother
and her sister sent her the same *Good Housekeeping* essay by a
woman who rued the loss of her husband to another woman
because she had chosen not to have babies.

Her mother and father had visited her and Felix in August,
and it was clear to Carmen that they were proud of her but

uneasy with her career. They were suspicious of her neighbors, who all seemed to be involved in the movie business and all seemed to have—at least based on the stories they'd read in the Hollywood fan magazines—questionable morals. She could tell that her father had the same doubts about Felix he'd had since she had first introduced the writer, then her fiancé, to him. There was something about Felix that rubbed Richard Tedesco the wrong way, something the older man didn't quite approve of. It may have been the way that Felix tried to ingratiate himself to her father. "Sucking up" was the expression Carmen herself had used after their first dinner together, when she was explaining to Felix that her father had spent enough years making up crap to sell cigarettes and soap that his bullshit meter was infallible. She understood Felix's insecurities, but he should have had the spine or the common sense to stop dropping names as soon as he mentioned Clayton Moore—the Lone Ranger—and her father observed, "We did a Cheerios commercial together. He was a consummate professional. Quiet and good with the kids on the set. Never said a word about himself."

But once again that past August, Felix had fortified himself with bourbon before meeting his in-laws for dinner their first night in California, and by the time they'd all finished their appetizers, her parents were exchanging glances or her father was sitting back against the leather booth, his arms folded across his chest, and staring over Felix's shoulder at the fish in the res-taurant's aquarium. Felix just couldn't stop pretending he was the Crown Prince of Hollywood because his father was an A-list director and he himself had a few screenplay credits. By dessert, Felix was getting the rapier-like slice of the Richard Tedesco side-eye.

She wanted to tell Felix, this isn't who you are. This isn't the man I married. This isn't how you are when we're alone, and this isn't the man I love.

And so when they said good night to their parents and sent them off to the hotel, when it was just the two of them in their jazzy little Thunderbird (a wedding gift from Felix's parents), she started to tell him all that. But he was morose and drunk and she wanted him to focus on the road, especially when she thought of how his poor sister had died. And so she said nothing, and an idea came to her and it gave her pause: what if this *is* the man that I married?

.　.　.

And now these white men with their Russian accents were telling her to get up off the ground, this dry Serengeti soil, barking their orders. They were commanding her and Reggie and Felix to stand up. She looked at her husband and the tawny dust that his tears had glued to his face, and how he wasn't moving.

"Get up!" one of the men hollered at him, kicking him in the ribs with his foot, the sound of his boot against Felix's side reminiscent of the thud of her mother's mallet on chuck steak on the cutting board. (What women's magazine recipe was that? The one with the dry onion soup mix? That revolting powder that came in the packet?)

Instead, Felix curled up into a ball, but Reggie took him by his arm and whispered urgently into his ear, "You're going to stand up and I'm going to be right beside you. You're okay, Felix, and Carmen's okay." Then, with a strength that Carmen had always suspected Reggie had but had never seen, he practically lifted her husband to his feet.

Felix glanced at her furtively, ashamed, but Carmen was ashamed, too. She was mortified that she had seen so deep into her husband's soul—it was pornographic—and she was almost as disgusted by her reaction as she was by his.

"This way, move, now," the fellow was telling them, and he started to march them toward the second of the two Land Rovers.

"Carmen, I'm sorry," he sniffled. "I'm sorry." His apology only annoyed her further. He sounded like a little boy.

"No," she told him, feeling more like his mother than his wife. "You're right to be scared. We should be. But . . ."

He wiped at his eyes with his fists.

"But we'll be fine," she told him. She wasn't so sure about their African porters and Muema, the lone surviving guide, and she wasn't even so sure about Charlie Patton. But the white people from California? She had the sense this was all about them, and they were far more valuable alive than they would be dead.

CHAPTER SEVEN

Terrance Dutton

Terrance Dutton was among those spotted in Washington, D.C., last month, listening to the Rev. Dr. King, Jr., Mrs. Medgar Evers, and other speakers. The actor has always been a little "outspoken" when it comes to the changing politics of America, and most people in Hollywood know that to work with the Negro actor means playing as much by his rules as theirs.

—The Hollywood Reporter, SEPTEMBER 15, 1963

They changed the tire and they left the camp.

The fellow who was driving didn't look like the plantation scions who wanted to make sure that Terrance and his family never "forgot who they were" (the words of one elderly descendant of a local general from the Lost Cause), other than the fact he was white. He was too solid and boxy to be the sort of southern white boy who drank booze with sprigs of mint in a highball glass, and he lacked those eyes that could transform in a blink from condescending but kind to acid if a Black man said the wrong thing. He was muscular and, it seemed, a little battle-scarred himself. He exuded weariness—maybe a war, Terrance surmised, but maybe a lifetime of petty degradations he himself had endured in one communist country or another—and the little hair he had on his head was as short as two-day-old beard stubble. Meanwhile, his partner, the one in the last row of seats in the Land Rover with a rifle slung over his shoulder and a pistol aimed at the back of their heads, seemed rather self-satisfied. Pleased with how things were turning out. Both of their captors spoke English, but Terrance couldn't decide how fluent they really were. Terrance wasn't positive, but he suspected that the rifle might have been one of Charlie Patton's weapons.

The Land Rover had three rows of bucket seats and a solid row in the back. The driver was alone in the first row. Billy and Margie Stepanov were in the second. Their guard was in the fourth. And he and David and Katie were wedged together in the third, though Katie was more in her husband's lap than in the bucket seat.

The camp was growing small in the distance as they bounced along the savanna, and Terrance was feeling more anger than fear. Yes, there was the helplessness of having to accept treatment like this because these two men had guns and they didn't, and, yes, there was the unmistakable reality that these bastards were part of a group that had coolly shot an unarmed grandfather and two rangers—one who had his rifle out and was going to try to protect the Americans, but one who had simply failed to drop his gun quickly enough. Terrance was frightened, readily he could admit that to himself. But he was also furious. How the fuck had he escaped the humiliations great and small that dogged a Black man in huge chunks of America, only to wind up with two white guys holding him at gunpoint in Africa? Was there no place on the planet where he wouldn't have to calculate whether a slight was worth a response or whether he should let the indignity breeze past him? Was there no place in the world where he wasn't going to—in this case, quite literally—have to fight to survive?

. . .

He'd gotten death threats before when they'd been shooting on location, especially the two times he'd agreed to film south of the Mason-Dixon line. There was the cop drama, some of which was set on the Outer Banks off North Carolina, and there were those nightmarish six days when they'd filmed in Mobile. He hoped he'd never have to film again in the South, but he knew that his clout was limited. (How hard had Natalie Wood worked to get the authority from the studio to pick even one of her films? She'd told Terrance it was practically a cockfight when she announced that she wanted to be in *West Side Story*.) At least he would *try* never again to film in the South. But Tennessee would always be the deal breaker, his line in the sand: if he was ever sent a script for a picture that was set in Tennessee, either he'd put in a rider that his scenes were to be filmed anyplace but Tennessee or he'd pass. Now that he had moved his parents to California and his sister and brother-in-law lived in Chicago, he was never going to set foot in that state again. He doubted his parents or his sister would either. His parents had gotten a dog last year, an adorable little mutt from the shelter that was part terrier and, they joked, part pig. They doted on that animal like it was a newborn baby and he asked them why they'd never had a dog when he and his sister had been kids, given how much they adored having a pet. And it was only after the question had escaped his mouth that he had the flashback: they had had a dog. And someone had poisoned it. He was too young to have more than vague, inchoate memories of the animal, because he'd been three—maybe four—when someone had killed it, but he'd figured out early on how the dog's murder had devastated his mother and how he should never, ever bring it up. And soon the memory was buried deep in the sludge of the hippocampus, unrecoverable until his parents, safely in Southern California, had gotten another pet and the lugubrious recollection had been exhumed.

Sometimes he took bizarre comfort from the fact that the local galleries had refused to include his paintings and sketches in their student art shows when he'd been an adolescent because he wasn't white. His work was good enough, and at the time, when he was thirteen and fourteen, he'd been devastated by the unfairness of it. But, in hindsight, the consolation prize of that discrimination was that instead of growing into a starving painter, he had wound up a pretty damn wealthy actor.

It was only in the last year or so, after Kennedy was shot, that he had begun to take his death threats a little more seriously. Before that, even though he'd grown up with a kid whose uncle had been lynched, he'd written off the always anonymous warnings as the rantings of racist crazies. Why in the world would someone bother to take out an actor? And it hadn't even seemed logistically possible. He was usually in crowds, and movies had pretty solid security. But then Medgar Evers was shot in his own driveway in Mississippi, and the president was assassinated in Texas—and there were enormous crowds lining the streets in Dallas that day—and so he'd actually informed the police of the two threats he'd received in the last year. Had they viewed them as legitimate and frightening? The cops in northern Vermont had. But the ones in Albuquerque? He was less sure. Nevertheless, the studio had brought in extra security in both cases. He was encouraged to stay inside his trailer in New Mexico for long spells, baking in the tin can that had a small window and a crappy little fan to cool what seemed an increasingly inhospitable oven.

Of all the threats he had received over the years, the most deplorable might have been the ones he had gotten recently, only about three weeks before Katie and David's wedding. The wedding was going to be at the Beverly Wilshire, and someone from the hotel had leaked the guest list. The press reacted to the idea that Katie's Black friend Terrance Dutton was going to be among the people in attendance—and, the reporters supposed, whatever Black woman he was dating—with its usual tolerance. Katie was viewed as both headstrong and eccentric, the sort who, if she weren't an actress, would have been among those people in the North and the East who were regularly riding those buses into the South to face off against the fire hoses and police dogs. But she had gone once. When Terrance had suggested that she and some of their friends take a stand and join a group of freedom riders, she had joined him. But she was the only one. Everyone else had passed. Their excuses, invariably, were work. So, he and Katie had gone alone, getting more threats, and making more headlines. They'd had to stay in separate hotels, but still the gossips had a field day. According to both of their agents, it had probably cost them some roles but perhaps had gotten them others. They'd never know.

In any case, Terrance was on set in August, the month before the wedding, wrapping a drama about a Black family in Detroit that was almost (but not quite) torn apart when the teen son wants to become a recording star instead of following his father into the auto plant. It was the first time that Terrance had played a man old enough to have a teen child. He'd supposed Michigan was safe ground, but the idea that he was going to be at Katie's wedding had resurrected all the *Tender Madness* innuendo: the idea the movie had suggested that his and Katie's characters had kissed and the subsequent rumors that they were lovers, but the scene had been cut.

Which was, of course, precisely what had happened: they had kissed. They had kissed through seven takes and he had taken off her blouse seven times. The director (or, more likely, the studio) had decided to end the scene at the point where it seemed inevitable the characters would kiss, but audiences in places like Spartanburg, South Carolina, or Richmond, Virginia, could tell themselves that Katie's character had come to her senses. Or, even if she hadn't, at least they didn't have to see America's sweetheart making love with Terrance Dutton.

Nevertheless, some of the Michigan papers republished some of the press photos from *Tender Madness* while he was on location, one that was decidedly steamy, and the vibe on the set grew tense. The threats were more vile than usual, more disgusting, and they involved castration. Whoever was mailing the studio had also discovered the Detroit hotel where the cast was staying and left telephone messages with the clerks at the front desk that were as coarse as the letters that MGM was receiving. But, as always, whoever was behind the threats was as cowardly as they were hateful, and never showed themselves.

Still, Terrance was glad that he had gone stag to Katie's wedding. He'd almost brought Felicia, but he feared that would only reignite a romance, and that wasn't fair to her. He liked her, but he didn't love her. There was, obviously, a chasm-like difference between the two feelings. The problem was that they were so damn good together: at restaurants, in bed, at the bowling alley in Crenshaw a couple blocks from the high school where she was an English teacher. He constantly had to remind himself that loving someone's company a couple of days or nights a week was just not the same as loving someone so much that you wanted that company all the time and felt a little unmoored when you were going to be away from them for any real length of time. He knew that she loved him that way, and that wasn't actorly narcissism. Moreover, she wanted children, and, at least right now, he didn't. What if he did bring her to Katie's wedding and whoever was sending him the threats chose that Saturday to try something violent? What if she were injured (or worse) because he'd brought her along as arm candy? Horrifying. Horrifying and despicable.

At one point at the wedding, when he was standing near the bar sipping a Manhattan (minus the cherry), the bartender uncorked another bottle of champagne with a great pop, and a couple of the drunken guests clapped. A tiny, pretty woman with white-blond hair in cherubic curls, an actress whose name escaped him, extended her champagne flute like a street urchin, imploring the bartender for more. Terrance turned away and gazed at the dance floor, and realized that he was one of the only guests between the ages of twenty and seventy who was still sober. Certainly, the dancers were feeling no pain. Even Glenda Stepanov, the toxic witch who somehow had birthed a lovely creature like Katie Stepanov, was tipsy: she kicked aside her heels as she was twirled around the floor by Katie's agent,

Peter Merrick. And Terrance felt, as he did often, at once absolutely invisible and an awkward, flagrant outsider.

. . .

"You don't sound like you're from around here," Terrance said to the guy behind him with the pistol and the rifle hanging off his shoulder. It was a trial balloon, an attempt at conversation. It couldn't hurt to remind their captors that the five Americans in the Land Rover were human beings, too. At least that's what he was thinking when he turned around and opened his mouth. Now that he'd heard his voice, he thought how being human didn't necessarily help in the United States, and it probably wasn't an especially compelling reason to keep someone alive here in the Serengeti. Nevertheless, when the guard just glared at him and said nothing, Terrance decided to press: "My name is Terrance. I'm guessing you don't want to tell me yours, but I'm Terrance."

"Stop talking," he said in that accent, and then he leaned forward and placed the pistol against the side of Terrance's skull. He continued slowly, enunciating carefully, though his accent never wavered. "Say one more word and your brains will be on the back of the seat ahead of you."

He felt Katie's fingers on his forearm, pressing hard into the skin. He got the message. He put up his hands in a sign of surrender, his heart thumping hard now in his chest, and the fellow pulled back the gun. He looked satisfied.

Outside the vehicle, no more than fifty yards away, Terrance saw a dozen elephants grazing, and one giant with great tusks looked up at the vehicle, no doubt trying to decide whether it represented a danger. *Well,* Terrance thought, *not to you, old friend. Not to you.*

CHAPTER EIGHT

Felix Demeter

*Our inside sources tell us that Oscar-winning director Rex Demeter
is no fan of his son Felix's latest film. "He thinks he's Ben Hecht,
he thinks he's Billy Wilder. He's not. At least not yet. He thinks
because I'm his old man he automatically has some writing chops,"
Rex was overheard saying while holding court and savoring the lob-
ster bisque at Fred and Wally's on Wilshire.*

—*Movie Star Confidential*, JULY 1962

Felix tried to stop shaking, but he couldn't. He could feel the
blood in his head, in his temples; he guessed he could feel it
everywhere. He was hot and he was humiliated, but none of that
mattered quite as much as the fact he was terrified and his body
was trembling. Two of the men who had thrust them into the
second Land Rover were in the vehicle with them, one driving
and one in the back with a couple of guns. He had the taste of his
vomit in his mouth, and there was a tendril still staining his shirt
that he had tried and failed to swipe to the floor, and while it
might not in fact have been stinking up the whole rig, he sure as
hell could smell it. He supposed that Carmen could too. She was
gently holding his hand and stroking it, but she couldn't look at
him—or she wouldn't look at him—and he couldn't blame her.
But he hadn't been able to help himself. He just hadn't. He had
seen people killed. Shot. There were those rangers. There was

poor Juma. And maybe Charlie Patton. God, he had thought they were about to kill him (and he thought they still might).

The two Land Rovers were starting away from the camp in a small convoy. Behind them, the camp was being ransacked. The attackers didn't seem to be disassembling it; they were just taking the things they wanted or needed. His first morning in the Serengeti, Felix had supposed tearing down the camp would be a monumental task, but Patton had told him that with a good crew, the village could be created and taken apart in a couple of hours. (This was, Patton had implied, a good crew.) Three or four of the crazies from Russia or Romania or wherever had been ordering Patton's African team around when the Land Rovers were leaving, and he had no idea whether the interlopers had the slightest idea what they were doing, but it probably didn't matter: by lunchtime, they would have stripped the camp of its assets.

Reggie had started to say something to Carmen as the car had begun accelerating over the grass, but the guy behind them had swatted the back of the publicist's head (and swatted it hard) and told him to shut up. None of them were to speak. None of them were to say a word.

Felix gazed out the window and saw that the giraffes that had been at the watering hole moments ago had vanished, but the wildebeest and zebras and a couple of elegant impalas had returned.

Assuming, of course, they had ever even left.

.   .   .

Felix Demeter knew that he would never be mistaken for one of those Horatio Alger pluck-and-luck sorts of Hollywood success stories. He wasn't even sure he viewed himself as successful—or as successful as he should have been by now, at thirty-five, given the reverence the community had for his father.

He vacillated wildly between seeing himself as a serious A-list screenwriter who was asked to work on very good projects, and as a hack already flirting with middle age who had one solo credit and three co-credits to his résumé. Of those four movies, one had been a box office grand slam, two had been mediocre in every imaginable way (the grosses and the reviews), and one an absolute bust. His solo credit had not been the big winner. His father, who had three little gold men in his screening room in the family home in the Canyon, two for directing and one an honest-to-God, can't-make-this-up Best Picture Oscar, was still working, and his films, invariably, utterly destroyed everything Felix touched. If he died anytime soon, Felix supposed, his obit—if anyone even bothered to write one—would be more a biography of his father than a litany of his own accomplishments. His life, so far, was largely one of proximity to one human's success (his father, Rex) and another's tragic death (his sister, Olivia).

Felix had nothing lined up after they returned from this ridiculous odyssey into Africa, and he would have preferred to have remained behind in Los Angeles to try to prospect for work.

Still, he took comfort that even here in the Serengeti he was surrounded by people who could further his career. Carmen alone wasn't ever going to be the catalyst that got something made, but her best friend, Katie, sure as hell was. And her agent, Peter Merrick, wasn't a bad ally to have. Neither was Reggie Stout, both Katie's and Carmen's publicist. God, Reggie knew everyone in Hollywood and, despite the whispers that sometimes trailed him, was venerated. The man was a fixture and, for a person who owned a public relations agency, considered scrupulously honest. Perhaps it was that war hero vibe. Perhaps he really was the last genuine man in L.A.

Felix saw Peter Merrick having breakfast alone at the hotel their first morning in Nairobi, before they started south into the Serengeti, and descended upon him like a hawk on a chipmunk.

He had seen him at the wedding and then a week later at the airport and then on the plane, but he had managed absolutely zero solo face time with him. Or, for that matter, with the bride or with Reggie. God, Peter and Reggie were like Katie's bodyguards. But the agent was alone now with his eggs Benedict and a pot of coffee, and so Felix sat himself down across from Peter, grabbing one of the three empty seats at the table. Carmen was still upstairs in their hotel room, savoring what she knew would be her last brush for a week and a half with indoor plumbing, a porcelain tub, and a decent mirror to put on her face. Only after Felix had unfolded the napkin and planted his flag on this coveted spot of ground did he excuse himself to pile cheese and fruit on his plate from the buffet and order an omelet from the waiter in the white coat and red fez who was easily as punctilious and proper as a Buckingham Palace butler. When he had returned to his seat, he worried that he had grabbed too much food and looked like the sort of traveler who'd never seen a hotel spread this lavish, and quickly—reflexively—dropped the dad card, telling Peter how highly his father thought of the agent. It was a complete lie. His father, as far as Felix knew, had never even crossed paths with Peter Merrick.

The agent sipped his coffee and seemed to be looking past Felix. His eyebrows, bushy and silver, hung like strands of Christmas tree garland over his eyes. "Have your father and I even met?" he asked. "Your father is repped by Ted Hoffman at DKM and has been forever. Since the dawn of time."

"Maybe you met at a gala or a premiere or something," Felix replied, hoping vagueness made him sound more truthful. "But he speaks very highly of you."

"That's very nice. When we get back, I'll be sure and tell Ted that and ruin his day." Peter was wearing a white polo shirt, and the shoulders were stretched tight. He was tan and his hair, though entirely white, was thick. He was in his early sixties and his face was suitably lined, but he still had the aura of a much younger man. His response was meant to make Felix shiver ever so slightly and it did. Inadvertently, either Felix had implied to this super agent that his father was looking for new representation (which sure as hell wasn't the case), or his pathetic attempt to suck up to Peter had been agonizingly clear. He considered backtracking right now but took comfort in the reality that they would be together in the middle of nowhere for the next eleven days, and he would have plenty of chances to straighten this out if, it seemed, he needed to. And so, for the moment, he simply skewered some kind of fruit he had never seen before and hoped to God it wasn't going to give him the trots.

"I liked your wife's last movie," Peter continued, choosing to change the subject and have mercy on Felix.

"Carmen's amazing," he agreed, though a part of him had wished that the agent had brought up his own last movie. He was only one of the three writers in the credits, and much of what he had penned had been discarded well before they started shooting, but none of that mattered. His name was on it.

"She is. Very talented girl. How did you two meet?"

"A party. No meet-cute."

"You're a writer, you can do better than that."

Felix poured a little cream into his coffee and looked around the dining room. At the hallucinatory colors of the frangipani and bougainvillea and kaffir boom. At the trophies of different kinds of dead antelope with all manner of horn on the walls. At the two taxidermal giraffes under the dome in the center of the room, overlooking those long white linen-clad tables of fruits and cheeses and biscuits. When he'd walked past one, he'd realized he would have been roughly eye level with the damn thing's nuts, which, thank God, someone had had the good sense to lop off since they were parking the corpse in the dining room.

"Okay," Felix agreed, hoping to rise to the challenge. He sat forward in his seat, a plush armchair with butterflies on the upholstery that in his opinion would have been more appropriate in a library in a castle in Scotland than a hotel dining room in East Africa, and began, his voice epitaphic, "Olivia—my kid sister—had just died in a car accident."

"The one on Mulholland? I had forgotten."

"Coldwater Canyon, technically. But, yes, within yards of Mulholland."

He had the agent's full attention now and decided to bare it all. Milk it for every bit it was worth.

"Her funeral was on a Tuesday, and I was a mess. She was twenty-five, I was thirty. *Amsterdam* had just bombed—though not because of the script."

"It's not a bad script," Peter agreed, which wasn't precisely the enthusiasm Felix craved, but he wasn't going to be deflected from his narrative. It was his second movie, and he thought it was pretty good for a sophomore effort.

"Thank you. It's really not. Still, I was unprepared for its truly epic failure. And then Olivia died."

"Was killed."

"Yes. Was killed," he repeated. "Obviously, my parents weren't doing well. My mother was a mess, and my father wasn't doing much better. And my father has, as you probably know, more ice than blood in his veins. Think of that ball cap he wears when he directs." Felix was prepared to reveal what was embroidered across the front: NOBODY MOVES, NOBODY GETS HURT. But Peter nodded knowingly as he sipped his coffee, and so Felix continued, "None of us handled Olivia's death very well."

"How do you 'handle' something like that well?" the agent asked, but it was a rhetorical, sympathetic question. "No parent wants to outlive a child. No mother wants to outlive her daughter."

"No," Felix agreed. "Anyway, I started drinking at the reception after the funeral. I started at the reception, continued at the bar at the Chateau Marmont with a couple of friends who wanted to console me, and continued alone at my apartment in West Hollywood."

Peter folded his arms across his chest. "Your sister is killed by some drunk where Mulholland meets Coldwater, and you drove home drunk from a bar?"

"Nope. Left my car there and got a cab."

"Good for you."

"I was making nothing but bad choices that week, but none that were going to hurt anyone but me. I mean that. I blew off a meeting with Paramount. I didn't show up for a lunch with a director—who shall remain nameless, because he was seriously pissed off at me. There's a pool at my apartment, and I passed out there on the concrete in the middle of the day, the sun dead overhead, and burned the shit out of my back. Wound up in the ER with second-degree burns. I wasn't answering my phone, I wasn't opening my mail. I was an absolute mess. I loved Olivia, and the world seemed a really shitty, really heartless place."

"Oh, it is. Make no mistake, Felix: the universe doesn't give a rat's ass about any of us."

The waiter brought him his omelet and called him "bwana." He'd heard the Swahili word in safari movies and was momentarily taken aback to hear himself called "the man" or "the master" in person. He thanked the waiter and stared at his plate. It was the largest omelet he had ever seen in his life: it looked the size of a pizza cut in half. A small pizza, but a pizza nonetheless. The waiter was watching him, and he realized he was supposed to take a bite. So he did.

"Scrumptious," he said, though the eggs tasted different here, which made him uneasy. It was also a little chewy. "Hell of an omelet. Thank you."

The waiter bowed and left them alone.

"When I wasn't answering my phone, a friend of mine came by to check on me," he continued. "It was Friday by now, and I hadn't left the apartment or the pool. Apparently, I answered the door in my underwear, and I had done a real half-assed job of applying Noxzema to my back—except, I gather, to the back of my legs, where I had slathered the goop on like I was painting the side of a house. He cleaned me up and got some coffee and food in me. He looked at my sunburn and dragged me to the ER, where they gave me something a little better than Noxzema for my skin. And then, when I was sober and marginally less disgusting, he convinced me to go to a party, though I didn't drink anything but club soda when I was there. And that's where I met Carmen."

"I suppose you talked about Olivia that night."

Felix wasn't sure what to make of the agent's observation. He made it sound like he had used his sister's death to pick up a starlet. "Carmen's smart, she reads the papers. She knew and put two and two together. I didn't bring it up. She also knew that *Amsterdam* had flopped, and the whole idea that she was willing to talk about my latest movie debacle impressed me. She made me want to open up."

"A lot of people avoid our failures. Just pretend they don't exist."

"It's true."

"Tell me something."

"Sure."

"Which had you more upset? The fact that *Amsterdam* tanked or that your sister was dead?"

He saw Carmen standing in the entrance to the dining room, scanning the tables for him.

"I'll know if you're lying, Felix. I really will," Peter continued, and though Felix had never been arrested, he had the feeling that this was, at least a little bit, what an interrogation felt like. He could sense the strange intensity in the question and in the way that the agent was pressing him. It wasn't bullying, but he still felt intimidated and scared. Transparent. Quickly he stood, waving at Carmen and then motioning at the empty seats at the table.

"My sister," he said to the agent, hoping he sounded just a little indignant, even though on some primal level he knew he was lying. "Obviously." Then he kissed his wife on the cheek and told her that the kitchen staff made an omelet that was fluffy and light and delicious. Lying, he understood, was a reflex of his, and he supposed this was what made him a writer.

.   .   .

There were only five of them in the Land Rover, counting their two abductors, and so Felix assumed that the six other Americans were wedged into the first one. The vehicle that had a bunch of windows shot away. But he guessed some could be back at the camp, waiting to be tossed into one of the lorries. Or, dear God, dead, too. The problem was that the other Land Rover was just far enough in the distance that he couldn't see where everyone was, and now they were separating. Fanning out. Already the first vehicle was disappearing from view.

He tried to convince himself that the others, wherever they were, were fine. They had to be. They couldn't be dead, he reassured himself. Their captors had demonstrated that they were willing to kill Africans, but this had to be a kidnapping and they certainly wouldn't risk the wrath of the United States by murdering Americans. Not possible. It just couldn't be possible.

They'd been driving fifteen minutes, and when Felix turned around, he noticed that Reggie was rubbing the back of his skull, where he'd been hit, with one hand. His other hand was in his front pants pocket. They passed a herd of wildebeest and then a field with baboons, including four small ones—children—climbing up and down a tree with a slender trunk. They were playing a game, it seemed, trying to pull each other down before one could reach a branch about ten or twelve feet off the ground, and he was reminded of a new kids' toy called Chimp to Chimp, where you had to use little plastic monkeys with S's for arms to lift other identical monkeys off the table. Whoever could lift the most chimps off the table and create the longest chain won.

Felix allowed his gaze to linger for a moment on Reggie's hand in his pocket. He saw the tip of a jackknife and realized the publicist was either trying to flip open the blade or, perhaps, sur-reptitiously remove the knife. Rubbing his head? It was a magi-cian's distraction, a bit of vaudeville misdirection for the guard in the back row. Felix considered stopping him: reaching back and putting his own hand on top of Reggie's forearm, because he didn't want the other man to do something that might get them all killed. He was afraid that the guy, because he was a vet-eran and happened to have a little pocket knife with him, would try something stupid.

But he didn't want to risk drawing the attention of the guard with the guns behind them. That scared him too.

God, everything scared him. Everything. He had to pee, he had to pee badly, and he knew it was more because he was frightened than because of the breakfast coffee.

He spotted a lone ostrich in the distance, and the big bird seemed fearless to him. He wondered what that was like—to be stoic, to be strong, to be unafraid—as his eyes, once more, began welling up.

CHAPTER NINE

Margie Stepanov

The rumor is that Katie Barstow's wedding dress is being designed by MGM's legendary costume designer Helen Rose. But the actress was spotted at a bridal boutique on Santa Monica with her sister-in-law, Margie Stepanov. Margie is married to Katie's brother, Billy, and very likely a bridesmaid. And so it's possible that Katie was merely picking out dresses for her entourage. We would know if the star had had a falling out or a couture disagreement with the venerable Miss Rose.

—*The Hollywood Reporter,* JUNE 15, 1964

Margie put both of her hands across her belly as the Land Rover bumped along, and she thought of the child inside her. The link had been the baby baboons they had just passed. She was terrified for herself, but she was filled as well with self-loathing for being here in the first place. She should have listened to her physician; she shouldn't have come. She had jeopardized the kid. (Already that's what she and Billy were calling the fetus. The kid. It worked for them since they had no idea whether it was a boy or a girl, and the reality that she had not had any morning sickness further solidified the nickname in their minds. Their baby was jaunty and easy and unflappable: the kid was such a trooper that he or she didn't even make Mom vomit.) Neither the monster who was driving nor the one who was in the last row of seats and pointing a gun at them had even bothered to wipe the remains of poor Juma's brains off the window.

Billy was a shrink and had said, half joshing but half serious, that children had formative experiences in the womb and the kid—their kid—would benefit from the Serengeti. He or she would absorb all the happy chemicals that Mom was creating as she communed with lions and elephants and giraffes.

Well, that supposed it was a joyful excursion. If Billy was right, she shuddered when she thought of what she was doing to the kid now.

She was in the Land Rover with the rear and side windows that had been shattered, and a new tire pressed into service to replace the one that had been shot. But they hadn't been allowed to wipe the glass shards off the seats, and though she didn't think her ass was bleeding badly, she could feel the way at least some of the shards had cut through her khakis and sliced into her skin. Billy had managed to staunch the bleeding where pulverized slivers of glass had shredded a part of her shirt and gashed her stomach, but it wasn't as if he had sealed the wound with gauze and an antiseptic: he'd poured some canteen water on the cut as the Land Rover sped away and then pressed a bandanna firmly against the laceration until the bleeding stopped. It started again when he removed it, though he pulled it away from the skin as gently as he could, as if her stomach were an unopened Christmas present and he didn't want to tear the wrapping paper. But she thought it was starting to scab over now. Still, she was afraid the cut would only get worse. She feared an infection, either from the broken glass or the bandanna or even the tepid canteen water.

There were also bugs trapped inside the vehicle with them because they weren't allowed to open the roof, and the insects were too damn stupid to find their way to an open window or through the broken glass. One moment, they would be flying into the windshield, trying to escape, and the next they would be landing on the humans' arms or getting caught in their hair. She tried to shoo some of them through the shattered window beside her, but she dinged her fingers when she tried and the last thing she needed was yet another cut.

They could no longer see the other Land Rover that had left with them because the two vehicles had spread out in different directions. But she was pretty sure that she had only witnessed Felix, Carmen, and Reggie being shoved into it before they had left the camp. She was not 100 percent certain because it had all happened so fast and she had just seen Juma and the rangers shot dead, and then she was sobbing in a way that she never before had in her life. But in this vehicle, she could account for Billy (thank God) and Katie and David and Terrance.

It crossed her mind that it was the agent who was missing. Merrick. Peter Merrick. So was Charlie Patton. Or at least she had no idea where he was either. The last she could recall, the two older men had been laughing together over breakfast in the dining tent. Patton had just taught the agent an expression, and the two of them had shared it with her as she passed them on her way to see the giraffes at the watering hole.

Still drinking their booze.

Something like that.

Or, in the past tense, if you were back in Arusha or Nairobi. *Still drank their booze.*

It was the way a guide hunter would describe a safari that had all gone to shit because the clients were cowardly or stupid or cruel—because they snapped at each other or the woman tried sleeping with the hunter or the man was spooked by a buffalo or asked the hunter to bag his rhino for him—but it was part of the code that you never spoke ill of the people who were paying you well to find them their trophies. And so, if the safari had become one long annoyance, a hunter, when asked about it, would nod and murmur, "Still drinking their booze."

And that was it. Hemingway, according to Patton, had co-opted the expression in a short story, and some of the hunters who read it had thought it was a betrayal—as if Hemingway had shared a secret code with the world.

Up until that moment in the breakfast tent, Margie supposed, no one in this group had been cowardly or stupid or cruel. But, of course, this was just a photo safari. So no one was ever leaving their Land Rovers when they spotted animals. No one was trying to "collect" (and that was the euphemism that Charlie and Peter seemed to use instead of "kill" or "shoot" or "slaughter") a lion or leopard or buffalo.

And she rather doubted that Katie Barstow or Carmen Tedesco had tried to seduce Charlie Patton.

But then it dawned on her. The reason that Peter Merrick and Charlie Patton were laughing about such things was because Merrick was staying an extra week and Patton was taking him hunting in another section of Tanzania. Merrick knew at least something about guns. Maybe the two of them weren't in either Land Rover because they were hatching some sort of scheme to rescue the rest of the group.

No. That wasn't happening. She was trying to think like a screenwriter, and this wasn't a movie and those two older men weren't going to save them: this was real life and if Peter or Charlie weren't in one of the Land Rovers, it was probably because they were dead. That was the difference between a horror film and a real horror. No one was going to appear suddenly on the horizon—the cavalry coming over the hill—and rescue them.

.   .   .

Juma's patience was endless, Margie decided, a guide whose affection for the natural world never waned, no matter how many times he was out here in the Serengeti. And, clearly, he had been out here a lot, once upon a time as a cook boy, then a porter, a gun bearer, a head man, and now the chief guide for Charlie Patton, whose company these days brought far more Westerners to see the animals than to shoot them. He loved to speak of his grandchildren, whom he had taken on photo safaris since the creation of the reserve, sometimes having them travel in groups of two or three on the vacant seats of the puddle jumpers that flew from Arusha to the grass strip near Wasso.

By the end of the first day, Juma already had taught Katie Barstow's group dozens of small facts that she thought would stay with her forever: a hyena's poop was white because it ate so many bones; a topi was distinguishable from other antelope in a heartbeat because the coloring on its hind legs was reminiscent of blue jeans; a zebra's striping was as unique as a human's fingerprints, and zebra babies could instantly recognize their mothers in the herd.

Now, at the end of the second day, they were all drinking around the fire outside the dining tent, most of them sitting in canvas camp chairs, but Juma and Charlie were standing. The two of them were drinking tonic water, but everyone else was sipping gin or hot black coffee. There was a surprising chill in the air, and Margie finally decided she was just cold enough that she climbed from her seat and plopped herself into Billy's lap, curling up against him for warmth like a small child. The stars stretched forever here, a quilt that spread beyond the horizon and offered a zodiac one constellation at a time. Each star was a bright pinprick, and Margie imagined little astronomy projects she would find in magazines that she would share with her child someday: black construction paper and colored chalk, using nail scissors to punch holes in the firmament, a bedroom light without a shade providing for her child the light of the cosmos.

Billy wrapped his arms around her. "Your fingers are like ice," he observed and kissed her neck. She rapped his chest with one little fist because he had given her the chills on purpose. He did it all the time. He thought it was funny: he'd told her that he'd never met a person who got goosebumps as quickly.

"Soon you will be too big for Billy's lap," said Katie. "You'll be a big, beautiful, pregnant whale."

"Nope. She'll still climb into my lap whenever she pleases," Billy told his sister.

"Yes," said Margie. "I will." But she wasn't nearly as confident as she sounded. Once Billy had made a joke about his first wife and how plump she had grown when she had been carrying their son. He hadn't meant anything by it, but the remark had stayed with her.

"Tomorrow we want a leopard," Charlie told them all. "I feel . . . leopardy."

"Whenever bwana feels leopardy, watch out," Juma said, chuckling.

"Is it because we'll actually see one or because bwana will take us on a wild goose chase that will leave us all exhausted and cranky, but we won't get anywhere near one?" Margie asked. Billy rocked her a little bit. She snuggled deeper against him.

"We'll see one," said Juma. "I thank Jesus none of you wants to shoot one—"

"This week!" said Peter Merrick, who Margie supposed wanted very much to kill one when he was alone with Charlie next week, after the other Americans had returned to the United States.

"Yes, this week. When bwana feels leopardy, he means it. Ten years ago, he felt so leopardy he nearly got us both eaten by an especially smart cat."

"Oh?"

Everyone looked back and forth between the hunter and the old guide who had been with him for so many years in one capacity or another. Charlie said nothing for a moment, staring skyward at the great star-speckled quilt above them. Finally, he offered a few details, careful to protect the anonymity of his client. The gist of the story was pretty simple: a guest from the American South had wounded a buffalo, angering it and sending the injured animal into the brush beside a kopje with trees growing up and over the boulders. Charlie had murmured that he felt leopardy, but so far they had seen no sign of the big yellow animal with rosettes, and so Charlie and Juma began creeping on their stomachs toward where they thought the buffalo might be stewing. Sure enough, the damn thing charged and charged fast. A buffalo's head is virtually bulletproof, and its horn will poke a hole through a man that's as thick as a rolling pin. You have to aim for the nostril if it's racing toward you at thirty or thirty-five miles an hour and hope to obliterate the brain. But Charlie did precisely that, and Juma exhaled. Unfortunately, no sooner had Charlie accomplished that monumental bit of marksmanship, dropping a justifiably ornery buffalo in its tracks, than a leopard bounded from the branch of a tree and was about to leap on the hunter. Juma didn't have time to raise and aim his own rifle, so he swung it like a club, stunning the animal in midair.

"Then did you shoot it?" Margie asked. She hoped not. The whole story and the idea that Charlie Patton and Peter Merrick were going to spend the next week slaughtering things disgusted her.

"No. Didn't have to," said Charlie. "The cat turned and ran off."

"But when Charlie says he feels leopardy, stay in the Land Rover. Stay in your tents," Juma added.

"It's a violent world," murmured David Hill, and Margie couldn't help but wonder if her husband's childhood pal was thinking of things his father had done or alluded to at one point or another. Billy had told her two or three stories that David had shared with him that had left her shaking her head. MK-ULTRA. That was the name of the CIA task force he worked for, and she wasn't allowed to tell anyone. David didn't know quite what it was—he'd just overheard his father use the term on the telephone—and so Billy didn't either. But one time when David was in his mid-twenties, he was making his father a drink while visiting his family in Washington, and he'd dropped the cap to the whiskey bottle behind his parents' bar. It was during the period when his aimlessness was a source of frustration to his mother and father because he had no idea what to do with a degree in art history, since he had no desire to teach. He'd had to climb behind the bar to retrieve the cap, and there—in addition to the bottle top—he'd found the carbon copy of a phone message from Frank Olson. He was calling from the Statler Hotel in New York City. Olson was some kind of CIA spook who worked with David's father, David had told Billy, and he'd killed himself by diving from his hotel room on the tenth floor. What so disturbed David was that the message, taken by his father's secretary, made it clear that Olson had been calling over and over for two days—the two days before he'd fall one-hundred-plus feet to his death on a Manhattan sidewalk. And then there was that Ken Kesey strangeness, and that was well before Kesey wrote *One Flew Over the Cuckoo's Nest*. Something about the CIA and LSD. David only revealed these stories to Billy when the two of them were drinking, and Billy only shared them with her when he was feeling wistful after sex. It was pretty damn peculiar pillow talk, but she knew Billy's anxieties as well as anyone. At least she hoped she did.

"It is a violent world," Billy agreed. "But the violence among the leopards and buffaloes? A hell of a lot more natural than the nightmare across the border in the Congo. I don't know who's more dangerous: Mobutu and his crew or those Simbas in the east—in that province that tried to secede."

"Oh, they all hate us," said Charlie, his tone flat. "Or at least they should. Trust me, I've lived here my whole life, so I know: we have earned their wrath. The UN has boots on the ground, but I'm honestly not sure how that will help."

"And you know the Russians are involved," Billy added. "You just know it."

Charlie looked deep into the fire. "Yes," he said. "We do know that. And as dangerous as a leopard or a buffalo might be? Nothing compared to the Russians—at least the crowd they send here. I know that, too. If I ever tell any of you I'm feeling . . . Russiany? Duck and cover. And pray."

Then he raised his glass in a mock toast, stood, and said good night.

.   .   .

And now Charlie was gone, and she had no idea where.

And Juma was food for the jackals and vultures. Instead of driving them around in one of the two Land Rovers, seated behind the wheel in the front seat, he was but a corpse on the grass and splatter on the outside of the window. She felt a lurch in her stomach and wished to God it were morning sickness, and looked down at her fingers atop her belly. She had been mistaken: the cut wasn't quite scabbing over yet. It was still oozing. And it stung. She gave Billy a small smile and shrugged. He reached again for the bandanna, but the damn thing was filthy and she shook her head.

Instead, she pressed her hands flat on the seat and raised her bottom slightly into the air. Then she used her fingers like tweezers to pull a shard of glass from the back of her khakis. It was the width of her pinky and almost as long. It was beautiful and sharp, an obelisk that caught the sunshine as it streamed into the vehicle. There was blood on it, too. She studied it, not taking her eyes off it until a mosquito landed on the back of her hand holding the glass, and she swatted the insect dead.

CHAPTER TEN

Peter Merrick

*Peter Merrick is not recognizable the way his clients are, such as
Katie Barstow and Paul Sellars. But three of his clients took home
Academy Awards last week, and the super agent's face gets him
a table at any bistro or brasserie he wants—including Musso and
Frank, what might be Hollywood's oldest restaurant.*

—*The Hollywood Reporter,* APRIL 7, 1962

Peter Merrick had grown up in Sacramento and hunted deer
avidly as a teenager with his father and grandfather in Montana, most of the time using a rifle but once bagging a buck and
another time an elk with his grandfather's old-fashioned muzzle-
loader. It was his grandfather who'd first paraphrased Audubon
for him, teaching him in that wonderfully gravelly voice of his
that the outdoors isn't a place given to boys or girls by their
parents; nature is a place you're borrowing from your kids. His
grandfather believed that the slow walk in the woods or up the
mountain was more important than whether you succeeded in
tracking and dispatching your prey. He wanted his grandson to
tread gently and kill cleanly.

Peter had been too young for the First World War and too
old for the Second—at least for combat. He'd been in Southern
California for twenty years in 1942, having gone south in 1920
to attend the new state university there, and months after Pearl
Harbor was recruited by Jack Warner, who had somehow gone

from running Warner Brothers to being a lieutenant colonel in the army, to join the FMPU: First Motion Picture Unit. By then Merrick was an agent with his own table at the Brown Derby (near Warner's own table) and his own booth at Chasen's. The FMPU took over the Hal Roach Studios, christened the complex "Fort Roach," and began making morale movies and training films. Warner wanted Merrick because he knew the agent could help convince the likes of Clark Gable and Bill Holden to participate, and because—unlike almost everyone else associated with the project—he actually owned a gun and had discharged a weapon. He was also, Warner discovered, an immensely capable administrator. He got things done.

Now, as Merrick peered at the invaders (because, he thought, that's what they were) from behind a thick baobab tree, watching them ransack the camp, he wished he had a rifle. The safari staff was working at gunpoint to load the food and petrol into one of the trucks. He wanted to say the white men were Russian, but he wasn't completely sure.

In any case, he didn't have a rifle. He owned two, and one was back in his bungalow in Santa Monica and the other in the lorry with most of Charlie Patton's portable armory.

And what might be even better than one of his own rifles, if he had to be here in the Serengeti right now, would be the elephant gun that Patton had rented for him when he had taken care of his hunting license. The license allowed him twenty-five plains animals, ten rabbits, as many birds as he wanted, and a hippo. He had no plans to bring home anywhere near that many dead animals. He sure as hell had no need of a hippo. (God, how many people showed up to see the taxidermist at Zimmerman's in Nairobi hoping to have the gargantuan head of a hippo dipped and shipped?)

He watched the men throw the bodies of the two dead rangers and the dead guide into the back of one of the lorries.

He wasn't sure how he and Patton had gotten separated or where the hunter was now. Hadn't they both gone behind this

baobab to pee so the women could use the toilet tent before set-
ting out for the day? But then all hell had broken loose, and so
much was a blur.

He'd heard the pop of the guns and one of the Land Rovers taking off—and then screeching to a stop. He'd seen the rest
of the safari guests herded into another vehicle at gunpoint and
considered emerging from behind the tree with his hands up.
Surrendering to these . . . kidnappers. That's what he supposed
this was. A kidnapping. But he didn't believe he was hiding here
out of cowardice. He thought, for better or worse, that he was
being brave. His plan, as much as he had one, was that once the
porters, working at gunpoint, had finished loading the truck and
everyone had left, he would track down some Maasai villagers
and then together they would find more rangers and figure out
how to rescue Katie Barstow and her entourage. They'd passed a
Maasai boma yesterday when they had been skirting the edge of
the reserve, and it had been well into the afternoon. That meant
it might be walkable. It was to the southwest. He would try to
get there.

This all assumed, of course, that he didn't get himself eaten.
Or that they didn't spot him behind this tree and shoot him for
trying to evade capture.

He guessed Patton's tent was about forty yards away. They
hadn't searched it for provisions or torn it down yet.

And so he made a decision: he would sneak to that tent first
and see if any of Patton's guns were there. Most were in one of
the lorries, but not all. Maybe the rifle that fired the .375 H&H
Magnum would be in the tent. Or, if not that one, he presumed
the .38 Smith & Wesson might. A single weapon wouldn't help
much with the men back here at the camp: there were at least
three of them still here and probably a few more he hadn't spotted. But it might give him a fighting chance against any one of
the creatures out here in the savanna that would eat him as hap-
pily as it would a solitary klipspringer or oribi it found alone in
this endless ocean of grass.

. . .

Just yesterday, he had been in the third of the four rows of seats in the Land Rover, Terrance Dutton right beside him and Reggie Stout in the back. Katie Barstow and her husband were in the second row. They were traveling along the Mara River because Juma had heard that wildebeest were massing on the northern bank and there might be a crossing. But now Katie was pointing at the roll of toilet paper that the guide kept, among other critical provisions, in the front passenger seat to his left. For a movie star—for a woman who'd grown up in Manhattan—her utter lack of squeamishness impressed the hell out of him. But, of course, this whole safari was her idea, and he'd known her long enough to see that she was, as the movie mags liked to say, "as down to earth as your kids' favorite babysitter." Reggie knew as well as he did how toxic Katie's childhood had in fact been, though she always insisted that her older brother had borne the brunt of it. Still, Reggie was the one who had masterminded the public persona of Katie Barstow. Sure, people in the know realized that she was Roman and Glenda Stepanov's kid: a Broadway pedigree and serious Upper West Side scratch. But in Seattle or Tallahassee or Indianapolis, she was just that sweet, innocent, good-natured girl you hoped your son would date.

They stopped and Juma climbed out of the vehicle and looked around for animals. When it seemed safe, he nodded, and Katie grabbed the roll of TP and disappeared behind some thorn brush.

Peter knew that his first wife would never have put up with this nonsense. Neither would his second.

He stared at the ceaseless blue sky and squinted, enfeebled and enervated by the sun. The air was thick and heavy, and in the distance he saw a copse of trees, serried like soldiers. He couldn't believe that he'd forgotten his hat once more at the camp. His forehead had been red yesterday afternoon. If he weren't careful, it would hurt like hell by this evening. On the bright side? All this sun made his client even prettier. Yes, Katie had been an ingenue and always been seen as girl-next-door wholesome, but she still had just enough Stepanov inside her to add a pinch of exoticism to the look. It was, Peter realized, an unspoken part of her appeal.

When both Juma and Katie were back in the jeep, David asked her if she felt better.

She kissed him on his cheek. "I never felt bad," she told her husband. "I had to go to the bathroom. Big difference. Also?"

Everyone waited.

"On the other side of that brush? Two of the cutest little dik-dik antelopes appeared out of nowhere on the rocks. They couldn't have been more than a foot and a half tall. I may have a flush toilet in California, but I see nothing like that from the bathroom window."

"Maybe you will when we're settled in at the ranch," David said.

She arched a single eyebrow. "Unlikely."

They continued in silence for the next ten minutes, except for when Juma would point out animals to them: buffaloes or baboons, a crocodile in the shallow waters of the river near dozens of dozing hippopotamuses (some with birds picking the bugs off their backs), warthogs with their babies, and all kinds of vultures. A lappet-faced vulture in one tree, an Egyptian in another, and a pair of Ruppell's in a third. His eyesight astonished Peter. His own vision was a disaster without his eyeglasses, but this old guide saw things like a solitary cheetah or a lone rhinoceros at incredible distances.

Suddenly Juma started to accelerate, racing across the track in the savanna cut by countless other Land Rovers and jeeps, and Peter and Reggie exchanged glances. Their guide, with that remarkable sixth sense of his, knew something was about to happen. There was something they had to see, and so it didn't matter how badly he bounced them around in the back of the vehicle. In the distance, Peter noted the other Rover was paralleling them, plunging ahead with the same ferocity. And then, a moment later, there it was. Juma screeched to a stop on the southern side of the Mara River, kicking up dust, and Muema, who was driving the other vehicle—the one with Felix and Carmen and Billy and Margie—halted right beside them. Across the river, perhaps a hundred yards distant, were thousands of wildebeest pacing back and forth along the northern bank and many hundreds of zebras. A few at the front were staring into the water, some pawing at the dirt where the bank started a twenty-foot slope into the river.

Juma took out his binoculars but remained behind the wheel. So did Muema in the other Land Rover. But the nine Americans all stood on their seats and looked over the sides of the vehicles, the open roofs raised a good two feet above them. Peter got out his Leica and studied the animals through the camera. Reggie was using a twin-lens Rolleiflex that managed to look both like a boxy antique and a complicated tool for an astronaut.

"What are they waiting for?" David asked. "Why are they just standing there on the northern bank?"

"They want to be sure it's safe," Katie answered, and Peter watched Juma nod approvingly. "Or as safe as possible. There might be crocodiles in the water. Or a big cat waiting to grab one in all that high grass here on the southern side." David handed her the binoculars they had brought and, like Juma, she scanned the herd and the water before it.

After Peter had taken a photo, he let the camera hang like a medallion across his chest and reached into his pants pocket for his cigarettes and lighter. He hadn't smoked since breakfast because his doctor had told him he'd live longer if he stopped. But now that he had taken a picture of the wildebeest massing and all they could do was wait, he grew bored, which was usually when he smoked.

As he was snuffing out the cigarette in the ashtray in the armrest of the door, the crossing began. The animals started to run down the steep bank in three spots, a thunderous, three-column charge that caused the Land Rover to rock gently.

"It's like an earthquake," said Terrance.

The northern side of the river grew veiled by dust, but the shallow water, which had been so still a moment ago, began churning as the wildebeest tried to run or dogpaddle across it, some snorting and bellowing, others splashing forward in silence as best they could. Soon the first animals were climbing the southern bank and continuing across the plain, utterly oblivious to the pair of Land Rovers or simply not caring. Only when they were a quarter mile away did they pause: they were eating, Peter realized, calm and content. Little by little, more of the animals joined them.

"Looks like they're all going to make it," David said, and Peter couldn't decide if he was disappointed or relieved. But it didn't matter, because no sooner had David spoken than everyone in the car saw that he was mistaken. Katie let out an actual, nontheatrical gasp: a lioness had leapt from the high grass no more than twenty feet from where they were parked and pulled a wildebeest from the queue and wrestled it to the ground. The victim kicked his legs into the air for an agonizing half minute, because the lioness hadn't killed the animal quickly by ripping a hole through his neck. Instead, she wrapped the wildebeest's whiskered snout—mouth and nose—in her jaws.

"She's smothering him," Juma told them. "The animal can't breathe. He's suffocating. That's often how lions do it."

"Why?" Katie asked.

Juma shrugged. "Lots of reasons. Sometimes so their prey can't bleat for help. Sometimes so the lion is controlling the horns and the wildebeest can't defend itself. I've seen them kill baby buffaloes that way, too."

The wildebeest pedaled his legs one last time, a weak and

ineffectual poke at the air, and then grew still. The lioness looked down at the dead animal and then up at the humans staring at her from the openings in the roofs of the Land Rovers.

"She looks a little guilty," Reggie observed. "She looks like we caught her with her paws in the cookie jar."

"Are you okay, sweetheart?" David asked Katie.

"Yes. I'm fine."

"At least it was bloodless. She didn't open the poor bastard's neck," her husband said.

Peter shook his head and pointed at the river. His attention had been caught because the zebras at the back of the columns, most still on the grass before the riverbank on the north side, had stopped. But then he saw what they saw: two wildebeest were thrashing in the water, and already it was too late for them, also. Crocodiles were wrestling them into the foam. Whether they died because they drowned or they died because they bled out in the Mara River, they weren't making the southern bank.

.   .   .

Now Peter was creeping on his stomach. Sometimes he would use his elbows like feet and drag his body forward with his head raised so he could see both what the men were doing and where he was going: what he could hide behind next and how close he was to the back of Charlie Patton's tent. But more often Peter was keeping his body as close to the grass as possible, his head down and his nose or his cheeks scraping the savanna. He was inhaling dust through his nostrils. He thought of the snakes that might be watching him. He imagined a cheetah that supposed he was just far enough from the other humans to be safe game.

He would have given a great deal to have had Patton with him right now. Or Reggie Stout. Or Terrance Dutton. He was probably deluding himself, but if he had had even one of those other men with him, as a pair they might have a fighting chance to retrieve a couple of guns and . . .

And what?

Stout had shot human beings in the war, he supposed. But that was in a very different situation. A battlefield, for God's sake.

And Charlie Patton? He'd "collected" animals. Not blasted humans.

And Terrance Dutton? He was just an actor. Opinionated and strong-willed, yes, but he still spent his days playing make-believe.

And as for Peter himself, he'd shot deer and elk, but never had it crossed his mind that someday he would want (or need) to aim a rifle at another person. He thought he would be capable of pulling the trigger, but only because the men who had descended upon the camp had murdered a couple of rangers and Juma. But had he the aim? He hadn't been hunting in three years. Who could say what remained of his marksmanship. He had expected that his first day with Charlie Patton would be nothing but target practice. The second day, Charlie might let him shoot a zebra. That was Charlie's plan, at any rate. Shoot something easy. Something that trusted humans. Something not likely to get them killed flushing it out from the brush if he only wounded it. By the third day, with any luck, he would be reacquainted with the feel of a rifle and more comfortable with the light in the savanna: because the light here was different from Montana, that was clear. Good Lord, he'd seen a full rainbow, horizon to horizon, the other day, the sky behind it the deep, flat, beautiful gray of a thunderhead. An hour before, the sky had been cloudless, a robin's-egg blue.

And now he was at the back of Charlie Patton's tent. The interlopers had finished looting the dining tent, which meant soon they would be ordering the staff to disassemble whatever they needed (or wanted) from the guest tents. He heard them no more than forty-five or fifty feet away. He pulled up two of the spikes that pinned the canvas to the ground and slid underneath it. He saw the cot and he saw Charlie's bag. He didn't see any of the man's rifles. But there on top of the camp table was the .38. The Smith & Wesson pistol. It was beside the cot, which meant he had to crawl underneath the mosquito netting. He caught his elbow and then his boot in it, but soon he had the gun. Much to his relief, it was loaded. He thought he might see if the hunter had a box of bullets in the tent too when one of the Russians or Ukrainians or whatever the hell they were started to unzip the tent flap. He collapsed behind the cot, buying himself at best another minute or two before he was discovered, wondering whether he had a prayer in hell even with the pistol in his possession. What was he going to do, shoot the guy? He'd simply be massacred by the others when he started to flee. And he couldn't try and sneak out the back of the tent on his belly, because he would have to move the mosquito netting first.

But then he heard someone calling into the tent, and Peter once again was left alone. Whoever had been there had just turned around and left to supervise or take on some other task. Peter closed his eyes and, though he hadn't set foot in a church since his second marriage, said a small prayer of thanks in his head. Then he worked his way beneath the netting and underneath the back flap of the tent. He saw a lone acacia in one direction and thorn brush with some kind of thick tree with leaves and branches in another. He tucked the pistol into the back of his khakis, the grip against his spine, and crawled toward the thorn brush and that fat tree: it would give him more cover than the single acacia. If someone saw him, he hadn't a chance. Best case, they'd yell for him to stop. Worst case, they'd shoot him as easily as they might a solitary Thomson's gazelle.

But he made it. He was sweating and filthy, and his bare elbows were bleeding from the dry ground. His chest hurt like hell, and he wondered if he was about to have a heart attack. Now that would be ironic. But as he leaned against the rough

bark of the trunk, shielded by the brush, the sound of the criminals—no, they were worse than that; they were murderers, for
God's sake, they were murderers—was mostly a distant murmur
punctuated by the clink of metal as struts and supports and pots
and pans and jerry cans were tossed into the lorries, and his
heart began to slow. With any luck, the men on the other side
of the brush would be gone in an hour or two and he could start
toward that Maasai boma. If he could make three or four miles
an hour on foot, he might be there before dark.

Assuming, of course, that he could find it. And that he didn't
get eaten.

He closed his eyes. No, he wouldn't get eaten. He hadn't
survived so far just to wind up as lunch for a leopard or lion.

When he opened his eyes, he understood he was wrong.
Absolutely and completely mistaken. He sensed the animal before
he saw it. There, on a branch above him, was a leopard. Maybe,
Peter thought, I have it too: Charlie Patton's sixth sense. I had
felt leopardy (or something), and there it was. The animal.

Slowly he reached behind his back with his right hand for
the Smith & Wesson, walking his fingers like small, elderly legs.
What was that children's rhyme? Itsy bitsy spider? He hadn't had
kids, so if he'd ever said it or sung it out loud, it had been over
sixty years ago with his mother. When he'd been a child. But
he recalled the beginning of it, as once more his heart started
to thump behind his ribs. Now he was touching the grip of the
pistol with his fingertips. He would shoot the animal and run,
because the gunshot would alert the sons of bitches at the camp
to his presence. He would aim for the head, even though that
was a smaller target than the body and who the hell knew what
kind of aim he had. But he couldn't risk a gut shot that only
wounded the creature and left her both hungry and mad. He
wrapped his fingers around the grip and was just starting to slide
it from his waistband when the leopard sprang from the tree,
leaping not onto the ground but onto him. Reflexively he tried
to shield his face and his neck with both arms. What was it Pat-

ton had once said? You hoisted your rifle perpendicular to your throat and hoped the damn thing would bite down on the barrel until help came. The handgun was utterly forgotten. But it was too late. He saw the big cat's haunting amber eyes for a brief second as a front paw clawed away his arms with the ease with which he would whisk away a mosquito, and the barbs on her hind feet ripped through his shirt and slashed open his stomach. Then he felt the sting of the animal's bayonet-like teeth slicing through his neck and tearing open his throat, all but severing the human head that no longer had voice—there was no scream—from the human body.

Meanwhile, the men at the camp continued their work, most of them oblivious to the leopard that now was dragging her prey to the nearby kopje, where she had cubs waiting to feed. The two porters that saw it took note, and the younger of the pair wondered aloud at the possibility of retrieving the headless corpse before it was devoured as an act of kindness to the person's family, but the older man told him that would be dangerous and futile. The Russian supervising them snapped at them to let the body be, and the younger porter shook his head ruefully and continued loading the truck.

CHAPTER ELEVEN

Katie Barstow

"I've dated actors. You all know that," said Katie. "And you all know that it never worked out. So, why not date a nice man who has nothing to do with this crazy business?" Of course, that nice man will soon be her nice husband. Moreover, Katie has known David Hill since they were children and David was Katie's older brother's best friend.

—The Hollywood Reporter, AUGUST 11, 1964

Most of the time, Katie gazed out the window that was a little dirty with dust but not splotched with the smudgy remnants of Juma Sykes. Once more, she and David were sharing a seat in the Land Rover.

None of the Americans were supposed to speak and no one really wanted to talk, but the guard in the very last row was no longer threatening them each time one of them murmured something softly. Billy asking Margie how she was feeling. Margie asking the driver if she could reach forward for the toilet paper because she wanted to clot some of the blood from the glass shards that had cut the backs of her legs. David one time pointing out a harem of impala, as if this were just another day of sightseeing in the Serengeti.

The other Rover that had left camp with them was long gone. The two vehicles had spread out in different directions.

She glanced at her watch and saw they'd been bumping along for nearly forty-five minutes.

Katie sighed, scared, but grateful that she had her husband and her brother and Terrance with her. She was no longer afraid that she was going to be killed—at least anytime soon. David had reassured her that this was a kidnapping, he was sure of it, and the new government in Dar es Salaam or the studio or the American government would pay the ransom and they'd all be released. It shouldn't even take all that long. So, the fear was mostly of what ordeals loomed in the meantime. In her immediate future. Would they be chained in some rat-filled shack with a tin roof outside the reserve? Tortured in some way that was not merely horrifically painful, but disfigured her in a way that would end her career? And what if Margie lost her baby? At one point, Billy had speculated that the kidnappers might approach Charlie Patton's company for the ransom, alerting his office in Nairobi that they had the once famous hunter and nine of his guests, but there was no way Patton had the kind of money that would make kidnapping him and the nine Americans he was hosting worth the effort. Their captors? David was right: they were more likely to call the embassy to start the negotiations.

They passed a great herd of elephants, and if Juma or Muema had been driving, they would have stopped and one of the guides would have shared some remarkable minutiae. Or David would have taken a beautiful photograph: he was an immensely gifted photographer, and just this morning she had been thinking how she couldn't wait to see what was on his rolls of film from this trip. Terrance might have sketched some detail on the pad he had with him. Or, if Charlie Patton himself had happened to be in the Land Rover, he would have told them a story that might have been horrifying, but might just as likely have been very sweet: something about an old elephant with tusks as tall as a human that a guest had shot as the bull charged, or a mother elephant so proud of her little one that she had nudged him in front of the camera on a safari where they were only taking pictures. You just never knew with Patton. He was a raconteur, but he was wholly without a filter or the slightest instinct for his audience. He still seemed to live with one foot in another era, the world before the war, and sometimes seemed to think it was 1934—not 1964.

She studied the muscular fellow who was driving. When Margie had asked him for the toilet paper for her cuts, he'd obliged. Now their eyes met in the rearview mirror, and he returned her stare. He looked almost bemused, but she'd witnessed his ferocity when they'd overtaken the camp. All these men had, when necessary, the viciousness of wild animals. No, that wasn't right. They weren't madmen. They had the calculated, almost erudite cruelty of paid assassins. She smiled at him, an instinct. It was what she did. He didn't smile back. At first, she'd pegged him for twenty-five. Now? Probably thirty. He was at least her age. His brown T-shirt hugged his chest and his biceps like Saran Wrap, the hair on his arms so blond it was almost white. His pants were loose, as was his bandolier of ammo. She turned around to glance at the fellow in the back row. His rifle was across his lap, but his pistol was in his hand and she could see that the safety was off. He motioned for her to turn around, and so she did.

But an idea had come to her. She'd seen the driver slip his pistol beneath his seat. It was easily within his reach, but it would still take him seconds to retrieve it.

Based on where they were all seated in the vehicle, David and Terrance could jump the fellow behind them, and Billy could attack the one who was driving. Yes, the brute was strong, but he was also behind the wheel of the vehicle, one hand steering and one arm lazily recumbent on the shift. He'd be distracted, and Billy would have the element of surprise. The fellow would not be able to simultaneously fend him off, steer the Land Rover, and reach for his gun. They were no longer moving especially fast across the clay track. The Americans could mutiny. By the time the beast in the front seat had fended off her brother, she

and David and Terrance would have control of the back and one
of their guards' weapons. Maybe they'd have both the fellow's
pistol and his rifle.

She was mostly in David's lap and so she whispered into
her husband's ear, "We can get the gun behind us. Grab it. You
know Terrance will join you once you move."

He continued to stare straight ahead, clearly thinking about
the idea. She pointed out the window at the elephants as she
added, her voice little more than breath, "Billy could get his
hands around the neck of the driver. Or maybe grab the wheel."

David seemed to understand the ruse of the elephants and
craned his neck to look at them.

"Tell Billy," she murmured. "Lean forward and tell him. We
outnumber them."

He nodded but didn't move. Katie supposed he was waiting. He was smart—the son of an OSS veteran and then CIA
officer—and no doubt envisioning the best moment for the
group to act.

.   .   .

When she was out and about in L.A., the rule was simple:
keep moving. As long as she kept walking—and walking briskly,
the gait of a born New Yorker—the photographers didn't notice
her and the autograph seekers who did didn't have time to rifle
through pockets and purses for a pencil and a scrap piece of
paper. If she stopped? The crowds gathered fast. She was chum
for the sharks.

The first time she went to visit David at his gallery, she drove
there herself and parked behind the nearby Italian restaurant
where, if she called ahead, the owner always had a spot waiting.
Her autographed picture, as well as a movie poster from her hit
The Academy, hung by the coat check. Then she walked through
the alley to Brighton Way, her scarf pulled tightly around her
face and sunglasses the size of goggles perched on her nose, and

beelined into the gallery. The billboard at the corner for Lanvin perfume, a black cat gazing at the black bottle, was peeling, the paper falling away like long strips of cucumber rind.

The first time she'd seen David in California was when Billy had brought him to her house. Two days later, they'd had lunch with her brother and Margie at Billy's little bungalow, and Billy had joked how reminiscent it was of that afternoon when Nick Carraway had brought Jay Gatsby to his humble little cottage for a reconciliation with Daisy Buchanan, and for a moment Katie thought Billy was suggesting that she and David were on the cusp of a poignant, powerful romance. But that wasn't what he meant, she quickly realized: rather, he was embarrassed that his new post-divorce digs were so modest. The following week, she and David went to dinner alone, twice in five days, evenings that could only be construed as dates. The second time he'd kissed her good night, a chaste, dry peck on the cheek after he drove her home. It was unsatisfying because despite their two dinners together, she was honestly unsure whether the kiss was, by design, the polite kiss of her older brother's friend, the kiss of a person she'd known since she was a little girl, or the shy kiss of a suitor who just wasn't sure how aggressive to be with a movie star. If she had been confident that it was the latter, she might have given license to her more prurient instincts and pulled him through her front door and into the living room with its plush carpet and faux zebra couch.

No one spotted her as she walked to his gallery and so no one trailed her when she went inside.

And the place was empty.

Not the walls, which had bold, imposing paintings that stretched almost to the ceiling, and not the floor. Scattered around the room were bronze sculptures of creatures that looked to be monster birds: beaks and feathers, but also arms and legs. They were the size of adult people, and they had talons instead of fingers and toes. Their eyes and ears were as human as their bills and mandibles were avian.

Some of the canvases on the walls had been created by an artist named Martin Deedes, who thought he was the next Max Ernst: he crafted great surreal oil paintings and collages of fairy-tale icons in art deco cityscapes. Deedes was a pal of Ken Kesey's and claimed that most of his images were born when he was tripping on LSD, often with Ken and some filmmakers who called themselves the Merry Pranksters. David said he suspected there was some weird connection between his father and Kesey, but he himself had never met him and Deedes had never brought the novelist into the gallery. Kesey hadn't been able to come to his friend's opening.

And then, prominently displayed by itself on one wall, was the painting by the Soviet artist. The woman who had defected, most of whose work was at the museum. Nina . . . Nina something. She was famous for defecting, and she was famous as a painter, and if Katie had not been alone she would have been flustered that she could not recall the woman's last name. The painting was brand new, and David might have hung it that very morning. The image was a life-size vertical of a steelworker, the deep runnels of sweat on his chest so palpable that Katie wondered briefly if the piece was some sort of mixed media. David said that he had gotten the painter to allow him to represent this one piece because, she told him, she wanted his gallery and his radical tastes to succeed. Katie suspected there was more to it than that: she wouldn't have been surprised if someday she learned that David's father had had something to do with the woman's defection—neither she nor David believed that David's old man worked in something as innocuous as personnel—and now the painter was doing the man's son a favor. Or, perhaps, David and this Russian woman were lovers.

She was disappointed that nobody was in the gallery browsing, and although the glass door was unlocked, there wasn't even a shop girl behind the sleek Danish modern desk—which was Katie's favorite thing in the room and the one thing that most assuredly was not for sale. The place and the feeling it evoked in her right now reminded her of a moment when she was eleven and she and her mother went to see a Wednesday matinee of one of her friend's shows. It was at a small, down-at-the-heels theater in the West Village that Katie had never been to before, and the seats were ragged. She counted, as she did always to the best of her ability, the number of seats in the venue. This one was easy. There was no balcony and no mezzanine. There were a total of seventy. Seven rows of ten. The theater, even though it was a legitimate off-Broadway venue and the usher had handed them traditional playbills, was depressing and sad. There was not a single soul in the house for that performance other than the two Stepanovs, and when Katie had met her friend backstage after the show, a grown-up in the cast who had been in the wings that moment as well said, "Nothing like disappointing two people. Tonight, we should disappoint twice that many." The show closed the following week.

But that afternoon, Katie had hugged her friend and told her how amazing she was, all the while thinking to herself that she couldn't have done it. She couldn't have found it inside herself to put on a show for an audience of two. And suddenly both she and her friend were weeping in each other's arms. Their mothers were confused, and later that night Katie would explain to Glenda why she had started to cry. Why her friend had started to cry. At dinner she asked her father to find a role for her friend in a better, bigger show, but it never happened and Katie went to Hollywood and lost touch with the girl. She'd heard her friend was married and living in Westchester and had two little kids.

Now she was about to call out for someone at the gallery. Perhaps shout "hello" into the hollow air. But then David emerged from the small office he kept in the back, and there was another man with him. The fellow was a decade or so older than he was, and he was wearing a black suit and carrying an attaché case. Katie felt a little rush of joy at the idea this might be a client who had just spent gobs of money on one of the monster birds.

David was unwrapping a stick of Fruit Stripe gum and putting it in his mouth, and he stood a little taller when he saw her: happiness did this to people, and more times than not, her presence simply made people happy. "Well, this is a surprise," he began. "Katie, this is my accountant, Cal Lemont. Cal, this is Katie Barstow."

The accountant smiled at her and for a beat said nothing. He looked at her like she was a Martian. Or she was an alligator walking upright on its hind legs. Or one of the monster birds come to life. It happened. This was as common a reaction as was the adulation of the autograph seekers. Then he looked at David, the realization dawning on him that he had just heard David Hill call this movie star by her first name and they were, at the very least, friends. She extended her hand to Cal so he could shake it.

"Really love your work," the fellow said, gathering himself. "So does my wife and so do my girls."

"Thank you," she said. "How old are they?"

"Missy is forty-three—"

"I just meant your children. Your daughters."

Cal put down his briefcase on the Tuscan tile floor that David had added to the gallery and shook his head good-naturedly at his own awkwardness.

David laughed, and that diminished everyone's embarrassment. "You have three girls, right, Cal?"

"I do," said the accountant. "They're sixteen, fourteen, and nine."

"You have a handful," she told him. "Or, at least, I was a handful at all of those ages." But was she? No, she wasn't. It was her parents who were the handful. Their demons and the way they quite literally tortured poor Billy and would have continued to torture her if she hadn't served a more important purpose: a public affirmation of their genetic theatrical talent.

"Oh, she knew precisely how to drive her older brother crazy," David said, as if he had started to read her mind but only intercepted a part of the thought. "Her brother and I have been friends forever."

Cal took this in and looked back and forth between David and her. "So, you two have known each other since you were children?"

"I knew Katie when she was six years old and singing 'Come On-A My House' from the window seat in the family dining room. She used a soup ladle as her microphone. She would stretch the neck hole of her modest little sweater over her shoulders so much it ripped—so it looked like a strapless gown."

"I'm gonna give you candy," Katie said, purring the lyric that had become a part of the Stepanov family lore for its spectacular inappropriateness when it came from the lips of six-year-old Katie.

"Ross Bagdasarian," said the accountant.

Katie was impressed that he knew this. "And William Saroyan," she added. "They were cousins and wrote it together. The tune is based on an Armenian folk song."

"Katie's father has passed away, but he was friends with Saroyan. Broadway is a very small world," David told his accountant.

Cal seemed to think about this. "I'm going to ask this with whatever is the accountant equivalent of attorney-client privilege. I won't tell a soul what you tell me—not even my wife."

David seemed uncertain, a little wary. "So, it's a question for me?"

"I guess it's a question for both of you."

She and David exchanged a glance, and she knew he was thinking the same thing she was: he had nothing to worry about. The accountant was starstruck. It was actually kind of adorable.

"Go ahead," she said.

"Are you two dating?"

David was silent, which might have been an answer itself. But she wasn't going to make the mistake she had made the other night after dinner, when she had accepted his subdued kiss on the cheek and done nothing more than say good night. If he was involved romantically with that Russian defector, this was a way to find out—or, at least, glean a little insight. "Yes," she told Cal, "we are." Then she went to David's side, stood on her toes, and kissed him fully on the lips, the sapid taste of the fresh stick of gum on his breath.

Before the accountant left, she gave him personalized autographs on gallery stationery that he could bring home to all three of his daughters.

. . .

The packaging for the Fruit Stripe gum had colorful stripes: a psychedelic zebra, David had remarked one time back in Hollywood. He told Katie that he went through at least a pack a day before they met and even more when they started to date because she admitted to him that she liked the taste of it on his breath. He had brought gobs of it to the Serengeti, and they had joked about the striping the first few times they saw actual zebras.

Katie glanced at him now in the Land Rover, waiting. Wondering. Was her plan a pampered actress's idiotic fantasy? Was she keeping her panic in check with the sort of delusions that screenwriters created for her and her peers who lived on soundstages and backlots?

Maybe.

But the driver looked a little woozy from the heat and from staring into the bright sun as he drove. His eyes were heavy, his gaze glassy and nebulous. Billy would not be able to take him in a real fight, but he didn't have to: all he needed to do was distract him for a couple of seconds, because David and Terrance would do the rest. His pistol was under the seat, for God's sake. Why was David not leaning forward to whisper into Billy's ear? So few words were necessary: *Terrance and I will get the guy behind us. You jump the driver. On three.*

She elbowed David discreetly. She could see it all so well in her mind, the blocking clear and precise. She, too, would help. She would fall into the lap of the fellow behind her and press herself flat on the rifle. David would grab the guard's wrist and point the handgun straight into the air, Terrance then prying it from their captor's fingers. Meanwhile, Billy would ambush the driver. They could do this. They could. Stage combat, but real.

On three.

But David stared away from her out the window and the Land Rover bumped along, and her fear morphed into frustration.

"David?" she said softly but intensely.

He shook his head, a movement that was barely perceptible but still clear. She wanted him to meet her eyes, but he wouldn't, and she began to suspect there was more to the way he was ignoring her than a simple refusal to take her seriously.

Billy turned around to look at them. He must have overheard her. When he did, the driver seemed to wake up. "Eyes forward," he snapped.

Once more, Katie studied the driver's face in the rearview mirror. She had supposed he had been staring ahead at the grass and the track as he fought somnolence. She was wrong: he was watching them carefully too, one eye on whatever passed for a road in this part of the Serengeti and one on the five Americans. She hoped this was why David was sitting there, unmoving, and not because he was afraid. But she honestly wasn't sure.

CHAPTER TWELVE

Billy Stepanov

Billy Stepanov, like all psychologists and psychiatrists, won't speak of his clients. But rumor has it that many are the stars we see on the big screen who have the sorts of problems that are no different from the milkman's: they just have the money to "talk" about them.
—*Movie Star Confidential,* DECEMBER 1962

It was pavement. Shitty pavement, but still asphalt. A single lane. One minute they were in the reserve, and the next they weren't. They were on a real road for the first time in days. Occasionally, they would continue to spot a few wild animals, largely impalas and gazelles, but most of the creatures they saw now, other than birds, were the great herds of Maasai cattle and goats. The shepherds usually were boys, but not always: he saw a couple of old men holding their long crooks sideways against the back of their necks. He saw women carrying water and children carrying water, sometimes using petrol cans and one little girl using a pair of metal buckets so rusty they looked like terra-cotta pots with handles. And all of them were walking in sun that cooked you, whether you were out in the open in the grass or inside the kiln of a Land Rover. If he survived this, he thought to himself, never again would he take tap water for granted. Never.

Both the driver and his partner in the back spoke English, but the one in the back seemed more fluent. Still, Billy knew that he shouldn't assume anything: though the driver's accent was Russian or Ukrainian or whatever, it was certainly possible he understood any and every word that they said. Earlier, Katie had been whispering something to David, but he hadn't heard what and the fellow had ordered them all to quiet down. He decided enough time had passed that he would venture a question. He leaned forward and directed what he hoped sounded like a polite but confident inquiry at the driver.

"Can you tell us where we're going?" he asked.

Margie nudged him. She was worried he was only going to get them into more trouble. But he was scared for her; he was scared for the baby inside her. The kid. He was worried about the gash across her stomach and the smaller lacerations she had from the broken glass. He had vowed as soon as his first wife was pregnant with their first child to always ask himself, what would my mother or father do in this situation? And then, more times than not, do the opposite.

When the driver ignored him, he went on, "Excuse me. My wife is pregnant and one of her cuts is still—"

With the back of his left hand, without taking his eyes off the road, the driver smacked him so hard in the nose that Billy fell back against the seat and felt whirling pinwheels of pain and saw white lights behind his eyes. He'd heard the bone against bone over the growl of the Land Rover's engine, and then he heard Margie shriek once and felt the Land Rover speeding up. The guard in the back was laughing. He opened his eyes because his nose was running and there was something wet on his lips, and he understood it was blood.

.   .   .

It was like the time (the one time) that Roman Stepanov had belted him. Usually the corporal punishment was meted out by his mother, and usually it was far more creative than mere spanking or brute violence. There was the front closet that, for reasons he couldn't quite parse, scared the shit out of him when he had to be inside it alone. It was big and had a light, but the switch was outside the door and Mother always shoved him in there in the dark. And then locked the door. He'd sit on the floor, his knees at his chest and his arms hugging his shins, and be eye level with the bottoms of furs and dusters and wool coats. When he grew tired, because invariably Glenda would box him in there for hours, he'd curl up on the floor next to the galoshes with the tin buckles he hated, his mother's leather boots that smelled of the street, and umbrellas musty from their work in the rain.

And then there were the nights when she would use her husband's old neckties to bind his ankles to the chair in the dining room until he had cleaned his dinner plate. When one of the Irish girls was sticking around to clean up after dinner—to this day, Billy didn't know why some nights his mother had them stay and some nights she didn't—they knew to look away. They were better cooks than Glenda, but largely because Glenda was a terrible cook. In Billy's memory, he was more likely to eat what they prepared than what his mother concocted, but he was unsure whether it was because he wanted to be polite or because their brisket was better than his mother's mussels and clams.

There was no "worst" punishment, but among the stories he thought about most in the small hours of the night now that he was a grown-up was the underwear. Katie was just starting to walk, he believed, and so he supposed he was six. But memories, he knew, were fuzzy, frangible things. Perhaps his sister was only six months old. Perhaps she was as old as two. Which meant he could have been five and he could have been seven. His misbehavior had occurred when they had gone to the doctor. Just a checkup. But, apparently, he hadn't wanted to strip down to his underpants. Eventually he had, but whatever the reason, first he'd made a stink. And so, when they got home, she made him take off all of his clothes but his underpants and spend the rest of the day in them. And only them. She wouldn't allow him to retreat to his bedroom, even when she had a friend over for tea.

In some ways, he guessed, it had all made him a better father, even though he'd had one psychology professor who had hinted that it would, someday, make him a terrible parent if he didn't watch himself carefully. The professor, knowing that Broadway ran in his blood, quoted *South Pacific* to make his point, observing almost ruefully, "You've got to be taught to hate." Arguably, that childhood had made him a terrible first husband in ways he was still analyzing, but he loved little Marc madly and had striven mightily to be a kind and forward-thinking father. He had never spanked the boy, not once. He and his ex-wife both bought into what his mother referred to dismissively as "all that Dr. Spock mumbo-jumbo." He sure as hell would never lock their boy in a closet.

The one time that Roman had hit Billy, he'd hit him hard, which more than anything was why it had come back to him that moment in the Land Rover. His infraction? When he was seventeen, he'd said something dismissive over a Monday night dinner, the whole family together at the dining room table, about his kid sister's performance in one of their father's shows. Then, in a moment of classic teenage brinksmanship, he had dug in his heels and refused to apologize to either his sister or his father, which caused the event to escalate. And suddenly, out of the blue, his father backhanded him, sending him falling backward out of the chair and onto the thick Oriental carpet on the floor.

Yes, his parents had raised Katie in ways that were cruel too, but they were demonstrably less sadistic than the ways they treated him. It wasn't that she was a girl and it wasn't that she was younger and it wasn't that she was a second child and they had figured some things out by then. It was just that she was . . . Katie. Even at two and three, you just knew that she was going to be a star, and so Roman and Glenda Stepanov were constitutionally predisposed to be gentler with her.

Or, at least, to not risk disfiguring her.

Katie claimed not to recall much of what she had witnessed

them do to him—though fuzzy snippets had stuck, and they'd discussed some of the stranger moments when his first marriage was unraveling—but he supposed that she really had repressed much of it. Nevertheless, she hated her mother as much as he did, and she had hated her father until the day he died as much as her brother had. Billy supposed it was why he was so very close to a kid sister five years his junior.

Still, the mind was the damnedest thing: repression was a gift reserved for the Katie Barstows of the world. Mere mortals like him? Too often you couldn't mine the recollections that might keep you sane, but instead held close the memories that someday would kill you.

. . .

The Land Rover left the pavement and continued, based on the sun, to the west on grass that had been grazed almost to dirt. They drove for thirty minutes, once again occasionally spotting wild animals—warthogs and wildebeest, more gazelles, a small group of elephants—and then he saw ahead of them a kraal, a Maasai livestock pen. They coasted to a stop before it, and Billy saw that it was made from poisonous candelabra branches and thorn brush and some spiky wood he couldn't identify. Nearby he counted eight round huts built mostly from cow dung and mud. He saw neither people nor their herds: not cattle or goats.

"It's deserted," Margie murmured.

He nodded. The group had either moved elsewhere or been evicted by their kidnappers. He was still holding a wad of toilet paper against his nose, but he thought the bleeding had stopped and so he gently pulled it away. It was sore, the pain coming in waves. He decided it wasn't broken, but he really had no idea.

The driver reached under his seat and pulled out his pistol. Then he hopped from the vehicle, lifted the hinged timber that served as the gate to the kraal, and went inside. The fellow in the last row of seats, who Billy had begun to suspect was a mercenary of some sort—a hired gun who had seen all manner of carnage over the years—told them to stay where they were.

"Do you think the others are going to be brought here too?" David asked softly.

Billy wasn't sure whether his friend expected an answer or was just thinking out loud, but he answered him: "No. I think we're in at least two groups. Maybe three. They've definitely separated us."

"I agree," said Terrance.

They watched the driver wander into each and every hut, spending no more than a few seconds in each, before emerging. Apparently, he was making absolutely certain that each was empty. When he was done, he yelled that the place was clear, and the fellow in the back told them to get out too. Then their driver ordered them to walk fifteen feet from the Rover. It was a strangely precise order. He was pointing with his pistol.

"Fifteen feet?" David whispered.

Billy shrugged and climbed out first, helping Margie from the vehicle next. He saw the blood on the front of her shirt and the back of her shorts and experienced a small shudder of anxiety. God. Out here, untreated, a cut like that could kill you. Holding hands, they walked roughly five yards from the Land Rover. Katie and David and Terrance were right behind them. Once they were lined up, the driver took Katie by the arm, but David jumped in.

"Please," he said, "let us stay together," but the fellow paid him no heed.

"What are you going to do to her?" Billy asked, as Margie leaned into him, trembling. The driver ignored him, too.

Katie didn't resist as he pulled her into the farthest of the huts. She looked as if she might finally be about to break down. And then she was gone. The fellow who'd ridden in the back had holstered his pistol and was now aiming a rifle at the rest of them. Billy checked his watch over and over, and while it felt like the driver and his sister were gone forever, only four minutes elapsed until the driver returned. Then he tried to take Margie, but Billy wrapped his arms around her, her small face sniveling against his shoulder.

"I'm going with her," he said.

The one with the rifle said, "You're not. Don't make this worse for her or for you." His tone had a glimmer of understanding to it, and so Billy pressed his case.

"She's pregnant. She's cut. I'm not leaving her alone," Billy insisted.

The kidnapper sighed deeply, epically. Almost ruefully. "Fine," he said, and for a brief second, Billy thought he had relented. But then he sidled up to him, slung his rifle over his shoulder, and pulled out his pistol. With his left hand he squeezed Billy's nose where the driver had hit him, and with his right slammed the grip of his pistol into Billy's kidney. It was an excruciating combination, and he collapsed to his knees, as Margie was led, sobbing, into another of the huts.

He looked up at David. "What the fuck is with you?" Billy asked his friend, and his voice sounded to him like he was trying hard not to cry. Because he was. "You just let her be taken. Katie. My sister. Your wife. You didn't even try—"

"Yours was pretty token resistance, Billy. We can't do a damn thing but what they tell us. They have guns. You might have noticed."

And then David was taken away too, and so Billy and Terrance were left alone for a few minutes with the one with the rifle.

"Why?" Terrance asked him, his voice absolutely even, as if he were inquiring of a conductor why a train was running late. "Can you at least tell us why you're doing this? I assume there's a payday in it for you."

Their captor seemed to brood on the question as if he were deeply contemplating his response. "Why do we do what we do? Sounds like you want from me the meaning of life," he said, and with that accent of his, the last word sounded lyrical. "Do any two people have the same motive for—your question—why we do what we do?" He raised his eyebrows and dipped his chin, answering his question himself by suggesting it was unanswerable. But it wasn't. He just wasn't going to reveal anything.

"You're speaking generally."

He smiled at Terrance. "Now, let me ask you something, Mr. Movie Star. Ever had a broken rib? Open your mouth again and I will have to break one or two with the butt of this rifle. And that will hurt like hell. So, what say we drop the questions? Shall we?"

And then it was Billy's and Terrance's turns, each of the captors escorting one of them.

Billy was not surprised to see that the place was windowless. There was only a vent—sealed at the moment with what looked like a car seat cushion—and a spot where someone or some family had once built their fires. He could stand up in the middle, but they weren't going to let him stay there. The driver walked him to a section with what he supposed was a sleeping pallet. There he was told to sit down, and his feet were tied together with a twine that Billy knew was going to rub raw his ankles through his socks far worse than his father's old neckties, the cord then wrapped around a pallet stanchion that had been dug deep into the ground. He could sit or lie down, but he couldn't walk. Then the guy tied his hands.

"Don't call for your friends," the driver warned. "Don't call for anyone."

"And if I have to fucking pee?"

The driver shrugged unconcernedly.

When he left Billy alone, he closed the door and the hut was darker than night. There was a little blood trickling from his left nostril, and he wanted to wipe it away. Had they tied his wife this way? His sister?

God, the women. And David hadn't really fought in the slightest for Katie. Here he was the son of . . .

And that's when it clicked: maybe this kidnapping was all

about David. He was the son of a CIA . . . something. Wasn't it possible that David's father was involved in a clandestine operation in East Africa, and these Russians had taken the man's son and his wife's safari party to gain some sort of leverage? An upper hand to convince the Americans to back off or dial down whatever the hell they were doing?

He opened his eyes as wide as he could, aware that the pupils would never open wide enough for him to see a whole hell of a lot. Still, he rolled his head in all directions, hoping to find any pinpricks or markers of the world outside these walls.

This was worse, a thousand times worse—and he would never have guessed this was possible—than the front closet in his childhood home in which his mother would punish him. Yes, the closet was dark, too, and it had its penumbra of ghosts, the stink of boots, and that dangling freak show of his mother's fur coats: but it didn't have snakes and spiders and, he guessed, whatever rats called the Serengeti home.

CHAPTER THIRTEEN

Benjamin Kikwete

And while Katie and her guests will be far from most modern ame-nities we take for granted, Charlie Patton—who we spoke to in Nairobi—said that his team is capable of bringing many aspects of civilization to the Serengeti. "My guests sleep well, eat well, and—most importantly—drink well," he told us. "And the men who work for me? I trust them with my life."
                    —The Hollywood Reporter, NOVEMBER 9, 1964

Benjamin's hands were bound at the wrists, but he was able to bring them to his face and use his thumb to brush a determined fly off his cheek. Patton and the Americans were gone.

He counted the men in the truck with him, and altogether—counting the porters, cooks, Muema, and himself—there were twelve of them wedged in the back. That meant there were two porters or cooks he couldn't account for. Perhaps they were in the little pickup, the last of the convoy, with the corpses of poor Juma Sykes and the rangers. Or maybe they were dead too. The staff hadn't torn down the camp, but Patton's men had been ordered to gather the food, the petrol, and the hunting rifles, working at gunpoint, and now Benjamin and the others were sitting in the back of the second largest of the three lorries, all with their hands and feet tied. The truck wasn't moving. It was still parked at the edge of where the movie star and her friends had camped last night.

He was sitting beside Muema, the second guide. Only Juma had been more senior. Muema, though shaken himself, had been trying to comfort the rest of the group, and his reassurances had made Benjamin feel better. At least a little better. But the intruders had murdered Juma and the two rangers, that fact remained, and their cavalier disregard for life had meant that Muema's faith that all would be well was rather like aspirin for a broken leg. It helped, but only a little.

"They're not just kidnappers," he was telling Muema now, speaking quietly both because he didn't want to anger the white guy who was pacing back and forth with one of the rifles he'd taken from Patton's armory, and because the porters and cooks were already frightened. "They're Russian kidnappers. I only saw a few of them, but I saw and heard enough to know. They're Russian. And you know what happened when Charlie took some Russians hunting a few years ago. I was there."

"I know."

"It was a nightmare."

"As is this."

"And if this was just about hostages, they wouldn't have killed—"

"Once you kidnap Americans," Muema said, shaking his head as he cut him off, and whispering into his ear, "you're in so deep, you might as well kill any African you like. If you're caught, you're dead anyway. I'm going to lie to everyone else to keep them calm. I am balancing the fact they have not killed us yet with the fact they were willing to shoot my friend and two rangers. But Benjamin? We are surrounded by hyenas. I don't know the way out, but if we don't find one or they don't get what they want? Yes, they very well might kill us too."

Benjamin took this in. He felt the same way. "Are they poachers?" he asked. "Or were they poachers? Is that part of this?"

"No. Look at the back of that one over there," he said, and with his head he motioned at the shirtless fellow holding the

Kalashnikov with two hands, the barrel pointing at the ground. There were no deep bruises or creases in the skin along his shoulders. If he were a poacher, there would be. Poachers used wooden bars like yokes to carry from the reserve the tusks or horns or even the meat they carved from the animals they killed illegally.

"Where do you think they're taking us?" Benjamin asked.

"I have no idea."

"I understand why they killed the rangers—"

"I don't. They could have just disarmed them. They had all the surprise," said Muema. He gazed up at a trio of bee-eater birds against the blue sky. "And look at Juma. He was unarmed and had his hands up when he got out of the Land Rover. I saw it. I saw it with my own eyes."

"Juma was like an older brother to my father."

Muema nodded. "You saw his instincts. Protect the guests. He tried to get as many to safety as he could."

It seemed that Muema was about to say more, and Benjamin waited. But then he saw why Muema had grown silent. One of the men who had overtaken the camp and shot the rangers was approaching the front of the lorry, twirling the keys in his hand. An idea came to Benjamin and he told himself it was just a possibility: it wasn't a certainty. It wasn't an absolute. But he thought of what Muema had said, and he understood now what the guide was suggesting and why he viewed their plight as so dire: all of these men in the truck knew the faces of the criminals who had murdered the guide and the rangers and, possibly, the porter and the cook he couldn't account for. They could identify these men for the police or the army or in a trial.

And that alone might be a reason why they wouldn't be allowed to live—why they couldn't be allowed to live. Perhaps they really were all going to be driven somewhere to be executed where their bodies would never be found.

. . .

Kenya hadn't the gold of Congo or Tanganyika, but there was a mine near Lake Victoria that was owned by Europeans, as well as a tremendous refinery to process the mineral. Near that mine were the ditches and ravines and sewage pits where men and children—lots of children—would dig by hand, hoping to find a few nuggets or a little gold dust. Benjamin's grandfather had done that as a teen before getting a job at the European mine. The working conditions there weren't much better, but he made a little more money. He was deeply religious and (at least according to Benjamin's father) steered clear of the prostitutes who worked the streets and the bridges over the river so filled with sewage and poisons from the mining operation that some days dead fish floated on the surface like water lilies. He ate as little as he could, and thus saved enough cash to return to Nairobi to marry Benjamin's grandmother. Most of the time that he spent mining he was sick or hungry, and his back never recovered. Before he died, Benjamin's grandfather told him of the line of hovels on the far side of the river where you sold the gold dust and flakes you hacked from the ground or panned in the fetid water. The buyers were Africans, but they, too, had European masters. Many, like Benjamin's family, were even Kikuyu.

The lesson that his grandfather took away from his adolescence and his year at the gold mine—other than the rather obvious one that he wanted his children and grandchildren to have nothing to do with gold—was that survival depended on white people. As a boy, Benjamin watched his father and his grandfather argue about this, but the debates never grew heated. Neither man had a temper. Still, Benjamin could see the generational difference, how his father saw the English for the slave masters they were and the potential in African independence, while his grandfather had the fatalism and acceptance that came from growing up beneath British boots. He had seen the severed heads: the skulls of the workers who'd died in mining accidents decorating the street side of a wealthy Brit's flower garden. There they were, human trophies posted on pikes beside the buffalo and rhino heads that sat on the ground amid rose moss and weeping ferns. The Belgians across the border were even more likely to decorate with dead Africans, because they were using the corpses of rebels: it was, for them, a reminder of who was in charge.

Nevertheless, Benjamin never lost sight of the reality that his father worked for a white man: Charlie Patton.

And, for better or worse, so did he.

. . .

There was a difference between pursuit predation and ambush predation. Examples of the former, Benjamin's father had taught him, were most (but not all) of the big cats and the birds of prey. The hunters. The stalkers. The latter were such creatures as the crocodile, that would lie in wait in the water. The lion could be both. One might trail its prey a long time; another might be lazy, absolutely content to wait in the brush for the solitary gazelle to wander off. It might hinge upon how hungry the cubs were.

And humans? They were both, too, though the biggest factor was what they were after and why. They might sit for hours in a blind awaiting a buffalo, but they might track a particular bull elephant for days if they thought his tusks might near (or top) a hundred pounds each. But, as with the lion, it also depended upon whether the human was hunting for sport or survival. His father only saw the hunters so wealthy they didn't need the animals that they killed. They slaughtered animals solely for trophies.

And, thank God, his father had never seen men such as the group that had taken the Americans and now was driving off with Charlie Patton's crew. Two men were in the back with them, both armed with rifles—one that Kalashnikov—while a third was driving. Benjamin watched the men from the corner of his eyes, knowing he didn't dare stare at them. He felt his internal clock racing in much the same way it did when he was doing work as pedestrian as assembling a camp before the guests arrived or as exciting as rumbling across the savanna because someone had spotted a rhinoceros. In this case, the countdown was until this lorry stopped. He and Muema and the others dramatically outnumbered the men who had taken them. But the Black men were bound, and the white men had guns.

He recalled some of the movies his father had taken him to over the years. What would James Bond have done in *Dr. No*? In *From Russia with Love*? Or what would the British POWs have done in *The Bridge on the River Kwai*? He'd been thirteen years old when he'd seen that one, but he'd been old enough to be moved by the very specific heroism and selflessness of the prisoners.

But that was all make-believe. All of the movies were make-believe. Certainly, the Americans on this safari were incapable of saving themselves. They were all from Hollywood and he doubted any of them had ever done anything heroic, except maybe Reggie Stout. After all, they hadn't ever had to, and they didn't have to now. They were being kidnapped, and either someone would pay for their release or the government would swoop in and save them. Because unlike the men in the back of this truck who worked for Charlie Patton, rumbling now toward some spot where each and every one of them might be gifted with a bullet in the head, they had value. But men like Benjamin? He had none.

At least in the eyes of most of the world. His mother would disagree. So would his father.

These men who might kill him had ambushed the safari, but it was clear they were fundamentally pursuit predators. This was all part of a very-well-coordinated plan. They had stalked the safari, they had trailed it. And, finally, they had attacked it.

Benjamin, on the other hand, was in no position to be a pursuit predator, and so that meant he was, by definition, prey.

Or, just maybe, an ambush predator. Unfortunately, it was

unlikely he had the time to lie in wait, because any moment they might arrive at their destination: the ravine or the river or the kopje where their captors might execute the whole bunch of them sitting now in the back of the truck. They'd march them one by one from the vehicle, line them up, and shoot them.

"Muema?" he murmured.

The guide looked into the distance but didn't respond.

"You really believe they might kill us?" Benjamin pressed.

"I think it's possible, yes. But I don't know it for a fact. And neither do you. I may be mistaken. If they really wanted to execute us, they could have done it back at the camp. Just thrown our corpses into the lorry if they have some special place to bury us."

"Then we're just being kidnapped, too?" *Just.* What a concept. *Merely* kidnapped.

The guide glanced down at his bound wrists and then brought his fingers together as if in prayer. There was beauty in the gesture, but also fatalism. Benjamin recalled the Swahili word for freedom that was synonymous now with the liberation of the East African nations: *uhuru*. In some cases, that birth was bloody and violent, in others a transition that surprised everyone with its peacefulness. It was impossible to know what turns the upheaval would take: even the Americans on this safari had come from a nation born via a bloody cesarean, a revolution against one of the very same European nations that had demanded such fealty from East Africa.

Well, if they do decide to execute us, Benjamin decided, I am not going to die on my knees. Even a Thomson's gazelle will fight to the end against a jackal; even a buffalo with half its insides obliterated by a Mauser will charge if it can walk.

"It's time to attack the bastards," he said quietly to Muema. "We swarm the two back here. Then we jump the driver when he stops—or we jump out the back if he doesn't."

"Your father took you to too many movies, Benjamin. Most of us would get killed."

"We may all get killed if we don't."

"Have you ever seen a man fire a Soviet assault rifle? That one gun could wipe us all out in seconds."

"I have," he said. "I was there for the elephant massacre. The elephant slaughter. They all had Kalashnikovs. My father and I were both there."

When the guide remained silent, Benjamin told him, his tone as urgent as it had ever been in his life, "Muema: I'd rather die charging like a rhino than bleating like a goat."

CHAPTER FOURTEEN

Felix Demeter

Doris Day and Audrey Meadows both cringed when asked about the beach scene in "Bermuda Shorts." Although Felix Demeter—yes, progeny of director Rex Demeter—is only one of the four writers credited with the 93-minute disaster, insiders tell us that the grating sand-in-your-suit dialogue is all his.
— *Movie Star Confidential,* FEBRUARY 1962

There it was: a pocket knife. A Boy Scout knife. Reggie Stout had a fucking camping knife in the fingers of his left hand, his right hand shielding most of it. But for a brief moment, Felix had seen it. He'd had a knife just like it himself when he'd been a boy. And, it seemed, this PR man had one too. Still. At the age of forty or forty-one.

Its body was black, though the metal was supposed to look like tree bark, and it had, Felix believed, a flat-head screwdriver, a can opener, a bottle opener, and the knife blade. But the blade couldn't have been more than three inches long when you flipped it open. Did Reggie really believe it was any match against a rifle—plus the gun their driver was packing?

But it seemed that Reggie was scheming. He leaned forward, adjusting one of his socks, and whispered something to Carmen.

"What?" Felix asked his wife, his lips barely moving. "What is he doing?"

She shook her head vaguely, ignoring him. Whatever Reggie was planning—whatever Reggie and Carmen were planning together—it did not involve him. They knew the depth of his cowardice. It was among his defining features: his eyes, his hair, his craven soul. He was useless.

Casually, she took off the scarf that she had tied around her neck, the scarf that had seemed to begin each day in Africa there but by lunchtime was covering her hair and her ears against the dust and the sun. She was holding it in her hands, stretching it out. It was yellow, just like the one that Joseph Cotten had used to strangle Marilyn Monroe in *Niagara*.

He wanted to press her, but he was trembling and he was afraid to draw further attention to her or to Reggie. Because now he knew. He knew. And he didn't know which scared him more: the idea of his wife and this PR flak doing something dangerous or, like him, doing nothing at all.

.   .   .

And yet, just yesterday, neither his wife nor Reggie Stout thought he was such a pitiful child. God, along with Charlie Patton, Peter Merrick, and Reggie Stout, he and Carmen had had a rather good time. The five of them were sitting on two big blankets eating lunch: Coca-Cola and sandwiches made from cheese and leftover gazelle from last night. It was before they raced to the Mara River like Indy car drivers to see the great crossing. He had been thrilled by the company, because it was another chance to bond with Merrick and show the agent that he was (or could be) a force in his own right. He wouldn't drop his father's name (he wouldn't drop any names) the way he had during their first breakfast in Nairobi, and he would play entirely by the rules of etiquette that seemed to apply here on safari: you didn't try and leverage who the hell you were professionally in real life (because, except for Patton, this sure as hell wasn't real life), but instead shared the details of your life that were genuine and personal—that is, if you spoke at all of your life back in America. Mostly you focused on the way the sight of a rhino in the wild changed you. Because it did.

And, suddenly, he wasn't thinking about what he could say that would make him sound smart, or whether he needed to jump in so he wasn't forgotten in the conversation. Charlie Patton was talking about elephants.

"There really is such a thing as an elephant nursery," he was saying. "An old girl, not likely the mom but maybe the grand-mom, keeping an eye on a bunch of the young ones. I always enjoyed it when I stumbled upon an elephant nursery."

"And yet you never had children yourself," Carmen said.

"Never even married," he replied, and Felix thought for a second that Charlie was going to say more, perhaps file this real-ity under regrets. But he didn't, instead continuing as if he had never paused. "I also love it when I come across some new mother trumpeting the birth of her son—or daughter. Elephants are smart: they love daughters, too. They'd like your Betty Friedan."

"And yet you hunt them," Carmen reminded him. It was an observation, but there was a hint of judgment in the tone. "And you will too, Peter, next week."

"Honestly? It was usually the old men I was collecting," Charlie said. "The ones who'd been kicked from the herd or had chosen to leave because, well, it was just their time. Their backs are moss, their ears are rags. Their tusks are broken, but still, it seems, too damn heavy for them to manage. You can tell from their tracks that they're dragging their feet because it hurts like hell just to walk."

"Well, that doesn't sound very sporting," Peter said. "It's never a fair fight because we have the guns. But shooting an old codger like that? I don't know . . ."

"You want a raging bull, do you?" Charlie asked the agent. "We can do that, too. But my days of wanting to take down some elephant in the prime of his life? They're over. I cried the first time I collected one like that. I got a little teary two years ago when I finished off what I supposed was my last one. And I only shot him because . . . never mind."

"Because your guest dropped his gun and ran," said Carmen.

After a long pause, the hunter confessed, "No. But he wasn't squeezing the trigger, either."

Felix looked at Peter, wondering how the agent would respond to the idea that another guest had frozen. Finally, Peter said, "An old dog can break my heart. The white whiskers, the milky eyes. The weak back legs. The only time I saw my father cry was when a dog of ours died. The dog was so old he could barely walk, and so my dad used to pick him up and carry him outside so he could do his business. And he was a black lab, and so even at the end he probably weighed sixty or seventy pounds. He was deaf, he was blind. An old elephant must be even worse. Sadder."

"I agree. But why do you think that is?" Reggie asked, not directing his question at anyone in particular. "Because it's so smart?"

"Perhaps," said Peter. But then everyone turned toward Charlie Patton and waited like schoolchildren for him to weigh in.

"First of all, it is smart. But that's not what I was getting at. It's because if you don't kill it, eventually it's going to die alone and be eaten," Charlie told them. "And, most likely, eaten alive. That's certainly the case with old lions. When I took an old lion, I was saving it from that sort of fate."

"Hyenas?" Felix asked.

"Precisely. I remember one old fellow who had once been very regal. You could tell. Earned his crown. But those days were behind him. Long kicked from the pride by a younger, tougher male. Still had a gorgeous mane, but he was all ribs and you could see the scars on his hide. A road map. His roar was more of a cough, and he had a hobble to his gait that was painful to watch. For all I know, he had a broken bone in a foot or one of his rear legs. And, yes, the hyenas were circling."

The safari had seen three spotted hyenas their very first day. They had heard some last night while they were tucked in their tents. "Hyenas are ugly," Carmen said.

Charlie nodded. "They are. Why Noah grabbed a pair for the ark is beyond me. Damn things have a canine snout and a koala's ears. And they're so slow that practically everything they want to eat is faster than they are, so they pick on the very old and the very young—and, of course, the very dead. The Maasai have a great name for them."

"For hyenas?" Carmen asked.

"Yes. Sometimes they call the bastards 'limpers' because their walk is so odd. There's a great fable. A crow tells a bunch of them to stand on each other's shoulders so they can stretch tall enough to reach the top of a tree where some tribesmen have stored their meat. But the crow was just tricking them. Knew they would try to steal something that wasn't theirs, because they're such loathsome creatures. There was no meat at the top of the tree. Not a scrap. Anyway, the hyena at the bottom couldn't hold the ones above him, and so he struggled out from beneath them without warning them. They all fell, of course, and the species was left lame for eternity."

"That old lion you were thinking of," Felix mused. "Did he know the hyenas were near?"

"Absolutely. Hyenas are anything but subtle. I'm sure he smelled them and then he heard them and then he saw them. And, if the time had come, he would have put up a good fight. He would have lost. But he was proud. He would not have gone gently into that good night. He would have burned and raged. Nevertheless, in the end he was going to be their dinner—and he would have been breathing when they started to dine."

"Was it an easy shot?" Peter wondered.

"Technically, yes. Emotionally, no."

Carmen dabbed at her lips with one of the cloth napkins the porters had set out on the blanket. Then she looked at the hunter and asked, "Did you consider shooting the hyenas instead?"

"Heavens, no. The hyenas were just being hyenas. If those ones didn't finish off the lion that morning, three or four would have the next day. Or the day after."

"I actually had a couple of pet turtles on Okinawa. We did. Four of us. They were the soft shells," Reggie said. "Most of the time, we were trying not to get killed. But a friend of mine found these two in some muck in a bomb crater, and one was missing a leg and the other had big cuts on his face. He was missing an eye. And suddenly, we had built them a turtle tank out of an oil drum and were foraging bugs and worms for them. They became like mascots for us. Some fellows were superstitious and told themselves that so long as the turtles stayed alive—we named them Mike and Ike, after the candy—they'd stay alive."

"I have a feeling that didn't end well," Felix said.

Reggie shrugged. "No. The turtle tank was blown up by a mortar shell. And the next day, two of the GIs who helped build the turtle tank were killed, too. Anyway, we were all shaken up by Mike and Ike's deaths in ways we hadn't expected. Let's face it: they were turtles."

"They died quickly. That's the best thing that can happen to an animal," Charlie said.

"We're animals, too. But I think the timing matters," Felix said. "You're talking about old lions and old elephants and wounded turtles that may also have been pretty old."

"And?" asked Charlie.

Felix almost didn't answer. Opening his mouth a moment ago had been a reflex; for a change, he wasn't thinking about what he should be saying. "And," he said finally, "quick is relative. My kid sister died quickly, but whether she had thirty seconds or three minutes before her heart stopped or her brain stopped or whatever stopped, she must have been so scared. So horribly, unbelievably scared."

Carmen smiled at him gently and Reggie was nodding.

"How did she die?" Charlie asked.

"Car accident. Another car slammed into her."

"Well, when human animals"—and he emphasized the word *animals* in a way that sounded affectionate to Felix—"die out here, it's not because of automobiles."

"No," said Reggie, and he chuckled. "It's because, I suppose, we get eaten."

.   .   .

It happened fast: the deaths. Not as quickly as a bullet taking down an old lion or a mortar obliterating a pair of wounded turtles, but it unfolded with a speed that astonished Felix. And, either because he hadn't had the time to think or because he was simply fed up with being a child, he jumped into the fray.

Carmen lunged forward and wrapped her scarf around the driver's neck, pulling it tight at the same moment that Reggie plunged that little jackknife into the neck of the guy behind them. And so Felix dove across the seat and grabbed the man's rifle barrel, and while he wasn't strong enough to wrest it from the guard's hands, he could keep it aimed up toward the roof, while over his shoulder Reggie kept stabbing the fellow and the blood splattered him like marble-sized drops of rain. The Land Rover careened off the track and into the grass as the driver lost control, and then he jammed his foot hard on the brake and everyone in the vehicle was thrust forward, especially Carmen, who fell between the front bucket seats and into the dashboard. But she held on to the scarf and broke the guy's neck. Felix saw it and he knew, even as he and Reggie and the guard were falling against the seats ahead of them, that his wife had snapped the driver's neck. His head whipped forward and then backward, and then his hands and his body went limp—which meant that his foot slipped off the brake and the Rover sped forward and smashed into a copse of acacia and rolled onto its side.

Which was when the rifle went off.

At first, Felix thought that he had had the wind knocked out of him. He knew the feeling because it had happened before, playing pickup football as a boy. One minute he was running and then he was being tackled and then he couldn't breathe. They were all on their sides in the Land Rover, and both of their captors were dead. But then he saw Carmen's face—the horror and the fear, so much worse than it had been at any point this awful morning, when she had been so very, very brave—and he saw that she was staring at his chest. Reggie was, too, and he seemed just as alarmed as Carmen. And so Felix tried to gaze down, but his neck wasn't quite right, and the combination of the fact that he couldn't breathe and the looks on his wife and her publicist's faces had him scared. Reggie pressed on his chest, and Felix wanted to say, *No, please, no, don't do that; that will only make it hurt more and make it harder to breathe,* but when he tried to speak there was so much fluid in his throat and his mouth that it was impossible. It was running down his cheek and his chin.

Which was when it dawned on him. He'd been shot and was about to die too. Just like their captors. He hadn't had the wind knocked out of him. He'd been shot at point-blank range by a fucking rifle. He was going to die, and just like his sister, it was going to be in a goddamn car. He felt a great wave of terror because this was it, this really was it. He thought of the Dylan Thomas poem that Patton had quoted just yesterday when they'd been having that pleasant lunch on the grass: he didn't want to rage, he just wanted to cry. But even that was too much. A healthy poet could write about the dying of the light, but a dying writer, a human whose blood was running from his chest like a garden hose? There was no energy to rave, no resolve to rage. There was only soul-crushing fear.

There were so many things that he wanted to say, but he couldn't, and already he was sinking, fading, the people around him growing foggy and far away, their words as distant and indecipherable as if they were trying to tell him something and he were underwater. But one idea ameliorated the horror and the despair a little bit. Made it bearable. And it was this: Carmen was proud of him. Surely, she was. She would think more highly of him because he had joined her and Reggie. In the end, he hadn't been sniveling and mousy and pathetic. He had helped. That was, in fact, among his very last thoughts: I've been shot just like Charlie Patton's old elephant, but unlike that creature, I will have left this world fighting. I died like . . . like . . . what was it they had called themselves at Katie and David's wedding? When they were toasting? The lions of Hollywood. That was it. And that was me. A young, roaring, ferocious lion.

I have died like one of the lions of Hollywood.

CHAPTER FIFTEEN

Reggie Stout

*Luke Barker's suicide surprised even the most jaded West Holly-
wood detectives. The thirty-six-year-old stockbroker was found dead
in his apartment on Christmas Day by the building superintendent
and Reggie Stout, publicist for so many of Hollywood's biggest stars.*
—Movie Star Confidential, JANUARY 1961

Carmen was weeping, and so Reggie held her racking body
close and murmured, "Shhhhhh," over and over, the sound in
his mind a bicycle tire losing its air after a puncture. He'd whispered just like that three times in the spring nineteen years ago,
though back then he was comforting men who were dying, not
a woman who'd suddenly been widowed. He was holding those
soldiers' hands or sitting beside them or, in one case, smothering
an abdominal wound with sulfanilamide because that was what
he found in the dead medic's bag. He had supposed back then
that whenever he returned home (if he returned home), he'd
never see another person shot. He'd never again see the human
body savaged by that sort of violence. He thought that was all
behind him.

Apparently not.

"Shhhhhh," he whispered again, rocking Carmen ever so
slightly. She had a bad cut on her forehead, but foreheads didn't
bleed much. Still, she was going to have a black eye, that was
apparent, and he worried that she might have a concussion—

and, if she did, what he should do. And he himself was hobbled: if he were to self-diagnose, he would say that he had sprained his left knee and pulled his left hamstring. He had also done something, though he couldn't say what, to his left shoulder. It hurt like hell, at least as much as his leg.

They were standing outside the toppled Land Rover, and as he had held Carmen, he had turned her, almost as if dancing, so she was facing away from the vehicle and could not see the three corpses inside it. The thing looked to him like a giant dead beetle. She was sobbing over Felix, but he also suspected this was a reaction to the fact that she had killed a man. They both had. They had, in fact, killed two men. And, yes, they were responsible for Felix's death, as well.

"We can't leave them in there," she said, sniffling, pulling away from him, but still speaking mostly into his shirt.

"They're better off in there," he said.

"They'll . . . they'll cook!"

He was surprised she was so explicit. He shuddered to think what condition the bodies would be in by the time a ranger or bush plane spotted the vehicle. The decomposition in this heat inside a metal box? The insects? It wouldn't be pretty. But, still, it seemed to him much better than being devoured by jackals or vultures like common carrion. Eventually, if he and Carmen survived this, they could have the bodies retrieved and whatever was left of Felix could be properly laid to rest, the ashes or the remains returned to California.

"We have to bury them," she continued. "We'll bury them and put a marker so someone from the government can find the bodies."

Bodies. Plural. She was thinking even of their captors. He guessed she was feeling guilty. As was he. He had to remind himself that these men had shot Juma—or men from their group had. They had murdered the rangers. They were killers. He wanted to make her see reason, remind her that they themselves were injured and didn't even have a shovel. And this ground?

Pretty damn hard. They couldn't bury anyone. Certainly, they couldn't dig a hole deep enough to prevent the corpses from being exhumed and scavenged. But he didn't want to argue with her. When she calmed down, she would see the reality of their predicament. She would understand that they had to get out of here and get help. They couldn't remain beside the Land Rover, because eventually the other abductors would wonder why this vehicle hadn't reached its destination and they'd backtrack. Whoever had attacked the safari was likely to get here long before rangers or rescuers—assuming anyone was even out there looking for them yet. He had no idea when or how often rangers were supposed to check in, but he realized that was his big hope. Someone soon would go off in search of the missing rangers.

And so he held her and rubbed the small of her back, while in his mind he started to make an inventory of the things he would look for inside the Land Rover. Things they would need as they tried to cross the savanna. The most important items were the guns and the water. But he had a feeling there was a lot more in there they could use. Hats and sunscreen. Maybe there was aspirin in the glove deck. He had no idea whether they could reach help before dark, and he wanted to be as prepared as humanly possible.

His mind paused on those last two words. Humanly possible. This seemed the last place on earth where two humans could survive. At least two humans who, unlike the Maasai, didn't have the slightest idea what the hell they were doing. And then, instantly, he recalled Okinawa, and the pit vipers, the sea krait, and the myriad insects and jellyfish that lived on the island or in the waters around it. He had survived Okinawa. Somehow, he and Carmen would survive the Serengeti.

He looked up at the sun. Nearest civilization, he guessed, was west. Congo. He hadn't followed the news there the way others on the safari had before leaving California, and he didn't know many details. The names Mobutu and Mulele rang a bell for him. The Simba rebellion. Mobutu was backed by the West. That meant the Simbas were backed by . . .

He had no idea. The Soviet Union? The sons of bitches who'd attacked their safari?

Or were the Simbas revolutionaries who wanted an independence unencumbered by the East or the West, which, whether it was Belgians or Germans or English, had exploited East and South Africa forever? Since they had first set foot here. Copper. Cobalt. Diamonds. Gold. Uranium. They mined it all, often with slave labor and always with exploited labor.

But it was the idea of the uranium that had stayed with Reggie, and that was because of Okinawa. Most of the uranium that the Americans had used in the bombs for Hiroshima and Nagasaki had come from a Congolese mine owned, at the time, by the Belgians. So, he was, perhaps, alive today because of that mine. He had no doubt he would have been part of the invasion of the Japanese home islands if the United States hadn't dropped those two bombs and Japan hadn't surrendered.

Which brought him back to where he and Carmen should go. Which direction.

Did that matter?

Yes. Good God, it was everything. They had to get out of here before they were eaten or died of exposure or infection or dehydration. The air was broiling, heavy with heat. It wasn't humid the way Okinawa had been, but just standing here was searing his skin and making him tired. They had gone back in time to a world without people, a cosmos of rivers with prehistoric-looking hippos lounging like boulders in the shallow water and crocodiles with mouths that could tear antelopes the size of ponies in half. And on the land? There were too many predators to count, too many cats or snakes or bugs or trees—Jesus, there were trees and shrubs here at least as lethal as the ones on Okinawa—that could do the two of them in. What mattered now was finding other humans: humans who, at the very least, didn't want to kidnap or kill them.

Which was when the realization, formless and fuzzy at first, began to grow firm in his mind. What had he been thinking when he had taken out his Boy Scout knife and killed their guard in the back seat? Yes, he and the driver had been willing to slay their African guide. They had been willing to execute the rangers. But they were never going to murder Carmen or Felix or him. At least they probably weren't. At least not until they had gotten their ransom. He and the other two Americans, after all, only had value when they were alive.

Still, who was to say when that would have happened or what might have occurred after they got their money? The kidnapped often were killed, whether they were a famous pilot's baby boy or a millionaire's twin granddaughters. So, he shook his head, trying to cast aside the second guess as if it were a fly in his hair.

Carmen pulled away from him and wiped her nose with the sleeve of her blouse. He noted how quickly her eye was swelling shut.

"Fine," she agreed suddenly, coming to her senses. "We won't bury them. We'll roll up the windows. At least that way, they won't get eaten."

Roll up the windows. The car was on its side, closer to upside down than right-side up. This, too, was the irony of language.

"I'll handle it," he told her. "I'll also retrieve a few things. Why don't you get out of the sun?" He pointed toward the branches on the side of the acacia farthest from the vehicle.

"Which way should we go?"

Again, he glanced up at the sky. There wasn't a cloud to be seen. Nothing but the cerulean heavens that marked this part of the world when it wasn't raining. There seemed no in-between. There were either torrential rains and gunmetal skies, or there was a blue so vibrant it belonged in a stone on a ring.

"West," he decided.

"Because we might find some Maasai?"

"That would be great. I honestly don't know what we'll
find, but I think it's the fastest way to civilization."

"Okay."

She walked toward the shade, almost stumbling once, and
waited there, a solitary woman who looked like she had but one
eye and a gash across her forehead—a woman who, just hours,
ago, had been a movie star.

.   .   .

When Reggie Stout had returned to America after the war,
there was no Mattachine Society. Not yet. He heard rumors of
groups calling themselves Bachelors Anonymous or the Andro-
gynes. He knew that men sometimes met near the water in
Westlake Park (and he knew where), and he knew of at least two
bars in West Hollywood, one off of Sunset and one on Haci-
enda, where discretion was a little less necessary because everyone understood they were safe spaces for men of a certain (and
here was a word that was supposed to show empathy and psy-
chological understanding, but just made him cringe) proclivity.

For two years he saw ("dated" suggested too public a relationship) an actor his firm represented, but in 1953 the fellow
married. The man continued to want to see him, but Reggie
wanted nothing to do with married men: it wasn't fair to their
wives, it wasn't fair to them, and it sure as hell wasn't fair to
himself. There were the pool parties, but from the very beginning he felt too old. He wasn't, not in chronological years, but
he had just seen too much in the Pacific. He didn't want to sit in
his swimsuit on a diving board with actors or insurance agents
or doctors who had no idea what it was like to watch whole rows
of men collapsing—arms akimbo, blood spraying from them
like water from a wet dog—when machine guns opened up in
caves you didn't even know existed.

Then, until 1960, he had an on-again, off-again thing with

another veteran, a fellow his age named Luke (and he liked to be called Luke, even though he was born Lucas, because his father was a Baptist minister) who had been with the 101st Airborne. He'd dropped over Normandy, he'd dropped in Market Garden, and he'd survived both battles without a scratch. It was while being trucked into Bastogne just before Christmas that he was machine-gunned in the legs. Both legs. Right thigh, left shin. Right femur, left fibula. He was in the makeshift hospital that was shelled on Christmas Eve and was one of the few G.I.s who survived. He came home and worked himself back to the point that his limp was barely noticeable, and, through his uncle, got a job with E. F. Hutton as a stockbroker. They might still have existed in that liminal world between friends and lovers, but on the sixteenth anniversary of the hospital shelling, Christmas Eve, 1960, alone in his apartment, he took a Colt .45-caliber and shot himself dead. Reggie was the one who found the body, when Luke didn't answer his phone that night or again on Christmas Day. The stockbroker's family never asked Reggie why he had called the apartment superintendent and convinced the man that they had to open the door. Even Luke's father, the Baptist minister, never pressed.

Since then, Reggie had lived a rather monastic life. Rather. Not total. But monasticism seemed about right when he thought about the last time he saw Luke. His friend had cut short their lunch on December 21, because, he had said, he had some last-minute shopping to do for his niece and his nephew, and he wanted to get to the toy store and then clean up some trades at the office. He hadn't struck Reggie as depressed. Melancholic, yes. But they were both melancholy around the holidays. They had never spent Christmas Eve or Christmas Day together, but they always spoke on one day or the other. When Luke hadn't answered his phone or called him by lunchtime on Christmas Day, that sixth sense that Reggie was convinced sometimes separated the living soldiers from the dead kicked in. He intuited that something was wrong, and so he went to Luke's apartment and, with the super, found the body dead in the bed. It said something about his life, Reggie thought as he stared at the corpse while the super called the police, that the sight of a gunshot suicide was far from the worst thing he had ever seen.

No one ever suspected that Reggie killed the stockbroker, but the first cops on the scene and one of the beat reporters clearly believed that Reggie had called the super because of his (and here was that awful word again) proclivities. Reggie's name appeared in a few of the newspaper stories, and that fueled speculation and innuendo about what sort of relationship he might have had with the man. But the world continued to spin, and Reggie understood there were enough people in Hollywood like him, women as well as men, that it didn't derail his career. Besides, the industry appreciated him as a human being, and he was good at what he did. And, yes, he had survived Okinawa. If you walked away from that island, people were always going to cut you some slack.

. . .

There were four canteens full of water in the Land Rover, and he carried them all to the shade of the acacia. He had to crawl over the corpses of the three dead men to retrieve them, getting still more of their blood on his hands and his clothes, aware always of how solid were some parts of the human body and how gelatinous were others. But water was essential, and these were not the first corpses he had navigated in his life.

The vehicle seemed so much smaller to him when it was on its side. The dead seemed to fill it in ways that they hadn't when they were living. The smell of their sweat—and his—was as pronounced and pungent as the smell of the ocean.

One of the two bags of nuts had been torn open, but he picked most of the nuts off the underside of the vehicle's roof and put them into the other bag, the one that had not ripped apart in the crash, and brought that to the shade, too. The nuts on the clothing of the dead guard he left where they were. He took the rifle and the driver's pistol and the toilet paper and the little metal first-aid kit. There was a knapsack that he believed had belonged to Muema, the second guide, and it was hard work to dislodge it from beneath the body of the driver. But he did. He was able to wrench it from where it was pinned behind the man's back, one of the canvas straps wrapped partly around the steering wheel.

In it he found a map of the reserve, a lighter, binoculars, a compass, and a pack of cigarettes. He grabbed all of that and then emptied the knapsack, including a week-old newspaper and a paperback novel, also onto the underside of the roof, where he would leave it.

For a moment he gazed down at Felix. He'd seen his share of dead faces, and he was never going to categorize any of them as "at peace." They'd all died violently. Felix was no exception. One eye was open, one closed, and he looked inexorably and inconsolably terrified. Reggie shut the eye that was open and brushed a lock of chestnut hair off his forehead. He tugged off Felix's wedding ring, unstrapped his wristwatch, and found his wallet in his pants pocket, because he knew that Carmen would want all of that. Then he pulled the folds of the man's ragged shirt back over his chest, even though the blood on the fabric had already started to dry, epoxying the cloth to the wound, and then rested his arms there.

He noticed near the gas pedal a knife considerably longer and more dangerous than his Boy Scout knife (though that had proven sufficiently lethal a few minutes ago), and supposed it had belonged to the driver. He took that, too. Then he checked the pockets of the dead men, but he found only keys and some Kenyan currency. No wallets and no IDs.

He grabbed his safari hat and the Dodgers ball cap Felix wore in the heat of the day. He didn't unwrap Carmen's scarf from the driver's neck. She could wear her husband's cap, which was probably better anyway, because it had a bill.

Before leaving the vehicle for the last time, he rolled up the driver's window. Unfortunately, he couldn't roll up the open window behind it. The door was too badly dented, and the handle wouldn't budge. He struggled with it for perhaps a minute, but in the end he gave up. Maybe he was wrong and animals wouldn't crawl into the Land Rover and either dine on the three dead humans where they were or drag them outside into the well-grazed grass to finish them off there. No, he knew what he knew. By tomorrow morning, the bodies would be mutilated or gone.

When he was through, he returned to Carmen and sat down beside her and studied what they had. Everything except for the rifle and two of the canteens would fit into the pack. Carmen could loop one canteen to her pants, and he could hang the other off his. He would have her carry the pistol. He would tote the rifle.

"Who are they?" she asked. She was no longer crying. He wasn't sure whether she meant the two men in the vehicle or their kidnappers generally. He decided that how he responded didn't matter.

"I don't know," he said. "I just don't know. They didn't have wallets."

He opened the metal box that held the first-aid kit. There was a tube of Germolene antiseptic, all sorts of bandages and gauze, tape, small scissors, eyewash, Bayer aspirin, and a bottle of pills from which most of the label was gone. But the little wording that remained led him to suspect it was a prescription antihistamine that was not part of the original kit.

"Give me your hand," he said, and she obliged. He shook three aspirin into it and watched her swallow them without water. He handed her a canteen, but she shook her head.

"I'd rather save it. Just in case," she murmured.

"Okay." He squeezed some of the antiseptic onto his finger and ran it over the gash on her forehead. "Do you think you broke anything?"

"You're going to set a bone for me out here?"

He held up the tape. "This—and the aspirin—is about as good as it's going to get."

"No. I suppose I have some bruises to look forward to. And my eye must be a mess."

"Not that bad," he lied.

"You were limping," she observed.

"My left knee," he admitted. "And maybe a hamstring."

"Can you walk?"

"Absolutely," he said. "But I will tape up my knee and my shin. It might help—and it couldn't hurt."

"Until, as they say, you rip off the bandage."

He smiled at her small joke.

"You rolled up the windows?" she asked.

"Yes," he lied again. "I did." He was a deeply honest man, but he knew also that he was a very convincing liar.

She nodded.

And then, finally, they started away from the wreck and the bodies, walking west, the sun overhead. Paralleling them, perhaps two hundred yards away, were three hyenas. Limpers. They were off to the side of Carmen's face where her eye was swollen shut, and so Reggie hoped that she wouldn't (or couldn't) see them.

CHAPTER SIXTEEN

Margie Stepanov

Margie Stepanov, seen here smiling beside actresses Katie Barstow and Carmen Tedesco, may be a housewife, but in this lavender bridesmaid's dress at Barstow's wedding, she looked every bit the movie star, too.

—*The Hollywood Reporter,* NOVEMBER 9, 1964

It was, she supposed, late afternoon, by the way the sun had moved west: there were no windows in this hut, but the cow dung and mud had started to separate along one wall, creating a sliver of light. About two hours ago, one of the men had untied her and allowed her to pee, and then given her water and some sort of gruel. She had heard enough through the walls that she knew each member of their group had been marched out, one by one, and walked behind some brush and allowed (like her) to relieve themselves at gunpoint. They'd been given their allotment of water and a little of that porridge. Then they were brought back into their huts.

The cut on her stomach was painful, and she wished she could examine it. She wished she could see it. She tried to convince herself it was nowhere near the kid. Too high on her abdomen. She told herself it would have no effect on her baby. But she failed. Already, she feared, the infection was growing worse.

She recalled when they had all heard the first shots that

morning. No one had understood the magnitude of what was
occurring. She knew the term Billy used for that sort of under-
reaction: normalcy bias. We suppose the world will continue to
spin the way it always has. We tell ourselves that what we are
seeing isn't, in fact, the cataclysm that it is. She was the first to
scream, and for a moment, even in her hysteria, clearly Billy had
supposed that she was panicking about nothing.

If only she had been . . .

Now she noticed a flashlight beam and saw one of the captors returning. It was someone new, someone she had never seen
before—neither the driver nor the guard from the Land Rover
who had brought them here. He knelt before the sleeping pallet
on which she was restrained and shined the flashlight up on his
face so she could see him more clearly. He had moonstones for
eyes and dirty blond hair. He was good-looking, but she would
have thought he was drop-dead gorgeous if it didn't appear as
if his nose had been broken at some point and left twisted and
bulbous. God, she thought, poor Billy's nose might look like
that someday.

"Good afternoon," he said, his accent tinged with Russian.
At one point, perhaps, an hour ago, she had heard men speaking
outside the hut in Russian. He smiled at her. Then he put the
handle of the flashlight in his mouth and shined it on her ankles
as he unbound them from the post. He scooted forward and
untied her hands the same way.

"That should feel better," he said. He was, she suspected by
his carriage, the group's leader, though how many people he
led, she couldn't say. There had to have been at least eight to ten
of them at the camp that morning: two or three for each Land
Rover, and at least three or four more to supervise the porters
as they ransacked the site. But there may have been others. She
just had no idea.

But now she stretched her legs and rolled her wrists, and it
felt good. She wondered whether she should only speak when
spoken to. That was how she had viewed her first foray from the

hut, a few hours ago, when she had been taken outside to relieve herself.

"How are you feeling?"

"I'm okay," she said hesitantly.

"I gave your husband some aspirin. For his nose."

"Thank you."

"You're pregnant, yes?"

"Yes."

"One of my men told me. How many months?"

"Three."

"The child making you sick?"

Child. It was a peculiar choice of word, and she attributed it to English being his second or third language. But was it really any stranger than the way she and Billy referred to their baby as *the kid*?

"No," she said.

"Good. I'm untying you because I want you comfortable. More comfortable. But you can't leave this hut unless we bring you outside. I hope you are all home soon, including your child."

"So, this is a . . . a kidnapping?"

It was odd: now that the flashlight was pointed at the ground, she could barely see his face, and he could barely see hers.

"Yes, this is a kidnapping," he replied, and there was a lightness to his voice. It was reminiscent of the way she had heard Billy laugh when he was confirming something for his little boy that was obvious to grown-ups. *Yes, a starfish needs to be in the water to live. Yes, the sand does stick to our feet when we come out of the ocean. Yes, once upon a time you were as little as that baby.* These were all things that Billy had said to Marc when they had been at the Santa Monica beach that summer.

"Are you . . ." she paused, worried that she shouldn't be asking any more questions. Perhaps questions were like wishes in fairy tales and she'd been given her one and she'd used it. (No, that wasn't right. If this were a fairy tale, which it sure as hell wasn't, wouldn't she have three?)

"Go ahead," he said.

"Are you going to untie the others?"

"I untied your movie star friend."

She knew that he was referring to Katie, not Terrance. A woman. She supposed that also meant the three men were still bound to the sleeping pallets. "Thank you for giving my husband some aspirin. Is he"—and, again, her voice wavered briefly—"in a lot of pain?"

"Probably." He pointed the flashlight at his own nose. "But he'll live."

This fellow seemed so civilized, so unlike the man who had swatted Billy or the crew that had murdered a pair of rangers and Juma. She wanted to ask him his name, but knew she didn't dare. That was definitely going too far.

"How long will we be here?" she inquired instead.

He reached into her hair, and she was able to restrain a flinch. He pulled out a leaf and a twig and showed them to her with his flashlight. "Don't leave the hut," he told her, his tone at once kind and firm. Clearly, he had no intention of answering her question. "My boys are edgy. Do you know the expression 'trigger-happy'?"

"I do."

"Good." He dropped the leaf and the twig on the ground, and she thought he was going to leave her alone. He turned toward the entry and may even have moved slightly in that direction, and she regretted that she had not mentioned her own wounds, especially the cut on her stomach. He had that flashlight. Perhaps he would allow her to examine it. But then, as if he had read her mind, he paused and turned back toward her.

.   .   .

This morning she had awoken and put her bare feet down on the canvas groundsheet in their tent. Sunlight had pulled her from sleep before the porters. Each day one had arrived and called, "Jambo!" outside the flaps, and left a pot of steaming coffee, a little pitcher of milk, and two porcelain mugs on the ground before the tent's wide zipper. She'd felt the uneven earth beneath her toes and placed her hands low on her stomach, her way of saying good morning (and she said it every morning) to her baby. She saw Billy was still sleeping deeply in his cot. He'd awaken when the java arrived. Then she'd stood, a little awed that she was here, so very far from her and Billy's modest place in L.A., and climbed out from beneath the mosquito netting. Outside a bird sang, but she knew almost nothing of birds and had no idea what kind it was. Then she heard some snuffling behind the tent, the side where the porters had set up the bathtub, and went there. She had brought a nightgown to sleep in, but the first night she had opened her eyes around two thirty, sweating as if she were in a sauna, and since then had slept in only a T-shirt and underwear. Still, however, inside this tent she felt strangely invulnerable.

She carried the camp chair from the tent over to the tub and stood upon it. She peered through the strip of mesh that separated the roof from the wall, and there they were: easily two dozen wildebeest, walking and grazing, a procession no more than nine or ten feet from where she was standing on a chair. They were either oblivious to her or they didn't care. They looked, she decided, rather like thin cows with beards. There were no calves or babies in this group, and once more she touched the small of her belly. She had felt a special affinity on this safari for animals when they were spotted with their young. Juma had told her that wildebeest calves were precocious: running (and running fast) within weeks of their birth. They had to be quick learners if they wanted to live. Her kid? Lord, it would be months before he or she would be crawling. A year or so before walking. And running? She had no idea when toddlers began running.

She jumped when she felt something on her hips before realizing that it was but Billy's hands.

"You scared me," she told him. He lifted her down from the chair to the canvas.

"I'm sorry. But your bottom was irresistible. I hope you never return to nightgowns when we're back in L.A."

"There are wildebeest just outside the tent. They're within feet of us. Stand on the chair and peek."

"I thought I heard them," he said. He was sleeping in underwear and a T-shirt too, and she held the chair while he climbed onto it and glanced at them through the mesh. Then he hopped down.

"That's it? You just needed a peek?" she asked.

"You sound disappointed in me."

"Weren't you amazed?"

He shrugged. "They were wildebeest, that's all."

"That's all," she said, mimicking him. She poked him in the side with two fingers.

"I guess I've become a junkie. A wildebeest doesn't fly me to the moon anymore. I need lions."

"And elephants."

"Exactly."

She shook her head. "How will you ever again bear the boredom of L.A.?"

"Oh, I have a feeling the kid will bring plenty of excitement into my world. I remember when Marc was a baby."

"Babies aren't exciting for men. I'm not sure they're all that exciting for women. They're messy and chaotic, but—"

"It will be fine. It will be wonderful."

"Are you"—and she emphasized the word—"*excited* for today?"

"Yes. Absolutely."

"Even if you don't get your lion fix?"

"Even if."

"Don't take this for granted, Billy. This is special."

"I know."

She couldn't quite read his tone. If anyone understood the strange dynamics of a brother so thoroughly diminished by a younger sibling, it was Billy. He probably had patients in which he saw himself. Katie made more money than him (God, she made more money than everyone), and she was certainly more famous than him (because he wasn't famous at all), and . . .

And there was nothing else in Hollywood. Nothing. There was only money and fame.

Katie had been the Stepanovs' favorite child; now she was America's favorite daughter.

"Just because it's a gift from your little sister—" she continued, her plan to remind him that this was a moment that was singular and he should savor it. But he cut her off.

"I'm fine, sweetheart," he said. "I resent none of this."

She kissed him on the cheek. "I'm glad," she said. She didn't believe him, but she was pleased he was pretending to be content. That was half the battle.

From the other side of the tent she heard more rustling and for a moment imagined the wildebeest had moved toward the front of the camp. But then she heard a porter calling out, "Jambo, jambo!" and she knew the sounds were young men, and that their coffee had arrived.

. . .

Well, now. Billy had his excitement. They all did. And if he wanted inarguable cause for resentment, he had that, too.

For a moment the fellow with those blue eyes looked back at her from the doorway, and she wished he would shine his flashlight up again so she could see his face and try to gauge his intentions. The idea that he might rape her crossed her mind, and abruptly she felt her stomach turn and her body grew rigid.

"Tell me something," he said.

"Yes?" She didn't know what else to say. Did he know also

about the wound on her stomach? Had the driver told him and it had just now dawned on him to ask?

But, no, it wasn't that. "Why is your husband a Stepanov and his sister a Barstow?"

"She changed her name. Katie did. For the movies."

He seemed to take this in. "Should I be insulted?"

"Is that your name? Stepanov?"

"No, it's not," he told her, and she heard mirth in that short sentence, as if the idea that he would ever respond with his real name was utterly absurd. Which, of course, it was. "But Stepanov is a very common name. I know two families with that name."

"Then why would you wonder if you should be insulted?" She knew now—she knew it with a confidence that she hadn't felt about anything since they had been abducted—that he wasn't going to rape her. He wasn't going to hurt her. She relaxed.

"Because changing it is disrespectful to Russians. And to her family."

Now that she was sure he wasn't going to assault her, she found herself hoping that she could keep him here with her for another few minutes. Perhaps if she really won him over, he might untie Billy. He might untie all the other men.

"I think she was just doing what the studio wanted."

"Hollywood doesn't hate the Soviet Union."

"I wouldn't know about that. But they do make pictures for America, and they don't want to upset that apple cart."

"Apple cart? Who has apple carts? This is 1964."

"It's an expression. It means—"

"I know what it means. I was teasing you. I actually have family in America."

"Really?"

"I was jesting when I asked if I should be insulted. I know why she changed her name. I changed my name too. It used to be Washington."

"And now you're"—and she considered using the word *jesting,*

the way he had, but was afraid it would sound condescending—
"teasing me again."

He nodded. "My name was never Washington and I never
changed it."

She was surprised at his playfulness. He was rather funny. "It
wouldn't make sense for you to tell me your name. Obviously,"
she agreed.

"Obviously."

"Your English is excellent."

"I would make a joke that it was my native language, but
you'd probably believe that, too."

"Yes. I probably would."

"But you're not a gullible woman. So, why is that?"

She took a breath, buying time, unsure how far to press
him. Finally, she replied, "Perhaps because I'm scared to death?
Because I was tied up for hours? Because I'm here alone in the
dark? Because this morning I saw people murdered?"

"You don't need to be scared."

"I saw men killed."

"They were raising their rifles. They had guns."

"The guide didn't. Juma."

"But the person who shot him thought he did. My guy
thought he was raising his hands to fire." He shook his head,
a motion she could see even here in the deep gloaming on the
inside of the hut. "All of you have value when you're breathing.
None of you have value when you're dead."

"Unless you're a ranger or a guide," she said. God. She was
alive only because she happened to have been born in America.

"Yes. I have very little use for either rangers or guides. Nevertheless: I don't want to see them dead. I don't want to see
anyone innocent dead."

Innocent. So, here was the logic: you lived if you were innocent or valuable. She understood who could be pegged as one
or the other. But guilty? She had no idea how he defined that.
Since her captor was Russian, might the guilty be capitalists? If

so, it was apparently better to be valuable and guilty than worthless and innocent. But if this were a kidnapping, that meant these men cared a hell of a lot about money—more than even the most ruthless capitalists. It wasn't as if the most cold-blooded and merciless among the Rockefellers or Carnegies were shooting people seventy and eighty years ago.

"May I ask something else?" She saw him nodding in silhouette from the entry, and so she continued: "How much money are we worth? What are you asking for?"

"Are you asking the money value of a human life?"

"I guess I am," she agreed, though it was tragically clear that some lives had far greater monetary value than others.

"Well, I will ask you something in response, Mrs. Billy Stepanov. What makes you think we're interested in money?"

"You admitted this was a kidnapping."

He kicked at the ground with the toe of his boot, and the gesture was almost boyish. "I would say I was disappointed in you, but that would mean I was surprised. I'm not surprised. You're American. For Americans, it's always about the money. It's only about the money."

"But a ransom has to be—"

"No," he said, cutting her off before she could finish. "It doesn't have to be about money. There are things in this world that matter more. Now, it might be about money. I'm human. But have you looked for one moment beyond Africa's zebras and lions and giraffes? At the continent's people? Whole nations are rising up, and all you can see is the wildlife."

"I understand." She knew now that she hadn't won him over enough to broach the idea of untying the others. She'd been a bad student and a poor study, and she was angry at herself for disappointing him because of what it meant for Billy and David and Terrance.

But there was still her baby and that gash on her abdomen. She still had to look out for the kid, and this might be her last chance. "May I . . ."

He waited.

"My stomach. There's a cut there. I can't see it, but I think it's getting infected. Or already is infected. I also have some cuts I never really got to look at on"—she couldn't think of a euphemism for *ass* or *bottom*—"the back of my legs. The back of my hips."

"You're injured?"

"That might be too strong a word, But—"

Instantly he was back beside her with the flashlight. He knelt down on the ground and commanded her to pull up her shirt. She did, her embarrassment small compared to the relief that he was going to examine the wound.

"Why didn't you tell me?" he snapped.

"I was . . . afraid."

He shook his head, his annoyance evident. "Yes, it is infected." He then murmured something in Russian, and she was quite sure it was a curse of some sort. "I'll be right back. We might have something." And then he was gone.

She sat very still on the sleeping pallet and gazed into the dark, aware that whatever he had seen on her stomach had alarmed him. And so it alarmed her.

She tried to think of something else. What would happen if she went to the other room, the one with the entrance? She began to imagine what she might see if she stayed inside this hut but allowed herself a peek outside. Yes, she'd see the Land Rovers and the white men with guns. But might she also spot impalas or zebras in the distance? She focused on animals because it frightened her less than the idea she was hurt and the kid might be in danger.

And it was then that she felt her khaki shorts growing wet. For a second, she thought she had peed her pants because the dampness was warm, but then she felt a wrenching cramp that caused her to grunt and grab her abdomen, and it was followed almost instantly by a second one. And she knew. She knew. Whether it was because of the infection or the violent moment

that morning when her stomach had been sprayed with shattered glass or the relentless stress she had endured all day, she
understood what was happening. She bent over against the pain
and began to sob, because she realized that if there were actually
any light in this fucking hut, she'd see that her lap was awash in
blood.

CHAPTER SEVENTEEN

Terrance Dutton

There's certainly bad blood between the esteemed journalists here at Movie Star Confidential *and Dorothy Dandridge, but facts are facts: on Thursday night she was out* very *(and we mean* very*) late with married director Otto Preminger and on Friday night we spotted her having a* very *(and, again, we mean* very*) intimate dinner with actor Terrance Dutton. Both tête-à-têtes were at the Grotto on Sunset.*

—Movie Star Confidential, NOVEMBER 1957

The sky was a deep purple to the east and pink to the west, the kind of great stripes of color you never saw in L.A. They'd taken his watch, but he supposed it was nearly seven p.m. The Russian walking behind him was the smug fellow who'd been guarding them from the very last row of the Land Rover. He'd seemed taller to Terrance when he'd been sitting behind him, and Terrance realized only now that he himself had the height advantage. He made a mental calculation as he was walked behind the acacia to pee. He could probably move fast enough to overpower his guard before getting shot, but he doubted that he could do it quietly enough not to draw attention to the two of them. And if he attacked, he had to win—and he had to win silently. Because only then, in the dim light of dusk, did he have a prayer in hell of sneaking into the huts with David and Billy, untying them, and giving them all a fighting chance against these pricks. There would be three of them, and they'd have a rifle.

And he was feeling a particular urgency now. It wasn't simply that he had spent most of the afternoon tied up in the dark; it was that something had happened to Margie Stepanov. He didn't know what, but he'd heard her sobbing. Then he'd heard chaos, and at least a couple of the men who'd arrived in the jeep that afternoon running in and out of her hut. There was someone new in charge, a Russian with ice-blue eyes and a nose that a casting director would kill for if he ever needed a boxer, barking commands. Finally, one of the vehicles was leaving the boma, and if Terrance were a betting man, he would bet it was leaving with Margie.

He was taking small comfort from the fact that he was pretty sure Billy had heard the Russian yelling and the jeep or the Land Rover driving away, but nothing else. Margie's hut was beside his, but Billy's hut, thank God, was farthest away. It wasn't likely that the woman's husband had heard her sobbing; he hadn't made the connection between her cries and the commotion. He probably thought she was still in her hut too.

With some of the Russians having left—including that new guy, their leader—Terrance supposed the odds were even better if he could take down the one now waiting for him to unzip his fly. How many guards remained, including this character? Two? No more.

So, this might be his best shot. His one shot. And he'd heard Charlie Patton say often enough their first days here in Africa that when you had your one shot in the Serengeti, you damn well better take it.

. . .

The group from L.A. had caught up with Katie and David at the airline's gate at the airport in Paris. Terrance had seen people gawking, some with adoration for Katie, some a little annoyed

that this contingent from Hollywood was garnering such attention from the boarding agents and the stewardesses who were
soon to strut down the jet bridge ahead of the passengers and
prepare the cabin. They had at least an hour until they'd board.

Usually people in France cared less that he was Black, though
he knew the French had their own issues with pigment: Alge-
ria had only clawed its way free of France two and a half years
ago, and both countries had been badly scarred by the war—
though, inevitably, it was the Algerians who had lost more.
Much more. Now, however, as he watched a few people get out
their cameras, he decided to give them all a treat: when Katie
stood on her toes—a ballerina almost *en pointe*—to kiss him, he
turned toward the crowd with their Kodaks and put his hands
on her shoulders exactly the way he had in *Tender Madness*. They
kissed on the lips in that scene, though the kiss itself was cut. Of
course. As was the rest of the scene. But these travelers who were
shooting them now would look at their prints after they had
been developed and recall that scandalous moment from that
controversial movie. *Terrance Dutton and Katie Barstow, together in
real life! Kissing—and Katie on her honeymoon! Surely the gossip was
true! Surely!*

"My God, you look wonderful," she said to him. "You've
been traveling forever, and you still look fantastic."

"So do you," he told her. A white woman's lips on his cheek;
a Black man's hands on her shoulders. Merely salacious and
newsworthy at a Paris airport in 1964. But years ago, back in
Tennessee, it would have gotten his grandfather killed. It would
have gotten his father, at the very least, beaten. God, the things
they whispered about Dorothy and Preminger, and that was
Hollywood just a couple of years ago.

When they pulled apart, he shook David's hand, and then
the honeymooners started inquiring about their first two flights
and how they were bearing up. After all, they still had a long
way to go. And while the seven new arrivals in France had spent
much of the last day traveling from California, the newlyweds

had been walking the Seine and savoring Notre Dame. Sleeping late in their suite at the Hotel Lutetia. But, almost as one, the guests from America all said they were fine, though Billy Stepanov, ever solicitous, wanted to find a seat for his pregnant wife, and Peter Merrick wanted to find a bar.

"There's one about six gates down," David told the agent. "We have time. I'll join you."

And, just like that, the sexes separated, as if this were a Gilded Age dinner party, where the men went to one room to drink and smoke, and the women to another to . . . to do the exact same thing, minus the cigars and the serious booze. The six men left Katie and Carmen Tedesco and Margie Stepanov in orange Naugahyde seats at the gate, where they insisted they were content, and went to the lone bar in the concourse. Terrance and Peter took over a corner of the ebony balustrade near the window so they could appreciate the sun, both standing, while the other four men took the last empty table. Terrance ordered a martini and Peter a shot of Johnnie Walker, neat. There Terrance asked the agent about his plans to stay an extra week in Africa with their safari leader, Charlie Patton.

"I figured, what the hell?" Peter answered. He had both his forearms on the bar, the fingers of one hand around the glass, and, as he often did, Terrance saw a sketch or a painting—in the man's big fingers beside that squat tumbler of Scotch, and the reflection of the glass on the bar. "I used to hunt. Not much lately. Not at all in the last three years."

"Suppose you kill a lion. Will you have the head shipped back to L.A.? Is that still done?"

"That's a big supposition. Bagging a lion? Might be above my pay grade."

"A zebra then?"

"Ship the skin back? I doubt it. Maybe if my ex-wives didn't hate me, I would: have it turned into handbags for them. When I hunted in America, it was to be with my father and my grandfather. Be outside. In the wild. The woods? A cathedral for my grandfather. And I actually like deer. The taste. I have very fond memories from my youth of eating venison at my grandfather's in Montana."

"From a deer you shot."

He nodded. "Or one my grandfather shot. And Charlie Patton? He's a legend. He used to hunt with Hemingway. Taught Robert Ruark a bunch. So, when I heard that he was the outfitter that Katie had booked, it seemed a natural."

"It sounds like I should have heard of him."

"Nah. If you're not interested in collecting an elephant, why would you know his name? He's a dying breed: one of the last remaining great white hunters."

The last three words caused Terrance to snap his head up. His mind had begun to drift: he had been looking down at the bar and their booze, but now he was staring at Merrick. Merrick was gazing at the rows of bottles with their exquisite labels behind the bartender, a phantasmagoric collage of yellows and reds and impeccable graphics. He considered letting the words slide by, but Peter was a straight shooter and Terrance once more was on the balance beam he knew well: outrage on one side and acceptance on the other. He'd built a career walking it. "Great white hunters?" he asked. "What in the world does that mean, Peter?"

The agent turned to him and shrugged. "It means nothing. No need to take offense."

"I'm not offended, but it means something. Are there no great Black hunters? Or are there white hunters who aren't great?"

Peter swallowed the last of his Johnnie Walker. "I'm guessing you didn't see *Drums of Africa* last year."

"Missed it."

"You missed nothing. Atrocious movie. God-awful. But Torin Thatcher plays one."

"A great white hunter."

Peter nodded. "It's just, I don't know, the term that's used for a certain class of elite hunter. The colonials who would lead the more exclusive hunting safaris. They used to be called that."

That. Terrance noted that he didn't repeat the expression. "And they were all white?"

"Yes. This was Africa."

Peter saw no irony in that last sentence. But, then, why would he? The fact was, the *colonials* (Peter's word) had had their boots on the necks of the native Blacks for centuries. They still did in vast swaths of the continent. And in some countries where the Africans had fought for and won their freedom, they were now reenacting the civil wars that had plagued Europe and North America the last three hundred years.

"I'm sorry, Terrance," Peter was saying. "I won't use that expression again."

"Thank you. But you have nothing to apologize for. I was just taken aback by the term."

"I think he's an all-right sort. Charlie, that is. More good than bad. At least that's the impression I've gotten from the memoirs and articles I've read about him. From the letters we exchanged when I booked him."

"You did your homework."

"I did. But, as I said, I'd already heard of Patton." He motioned for the bartender to refill his glass. "Look, I'm not going to defend the man and what he's called. But I have a sense that . . ."

His voice trailed off, and Terrance waited for the agent to continue. "I actually feel a little bad for him," Peter went on after a moment. "I doubt his career is ending the way he would have liked."

This surprised Terrance. "How so?" he asked.

"I'm guessing here, but I think he's feeling a little diminished. Hunting isn't what it used to be. Fewer people do it, fewer people spend the money. The new governments have figured out there's a lot more dough from Americans and Europeans who want to photograph lions than kill them. Look at how little of Kenya or Tanganyika—where we're going—is now zoned for hunting. It's all about cameras, not guns. Wildlife experts, not hunters. And so Patton changed his business model and now guides the likes of us, instead of the likes of Hemingway. And if you're the sort of man that Patton probably is, that's a comedown. It's . . . unmanly. That's what I meant by a dying breed. I guess it would be like an actor of your stature suddenly having to pay the rent doing schlock horror movies with tiny budgets."

"Oh, I did my share of those," Terrance admitted, smiling, but he had been younger, and he sure as hell hoped he never again did another film where the flying saucers were those Wham-O Frisbees.

"And then there are the poachers out there. Killing elephants and rhinos. That must further deflate a fellow like Patton. They're doing it illegally and without proper, I don't know, respect for the animals."

"So, how do you think he'll treat us?"

"Patton? Oh, I suppose just fine. We're paying guests. Well, Katie's his paying guest. But you see my point. He's been reading the writing on the wall for years."

"And his staff will all be Black? Even now?"

"I think so. Maybe an Indian or two, but I doubt it."

"I don't imagine he's had a lot of Black clients," Terrance mused.

"Probably not," Peter agreed. "But you're American, and you're with a party paying him big dollars. He won't mistake you for a porter."

The words hung there again, and Terrance restrained his desire to snap at the agent for what the other man clearly supposed was a harmless joke—tell him there was nothing funny about a remark like that. But he didn't because Merrick hadn't meant anything by it. He may even have thought he was being reassuring. Besides, Terrance was going to be traveling with him for the next week and a half. And Peter Merrick was a powerful man in La-La Land. He pulled strings that Terrance understood

he would never see: he had to be careful. For all he knew, someday he might need or want Merrick to represent him. Actors
changed representation all the time. So, he kept his irritation
with the porter remark to himself. He hadn't climbed this high
on the Hollywood ladder by being combative over the things
that, in the end, didn't matter. He picked his fights carefully.

"I suppose Patton grew up in Tanganyika?" Terrance asked
instead.

"Kenya. Big estate outside Nairobi. A lot of native help and
farmworkers."

"Native help and farmworkers. This just gets better and better." Terrance chuckled when he said it, so he could make his
point about the baggage that accompanied an expression like
native help, but not offend Peter.

Still, the agent turned to look him squarely in the eye. "I
have just biased you completely and needlessly against the man.
I'm sorry. I didn't think. You might like him. I might like him.
I sure as hell hope we both do. I don't know him, but I promise you, Terrance, whatever faults and prejudices Charlie Patton
has, he's not Bull Connor."

"Good to know. I'd hate to think our host is going to turn
the fire hoses on me—or unleash the police dogs."

"Just the opposite. I got the sense from one of Patton's letters
that if he were a mercenary sort, he'd be fighting in Stanleyville."

"For or against the Simbas?"

"Oh, against. He's as capitalist as all the colonials. But he's
smart and, I honestly believe, decent. Or decent enough. At this
point, he wants Africa for Africans. Isn't that one side's slogan?
He just wants to be sure that whoever's running the place has
a good old-fashioned Western infrastructure in place. None of
this communist nonsense."

"The right alliances. NATO. America."

"Or, perhaps, General Motors. U.S. Steel. Esso. You know—
those alliances."

"Got it."

"At least that's how I read the man," Peter said. "And Katie and David have liked corresponding with him." The bartender had refilled his glass, and he took a sip.

"I didn't realize David helped organize this."

"Oh, David is very good at spending Katie's money."

Terrance heard the edge in the other man's voice. It surprised him, but only a little: Peter Merrick was known for his honesty, his candor, and for refusing, under any circumstances, to put up with anyone's bullshit. "He was the one who connected me with Patton so I could set up my little expedition after you all head home," the agent continued.

Terrance glanced over his shoulder at the table with the four-some to make absolutely sure that they couldn't hear the conversation at the bar. They were laughing at something, oblivious to Peter and him. "I couldn't help but notice a little something in your tone—about David and how comfortable he is dishing out Katie's money."

"It was just an observation. She's the breadwinner in that couple and he's fine with that."

"But he has that gallery."

"He has that storefront with crazy rent that's usually empty."

"Huh. I always thought it was a prestigious little place."

"It hemorrhages dough."

Terrance took this in as the agent finished his second shot.

"Make no mistake, I like David," Peter added. "I think his dad is CIA. Did you know that? Once upon a time, managed clandestine work against the Nazis. Now he's a paper pusher. At least that's the facade. 'Personnel.'"

"David told me something like that when Kate introduced us and we got to talking about our families. I had no idea his old man might be CIA, but it sounded as if he did something interesting in World War II."

Peter nodded. "Guy may have been a super spy, and he may

have been some bureaucratic underling. No idea. Either way, whatever he does now, it doesn't result in the kind of scratch that can prop up his son's ailing gallery. Damn thing's a hobby."

"David—"

"Look, David is good for Katie and she's good for him. It's just . . ."

"It's just what?"

"It's just that no man likes to be a failure in his wife's eyes. Especially given that pair's history. Remember, they grew up together back east. Same apartment building on the West Side. That's what I mean about how they could be so damn good for each other. And so when that gallery finally goes belly up? It won't be pretty."

"For their marriage."

"Uh-huh." He nodded at the four men behind them. "I don't know whether it's two years down the road or four or five. But Reggie Stout and I have talked about this. At some point, Katie Barstow's marriage is going to tank, and Reggie's going to have his hands full as her publicist and father confessor."

. . .

And so Terrance zipped up his fly.

And at the moment when the guard used his gun to motion him back toward the hut, he dove at him. Just threw himself into the fellow and drove him into the hard, dry ground. And he knew instantly that he had gotten lucky: the kidnapper's finger had not been on the trigger and so he hadn't inadvertently discharged the rifle. He hadn't even yelled, because he'd had his breath knocked from him when his body had slammed into the earth.

Terrance hadn't hit someone in decades. He'd been twelve, maybe thirteen, when he'd gotten into a fight with a couple of idiot white boys who'd jumped him, but he recalled keenly the pain in his knuckles when he pounded his fist into the side of his captor's face and the nauseating squishiness when he punched him in his Adam's apple. The guard was stunned, and Terrance was able to wrestle the gun from him. He stood up quickly and kicked him in the stomach and the groin to ensure his obedience, and pointed the rifle down at his chest.

"Make a sound and I kill you," he told him. He didn't recognize his voice: he sounded winded himself and more than a little crazy.

But the guy nodded sheepishly, gasping for air and curled up in a ball with his hands on his crotch. Beaten, it seemed. Absolutely beaten.

"Now stand up," Terrance commanded. He didn't move, and so Terrance repeated himself. "Get the fuck up."

He rolled onto his hands and knees and gingerly pushed himself to his feet. "You're Russian," Terrance said. "Why the fuck have you kidnapped us?"

The fellow was quiet and rubbed at his neck.

"Tell me," Terrance hissed. "Answer my question."

The guard seemed to be formulating his response. But then his eyes moved just enough that Terrance could see them even in the dusk, and he gave Terrance a tight-lipped smile. He brought one finger to his lips, the universal sign to be quiet. For a second Terrance thought there must be a wild animal behind him, a leopard or a lion, but would that have made the guard smile? Not likely.

Which was when he heard the dual clicks, a sound he knew only from movies, but a sound he knew well: it was a rifle reloading. It wasn't a big hungry cat over his shoulder, it was something that was, arguably, much, much worse.

CHAPTER EIGHTEEN

David Hill

David Hill laughed when he was asked about the artists whose modern paintings grace the main room of his gallery. "Reefer madness, I call them," he said, because they reflect a sensibility that can only be called marijuana chic. One critic who is particularly dismissive told us in confidence, "The people who would like them listen to Bob Dylan and the Beatles, but they don't have the thousands of dollars for paintings like these. Even Hill's movie star friends—people like Katie Barstow—aren't buying them."

The one exception might be the lone painting in the show by the Russian defector. But even that has left us all wondering: is she really a defector or is she a spy? Now that could be the plot of Katie Barstow's next picture!

—The Hollywood Reporter, MAY 20, 1964

His knees hurt from being straight for so long and his shoulders ached from having his hands tied over his head. It wasn't that they were stretching his shoulders so far: he could rest his hands on his forehead when he wanted. But, over time, they had grown sore. And the twine cut into his wrists if he moved his arms the wrong way. Had they restrained the others this way? What the hell were they thinking?

God, his father, who took pride in whatever the hell he actually did, never endured anything like this. He pulled strings, yes, but never the kind that cut into his own skin while he was kept tied up in the dark. Had he ever worked anywhere but New York or Washington, D.C.? No. Of course not. He might have moved spies around the chess board, or he might only have analyzed the findings of the chess pieces; either way, he wasn't in harm's way quite like this. Mostly, David suspected, he was involved with something shady involving brainwashing and drugs—or, to be precise, drugs to wash brains—and probably at the sort of distance that would always give him plausible deniability. That was the new CIA phrase, and he'd heard even his own mother use it.

But then, as far as David knew, his father had also never made the mistakes he himself had. Jesus Christ, he was an idiot.

He stared up into the dark, wondering where they had taken Margie. At first, he had thought it was Katie, but no, that was Margie he had heard crying. It wasn't that he recognized her sobs, because he had never actually heard them; it was just that he knew they weren't Katie's.

But then, he'd never heard Katie cry either. At least not in real life. At least not like that. Thank God. But he had heard her cry in the movies.

He tried to stay calm by thinking about his breathing. Slow, steady inhalations. But as the sun was beginning to set, it was growing harder. He'd been bitten by countless mosquitoes that afternoon, and already the bites on his forearm were itching. He hoped the itch would be the least of his problems. In some ways, the bugs were the worst of the torture—worse even than the aches and pains from being restrained by his wrists and his ankles, and fearing the small animals that he was sure would emerge in the dead of night to gnaw at his flesh.

No, they wouldn't make them sleep like this. Surely, they would untie them for the night, because no one, not even an idiot American, would try to escape in the dark in the Serengeti. He told himself they would come for him any moment now and feed him his supper, let him relieve himself outside, and then order him to stay in the hut until the morning. They wouldn't bind him again. They wouldn't bind any of them again. They'd post a guard outside in the boma, and the guard would sit by the fire and watch the huts to be sure that no one exited them.

But no one would. You'd have to be mad.

He wanted to call out to Katie to reassure her that they would be fine. He wanted to comfort Billy, because he supposed this must be a special kind of agony for him: David knew about the closet and Billy's childhood demons. He wanted to apologize to Terrance, who wasn't related to any of them and just happened to be one of Katie's close friends and, thus, had wound up in the wrong place at the wrong time.

But he knew that he couldn't do any of that. He didn't dare.

.   .   .

Katie had met Mary Quant when she'd been filming *The Courtesan* in London in August, and the designer had made her a black leather miniskirt—just for grins. It wasn't a costume. And when you were only five feet tall, a skirt with a hemline six or seven inches above the knees was, indeed, mini. Miniature. Katie wore it with white go-go boots (also leather) to the Marquee discotheque one night on a day they hadn't been filming, and the image had become iconic: checkerboard fashion, one reporter called it. She was with both Quant and Michael Caine in the photo, and David had felt a pang of jealousy. It was unfounded. He knew Katie wasn't the sort to involve herself with another man, especially now that she was engaged to him, but the idea that she drank with superstar fashion designers and danced with movie stars still left him a little unmoored. He didn't understand her friendship with Terrance Dutton. When he'd asked her if Terrance was an ex-lover, she'd said no; she viewed him rather, she insisted, a bit like she did her brother, Billy. And while he believed her, he had only barely been able to restrain a remark about how she never draped herself around

Billy the way she did around Terrance. She was like a human stole when she was with the other actor.

He saw the photo of Katie and Michael Caine in the *Los Angeles Times* while having breakfast alone: a cup of coffee at a diner on a side street near the gallery. The fact that he'd ordered two eggs instead of the omelet because it was a quarter cheaper—twenty-five cents—was pathetic and upped the ante on his self-loathing. He had to remind himself that one of Hollywood's biggest movie stars loved him and so he should love himself. Or, at least, not hate himself. But he had to figure out this gallery mess. He thought the publicity around his Russian defector's painting would drive traffic and sales, but all it did was encourage yet more interest in Nina herself. The painting sold, but she wouldn't share with him any others. He knew in his heart she'd only allowed him that one—an oil painting of a welder, shirtless, his hair a campfire of red and gold—because she wasn't going to sleep with him again and it was a farewell gift. She regretted their one night after the reception at the museum, mostly, he supposed, because she thought he was rather pathetic: he understood little of international politics—despite, she said ominously, who his father was, as if she knew far more about him and his family than she had ever let on—and spoke but one language. And, she admitted, until they had met she'd never even heard of his "little gallery."

Little gallery. It was blistering and dismissive. A dagger.

He and Katie had been dating a couple of weeks at the time. Sort of dating. They'd only gone out to dinner twice, but he had hopes. He told himself he had only wound up in bed with Nina because Katie was on location in Arizona and he and Nina had had too much to drink. Probably she was telling herself the same thing.

And yet, it had been fun for them both. Hadn't it?

Or, at least, it had been fun until he realized the next morning that he had just had sex with one woman while starting to see another—a woman who happened to be one of the world's biggest movie stars. But . . . still. The booze was no excuse. He had no future with Nina. Yes, she was sexy as hell, but so was Katie, and he *might* have a future with her. To risk a life together with Katie Stepanov (she would always be Katie Stepanov to him, never Katie Barstow) for one night with a hot Russian painter? Therein lay the path to madness. It was reckless, and he would have broken it off the next morning himself if she hadn't spoken first. Of course, it might have been nice if she hadn't been so damn quick to distance herself from him. God, it was as if the moment she opened her hungover eyes and saw his sad little flat by the pitiless light of morning, she wanted out of his bed and out of his apartment.

The painting? Letting him rep it wasn't a farewell gift. It was a sympathy gift.

When he sold it and mailed her her cut, he considered adding a note about what a fantastic *little* capitalist she'd become. Yes, the sale was going to keep the wolves at bay a bit longer, and it was also going to keep Nina in those furs she loved but needed in L.A. about as much as sled dogs. It fascinated him the way she remained news candy, even though it had been three years since she'd defected: she'd been in New York City for a reception at the Metropolitan and managed to elude her KGB handlers in arms and armor. The story she told the press was that the pair, a man and a woman, had been obsessed with a sixteenth-century crossbow with stag horns, and she'd simply walked backward until, before she knew it, she was in medieval art, then a ladies' room, then the great hall, and then Fifth Avenue. Then she had kicked off her heels and was running down Eighty-Second Street in her stockings. Given her family and the wonderful life she led in Moscow, the KGB hadn't seriously considered her a flight risk. They hadn't known how hard and fast she would fall for America.

He sighed. He'd failed when he'd tried to renegotiate the gallery rent last month, and he'd failed when he'd tried to get a soul from the very newspaper before him on the diner counter to review his new show. Katie said he was ahead of his time and the buyers had to catch up to the artists he'd selected. Well, the clock was ticking, and he didn't have much time left.

The waitress, a pretty girl no more than twenty-two or twenty-three, he guessed, with wide brown eyes and hair badly dyed blond, refilled his coffee cup without his asking and smiled at him. He supposed she thought he was in the business. The *right* business. Movies. He could feel how badly she wanted to be out from behind the Formica and in front of the camera.

"Thank you," he said.

"You're welcome." She put the percolator back on the counter behind her and then rested her elbows before him. "You come in here for breakfast a lot. But I don't think I've ever seen you at lunch, and I pull a lot of lunch shifts."

He wanted suddenly to lean into her. Lean near those elbows and hands, the fingers clasped in something like prayer. He wouldn't, and he told himself that the only reason he had the urge right now was because Katie had been doing the loco-motion (or whatever) with Michael Caine in a skirt the width of a belt. How pitiful was it that while his movie star fiancée was gallivanting around London nightclubs with the dashing young heartthrob from *Zulu,* he was reduced to flirting with a counter girl at a second-rate diner? Answer? Extremely.

"I like your coffee," he told her.

"No one likes our coffee," she said caustically. The she asked, "What's your name?"

"Michael," he lied. "Michael Caine."

"Like the actor?"

"Exactly like the actor."

"You're kidding, right?" She stood up straight and backed off a bit.

"I'm not. My parents are William and Becky Caine of Stam-ford, Connecticut," he insisted. He chose Stamford for a fic-tional childhood because one of his artists lived there, a fine art

photographer, and he owed him money, too. An actress friend
of Katie's had bought three of the artist's images, probably as a
favor to Katie, and he still hadn't paid the photographer his 60
percent of the sale.

"Is that a good thing or a bad thing?"

"To have the name of a movie star?"

She nodded.

"It's fine. It made him laugh when we met, because it's actually not his real name. But it is mine."

"You've met Michael Caine?" She sounded dubious. He
liked her instincts.

"I have," he said, and he knew he shouldn't be carrying on
this way. He understood why months ago he'd seduced the Russian painter (or, he occasionally tried to convince himself, why
he'd allowed himself to be seduced by her): Katie was living her
glamorous life in Arizona, he'd had too much to drink, and the
alcohol had fed the Machiavellian delusion that he could turn
around his gallery's fortunes if he could ink this Russian defector. Sign her. Represent her. Instead, later, he'd get that one
painting. But this sort of extracurricular dalliance with a pretty
girl at a diner was pointless; he would be kicking himself the
moment he rolled off of her. Either he had to fess up right now
that he was teasing her or thank her for a delicious breakfast
and plan never to come back here again. He'd only discovered
the unexpected satisfactions of lying in the last year, when he'd
had to start lying first to potential buyers—usually inflating the
résumé of the artists they were interested in or at least making
their biography more dramatic—and then to his creditors.

"What's your name?" he asked.

"Ashley."

She practically purred the first syllable.

"You know what I do," she continued. "What do you do?"

He put some milk from the tinny creamer into his coffee,
stalling. He took a sip.

"I own a gallery," he said, finally. It was taking what seemed to be Herculean strength to resist this temptation across from him, and so he reminded himself that absolutely no good could come from proceeding a single step further. He was engaged. He was engaged to a movie star. He was engaged to a woman with friends who were wealthy or influential or both: the sort of people who could afford the sort of sculptures and paintings that he wanted to sell in his gallery, and who were impressed that he had displayed a painting, albeit briefly, by the notorious Russian defector who was—even now, even still—the art world's flavor of the month. Just because Katie was with the real Michael Caine was no reason why he should be pretending to be a fake one.

"Art gallery?"

"Yes," he told her, and he was about to tell her his real name and that he was engaged, but before he could say another word she leaned into him once again.

"Need a model?" she asked, and that was it, his resolve was gone, as dry and empty as a birdbath in a drought. This girl obviously wasn't the financial lifeline he desperately needed, but she was about to provide a different, less tangible sort of succor.

·   ·   ·

David couldn't imagine how he could possibly be hungry, but he was. His stomach was growling.

He recalled how much he had enjoyed the breakfasts at the diner near his gallery until he fucked the waitress there and could never go back. The idea that she was a setup—a honey trap, to use the parlance his father would likely have used—and knew exactly who he was all along? He never saw that coming, but he guessed desperation made you an easy mark. God, who would have expected that the diner girl would be his downfall, and not Nina? He went to the waitress's place later that day, as they planned, and the regret was every bit as awful as he had supposed it would be. But it paled before the photos that some

bastard brought to his gallery two days later. He'd almost vomited when he saw them. Her little place was on the second floor
of a four-story apartment, and she hadn't closed the blinds. At
the time, he'd thought only how he liked the afternoon sun on
her skin.

His eyes were itching, and he was able to run his thumbs
over them. That felt better.

It was then that he heard the gunshot: a single pop and—at
the exact same time—the sound of a human being crying out.
A man, he thought, and he grew still more frightened. Instantly
his hunger was gone, replaced by nausea and the fear that he
might shit his pants, and he could feel that his heart was starting
to race.

He didn't know enough about firearms (in fact, he understood nothing) to know what kind of weapon it was, but it was
discharged not far from where he was bound to the pallet. It
crossed his mind that their captors had killed one of them, but he
told himself—forced himself to believe—that this was unlikely.
Impossible. Yes, things had gone off the rails, but there was no
way that they'd kill their American captives. They couldn't.
They wouldn't. It was far more probable that one of the guards
had shot an animal for food or to frighten it away from the
boma. That human sound? Had to have been wildlife. Had to
have been. Once more, he wanted to reassure Katie that there
was nothing to fear. Nothing at all. This would all turn out fine
in the end.

But he knew he was deluding himself when he heard the
second gunshot.

For the first time the idea grew real in his mind: I might
really be going to die out here. We all might.

CHAPTER NINETEEN

Carmen Tedesco

Carmen Tedesco is the perfect sidekick to Shirley MacLaine, her comic timing pitch-perfect as the eager young prostitute with very big dreams, a very big heart, and the common sense to know that what she does best is best done behind closed doors.

—*The Hollywood Reporter,* JULY 1963

The baobab was dead, listing at least twenty degrees, which was the only reason why she was able to scale it and reach that broad lower branch. The tree seemed as wide and round as a castle turret, but she was able to claw her way up the rough and stippled bark, though her first step had been into Reggie's cupped hands. With a strength that she'd always supposed he had but had never seen manifested, he hoisted her up onto the trunk and gave her just enough momentum that she could climb to that branch. She was easily eight feet off the ground and she had their pistol, and so while she was not safe, she was safer. She couldn't lie down, and she didn't dare fall asleep: if she did, the odds seemed pretty good that she'd tumble from the tree and best case break a leg and worst case break her neck. But if she stayed awake, she might make it through the night. She didn't think she had a concussion, though Reggie wasn't so sure.

Certainly, Reggie had to stay awake. By the time they reached the tree, he could barely even limp. Their pace had slackened inexorably throughout the endless afternoon. He tried a couple of times to clamber up the trunk, but it was clear that he was no longer capable of doing so. And so he was sitting below her with his back against the baobab and the rifle across his lap, watching their little fire. He tried to reassure her that his eyes were good and he'd shoot anything that got near him. They'd rounded up some scrub and scrounged a couple of dead branches and been able to start the small blaze, but they didn't have enough wood to feed it for long. Soon it would burn itself out. And then one man in the dark against a pack of hyenas or jackals or a couple of lions? He might get one, but he wouldn't get two.

"Aren't the stars beautiful?" he asked her. "Nights like these, I can almost understand why the ancients supposed heaven was up there."

"Reggie?"

"Yes, my dear?"

"I know you're trying to keep up my spirits, but I don't think we should be talking. I don't think we should be making any noise."

"You're worried about animals."

"I am."

"This probably won't comfort you, but any animals that might want to eat us already know we're here. The fire's a beacon. They smell us or see us. Some, I suppose, have been following us for miles."

"How far do you think we walked?"

"Not as far as I would have liked. I let us down. Or my leg did," he said. After a moment he added, "Somewhere between eleven and twelve miles."

"How did you come up with that number?"

"A bad guess. Normally I walk three miles an hour. I reduced it—randomly—to two and a third miles because I'm gimpy and pathetic, and we walked about five hours."

"Not counting when we rested." God, there had been some moments when she had been so hot and sweaty that she thought she was going to vomit. Heatstroke. Sunstroke. Whatever. She had melted. Puddled.

"Correct."

"You didn't let us down," she said. "I promise you that. You sure as hell did not let me down."

"We'll see."

"Why do you think they haven't come for us? The Russians?" She recalled him telling her that one of their abductors had used the word *mertv*. Dead.

"Maybe they have."

"And we've gotten far enough away?"

"And it's a big area. Two people don't leave much of a footprint here."

She thought about what he'd said a moment ago about the fire being a beacon. They almost hadn't started one, in the event their kidnappers were close enough behind them to spot it. Finally, after thinking about it long and hard, Reggie had decided that the savanna was sufficiently vast that it was unlikely a little fire would give them away.

"I keep expecting to see headlights. Or hear a Land Rover's engine. I fear I'll let down my guard and there they'll be," she said.

"Or a truck full of rangers. Imagine that instead."

She considered repeating back to him what he had just said to her: *It's a big area. Two people don't leave much of a footprint here.* But that would have been contrary and mean. And so instead she murmured, "I like that idea."

"You'll tell me if you need something?"

"Yes, but I have a canteen and aspirin and this pistol. What more could I possibly want?" She looked at the weapon in her hand. She had the safety on, but he had showed her how to flip it off and fire it. "You know," she told him, "I can't believe I could hit anything with this thing. The gun. I'm literally half blind."

"Not true. You have one eye that's in excellent shape. And a lot of people close one eye when aiming anyway. Besides . . ."

"Besides what?"

"You'll be firing, if you need to, at very short range. When the leopard has smelled us and is about to leap."

"Leopards have great hearing and great eyesight. But the canine predators have a much better sense of smell than the big cats."

"May I ask you something?"

She waited.

"Pardon my French, but how the fuck do you know that fun fact?"

"I read it in a safari guide on the flight from L.A. to New York. I've always been a smarty-pants." She recalled how Felix had teased her about that guide, making her laugh out loud on the plane, and when that memory came to her, it was accompanied by another spasm of grief. A literal spasm. She shuddered. It had been happening off and on all day as they walked, whenever she remembered her husband. She thought of their first kiss and their last kiss, and the last one pained her because it had been passionless and rote: a kiss before sleep in their tent last night, their lips barely touching. Last night she had yet to become, at least in her mind, Margot Macomber, because she had not yet witnessed Felix sniveling in the Serengeti dust. So why had their kisses grown listless of late? She had known that Felix had his issues with his father and she knew there was no friendship he would not try to exploit to further his career—and, she supposed, hers. But she had loved him. She loved him because he was wounded in ways that she wasn't, and she had loved him because of the things that they shared: movies and books and Irish Coffee at Tom Bergin's on Wilshire on Sunday afternoons. She supposed that if he hadn't died today, if somehow they had both managed to survive this nightmare, eventually she would have gotten past his behavior this morning and loved him the way she once had. There were so many worse things than being scared. She thought of the African novelist Muema had men-

tioned, Chinua Achebe, and the novel he had encouraged her
to read instead of Hemingway. She doubted the plot was in any
way reminiscent of her marriage at the end or the direness of her
plight right now—either would be too much of a coincidence—
but the title haunted her for both reasons: *Things Fall Apart*. Yes,
they did. It was inevitable. Nothing lasts. Just . . . nothing.

"Carmen?"

"Yes?"

"Just making sure you were okay. You'd gotten awfully
quiet up there."

"I was just thinking."

"About Felix?"

"Uh-huh," she said. "Most of today I've been in shock, and
the pain of his death has been dulled. Or my head hurt, and that
was all I was aware of. Or I just kept moving forward, as sick as I
felt, trying to get away from the Land Rover. Watching the sun.
Watching for things that wanted to kill me. Animals. A jeep or
lorry filled with kidnappers. But then I would remember Felix
was dead, and I'd have these tremors. They were almost like
seizures."

"Go on."

"I think I prefer it when I'm not in shock, and the waves
are just battering me. I feel better about myself when I'm really,
really overwhelmed by the loss. When it's physical. When it's
uncomfortable. When I want to tear at my clothes."

"You shouldn't ever feel bad about yourself, Carmen."

"I just suppose I'd be a better person if I were inconsolable.
If I were hysterical."

"Someday you'll play a grieving widow, and you'll use all of
this. Besides . . ."

"Besides what?"

"Your body and mind are too focused on trying to survive
right now to mourn. Grief? It's a luxury."

She knew he had more experience with death than anyone

she had ever met. She wasn't sure if he was correct about her specifically, but she knew she would nevertheless use his logic through the long night ahead to help rationalize her behavior.

.   .   .

There was a mini-golf course on Sepulveda with the usual sorts of obstacles: a waterfall, a windmill, and a hippo. But it also had a model of the Eiffel Tower on one hole and a twelve-foot-high fantasy castle anchoring another: pink bricks, yellow flags, and petunias lining the twenty-foot fairway to the palace entrance.

And that hole had a moat, and it was the moat that mattered if you were playing. The fairway narrowed like an hourglass, and the trick was to putt perfectly straight through the center. If you missed, your ball ricocheted back to the tee; if you tapped it too hard, you'd wind up in the drink.

But it was the castle that mattered to the movie magazine's art director. His vision? Shirley MacLaine and Carmen Tedesco popping out of the small turret with the nearby hole's Eiffel Tower right behind them. "It's perfect," he said. "The new movie is set in Paris, you two play a couple of chippies, and the Eiffel Tower looks like a giant phallus behind you." He said this as he stood in the awning of the snack bar, while Shirley and Carmen were seated on the snack bar stools and a pair of women applied their makeup. The young publicist from Reggie's firm, Jean Cummings, had just brought them each a bottle of Coca-Cola.

The art director was wearing a blue blazer with a Beach Boys T-shirt underneath it. He was probably fifty and had been doing this since the end of the war. Carmen watched how Shirley responded to being called a chippie, but she didn't seem perturbed. And so Carmen dialed down her own vexation at the word. The truth was, they were playing hookers in the movie, and so chippies was, arguably, a step up.

The photographer, a guy about the same age as the art director, was out by the castle, checking the light. He was wearing khaki pants with more pockets than Carmen had ever seen on a pair of trousers. He looked back at the snack bar and called to them. He asked if Miss MacLaine and her stylist could join him, and so Carmen was left alone with the art director, Jean Cummings, and the woman working on her face.

"Think you'll ever be in a pic your father-in-law is directing?" the art director asked her now.

Carmen didn't have to answer right away because the makeup artist, her breath a little sour with coffee, was finishing her eyeliner. It gave Carmen a moment to formulate her response.

"I'd be honored," she told him after the woman had stepped back to appraise her work. "I'd be honored to be in one of my husband's movies, too."

"You ever see the story we did on Rex?" he asked, referring to Felix's lion of an old man.

"I did," she answered. She had hoped to steer the conversation back to her husband and decided to try a second time.

But Jean was a step ahead of her. The other woman began, "I think Felix—"

"You remember the photos that went with it?" the art director asked Carmen, cutting off the publicist.

"I do," Carmen answered. "They were up at the Griffith Observatory. There was one of Rex near a telescope."

"A massive telescope. Now that was a phallus." He nodded, pleased that she had remembered it and proud of the image. "Yeah, those pics really worked. It was for that pseudo-science-fiction movie he did. But these ones of you and Shirley we're getting today? They'll be even better."

"They'll be fantastic," said Jean. The publicist was wearing a sleeveless black blouse and a skirt with a pattern that looked like it belonged in a Las Vegas casino lobby. Lots of teal and pink and orange blocks bouncing like dice against a white background.

"Why?" Carmen asked. "Why will these be even better?"

"Why?" He repeated the single word, and his tone had an edge of exasperation. She realized that she should only have said something about how grateful she was. Still, she was curious.

"Yes. Why do you think these will be better?" she persisted.

"Isn't it obvious? You and Shirley. No one really wants to look at a wrinkled old fart like Rex Demeter, no matter how many subliminal phalluses I put in the pic. But two pretty actresses and the Eiffel Tower? The subconscious will drool." There was a tree near them with indigo flowers that reminded her of foxglove, and he picked one of the blossoms off the sleeve of his jacket. "That's what I want. And that's what you want."

"To make the subconscious drool."

"Yes, little lady. Whether you admit it or not, that's what we do in our business. High art, low art. Good films, bad films. Good photos, bad photos. It's all about . . ." His voice trailed off as he searched for the right word.

She decided to help him. "The phallus?" she suggested.

She could see in his eyes and in poor Jean's eyes that she had just shot herself in the foot. Reggie Stout had once told her—gently, with an avuncular kindness—that a few people had hinted to him that she could be a bit of a smart aleck. She didn't have that reputation (not yet), and while he rather liked her sassiness, there were some people who didn't. She'd promised him that she would be more careful, and since then she had been. And so she added quickly, "I understand. I really do. It's interesting to me how carefully you work to strike that balance between conveying what's obvious in an image and what isn't. Thank you."

"Yes, thank you," agreed Jean. "Reggie and I are so appreciative of all that you bring to the party."

He bought it. He nodded at her and then at the publicist. She could see in his gaze that the two of them had sold it. Sometimes, she decided, she really was a pretty good actress.

And so, it seemed, was Jean Cummings.

·   ·   ·

How long had she been fighting sleep? She couldn't say, and she couldn't bring herself to look at her watch yet again. Between ten p.m. and midnight she must have looked at it over twenty times. On each occasion, the minute hand had crept forward no more than four or five minutes, though always she had supposed that she'd waited at least ten. It had to be well after midnight now. Her head was lolling around as if she had a broken neck, and it felt so very good when she would allow it to tip toward her collarbone. The yawns felt fantastic too. She was weak and knew she should ask Reggie to toss her the bag of nuts, but she doubted she'd catch it and she didn't want Reggie to draw attention to himself by standing.

It was also colder than she expected, but she was grateful for that discomfort: it might be what kept her alive because it was keeping her awake.

She tried to think of things that made her happy. The fourth-grade geography test on South America that she aced. The soft lips of the boy who kissed her when the two of them were standing in the wings after a rehearsal for the high school talent show. The Christmas tree when her father first plugged in those new lights. Dozing in the back seat of the car at night, her father and mother in the front, and her stuffed dog—she named him Moppet, though she didn't know at the time what the word meant, but her grandpa sometimes called her that—in her arms. Now that word was her favorite onomatopoeic. Moppet.

She recalled how much fun she had had doing press last year with Shirley MacLaine, and the movie mag where she and the other actress had been shot for the cover at a mini-golf course. Reggie had made that happen. He'd made sure that it wasn't just Shirley on the front of the glossy.

She also prayed. The Lord's Prayer. Over and over. That helped her stay awake too, and it gave her a semblance of comfort.

There had been a time when she had also known the Apostles' Creed by heart, but other than the first two lines—"I believe in God, the Father almighty, creator of heaven and earth"—it was gone. But she repeated those two lines in her mind, as well. She prayed that Felix was in heaven and tried to imagine what that was like. Angels? Did Jesus have a room waiting for him? Could Felix see her now in this tree? Was he with his sister, Olivia? One of the things she had loved about Felix was how much he had cared about Olivia and how acutely he had felt her loss.

Did she love her own sister that much? Probably not. But maybe. She just didn't love the way her sister judged her and thought that being a mother was such noble work. Carmen didn't disagree. She had supposed before this morning that someday she and Felix would have children. But she had other desires, other dreams. She took satisfaction in those things.

The night was alive with the endless chirping of insects, the cries and calls of birds she didn't recognize, and the deep lowing of a herd of wildebeest that must have been passing nearby. It wasn't quiet. Her and Felix's home—fuck, her home now—in West Hollywood was calmer. If there was a big cat skulking out there in the dark, she wasn't going to hear it. Or them. She recalled the birds she would hear when she was a girl growing up in Westchester. In the mornings, when she would be waiting for the school bus, she would hear woodpeckers, phoebes, and mourning doves. She tried to convince herself that the birdsong here—the night song—should be no more frightening. But it was. Of course it was.

Maybe she'd hear the hyenas before they attacked. The creatures really had sounded like they were laughing that one evening when they'd been near the camp: the high-pitched giggles of maniacs in a mental hospital. That's what she'd thought of. Even before Charlie Patton had told them all at breakfast the next morning that what they had heard had been hyenas, she'd known. She just had.

God, she really was a smarty-pants.

Her head was throbbing again, and she wondered how she had forgotten to stay ahead of the pain. She reached into her pocket and swallowed two more aspirin. It seemed like a lot of work to unscrew the canteen, so she didn't bother to wash them down with water.

The fire was out now. How had she not noticed it become a smoldering pile of red and yellow embers, and then nothing?

There wasn't a sound at the base of the tree, and she was glad that Reggie was keeping silent. God, to be down there alone in the dark? In the morning—and she was beginning to think they really might make it to the morning—she would have to ask him whether this was worse than Okinawa. She just had no idea.

She rubbed her hands aggressively over her arms, warming them, and blew on her fingers. She rested her head against the baobab trunk and fought the urge to close her eyes by looking up at the sky. And there it was: a shooting star. One second it was there, and then it was gone. Had she ever seen one before? She wasn't sure that she had. But it felt like a gift, an answered prayer.

"Did you see that?" she asked in a stage whisper, hoping that Reggie had.

When there wasn't an immediate response, she felt an acute spike of anxiety. Had he fallen asleep?

"Reggie?"

Again, nothing. Just the endless concert of the bugs and the birds and the wildebeest. He really must have dozed off, and the idea didn't frighten her as much as she thought it would. A part of her was even a little relieved. They both desperately needed to rest. But, still, she would have to wake him up.

She looked at her watch. And then, in horror, she looked at it again. It was three fifteen in the morning. Somehow, she had conked out for roughly three hours and not fallen from the tree. That was why she hadn't seen the last of their little fire disappear.

She wouldn't have thought it possible to sleep and not tumble from her branch, but she had. She really had. She'd slept for hours. Well, she was up now, and she better wake Reggie, too.

"Reggie!" This time it was more than a stage whisper. "Reggie, wake up!"

Still, there was only quiet below her. He wasn't waking up, he wasn't responding.

Which was when she felt a wave of dizziness and nausea welling up: he might be dead from a snake bite.

Or he might not even be there. A lot could happen in a couple of hours here. Hours? Good God, a lot could happen in a couple of seconds. Especially at night.

"Reggie: are you there?" Her voice had become a whimper that she didn't recognize, a little girl's plaintive cry to her father or mother. And, still, nothing.

She grabbed one of the tendon-like protrusions of bark on the trunk with her left hand and the branch above her head with her right. Then she leaned over and peered at the base of the tree where Reggie had been a few hours ago.

And she saw he was gone.

Still, she said his name once more, this time adding, *Please*.

But he wasn't there. There was no question about it, none at all.

And, she understood, she was alone. She was absolutely and completely alone.

CHAPTER TWENTY

Terrance Dutton

But Sammy Davis Jr. and his spanking new wife, the Swedish actress May Britt ("War and Peace," "The Hunters"), weren't the only interracial couple that caused heads to turn at the studio's Christmas party. Terrance Dutton may not have been flouting "the norm"—this is Hollywood, after all, not Dutton's "native" Memphis—but some guests were uncomfortable that his date was the Parisian ingenue Juliette Fournier, known for her alabaster skin.
                                        —*Movie Star Confidential*, JANUARY 1961

It had happened fast. Incredibly fast. He'd killed a man. He was breathing hard at the idea.

One minute he'd been zipping up his fly and then he'd been tackling the creep who was guarding him, wrestling the gun from his hands. And then he'd heard another one of these bastards with another rifle—there were those clicks he supposed he would remember forever—and he turned, but instead of dropping the gun, he'd just done it. Rammed the barrel of the rifle he was holding into the gut of the Russian who'd come up behind him, their driver, because he was that close, spearing him in the abdomen with the muzzle and knocking him down. When the other one, the guard who'd first brought him out here, managed to stagger to his feet and charge him, Terrance had fired, a reflex, just squeezed the trigger, the bullet hitting the son of a bitch in the chest. When he understood that the fellow was going to die slowly over the next few minutes and his partner was still on the ground on all fours, winded, he'd put a second bullet into the wounded Russian's head at point-blank range to put him out of his misery.

God, they'd christened themselves the lions of Hollywood at the wedding, and raised champagne to the idea. The seven of them, minus Katie and David, who were already in Paris, had greeted each other that way, half kidding but also a little smug, when they'd rendezvoused at the airport in L.A. a week later. The movie mags even called them that when they wrote about the safari: the lions of Hollywood. Well, he'd taken a life, but he was no lion. He was just . . .

He couldn't say. He did not feel remorse, but neither did he feel pride. He was focused only on survival.

Now he was walking his captor, the roles reversed, back toward the huts. He'd begin with Katie Barstow. They were getting out—they were all getting out and they were getting away—and he supposed they were taking this Russian bastard with them.

·   ·   ·

"You're Terrance Dutton."

The fellow had dirty blond hair and cheekbones sculpted with a detailing chisel. He stood six feet and change, was probably about thirty, and his safari jacket was well worn. They were standing near a fountain in the lobby of the hotel in Nairobi after breakfast as Terrance waited for the rest of Katie Barstow's entourage to arrive. Already Charlie Patton's porters were starting to load the first suitcases and valises into the lorry that was going to haul everything southwest into Tanganyika and the Serengeti.

"You must be Charlie Patton," Terrance said, though the moment he spoke, he realized he was mistaken. The man was too young to have helped Hemingway stockpile his dead things.

The other fellow laughed, shook his head, and extinguished his cigarette in the pedestal ashtray made from an elephant foot. "Far from it," he said. "I doubt I'm half his age." He had a pile of gear beside him, which looked to be mostly cameras and lenses. Then he extended his hand and Terrance shook it. "Phillip Tiegs," he said, and Terrance thought the accent might have been Main Line Philadelphia. He was definitely American.

"Are you part of the safari?" he asked. "Do you work for Charlie?" Terrance had considered asking how this Phillip Tiegs had recognized him, but he still supposed the fellow was a member of Patton's team. He'd sounded almost deferential when he'd said, *Far from it.* Or, just maybe, he was a movie buff. Terrance was recognized frequently back home in America.

"No, I don't work for Charlie. But some of the folks in this hotel, who don't normally get starstruck, were a little starstruck when they realized last night that you and Katie Barstow had checked in. This is quite some little honeymoon she planned."

"It is. I agree."

"You're in for a treat."

"You're a photographer, I gather," Terrance said.

"I am. I'm heading out today, too, but separate from all of you."

"Newspaper assignment? Magazine?"

"No."

Terrance considered pressing, but didn't. Instead he said, "I'm guessing this is not your first time."

Phillip shook his head. "But I'm not a veteran, either. This will be my third time out in the wild."

"Well, you keep coming back."

"I do. I'm trying to chronicle a problem, which, alas, makes me part of the problem."

"And that is?"

"Ecological catastrophe. People. You, me. Katie Barstow. Other than the Maasai, we don't belong here."

"In the Serengeti."

He nodded and said, "But I'm not going to lecture you. I don't lecture anyone. My plan is a book of photos that will tell the story much better than I can with words."

"Who are you with?"

"You mean who's my outfitter?"

"Yes."

"Didn't use one. Just me and a couple of porters and a guide. Fellow I used last time who knows the land as well as anyone."

"Any tips?"

"On getting a good photo of a rhino?"

"Sure. Why not."

"You may not. Maybe down by the crater you'll see a few. Or one."

"Ngorongoro."

"That's right. Used to be much easier. Obviously. But if there's a rhino about, Charlie will know. You should be fine, if the animal doesn't have a calf with her. And you don't get out of the vehicle. And you get close, but not too close."

Terrance thought about this. He'd learned a bit about trackers in South Dakota for a Western he'd done in 1959. "How would Charlie know? Something he'd notice in the landscape? Or do you just get a special sense for that sort of thing when you're out there enough?"

Phillip nodded. "Both. And he also has very solid guides."

"So, we're in good hands."

"Oh, I didn't say that. You're in Charlie Patton's hands."

Terrance stood up a little straighter. "Okay, I'll bite. Tell me more."

The photographer shrugged. "Ol' Charlie will give you a good show. You'll all get your money's worth. Or, I suppose, Katie Barstow will get her money's worth."

"But . . ."

Phillip looked at his watch, and it was clear to Terrance that he was stalling.

"You can't say something like that and not elaborate, man," Terrance pressed. "You just can't. You have to tell me more."

"You can when you didn't sleep much the night before because you stayed too late at the bar and now, the morning after, aren't thinking before you speak."

"Nope," Terrance said, smiling. "Not letting you off the hook."

"Fine."

There was an awkward beat, and Terrance considered whether he'd made a mistake pressing and putting Phillip Tiegs on the spot. He was about to let it go when the fellow spoke.

"Charlie can be an angry man," he said. "You may not see his temper. You may only glimpse his Papa Hemingway charm. Big-game hunter. Man's man. Whole persona. Storyteller—though half his stories are whopping fairy tales. But he doesn't much like the 1960s. Time has passed him by. That's the problem."

"Have you ever seen this anger of his?"

He chuckled and pointed at the pile of camera gear at his feet. "See that Rolleiflex? I bought it to replace the one he smashed with the butt of an elephant gun a couple of years ago on my first visit here."

"And he did that . . . why?"

"Because a Nairobi newspaper published a photo I took of an elephant graveyard."

"I didn't know elephant graveyards were real. Are they?"

"Yes and no. It's not as if old elephants create patches of earth where they can go to die. In my opinion, it's the opposite: They actually choose places that give them the best chance to live. They're too old to migrate and keep up with the herd, so they find a spot with water and food. But, eventually, it all catches up with them. They starve or the infirmities that get all old mammals get them. So, there tend to be sizable concentrations of dead elephants in some spots. A graveyard. But not really a graveyard, if you get my point."

"Why in the world did Patton care that you took a picture of one?"

"Because this graveyard? It was man-made. Patton was hosting a guy named Viktor Procenko. Colonel Viktor Procenko. Procenko was a military adviser working with Lumumba in the Congo—one of the hundreds the Kremlin sent. After Lumumba fell, the Soviets left. Except, before going home, Patton took Procenko and a couple of his communist cronies out on safari. These days, as far as Patton's concerned, all money is good money. He'll take anyone into the bush. Well, they all started drinking one night, and the Russians got Patton absolutely soused. Blotto. They thoroughly embarrassed an old-school colonial who takes great pride in the way he can hold his liquor. Then, when he was conked out, they went night hunting, using the lorries' headlights, a couple of gun bearers, and their AK-47s. They found the elephants. It was quite a massacre."

"How did you hear about this?"

"Procenko. He tried to drink me under the table right over there," said Phillip, pointing toward the hotel bar. "But not even a Soviet colonel can drink me under the table. Especially a couple of years ago. Anyway, the next day I retained a guide and went to the site. It wasn't hard to find. I just went to one of Patton's regular campsites."

"Did you name names?"

Again, Phillip laughed. "God, no. I don't pick fights with Soviet military advisers. But this is a small community. Procenko told enough people what he'd done—he thought it was rather funny—and everyone knew that Patton had been his host."

Terrance considered this. "Which ticked off Charlie Patton more? The idea that he had been outdrunk by a guest or that his guests had committed a rather egregious hunting faux pas?"

"A faux pas? They broke the damn law! And Charlie was responsible. He never went to jail, but I'm sure even he had to pay one motherfucker of a fine. Anyway, he thought I'd humiliated him by going out there and then telling some of our mutual acquaintances what the hell had happened. Publishing the photos. The combination of the humiliation and the fine? He was one pissed-off, over-the-hill hunter."

"Well, it sounds like you did embarrass him."

"He deserved it."

A woman almost as tall as Phillip and roughly his age came up beside the photographer and linked her arm through his.

"Ah, Nicole," he said, kissing her on the cheek and placing his hand on the small of her back. "Meet Terrance Dutton. I believe you've seen at least one of his films. *Tender Madness.*"

"It's a pleasure to meet," she said, and her accent suggested she was from East Africa. Like Phillip, she was clad for safari, and she, too, exuded cinematic beauty: a statuesque carriage and an impeccable, flawless face. She also had skin, Terrance thought, even blacker than mine.

.   .   .

For a moment, Terrance stood outside the hut where Katie had been taken, his rifle still aimed at the Russian. Here was the problem: it was dark in there. Who could say what this guard would do when either Terrance demanded he untie Katie or he himself went to untie her? It would be easy for the Russian to jump him. Terrance supposed there was a flashlight in the one Land Rover still parked in the boma, but even retrieving that was playing with fire. If he sent this guy into the vehicle to get it, who knew what else he might salvage? A pistol? A knife? He had, after all, been the one driving the damn thing.

God, a part of Terrance just wanted to shoot him. But he already had one dead man on his ledger; he didn't want two. And they needed this person. He probably knew where Margie had been taken and where the other guests—Reggie and Felix and Carmen and Peter—were being held captive. He might know the direction to drive to get the hell back to civilization.

And, if necessary, he might offer some leverage. It was quite possible they'd need some.

Terrance had searched him to make sure he didn't have other weapons on him and to see if he had any identification. He had neither. He had keys to the vehicle, cigarettes, and a silver lighter that was exquisite. It had a red and yellow five-pointed star, the hammer and sickle inside it, embossed on one side. It was likely Soviet army gear. But when Terrance had pressed him for details, he'd insisted he wasn't a soldier and never had been. Claimed it was his father's, but Terrance didn't buy that. It didn't look that old, and it didn't look like it had seen a lot of wear. He claimed his name was Glenn, but it was evident he was lying. He was making too big a deal about the fact it was spelled with two *n*'s, not one.

And so now, at Terrance's command, the Russian had paused in front of the hut where Katie Barstow was confined, about five feet ahead of him, but not close enough to the entrance that he could dive forward and lose himself in the darkness within. That had been among Terrance's fears, which was why he had ordered him to halt where he was. The fact remained, however, that now Terrance was at a loss over what to do. It was just the two of them, and still, it seemed, he had no good options. Which meant, he guessed, you went with the least bad option. And the least bad option was probably this: see if there was a flashlight in the Land Rover. He couldn't get Katie and David and Billy untied without one, and that was obviously his next step.

Which was when it clicked: he should untie David or Billy next, not Katie, so there would be two men against one. Screw the chivalry right now.

"Is there a flashlight in the Land Rover?" he asked.

"Yes."

"Where?"

"I don't know. Maybe the dashboard. Maybe under the seats. But there's one there."

"Okay. We're going to walk to the vehicle and we're going to get it. You're going to stand ten feet from the Land Rover—the far side—away from the huts, and I'm going to check. I will also keep an eye on you. You move, and I shoot you exactly the way I shot your friend."

The Russian shook his head. "That was point-blank. The range. You think you can hit me if I run even ten feet?"

"Not for certain. But are you really that sure I'll miss? And do you want to run into the wild at night? Unarmed? Think that's a good plan, buddy?"

The man's face was bemused. Terrance wanted him scared. He'd shot his partner—twice. Put a bullet into the bastard's skull. How the fuck was this character not terrified? Terrance had to admit, he was impressed.

"We see," the Russian said.

So, Terrance walked him to the far side of the Land Rover and ordered him to stand where he was. "Move and I shoot," he reminded him. Then he opened the passenger's-side door, one eye always on his captive, and glanced at the dashboard and the glove deck. He ran a hand underneath the front passenger seat. He stretched his arm and his fingers under the driver's seat. He reached deep into the well between the bucket seats. And he kept coming up empty. No flashlight. No pistol, either, and no knife. Briefly he thought he might have found one, based on the cylindrical shape—his mind imagined the barrel—but it was a battery, nothing more. He also found some peanuts and a bandanna. But not the goddamn flashlight.

He sat on that front seat with one leg dangling out the front door. "I can't find it," he said. "Where else might it be?"

The guy shrugged. "Maybe it rolled into the back seats." He seemed to be enjoying this.

Terrance could use this same process with the second row of seats: sit half in and half out of the vehicle with the door open, keeping watch over his captive. But if the flashlight had rolled into the third or fourth row? He was fucked. There were no doors that far back. You had to climb into the vehicle. He had to hope it was in the second row.

He rested the rifle on his thigh, his right finger on the trigger, and walked the fingers of his left hand like a spider under the seat. The idea there might be actual spiders there caused him to pause, but only for a second.

And, yes, there it was. The flashlight. It was smaller than he hoped, but it would do. The silver metal was starting to rust, but it worked. He jumped to the ground, satisfied, though he understood this was only the first step. Now he had to get Billy or David untied. After that, it would get easier. Not easy. But easier.

"Now you have a flashlight," the Russian said, smiling. "A flashlight and a gun. Good for you."

Terrance thought the ornery motherfucker might laugh. His moment of gratification at discovering the torch already had been undone. This creep just didn't seem to understand or care about the gravity of his situation. The precariousness.

"We're going to go into that hut and untie David Hill."

"You'll keep the lady tied up?"

"I will. Now move." He pointed at the hut where he thought David was restrained and motioned for his captive to walk ahead of him. When they reached the entrance, he said, "We're going inside, and you're going to untie my friend. I swear to Christ, you do one thing other than untie him, and I will fucking shoot you. You so much as hiccup or flinch, and I will fucking shoot you."

"You don't want to kill me. If you wanted to kill me, I'd be dead now."

"You're right, I don't. But I will."

He turned on the flashlight and put the slender tip of the handle in his mouth, the metallic taste bitter. He had to bite down on it with his teeth. He aimed the rifle at the Russian, and the fellow followed the light into the hut. He bent low as he entered the section with the sleeping pallet. And there was David. He squinted against the beam, but when the Russian knelt on the dirt floor and untied his hands, he said, his voice raspy, "Terrance. It's you."

Terrance didn't respond because his teeth were clenched around the flashlight. He didn't even nod. But he was shocked at the way they'd tied David up: it looked like a torture rack. Terrance's hands had been bound at the wrists and his legs had been tied to one of the posts that held the sleeping pallet, but at least he could sit or lie down if he wanted. David, on the other hand, had been restrained flat on his back, his hands over his head. It looked medieval. It looked excruciating. Terrance watched as the Russian untied David's feet and the other American sat up. Only then did Terrance spit out the flashlight. Instantly he picked it up off the dirt.

"David, holy shit. You okay?" he asked.

"More or less," David mumbled, rolling his shoulders.

"You're positive?"

"Yeah. I think so."

He eyed Katie's husband carefully. He seemed stunned, but not incapacitated. "Well, then: tie him up, this Russian," Terrance said.

"I'm not sure I know how."

"Pull his hands behind his back and loop the twine around his wrists."

"I wasn't even a Boy—"

"Tie him the fuck up, David! Just do it. Pretend you're tying your goddamn shoes."

David stood, a little wobbly, and asked the Russian to turn around. When he did, Terrance looked into his face, and the man grinned. It was as if he knew something, but Terrance couldn't begin to imagine what it could be.

"I think that will hold," David said, after working the twine. "But I'm not sure."

"Make sure," Terrance told him.

"I did my—"

"Make sure."

He watched as David pulled the cords and the Russian winced. Then Terrance used the barrel of his rifle to prod his captive outside into the center of the boma. David walked behind them.

"Let's get Billy next," Terrance said. "Then we'll get Katie. I'll guard this one while you untie Billy."

David seemed to be digesting this. He was responding to everything Terrance said with hesitation and unease, and while Terrance understood why—the poor bastard had been tortured worse than he himself had—it was frustrating the hell out of him. Where was his resilience? Why wasn't his adrenaline kicking in? "Did you hear me?" he asked him.

"Yeah. I did."

Terrance realized he was overestimating how much help David was going to be. He seemed more than stunned: he seemed shell-shocked. "Let's go," Terrance said to them both.

But right away they stopped, because they heard the sound of a vehicle, the engine swamping the birdsong and the looing of the wildebeest. It was racing through the dusk, but within seconds Terrance could see headlights.

Terrance looked at the Russian. "Maybe they're rangers," the guy said, but he was smirking.

"Bring him into the hut you were in," Terrance told David. His idea, as much as he had one, was to hide behind the Land Rover on the assumption that whoever was coming would park near it. If it was rangers, he would emerge and be grateful. But if it was Russians, he'd have the element of surprise and be close enough that he might be able to shoot one. Friend or foe, lady or the tiger.

At least, it was only a single vehicle. Still, how many people might be inside it? For all he knew, it was a fucking clown car with a militia of Russians piling out.

Let it be only one person, he prayed softly. Then he changed his mind: No, let it be many people, and let them be rangers.

And still David wasn't herding this Glenn—or whatever his name was—into the hut. He was just standing there, apparently so frightened that he was paralyzed.

"David, move him now!" Terrance said, his voice a bark he didn't much like.

Half-heartedly, David pushed him toward the hut, and the Russian responded in slow motion. But at least they were heading in the right direction. Terrance ran to the Land Rover and crouched down.

And then it was almost upon him. A jeep. Even in the twilight he could see there were two men in the front seats, but there could be more in the back. And the pair up front were white, which meant it was unlikely they were rangers. He brought the rifle to his shoulder and peered through the sight as the vehicle slowed. From this spot, he might be able to take out one of them when it stopped.

It was too dark to see whether the Russian with the crazy blue eyes was inside it, but he supposed he was.

And now it was stopping and Terrance had to decide: did he shoot?

Which was when he felt the twine around his neck yanking him back, his feet almost coming out from under him. He swung the rifle over his head toward whoever was choking him, but he missed, and so he dropped the gun and tried to wedge his fingers under the cord, but he couldn't breathe and it hurt like hell, and he was failing. The idea crossed his mind: This is where it ends. This is how I die. But he got a single finger under the twine, then two, and he was able to inhale just enough oxygen that he could use his legs to push his whole body as hard as he could into his attacker, and it worked. He sent them both careening into the Land Rover and then onto the ground, the guy's head banging hard into the earth, and when he looked around he saw that it was, as he expected, Glenn. Or whatever his name was.

And Terrance might have won. He might have been able to land a punch or a kick or get a finger into the Russian's eye, despite the way he was coughing.

But there was David—David, for fuck's sake!—grabbing one of his arms and tugging him away from his attacker.

"It's over, Terrance, stop!" he was yelling, "Let it go, they'll kill you!"

And then the men from the jeep were upon him—there were only two, after all—and the first of them took the butt of his pistol and slammed it into Terrance's cheek so hard that he really did see stars, understanding for the first time in the midst of his pain and shock that seeing stars was neither hyperbole nor myth. His ears were ringing. He was on his hands and knees in the dust. He blinked, trying to clear his head and focus on something more than the twinkling lights, and when he could see again, he saw those blue eyes. Yes, their leader was back. The one he could tell was in charge.

"This isn't a movie," he told Terrance. He was towering above him. "You're not making a film in Arizona or New Mexico. You're in Africa. There are a thousand ways to die out here, including pissing me off. Again."

It hurt to breathe. His throat. But at least he wasn't having the wind choked out of him anymore.

"I'll tie him up," said the fellow who had returned with him.

"Tie them both up," he said, and he picked up the rifle.

David looked crestfallen as the leader of the group approached him. The guy smiled cryptically when he was eye to eye with the gallerist. "Tie him up the way his father would. On his back. In the dark. Maybe take some cotton from the first-aid kit and stop up his ears so he can't hear, either. Isn't that what your father likes to do, David Hill? Isn't that what your father's people do?"

"I know nothing about what my father does. I—"

"MK-ULTRA. You have Ken Kesey's friend in your gallery."

"But—"

"We should tie you up, blindfold you, stop up your ears, and then drug you. Make your mind mush. LSD, right?"

Terrance tried to make sense of it all, but the idea that David Hill's father had something to do with LSD was too wild to believe.

"I'm torn," the Russian went on. "I'm supposed to send you to Moscow. Let the KGB interrogate you at the Lubyanka. I'm sure your father has told you about the prison. Maybe it was an inspiration for him. Possible, yes? But a part of me just wants to finish this here. I'm curious: did your father kill Frank Olson?"

"Frank Olson threw himself out a window."

He nodded slowly.

"Did your father dose him with LSD?"

"No."

"And you know this for a fact?"

"I just know my father."

"Oh, for fuck's sake, David Hill." He punched him hard enough in the stomach to double him over. "You know enough. Maybe if I shoot a kneecap your knowledge will improve." He reached for his pistol and had gotten as far as unlatching the safety when David caught his breath and began to speak.

"Why would my father tell me anything?" He raised his voice, and Terrance thought he might break down and cry. "I know he's CIA, but nothing else!"

"Do you know what we call him? Your father?"

David waited.

"The brain fucker. That's your esteemed father. He gives people LSD. He restrains them the way we tied you up. Exactly that way. He tries to empty their heads so he can fill them up with whatever nonsense he wants."

"My father is just . . . just a bureaucrat. He works in personnel."

"Desk job. Bologna sandwich at noon. Low security clearance." The sarcasm was thick.

"Yes! He's not even sure what he's going to live on when he retires!"

He sighed. "You know what, David Hill? I want to believe you."

"Thank you."

"But it's not up to me. Maybe you do know nothing about what your father does or Frank Olson or MK–ULTRA. Maybe. But we can let the experts at the Lubyanka decide for themselves." He gazed at David with disapproval, and no one said a word. David's eyes had gone wide and were darting back and forth among the Russians. Until a moment ago, Terrance had never heard of the Lubyanka, but two words had registered: *KGB* and *prison*.

Finally, the one who was going by Glenn started to speak, but his voice trailed off. "I need to tell you something . . ." he began.

"Go ahead."

"This one"—he pointed at Terrance—"killed Grissom."

"Killed him?"

"Yes."

"How?"

"Shot him. When Grissom took him out to piss."

He nodded, absorbing the news.

"Cooper?" It was Glenn who had spoken, and that's when it clicked for Terrance: the names. Glenn. Grissom. Now Cooper. Astronaut names. American astronaut names. Whoever these Russians were, they were identifying each other by using the names of the Mercury astronauts. John Glenn. Gus Grissom. Gordon Cooper. And Cooper, the one with cobalt marbles for eyes, was the leader.

"Yes?" said Cooper.

"I just . . . I just wanted to be sure you heard me," Glenn continued.

"I heard you," Cooper mumbled, before squatting to look directly into Terrance's face. "I guess that makes us even," he told him. Then he stood and kicked him in the stomach, and Terrance curled up, though he felt more winded than in pain. Yes, it hurt, but not like his skull, which was excruciating, or his neck, which still burned. For a long moment, Cooper did nothing but breathe heavily. Everyone waited.

"What do you mean by 'even'?" David asked, breaking the silence, and the unease in his voice was especially manifest in those last two syllables. That last word.

"Your friend," Cooper answered. "Your sister-in-law. Margie Stepanov. She didn't make it. She died before we could get her help. Just kept bleeding and bleeding."

"Oh, God, no. We were all supposed to go home and—"

"No. I just told you. You were never going home, David Hill. You were always going to Moscow. We need to find out how much you really know about your father. And the value of seven is not substantially less than the value of eight. Especially when we have movie stars to send back to America and that eighth is the son of the CIA's respected brain fucker—and we have that boy in the Lubyanka."

Cooper again offered that enigmatic smile, and Terrance thought it was over. They would take David and him back to their huts and tie them up. But something in David snapped, and he lunged at Cooper, frenzied and febrile, and managed to grab the pistol in Cooper's belt before Glenn could seize him by the shoulders and yank him off the other man. David spun away and held up the revolver, and for a split second Terrance couldn't tell whether he was going to shoot Cooper or was too surprised that he had managed to commandeer the weapon. But it didn't matter, because Glenn had a gun too, and he fired first and his shot instantly dropped Katie Barstow's husband. The body collapsed into the dust, his left hand falling limply on Terrance's thigh, and Terrance saw how quickly the blood was saturating his shirt. Just like that. The bullet had hit him in the side. The rib cage. It'd had to travel maybe six feet.

"I'm sorry," Glenn said, and initially Terrance thought he was apologizing to David. But, no. He was speaking to his boss.

Cooper glared at his comrade for a moment, but then calmed. He shook his head. "It's fine. You might have just saved my life. We'll say . . . it doesn't matter what we say. He was eaten, for all I care." He reached down for the pistol, which was beside David's right hand. David was still conscious, his eyes wide and alert, but his breathing was labored and weak. Then Cooper raised up his arm with the handgun and planted a bullet in the gallerist's forehead, putting him out of his misery exactly as Terrance had finished off the Russian he'd shot in the stomach. Cooper relaxed and said something in Russian to his men.

Straight away, the two of them lifted Terrance up off the ground, each grabbing him under an arm.

"Terrance Dutton," Cooper said to him. Terrance waited.

"Yes, your friend was going to Moscow. But you? You're just a movie star. You can still make it out of here alive. You can go home. But don't fuck with me again." Then, though Terrance could walk, the pair dragged him toward the dungeon of his hut. He looked back once at David's corpse, already as indistinct in the dusk as a fallen tree or one of those massive anthills that dotted the plains, haunted and mystified by the reality that they had called the man's father a brain fucker.

CHAPTER TWENTY-ONE

Benjamin Kikwete

"Some of my crew? Fathers and sons. The boys follow their dads into the wild. I view my cooks and porters and gun bearers—each and every man, whether he's forty-five or fourteen—as if he were my own brother," said Patton. "Trust me, they'll take excellent care of that crowd from La La Land."

—*The Hollywood Reporter*, NOVEMBER 9, 1964

The body, Benjamin's grandmother had told him, will wither, but the soul is a flower that only blooms brighter with age. You can't see the soul in a person's eyes, as some people suggested, because they will grow cloudy and blind. Rather you see the soul in a person's whole face. Look at the mouth (even one that lacks teeth, because teeth aren't maps of either happiness or fortitude), and look at the nose and the rivers of lines in the skin, and (yes) look at the eyes. But see those eyes as only one part of the map of the soul.

Benjamin stared at each of the faces of the men in the lorry, trying to gauge who had the soul—no, who had the stomach—to throw themselves at the two men, one with a rifle and one with a machine gun. An AK-47. In some he saw fear, in others resignation. He wished he saw rage.

"Yes, I agree. You want to be a rhino, not a goat," Muema was saying quietly to him, the older man's lips barely moving. "But you need to think like a man, not a boy."

"Waiting for them to shoot us all in a gorge? How is that manly?"

Muema tapped his temple with the tip of his finger and murmured, "This isn't the moment. You'll know your moment."

You'll know your moment. It was an expression Charlie Patton used. You'll know your moment when to shoot, usually. But Benjamin had heard him use it in other contexts as well when he was speaking to guests. When it was your moment with a woman. When it was your moment to finish the gin. When it was your moment to leave.

And then, and it felt like a sign, the lorry stopped, and the two men with guns stood up and raised their weapons. He could feel it: his moment was coming. The driver climbed out and took a cardboard box from the passenger seat. He placed it on the ground, reaching inside and handing out to the prisoners in the back the bags of potato chips that Charlie Patton's cooks had planned to make part of the lunch for the guests.

Benjamin opened his and nearly emptied the bag in a minute. Muema told him to savor them, and to take comfort in the fact they were being fed. This seemed further evidence that they weren't going to kill them. But Benjamin wanted to be ready for what was about to happen next: he could visualize it all perfectly in his mind's eye as if, yes, it was a movie. He saw the driver was planning to fill a pair of canteens from the water jug he had in the footwell of the passenger seat, and was likely going to bring those to the captives next. And that would be his moment. Insurrection. He would lean over the side of the lorry for the canteen, but instead of taking it, he would grab the driver's wrist and jump over the side of the truck. He'd wrap his manacled hands around the guy's throat. He'd use the driver as a shield and threaten to snap his neck. There were a dozen prisoners. Two men, even one with an AK-47, couldn't shoot that many attackers before the swarm engulfed the lowly pair like a pack of wild dogs.

And now the driver was approaching, and so Benjamin

angled his body and put both hands, though bound, on the side rail, and prepared to hurl himself onto his captor.

.   .   .

"You'll know your moment," Charlie Patton was telling this Russian colonel. The Russian spoke English fluently. Over the course of the past two days, Benjamin overheard that the fellow's father had worked for Molotov in his second stint as minister of foreign affairs in the 1950s, and one result was that his son had gotten a cushy post for three years at the Russian embassy in Washington, D.C., and the official's daughter had been allowed to exhibit her paintings in America. When Molotov's star burned out in 1956, the children had already discovered the benefits— the colonel had used the word *perks,* a term that Muema had defined for Benjamin later—of living in America, even though the son admitted that he dutifully returned to Moscow within months of their father's fall from grace. His sister, he said, had defected and remained in the United States.

Now Patton and the Soviet officer were talking about the moment when the colonel would collect his elephant. The plan was to head tomorrow into a part of the reserve where Patton suspected there would be a sizable herd. Viktor Procenko and his group already had bagged the other four of the big five: they had a lion head, tusks from a rhino, a leopard hide, and two sets of buffalo horns. Benjamin had just turned fourteen, and this was the first time he had accompanied his father as a gun bearer on one of Patton's safaris. He'd met Patton before in Nairobi but had never traveled with him into the Serengeti.

The colonel was one of five communists that Patton had in his shooting party. Benjamin had heard them referred to as soldiers one day and advisers the next. Procenko's eyes were a deep blue, and his hair had just started to recede. He carried himself more like an American than a Russian, in Benjamin's opinion, a testimony both to his swagger and his refinement. He moved seamlessly between Russian and English, and even knew some Swahili, Kikongo, and French from the time he had served in the Congo. And, Benjamin's father told him, Procenko was one of the few guests he had ever seen who was a better drinker than Charlie Patton.

"Oh, I'll know my moment," the colonel told Patton. "I always"—and there was a hint of condescension in the way he echoed the great white hunter—"know my moment." He raised his glass to Patton and the other Russians sitting around the camp table, swallowed the last of his gin and tonic, and crunched an ice cube between his teeth. Then he said, "I heard the Americans put a monkey in space. You know lots about monkeys, I suppose. What do you think of that, Charlie Patton?"

"I imagine they could have put a pig up there, too," the hunter replied. "And why not? The accomplishment was that they didn't barbecue the damn thing. Cook the monkey at blast-off or burn it up in reentry."

"A monkey. What a waste. The problem? Americans are wary of risk. You probably see that when you have American clients. We'll put a man up there. We won't waste a rocket on a monkey. We won't waste time on a monkey."

Patton nodded amiably and took a sip of his own cocktail. Procenko looked back at Benjamin's father and motioned for him to refill his own glass and top off Patton's. Benjamin could see in Patton's eyes that he didn't want any more, but he wasn't about to decline. And so Benjamin and his father brought the ice bucket, the gin, and the tonic to the table and did as they were asked. Another member of Procenko's group, a stout little man who laughed easily and was particularly kind to the staff, asked for another too, and Benjamin carefully scooped the ice into the glass and gave him a pour heavy with alcohol, because he had figured out on the first night that these Russians liked to drink and you didn't stint with the booze.

"The Americans have those seven astronauts," Procenko

went on. "The Mercury astronauts. And instead of using one of them to reach for the stars, they send a chimp. A monkey. Don't you think that's cowardly?"

"No, I wouldn't say cowardly," said Patton. "That's not the word I would use."

Procenko watched him, waiting for more. But it seemed Patton had nothing more to add. "Pathetic?" he pressed. "Is that a better word?"

"The goal, I suppose, was to test the rocket and not lose a man you've spent a lot of money training."

"So why not send up a watermelon?"

Patton shrugged. "Maybe the monkey had to press a button or two at a certain point. Maybe there was teamwork involved."

"You can train a monkey to do that? Push buttons at certain points?"

"Absolutely. Chimpanzees are splendid pack hunters."

Procenko shook his head. "It still doesn't matter. You want to be first. You want to put the first man in space, not the first monkey. And you want the element of surprise."

"Rather like all hunting and all predation," Patton observed.

"We weren't the first in 1941, and we paid for it."

"And Lumumba?"

Procenko rolled his eyes. "Same thing: he wasn't first. And in our case? You're either committed or you're not. We were not sufficiently committed."

"Is he in jail or on the run? You're with me here on safari, Viktor, and I can't decide what that means."

"It means Lumumba is dead."

His father had just screwed the top back on the gin and went perfectly still, gripping the bottle with both hands. He wasn't moving a muscle; it was as if he were afraid if he did, Patton and Procenko would remember he was there and stop speaking.

"You know this for a fact?"

"As you just pointed out, I'm with you right now. We all are.

We wouldn't be here with you if the man was alive. Mobutu and the Katangans—with the permission of the Belgians and the UN—shot him. They shot him and a couple of his allies."

"It wasn't the Americans?"

"Oh, they would have poisoned him. The CIA. That's how they work. Or made him go crazy. I could tell you stories, Charlie Patton. Everyone thinks the KGB is so nasty. But the truth? The CIA is just as ruthless."

Patton looked at his glass but restrained himself from having another swallow. He was doing his best to walk that tightrope of keeping up and pacing himself. Finally, he said, "Not surprised at all that the Belgians would countenance that: shooting Lumumba. But the UN? Not sure I buy that part of the story."

Procenko shrugged. "Believe what you want. Either way?" Here he gestured at the other guests. "We get to go home."

"But first you get your elephant."

"Which, I suppose, will be easier than a rhino." In truth, Benjamin hadn't thought the rhino had been all that difficult to find and kill. They'd had to crawl a long while on their bellies, but the creature had never known what hit him. Never turned and charged. Procenko was a good shot.

"Don't underestimate an elephant, Viktor."

The colonel raised an eyebrow. "I told you, Charlie Patton: I always know my moment." Then he leaned over and clinked his glass against the hunter's and said, "Drink up. That bottle won't finish itself."

·   ·   ·

But Benjamin did not jump. He didn't hurl himself over the side of the lorry and attempt to wrestle the driver to the ground. He would have; he knew in his heart he would have, despite the reality that his hands and ankles were bound. It wasn't cowardice that kept him on his rear in the back of the truck. It was Muema. The guide had listened to him and knew he was planning something, and with a strength that momentarily caught him off guard, Muema had grabbed his left wrist in both his hands and held him so firmly that he couldn't rise to his feet. Muema had pressed him into the base of the cargo bed.

And now the moment had passed. Muema gave him the canteen and Benjamin took one swallow, what he supposed was his share of the warm, coppery water, and then passed it to the next man.

"You shouldn't have stopped me," he told Muema.

"You would have been dead in a heartbeat."

"Well, we may all be dead in a few hours. What difference does it make?"

Muema shook his head. "No, they're not going to kill us."

"Don't try and reassure me."

"I'm not. They just fed us—"

"To keep us calm with false hopes."

"I was listening to those two," Muema said, and he nodded at the guards in the back of the truck with them. "They were talking about Shinkolobwe."

Benjamin shook his head. "I have no idea where that is."

"It's a mine. Or was a mine. Uranium. It's in the Congo."

"And you think they're taking us there?"

"It's far, so I don't know. Maybe the Simbas have gotten control. But if not to Shinkolobwe, then to a place like it. Another mine that the Simbas have taken. Maybe one closer."

"To put us to work."

Muema nodded. "The Soviets talk a good game when they speak of the rights of workers, but when it comes to a uranium mine on this continent? We have no rights. We'd be better off mining diamonds or gold in South Africa."

"My grandfather mined gold. It nearly killed him. It ruined his back. He was never the same, he told us."

"Uranium is worse. If that's what they want us for."

"So, we'd be Simba slave labor."

Muema brought his bound hands to his face and rubbed

his eyes. "Or Soviet slave labor. I don't know. I just know that this wasn't our moment. This wasn't your moment. You'll have another chance. A better chance. We all will."

The driver took back the canteens, climbed into the truck, and they started off. Based on the sun, they were driving southwest, which might indeed mean the Congo and the violent world of the Simba rebellion.

CHAPTER TWENTY-TWO

Katie Barstow

These are all actual "baby" pictures of Julie Andrews, Paul New-man, and Katie Barstow. Perky little Katie dressed up for Hal-loween as a pumpkin? Her mother, Glenda, says it was one of her daughter's favorite nights of her life. The child loved that costume so much, Glenda told us, that one year she insisted on going trick-or-treating in it on October 30—the night before Halloween. "Our neighbors laughed and laughed and thought Katie was adorable. The cookie and candy haul was insane," said the proud mom.

—Teen Screen, JULY 1962

She was crying because she was going to die, she knew this now, she was sure of it, and her ass was wet from peeing her pants, and in the blackness of the hut she could smell the toxic cock-tail of her urine and the damp earth beneath her pallet. Where had she smelled something like this? That fucking Halloween pumpkin costume. Her brother the shrink would say this was a manufactured memory—a memory someone had crafted from the stories of other, usually older people—but she knew it was genuine. It was her earliest memory. She knew the shame of trick-or-treating on the wrong night in a blob of orange fabric and cotton ticking that reeked like a dirty diaper in August. In hindsight, the stink was more Proustian than the reaction of the neighbors in the building: her recollections of their confusion and annoyance might have been manufactured from her conversations later with Billy and David and other people who lived on the same elevator line in the massive apartment.

Still, no shame or horror had prepared her for this: not even witnessing the cavitation of a human skull when Juma was shot with an elephant gun that morning. No, in the last few minutes, she had heard too much, and the fact she was hearing it all in the dark made it like a carnival funhouse, but real. She was virtually blind; no human eye had the capability to turn this darkness to day. There were the gunshots, three of them, but two at first. That's where it began, with men arguing, fighting, behind the boma and then inside the boma. The languages had been Russian and English. She had heard David, she was positive, and though she couldn't make out most of the words, she'd heard the wrenching fear in her husband's voice. And she'd heard Terrance Dutton speaking, and he was adamant and angry, which might have given her hope, but no one came for her. No one. Good God, was David even still alive? Were Terrance and Billy and Margie?

Margie. Margie. Katie asked herself over and over in her mind what she had done allowing her sister-in-law to join them on this safari. She should have insisted that Billy and Margie remain in California. Before all of that activity and the gunshots just now, maybe—just maybe—she had heard Margie, and the woman was crying, and then one of the vehicles had left in a hurry.

She was afraid she was losing her mind, but she was far more terrified that though this had begun as a kidnapping, something had happened and everything had changed and now it was going to be a massacre. The Russians were going to kill them all. Her feet were tied to the foot of the pallet and her hands were bound, but she could easily bring her fingers to her cheeks and wipe away the tears. And so, finally, she did. She wiped the rivulets of mucus that were streaming from her nose, too.

God, she thought, splaying her fingers because some were

falling asleep, I am oozing fluids everywhere. And that didn't even count the sweat.

This safari had been her big idea. Now it had fallen apart— Fallen apart? That was like saying Jack Kennedy's visit to Dallas had had a few hiccups—and when they all died, it was on her for bringing them here.

She wished she were being too hard on herself. She tried to convince herself that their deaths would be no more her fault than if the plane had crashed on its final approach to the airport in Nairobi. But she also understood that none of this self-flagellation mattered, because dead was dead and it was the only thing in the world you had no hope of changing.

Finally, she could stand it no longer and so she cried out. "Let us go!" she wailed. "Please! Let us go! Someone, please, tell me what's happening!"

And then she said the same thing softly—*Let us go. Tell me what's happening*—the words this time lost in her sobs.

·   ·   ·

Billy and this new woman in his life, Margie, were sitting with her at the wrought-iron table under the umbrella on the east side of her swimming pool. Katie thought Margie was smart and pretty and hoped that things would work out for her brother and her. But she had no idea. She hadn't realized that Billy's first marriage was crumbling until he had dropped the bombshell on her last year that he had moved out and he and Amelia were resolving the custody arrangements.

Custody arrangements.

God, what a concept. She was poor Marc's aunt and hadn't even known that his parents' marriage was in trouble until it was over.

"Sometimes, I miss living back east," Margie was saying, and she swirled the ice in her glass.

"Would you like more iced tea?" Katie asked her.

"No, but it's delicious."

"It's from a cannister. It's powder. The best thing about it is that it's sugar free but tastes like sweet tea," she said. She wasn't sure why she was telling them that the tea was instant. She'd discovered sweet tea on a movie set in Atlanta, and she associated the drink now with southern hospitality. Confessing that she hadn't even bothered to steep some real tea and chill the beverage before her guests arrived seemed the exact opposite of hospitality. But then she knew: her mother would have lied and told Margie some story about the work that either she or the latest Irish girl had done to prepare tea that was exquisite and special. Katie was being (one of her mother's favorite words) contrary because she didn't want to be her mother.

"One summer, Katie ate nothing but sugar-free iced tea from a cannister and peanuts," Billy told this new woman in his life. "Whole damn summer, that was it."

"How would you know?" she asked him, shaking her head at the story. "You were in college!"

"Mother told me."

Katie rolled her eyes. "I was getting fat."

"Mother told me that, too."

She was wearing a straw hat, and she hit him with it. He feigned terror and shielded his face as he groaned, "I'm just telling you what she said!"

"Did it work?" Margie asked.

"I lost weight, yes."

"You should tell the *Hollywood Reporter* or *Teen Screen*: it could be the Katie Barstow Miracle Diet," said Billy's new girlfriend, and for a moment Katie imagined suggesting the idea to Reggie. Sugar-free iced tea from a cannister or a jar, and all the peanuts you wanted. The weight would just melt away. Reggie would think she was kidding and laugh at the idea good-naturedly, and then suggest a healthier alternative, if she really wanted him to pursue this. She recalled how when *Teen Screen* had reached out to him for baby pictures of his client, she'd told him to check in with her mother back in New York. Katie had never expected that Glenda would send Reggie a snapshot of her in the pumpkin. She was sure it would be one from her first Broadway show. Or maybe that dinner at Sardi's when she was thirteen and her father let her have a glass of champagne, and she'd stared, mesmerized, at the opaline phosphorescence of the bubbles in the flute. Will I ever be this happy again? she had wondered, and for a long second, she had been scared. But the second had passed. Thank God. Those weren't baby pictures, but her mother had boasted often how pretty she looked in them, and how very much mother and daughter resembled each other. Had her mother sent the pumpkin pic because it really was a baby photo and she was following instructions, or had she sent it to torture her? Did she really believe that horseshit she'd told the magazine writer about their joyful, eccentric, *theatrical* evening trick-or-treating together with Billy on the wrong night?

"Part of Katie's team is Reggie Stout," Billy was telling Margie. "Owns a small but very powerful PR firm. So, what do you think, sis: should Reggie pitch the glossies the Katie Barstow Miracle Diet?"

Sis. Since when did Billy call her "sis"? She put her hat back on her head and watched a keg-chested seagull swagger along the coralline lip of the swimming pool. The house was at the edge of a cliff, and in the distance today—across the dry brown scrub that marked the valley—you could see Los Angeles, a little pink in the haze.

"I was kidding," Margie said before she had to answer.

"I was too," said Billy. He was gazing out into the valley and then asked, "Do you ever use the diving board?"

"Sometimes."

"Sometimes?"

"When I'm alone."

"That sounds sad."

"Sad? Why sad?"

"You should be using it at parties to encourage some old-school Hollywood bacchanalia. You need a diving board for the real madness, and you have one."

"I don't want real madness."

"When I was in high school," said Margie, "I had a teacher who told the girls we should always walk like we were on a diving board."

"Because it would make you walk with real confidence?" Billy asked. "Three or four athletic steps, arms swinging, and then, boom, you're up in the air?"

Margie shook her head. "No, I think it was just the opposite. We'd walk demurely. Little steps in straight lines."

"The things adults tell us," Katie said.

Her brother nodded. She knew that he, too, was thinking of their mother and father. But, mostly, their mother. "David says hi," he told her, and she understood the synaptic connection. Mom and Dad. Central Park West. David Hill.

She was happy for Billy that David had moved west. She thought that as his life was transformed by the divorce, it was good he had his best friend from childhood with him.

"Say hi back. Say hi for me. How's he doing?"

"He's excited about the gallery. It's looking good."

When she'd heard that David was opening a gallery, she'd been perplexed. What the hell did he know about art? She always assumed he would follow his father's lead and do something that involved international relations: the State Department or the Foreign Service or, maybe, the CIA. But Billy explained that David had studied art history at college and had an entrepreneurial eye. The gallery was never going to be trying to sell a Fabritius or Vermeer, but would instead be looking for the next Warhol. It would hang on its walls lots of hip modern stuff that would work well in the beach houses in Malibu. That was David's plan. But even that had left her a little dubious. Her father had bought a Mark Rothko painting from a show at—of all places—Macy's in 1942, and David's parents had looked at

it hanging in the Stepanov living room and been incapable of
mustering even a semblance of enthusiasm. Surrealism wasn't in
the Hill family's genes, she supposed, and a government bureaucrat wasn't likely to wax poetic over something so abstract.

"I'm glad," she said politely. "He was always my favorite of
your friends when we were growing up." This was true.

"You had a crush on him," Billy said.

"How in the world would you know?"

"Because you were always following us around. You didn't
follow around my other friends."

She smiled. "I did."

"Why?" asked Margie. "What was it about David?"

"Have you two met?" asked Katie.

The woman nodded, and Katie felt a slight pique: Billy had
introduced Margie to his childhood pal before he had introduced Margie to her. She tried to let it go. "He was nice to me
and he was cute," she replied. "A lot of Billy's friends were cute,
but not a lot of them were nice to me."

Billy gently ran his fingers over the back of Margie's hand.
"That's all it takes when you're the progeny of Roman and
Glenda Stepanov," he told her. "Someone's nice to you? You fall
for them. Katie and I are both beaten puppies that way."

"I am not a beaten puppy," she insisted.

"And you're not either," Margie reassured him.

Billy grinned, but it was derisive and self-mocking. "Well,
my sister and I are who we are because of that pair. Tell me
something," he said to Katie. She waited. "I know David loved
seeing you when I brought him by. He loved catching up."

"And?"

"Just curious: do you still think he's nice and cute?"

"Yes. Sure."

"You two should go on a date. I mean, you're not seeing
anyone."

"Are you fixing me up?"

"I guess."

She shrugged and thought, why not? They could have lunch at Billy's. It hadn't worked out with actors. Maybe it would with a man who'd known her when she was still Katie Stepanov, and had been a friend to her brother and her when they'd needed a friend—and a little kindness—most.

. . .

They answered her cries. Or, perhaps, they were coming to the hut anyway.

Two of them entered, one with a flashlight, and the beam cast flickering shadows that made her think of bad dreams and the childhood monsters that crawled out from under the bed. She was still weeping, and she asked them what was happening, to please, please tell her, but they remained silent, and she stopped asking questions when one of them untied her, helped her to stand, and walked her outside. It was not quite dark, but almost, and she saw the bright pinprick that was Venus against a deep purple sky and the first bold, bright stars to the east. The majestic profile of an acacia tree looked like a painting, and she might have stood there, struck silent by its beauty, if this had been just another night in the Serengeti.

The one who'd untied her instructed her to sit on the ground in the center of the boma, and then he started to round up stray sticks and branches and toss them into a pile in front of her. From a small dead tree, a kind she didn't recognize, he tore off skeletal twigs and added them to the mound too. When it was the size of a mother warthog, he lugged a jerry can from the back of one of the Land Rovers, sprinkled some fuel onto the heap, and set it on fire. She had been cold, and the warmth from the fire felt good on her face and arms. She rubbed at her wrists and her ankles, where she had been tied.

A moment later, a fellow who seemed to be in charge sat on the ground beside her, stretched his legs before him, and tried to hand her a canteen. In the light from the fire, she saw his fingers were gnarled. Not arthritis, she surmised, but likely broken in the past. Easily two of them and maybe three. She stared at the canteen for a moment but didn't touch it. She wondered if it had been poisoned and this was how they were going to kill her. Would they then add more wood to the blaze and toss her body onto the pyre?

As if he could read her mind, he winked at her, his eyes a piercing blue, and took a long swallow, and once more offered her the water. His face was lightly freckled. This time she accepted the canteen and drank some. The water was warm, but she chugged great mouthfuls. When she was done, he handed her a paper bag of mixed nuts, and she put a few in her mouth.

"Are the others still tied up?" she asked him after she had swallowed the nuts.

"They're in their huts," he said, not precisely answering her question. He had a trace of a Russian accent.

"Why have you brought me out here?"

"Because you sounded hysterical."

"Where is Margie?"

"She's in her hut."

She wanted to believe him, but she didn't. "She's pregnant, you know," she said. "And she had that cut."

"She had a few cuts. But we took care of them."

"I thought I heard her crying."

"You did, but not because of any cuts. She was, like you a few minutes ago, panicking. But she's fine now. She calmed down."

"May I see her?"

"No."

She started to ask why not, but stopped herself. She wasn't sure how far she could push this man. "I heard gunshots," she said instead. "Can you tell me—"

"We scared away a couple of hyenas," he explained, cutting her off.

Now she was sure he was lying. She was confident she

would have heard hyenas. Moreover, it had still been light out when there had been those shots. Would hyenas try and infiltrate a boma during daylight? She doubted it. Right now, there were neither goats nor cattle herded inside it. There only were humans.

"About the others—" she began, but he cut her off.

"I told you, they're fine." She could hear in his tone that she risked trying his patience.

"I'm sorry. I meant my other friends—the ones who were in the other Land Rover. There were three of them."

"I see. They're safe."

"And Charlie Patton and his team? Where are they? The ones who are still . . ." She let the sentence stagger and then sink like a stone underwater.

"Still alive?" he said after a moment, finishing it for her. "Is that what you're asking? The ones who are still alive?"

She sighed. The image of Juma's death and the murder of the rangers came back to her, causing her stomach to lurch. The man beside her was a beast. He was handsome—God, those eyes— and undeniably charismatic. But he was still a monster. (Perhaps that was the worst kind of monster: the kind who had blue eyes and small constellations of freckles, and yet was humanized by fingers made knobby by injury or illness. The fact was, Hollywood was awash with exactly that sort of predator.) "Yes," she said.

"They're safe. I suppose they're still in transit."

She decided not to ask where. She decided she didn't dare.

"Now," he began, clearing his throat, "I want you to do something. Or I will tomorrow."

"Okay."

"The negotiations have grown more complicated than I would like. So, tomorrow, I'm going to take a Polaroid picture of you. You're going to brush your hair and smile. And you're going to write a note, though you will be writing what I tell you to say. More or less. I'll want you to make it your own."

"Something has gone wrong with the . . . the kidnapping?"

"Negotiations are never easy. That's all."

That's all. Were people balking at the ransom? And who would that be?

"Of course," she said. "Whatever you need."

"Thank you. We'll deliver the note as soon as you write it."

"My brother, Billy," she said. "He's hurt, too. Worse than Margie, I think. One of your men hurt him."

"I regret that. You never want to bruise the fruit."

By now, Billy's face was likely fuchsia. "You hurt him badly. It was more than an apple with a ding."

"He'll recover. He'll get better."

"And no one else has been beaten?"

He said nothing, and his silence unnerved her. She had expected reassurance, even if she suspected whatever he said would be a lie. He threw a stick end over end into the fire. "Terrance Dutton. He tried to escape. We stopped him."

"How bad?"

"It looks worse than it is." A bird called out, and it sounded to Katie like an owl. "That's a hoopoe," he murmured, and he mimicked its high-pitched cry: "Hoopoo. Hoopoo."

"And the rest of tonight?" She wasn't precisely sure what she was asking. "You'll tie me up again. You'll tie us all up again. Is that the plan?"

"No, we won't tie you up. Most of you, anyway. Maybe Terrance since he tried to escape once. But maybe not even him. After all, you'd have to be crazy to try and escape in the night. Here? It would be a death sentence."

"But you'll keep us separated."

"Yes. But in a couple of days? Two, maybe three? You'll all be back in Nairobi. Then you'll fly home. And when you look back on this, you'll tell your friends in Hollywood that you just lived through a movie. And because it is you telling the story, Katie Barstow? They'll actually make it into a movie. What do you think? Could your Paul Newman play me?"

"Yes," she said, because she knew she was supposed to. But when she tried to take comfort in his scenario, she found it too rosy. It was a fairy tale. But she didn't dispute him. She merely stared into the flames and watched the sparks rise into the ever-blackening sky.

CHAPTER TWENTY-THREE

Reggie Stout

"I have clients who changed their names before our firm started representing them—at least three or four. You know who they are," Stout said. *"But I never asked anyone to change his name. I told people how I thought they should dress, but I never bought anyone the 'right' clothes. I try to treat my clients like grown-ups. Let's face it: you may not lose an adult when you talk to him like a child, but you're certainly not winning him over. Lord, even children know when you're condescending to them. There are people in this world who will sell their soul to be in the movie business, and the last thing I want to do is exploit that desperation or make someone beholden to me."*

—*Los Angeles Times*, SEPTEMBER 15, 1962

Carmen shrieked when she saw him, and then she was yelling, her voice so uncharacteristically frenzied and irrational that for a second Reggie feared she was going to fall from the baobab.

"I told you, I had to pee. I was no more than forty feet away," he said quickly but calmly when he was standing below her, trying to comfort and reassure her. He pointed at the spot where he had been standing. He could see her in the moonlight now that he was back at the base of the tree, and the terror in her poor, bruised face—and in her one open eye—was evident.

"No, you didn't, you didn't!" she wailed.

He wasn't going to argue with her. He had told her. She must have dozed off and he hadn't known. He took comfort from the idea that she hadn't shot him with that pistol when he'd emerged from the other side of the tree. God, his desire for a moment of privacy had nearly resulted in a bullet in his abdomen or his chest, when he'd supposed the big risk was getting eaten.

"It's okay," he said. "I'm here, you're here. And soon the sun will be up."

"It's not even three thirty in the morning!" she argued. "The sun won't be up for hours."

"Shhhhhhhh," he said. "We're fine."

And they were. More or less. His leg had stiffened up from sitting beneath the tree, but he had been able to walk and felt a little better now that he had been up and around. He'd popped some more aspirin. There really were only a few more hours of darkness, and that idea gave him hope. Perhaps at sunrise he could shoot them something for breakfast. A gazelle or a dik-dik. He'd find enough wood to restart the fire, and in his mind, he saw Carmen sitting across him, pulling meat from the antelope's leg. A cavewoman, he thought, and he smiled ever so slightly. Carmen Tedesco, smarty-pants cavewoman.

"How long were you gone?" she asked.

"Two minutes. Maybe three. Not much more."

"You could have been killed."

"True. But I could have been killed sitting beneath the tree, too. And I didn't really feel like peeing in my pants. Also? I was getting sleepy. I needed to walk around. Wake myself up."

"I might have shot you. By accident."

"Well, I'm grateful you didn't. Thank you."

He was just about to sit down when she said, "Now I have to go to the bathroom."

He considered making a joke about the way she had chosen such a modest euphemism for three thirty in the morning in the Serengeti—observing, perhaps, that the nearest bathroom was really very far away. But he knew that wouldn't go over well.

Nor would that old joke about how she should have thought of that before they got in the car. And so instead he leaned the rifle against the tree and said, "Let me help you down."

"Thank you. I'm sorry."

"Don't be. Just be careful with the pistol."

"The safety's on."

"Good."

Her feet had just touched the ground, and she was smiling at him sheepishly when her face, still streaked with her tears, changed in a heartbeat, her one good eye growing wide and her mouth opening into an O, a rictus of teeth and terror, and he felt the animal—whatever it was—jumping onto him, onto his back, throwing the two of them into the thick trunk of the tree, just as she started, once more, to scream.

. . .

There were four of them sitting around the folding table after lunch: Reggie and Katie and Juma and Charlie. The porters were starting to pack everything up and haul it back into the lorry. They were talking about jackals because they'd seen a pair sunning themselves in the dirt tracks carved into the dirt by countless vehicles that summer and fall. The animals had black backs and reminded some of the Californians of German shepherds.

"Oh, I've seen animals do things that suggest they're much smarter than we suppose and things that suggest we give them far too much credit," Charlie was saying. "I saw a lone jackal racing like a madman with a good chunk of a tommie—a Thomson's gazelle—in his mouth. There were a couple of hyenas hot on his tail. And he looked back at them, and when he did, pow. Ran headfirst into a baobab. For a second or two he was stunned, practically out like a light, and it would have been comic if this had been a children's cartoon. You know, one of those moments where the coyote gets conked in those Road Runner cartoons. Needless to say, the hyenas got to finish off the tommie. And then there are the elephants."

"I always heard elephants are smart," said Katie.

"They are. Very smart. I love them for that. But just like people, sometimes they show absolutely no common sense. For instance, they love to eat from the doum palm. When they come across some, they'll eat themselves into a stupor."

"Don't elephants have to eat all day long? Juma, didn't you tell us that just yesterday?" Reggie asked.

Juma nodded. "I did and they do. But they love the fruit from the gingerbread tree. The doum palm. Sometimes, they eat so much they get sick."

"You were in the war, Reggie. You must have seen some things that make your visit here seem rather tame," Charlie said.

Reggie shrugged but otherwise didn't respond. When he didn't say anything, Charlie took a swallow of his drink and went on, "I had a veteran and his wife out here two months ago. We were in one of the hunting reserves, and he nearly got himself mauled by a couple of hyenas. Thought he was invincible."

"Oh, I know I'm not invincible," Reggie said.

"The thing was, he'd collected his leopard, and so he thought hyenas would be easy."

"They're not?"

"They're different. Leopards are solitary beasts. They hunt alone. Hyenas hunt in packs. A leopard can rip out your stomach with one swipe of its claws. A hyena depends on its jaws."

"What theater was this veteran in? Pacific? European? Just curious."

Charlie smirked. "He was in England. I think he was some sort of code breaker. Real egghead. Never set foot on the Continent."

"I have no doubts that what he did was important."

"Probably," said Charlie. "Anyway, he saw a couple hyenas devouring a dead wildebeest—getting the leftovers—and got a

little too close. My fault, really. I wasn't paying enough attention."

"And?"

"And they're strong. Very, very strong. I had to shoot them
both when they charged the fellow. They would have tackled
him and eaten him alive."

"I suppose a man has no chance against a hyena."

"Not really. Unless he has a gun. Otherwise?"

"Otherwise what?"

"You just go for the eyes and pray. But, most of the time,
you'll still wind up dinner."

.   .   .

He had no idea whether it was a leopard, hyena, or jackal
snarling almost into his ear, he just knew that its proximity was
terrifying, and there were at least two animals, and one of them
had the brim of his hat in its mouth and the chin strap was
digging into the soft flesh under his jaw as his head was being
yanked back, and then the strap snapped and the hat was gone.
Carmen was howling, and he was pinning her against the bulbous trunk of the tree with his whole body, trying to shield her,
and then her wails were biblical, a keening far louder than the
hungry rumble from deep inside the animal's throat. The other
creature was pawing at his shoulders, trying to pull him to the
ground.

And that's when it clicked. These weren't leopards, because
hadn't Charlie Patton told him about a leopard's paws? The front
and back claws? If these were leopards, they would have ripped
open his neck by now. His face. They might have wrenched his
whole head off his body.

And leopards never hunted together. Charlie had said they
were solitary creatures.

He tried to punch the animal with his left hand, but he was
still facing the tree and so he was swinging his arm across his

body and his fist could barely reach his own right ear, and by then there was no power in the clout. He'd have to turn around and so he did, and—yes—they were hyenas, and so he pounded the nose of one with both hands, a reflex, but suddenly, somehow, his forearm was in its mouth and now he was yelling, too, his adrenaline no match for the pain as the animal's teeth sliced through skin and muscle and then crunched the bone there into pieces. Desperately, with his other hand, he plunged his fingers into one of the animal's open eyes, trying to poke it out, smash it like a black grape, and the hyena yelped, releasing his arm. He took his thumb and, as if he were hitchhiking, jammed it as hard as he could at the other eye, hitting the snout twice before he connected and the eye collapsed and spattered across his hand.

But still the animal wasn't retreating. Blind and hungry and now very angry, it lunged at him, and he brought his good arm in front of his face.

Which was when he heard the crack of the pistol at his side, and the animal dropped to the ground. The gunshot was loud, but not so close or near to his head that his ears were ringing, and so he was aware of the hyena whimpering at his feet, taking in great gulps of air. It sounded like a sick dog. He glanced back and saw Carmen had now extended both her arms, her right wrist in her left hand and the pistol in her right hand aimed at the second hyena. The beast took a step back, eyeing the humans warily, and Carmen fired once more. She missed the animal completely this time, and Reggie expected it would turn and run, retreating into the dark and the brush.

"Shoot again," he said, and she did. Once more, she missed.

And still the hyena held its ground as its mate or its sibling or whatever bled out at his feet.

She fired a third time, but now there was only an ineffectual click. The pistol was empty.

He reached behind him for the rifle with his one good arm, not taking his eyes off the animal that was watching these two humans, assessing whether it was safe to attack. He ran his fingers over the baobab bark until he found the barrel of the weapon and then the forestock. He grabbed it and was pulling it into the air when the hyena charged, and so reflexively he poked it as hard as he could with the tip, using the muzzle and sight as a spear, jabbing it, but the creature was so strong it was like using a matchstick against a wild dog. It sent Reggie sprawling back into Carmen and the two of them into the trunk of the tree, half on and half off the dying hyena, too weak now to protest. When the animal charged again, Reggie swung the rifle like a club, but with one arm the blow registered only enough to cause the creature to bounce away like a boxer who was barely grazed by a failed uppercut. Carmen took the pistol by the barrel and slammed the grip into the animal's head, once, twice, and then a third time, as it ducked and growled, but it didn't turn away.

Still, Carmen's frenzied beating had given Reggie the second he needed to get the rifle butt against his shoulder and a finger on the trigger. He got off the shot just as the hyena was meeting the tip of the weapon, and at point-blank range he blew a hole in the animal's side big enough to kill it instantly.

Or close enough to instantly.

It fell almost on top of the other hyena, and for a moment he stared at the two animals, one dead and one nearly dead. He was breathing heavily, as was Carmen.

"You saved our lives," he said to her, after a moment. "That was a good shot."

"I kept missing," she said, whimpering.

"No. You got off the shot that mattered. That first one. And then you bought us time when you were conking him with the pistol. Are you hurt?"

"I'm not. At least I don't think I am."

"Good."

She opened the backpack and started rummaging inside it for the medical supplies he'd taken from the Land Rover. But he realized how weak he was, how fast he was fading now that they had defeated the hyenas and his adrenaline was dissipating, and he slid to the ground against the base of the tree and sat beside the pair of dead animals. He couldn't believe how big they were. Beside them was his hat with the broken chinstrap. Only then did he grit his teeth and yank up the sleeve of his shirt to look at the ruin of his arm.

CHAPTER TWENTY-FOUR

Billy Stepanov

"Oh, Katie and I probably fought like all brothers and sisters grow-ing up," Billy told us, laughing. "She knew just how to push my buttons as my kid sister, and I'd wager I was a pretty typical know-it-all older brother. Our childhood was as run-of-the-mill as most people's. Yes, we grew up with Broadway in our blood—Katie sure did—but otherwise our parents were just like yours. Just like anyone's."

—*Movie Star Confidential,* DECEMBER 1962

Billy was unsure which hurt more: his nose or his back. His kidney. Both were throbbing like hell. And while his back had prevented him from getting comfortable, his nose was forcing him to breathe largely through his mouth. He supposed, if he lived, his nose would get better. The bones, if they were broken, would stitch. Oh, he'd be disfigured, but the damage wasn't per-manent. He was less sure about his back. His kidney.

The dark night of the soul.

The words came to him.

The poem didn't really have a name. St. John of the Cross had written it in the sixteenth century, and that was the title that scholars and theologians had attached to it. Billy had read it in a course on faith and mythology, and it interested him because of his own fear of the dark—that closet, the closet that was his childhood jail cell—and the journeys the mind took when confronted by such utter blackness. Imagination was toxic in the dark, a poison that likely spared no one. Certainly, it spared no child. In his last year of college, when he knew he was going to become a therapist, he had tried to decipher the links between psychiatric darkness and literal darkness, and had written his thesis, in part, about that. St. John of the Cross's poem was, in Billy's opinion, about the search for God, and because God existed for the writer in the firmament, Billy had wanted to title his thesis—with great import and pretentiousness—*The Oubliette.* Even his thesis adviser had had to ask him what the hell an oubliette was.

"It's a dungeon, but the entrance is in the roof. The ceiling," he'd explained.

"No door?"

"No door."

"So, it had . . . what? A ladder?"

"I suppose. Or they'd just drop the prisoner down. Push him, perhaps."

"But this hall closet in your parents' apartment," the professor had asked, wanting clarification, "it had a door, right? Just a regular old-fashioned door?"

"Doors, actually. Two of them. Side by side."

The adviser had taken a pencil and drawn a line through the word *oubliette,* and Billy had capitulated. "You know, don't you, that a lot of your thesis feels more like therapy than an intellectual exploration."

"I do know that," he'd agreed.

"Lord, I didn't know anyone had used that expression before Fitzgerald. 'Dark night of the soul. It's always three o'clock in the morning.' Something like that." The professor had grown ruminative.

"It often did feel like three a.m."

"What was the longest amount of time you can recall being locked in there?"

"I spent whole nights a couple of times."

"What did you think about?"

Now, in the dark night of the hut, he tried to recall what he had thought about, because as horrible as those nights were, they were a hell of a lot less frightening than this. And he wasn't concerned he had only one functioning kidney and the nose of a monster.

Mostly, he supposed, as a boy he had thought how unfair life was. How much he hated his parents, but how he hated his mother far more. He contemplated what would happen if he ruined the coats and boots and shoes in there by peeing on them like a cat. But he never did, because who knew what punishments Glenda Stepanov could invent that were worse (far worse) and that Roman Stepanov would tolerate because he just didn't give a damn? When he was first tossed into the closet, there had always been a sliver of light along the top of the two doors—not along the bottom because of the plush entryway carpet, and not where the two doors met because they met perfectly—and he knew as boy that the deep creepiness would really began later when his parents went to sleep and turned off the hall light. Because then that sliver of light would be gone, the last of the sun surrendering to the horizon and the sky utterly moonless. That was the dark night of the soul, where he would curl into a ball and shiver and cry until, somehow, eventually he would fall asleep.

When he self-diagnosed his own demons, he attributed his fear of flying to that closet. It wasn't really about being five miles off the ground, it wasn't the idea of traveling 550 miles an hour; it was about being trapped in a metal tube from which there was no escape. It was about claustrophobia.

At the moment, he was trying to remain sane and calm by thinking of his little boy, Marc. It took his mind off the relentless susurrus of the Serengeti's infinite array of vermin and bugs, and the pounding ache in his nose. Every breath sounded like a wheeze when he tried to inhale with his mouth shut, as if he himself were but one more of the myriad species of insects in and around the boma. He tried to move chronologically, finding memories from the moment the boy was born until the afternoon when Billy had dropped him off at his mother's house a couple of days before leaving with Margie for Africa. It was the last time he had seen him. He had taken the child to see *Mary Poppins* that day. His son had seen it with his mother when it had first premiered in August, but he'd loved it, and so Billy had taken him to it again. Billy hadn't seen it then, but he'd been inundated by the commercials and the billboards and he'd read the reviews, and so he knew what to expect. The cinema had been almost empty because the movie had been out for months, but that meant that Marc, who was only four years old and about three and a half feet tall, had had an unobstructed view of the screen, and they had been able to sit smack in the middle of the theater. Billy found himself focusing now on the scene in which Dick Van Dyke was dancing with the animated penguins, and he supposed that his mind was going there because penguins were wild animals and he was in a world of wild animals.

But the worst of the wild animals? The humans. The people who had kidnapped him. Perhaps they could be reasoned with—unlike a charging rhino or a hungry lioness—but they were at least as dangerous. And they were senselessly cruel. A lioness hunted to feed her family, and put its victims out of their misery quickly. Not so these men. They were just torturing them all.

He also passed the time in the hut by counting. There were sixty seconds in a minute, so every time he managed to count to six hundred without losing track, another ten minutes had elapsed.

They'd brought him a tin cup with some rice and beans and a little water for dinner, but he had no idea whether that was two hours ago or a mere forty-five minutes. They no longer had his wrists and ankles bound, but the luminescence on his watch hands was now gone, and so he couldn't make out the face. That was the other thing about the dark: it crippled a person's ability to gauge time, because the light never changed. He considered going to the entrance and peering out into the boma—surely, he'd be able to read the watch there—but they'd told him to stay where he was. He knew there was a guard outside. Was knowing the exact time worth pissing them off and getting tied up again? Nope. Absolutely not. He didn't think he could stand that.

And that supposed that tying him up was all that they did.

The one who'd brought him his rice and beans had joked that he should make a run for it in the night. He'd be better off getting shot in the boma trying to escape, because at least then he wouldn't be eaten alive.

Still, as he sat alone in the dark he imagined himself using that tin cup to dig his way under the wall of the hut. Isn't that what they did in *The Great Escape*? He'd emerge before dawn, maybe, and then he would . . .

He had no idea what he would do. Just none. He sure as hell wouldn't have a motorcycle waiting for him à la Steve McQueen.

And then, of course, there were Margie and Katie. He couldn't stop worrying about them. The fellow had reassured him that his wife and his sister were fine, as were David and Terrance.

"Can I see them?" he'd asked when the Russian had brought him his food. His voice sounded like he had a stuffy nose.

"No."

"But—"

"It's like you don't trust me," the guy had said. He was smirking, and Billy knew not to press. But the gunshots and the car engines had left him deeply unnerved, even when the fellow had promised him that the noises had been nothing, nothing at all.

And so Billy counted and thought of his little boy and the cartoon penguins, and just like in that closet, his own personal— fuck that professor—oubliette, eventually he fell asleep.

.   .   .

"So, the coaster had all this condensation on it from my soda. My apartment was an inferno and the ice melted, and when I picked up the glass, all these drops of water just cascaded onto the photo of my mom, and it was wrecked. Blotchy and smeared. And I was weeping and couldn't stop," the woman was saying to Billy. The recollection alone had the patient's eyes filming up, and he handed her the box of tissues. The cardboard design had big, garish daisies. Suddenly this spring, everything had big, garish flowers of one sort or another. Wallpaper. Album covers. Tissue boxes.

"I mean, my mother was the sweetest woman on the planet," she went on. "I loved her so much. She loved me so much. You know what that's like."

"I do," Billy lied.

"And that picture of her was going to be on the funeral card, and now it was worthless. And it was all my fault."

He didn't remind her that the loss of the photo was a bearable disappointment; that death tended to pervert one's view of the world, at least until the grief had begun to taper to mourning. Instead he said, his tone ruminative, "I suppose it felt rather like you had lost her again."

She blew her nose. "Yes. Exactly."

"Did you find another photo?"

"I did. It wasn't as perfect."

"Were your brothers upset about it?"

"No. They didn't even know that I'd been careless and ruined my first choice." She sat up. Her internal clock knew that their time was winding down. She used her middle fingers on each hand to push identical locks of cinnamon-colored hair back behind her ears, and then brushed her hands across her skirt. She was fine. Or she would be fine. It never ceased to amaze him how fucked up he was compared to the people he cared for. She reached into her purse and handed him the picture that she felt she had ruined. For a moment he was surprised she carried it with her, but then, no: it was inevitable that she would. She carried with her guilt and shame and disappointment the way most people carried car keys and wallets. He noticed that one of the drops had landed squarely on her mother's face, but he still had the sense that the woman had been very pretty. She was wearing a cardigan and holding a bouquet of tulips—yellow, he suspected, but that was conjecture because the photo was black and white—and they reminded him of the flowers that his first wife had carried when they had been married. The photo, Billy supposed, was from the 1920s.

He thanked her when he handed it back to her, and after she was gone, he went to his office desk and pulled out the wedding picture from his first marriage. The divorce had been amicable; he was still friends with Amelia. More or less. He saw her often because of Marc. But she fell out of love with him when she fell hard for another professor at UCLA. When they'd been married, she had hated more and more each month the way their lives were increasingly linked to Katie's, and what Amelia referred to dismissively as that whole Hollywood cabal. They were an inside, gated world, she said, one that depended upon the neediness of places like Rockville, Illinois (where Amelia had been born and where her parents and siblings still lived). When he pushed back that UCLA was the epitome of an ivory tower, she'd asked him if it ever creeped him out that every time his kid sister was in public, strangers' eyes would slither over her like spiders. They craved her: her beauty, her money, her status. And she ate it up, Amelia insisted. They all did. Actors and actresses. They devoured their fans' longing. It was the air that they breathed and the food that they ate. He defended Katie because Katie wasn't like that, not at all, but he had to admit that narcissism and self-importance marked a lot of the business. It was the armor that lots of actors and actresses wore, because the only thing *Movie Star Confidential* liked more than a movie star at the top of his game was one who had fallen hard off that pedestal and shattered into a million squalid pieces. God, to catch Katie Barstow out and about without makeup? It was like spotting a rare and exotic bird landing on the handle of your shopping cart in the parking lot while you tossed your grocery bags into the back seat of your car.

He supposed he was at least as responsible for the marriage burning out as Amelia. It wasn't that the professor was so magnetic; it wasn't that he himself was so repellent. But, Billy knew, back then he had not been especially communicative. He knew now he should have listened more and he should have talked more. Amelia said he was—and this was the expression she used—shut down. She said he was so shut down that some days it was like living with a stranger. She never knew what he was thinking and he never told her when she pressed. They'd been married two years one day when Katie was visiting, and his sister had kissed six-month-old Marc and said something silly about how he'd never be locked in a closet, no, never, and Amelia had asked her what in the name of holy hell she was talking about. Until that moment, Billy had never, ever told Amelia about the closet.

· · ·

It was still dark inside the hut when they came for him, waking him roughly, but when they brought him out into the boma, he saw the morning sky was rolling in like the tide. There was a shimmering band of orange to the east, and for a moment he studied the silhouettes of tree branches, some pendulous and some haggard, all potentially lethal. You just never knew here.

He could see by the light of the fire in the center of the boma that Terrance had been beaten too, his eyes slits, one cheek swollen, and a gash on his chin. Had he ever played a boxer? If so, his was that face after a fifteen-round TKO. But Katie, thank God, looked fine. Tired and scared, but it didn't look like she had been hurt. Neither she nor Terrance was bound, and Billy was relieved that they didn't seem to have any plans to tie him

up again, either. The guard told him not to speak—not to say
one single word. Billy nodded, supposing that Margie and David
would be escorted from their huts any second now, but when a
minute or two had passed and there was no sign of his wife or
his friend, he started to grow anxious.

"Where's Margie?" he asked. "And David?"

Instead of answering him—or, perhaps, it was an answer—
the creep jabbed him in his back with the butt of his rifle, hitting with surgical precision the spot that was most wounded and
tender, and sending him to his knees with a gasp. He looked up,
a beaten dog, confused, and one of the other Russians came over
to him and squatted like a baseball catcher in front of him. He
spoke very quietly.

"Your wife is fine. But she had a miscarriage. She's safe. She's
in a house outside the reserve with running water and clean
sheets. Do you understand?"

He absorbed the news: his wife was alive, their baby was
gone. The kid. No, the kid wasn't gone. Gone was the wrong
word. The kid was dead.

But Margie was safe. No, she was alive. Again, words. There
was a difference, and the difference mattered. She wasn't safe.
None of them were safe. "You're sure she's okay?" he asked, the
short sentence catching in his throat.

"Yes. Completely sure."

"But the baby—"

"The baby's dead."

He thought how he'd never told Marc that he had a half
sibling on the way. He hadn't told his ex-wife yet, either. He felt
another of those ripples of pain in his back that caused him to
grimace, and the Russian seemed to mistake the flinch for grief.
"Be a man, Billy Stepanov," he said. "You can have another
baby when you get home."

"It was my back," Billy said defensively, but now he was sniffling back tears. He didn't want to cry, but he could feel the tears

rising up inside him as readily as the bubbles floated up from the bottom of Katie's pool when he and Marc had played there just a couple of months ago and made faces at each other underwater.

"I see."

"And David?" Billy asked, fighting hard not to choke when he voiced those three short syllables.

"We had to shoot him. He's dead too." The Russian spoke so casually that the awfulness of the revelation took a moment to register. He'd revealed the fact that they'd murdered David Hill—Billy's brother-in-law and his oldest friend, a boy he'd grown up with in New York City—with the same offhand ease an airline gate agent might tell a passenger they'd be boarding the plane a few minutes late.

"Why?" Billy stammered, but now he was weeping. He could feel the wetness on his cheeks and his nose was a melting glacier, as his earlier conjecture came back to him: perhaps this whole thing hadn't begun because Katie was a movie star. David's father was CIA. So, perhaps, David himself was, too, the son joining the "family business" just as Katie had. And these Russians knew about David and that was really what mattered. Billy recalled that Russian defector. Nina Whatever. The painter. Maybe David or David's father had orchestrated the defection, and this was some sort of payback.

Either way, now his friend was gone. Just . . . gone.

"Why?" the Russian repeated, his tone calm and Socratic. "Because he did something stupid. But, to be honest, he was always going to be an inconvenience. I have a feeling he didn't know enough about the things that might have made him valuable alive and knew too much about things that made him too dangerous to live."

Billy looked across the boma at his sister, and it was clear that she had absolutely no idea. Her hair was even brushed. But, still, he had to ask. He had to be sure. He sniffed back a runnel of mucus and gathered himself as best he could. "Does Katie—"

"No. Your sister doesn't know. It didn't make sense to tell her since she needed to look her best for a Polaroid picture. She needed to be happy to write a note for us."

"A note saying—"

"Saying you would all like to go home, so please pay the fucking ransom."

"And Terrance? Did you tell him?"

"Your Black actor friend? Yes, he does know. And he has been instructed—as I am instructing you—not to tell your sister. Are we clear, Billy Stepanov?"

He rubbed his eyes and wiped his face with his fingers. "Where does she think David is?"

The guy was exasperated, and for a moment Billy cowered like a dog that feared a beating, a mendicant about to be rebuffed. But the Russian just rolled his eyes. "With Margie Stepanov," he said. "With your wife. This morning I told Katie that her husband had a fever and we wanted to take care of it before it became something serious. We told her that we sent him to the same safe house as your wife, where one of our doctors can look after both of them."

"One of your doctors?" He was incredulous.

"Yes."

"And she believed that?"

"She did."

"And why are you telling me the . . . the truth."

"Because your actor friend over there saw me shoot him."

"Terrance looks—"

"Terrance Dutton managed to get a gun. We got it back."

"But David? You killed David."

"And, if you keep talking, we will kill you."

The Russian stood up and put his hands on his knees. "When things are really bad—and things are really bad, Billy Stepanov, for all of you and for all of us—you start lying to yourself. You're some kind of head doctor, right? You know that. So, don't worry about your sister: she thinks her husband is alive. And it is in your interest to make sure that she continues to believe that fairy tale, too."

He was still crying. Not sobbing, at least. But he was still snuffling back snot and wiping away tears. He had managed to still his shoulders. But these people. How many had they killed? There were the rangers and Juma back at the camp, and now David and the kid. Yes, the kid was their fault, too: Margie would not have had the miscarriage were it not for this kidnapping. And he had no idea where Reggie and Carmen and Felix and Peter were. For all he knew, this Russian bastard was lying to him, and his wife was—

And that was the moment when he began to doubt that Margie was still alive, too. Maybe believing that it was only a miscarriage—*only* a miscarriage—was denial on his part.

"Cooper?"

The Russian who'd been talking to him turned around and waited. The fellow who'd spoken was the captor who was guarding Terrance and Katie.

"What?"

"On the radio. We picked up some conversation. It's not good. Some rangers found Shepard's Land Rover. Shepard was dead—eaten—and the Americans have disappeared. And—"

The fellow in charge cut him off and walked the guard a few feet away. They continued their conversation in Russian, but Billy, despite his despair at the death of the kid and David, despite his anguish that Margie was gone and might very well be dead, too, had not missed the three salient facts that had just been shared: the Land Rover that once held Reggie Stout, Felix Demeter, and Carmen Tedesco had been abandoned; someone named Shepard—likely one of their abductors—had been devoured by wild animals; and the other Americans had vanished.

He wasn't sure if their absence gave him hope or left him further wrecked.

CHAPTER TWENTY-FIVE

Carmen Tedesco

"I'm a fighter. I don't necessarily play fighters. But I know who I am and I know what it took to get where I am," Carmen told us. "So, every day I put on my big girl pants and I put on my big girl lipstick and I do what it takes. I do the work. When that camera's red light goes on, I'm ready."

—*The Hollywood Reporter,* JULY 1963

It had been hours now since the sky had grown from orange to blue, and they sat on the ground in the shade of the dead baobab. It was almost eleven in the morning, and, mostly, the vultures were keeping their distance. A half dozen were riding the currents of wind above them in a fashion that suggested they were having fun—they were gliding, their wings only occasionally flapping—but Carmen knew was more likely work. The birds were watching them, appraising them, waiting it out; they were waiting for one or both of the humans to die. Two of the vultures, however, were more brazen: they landed about fifty yards away, and Carmen imagined them as a human couple back home, passive-aggressively cooling their heels while the wait staff set their table at Musso and Frank.

"The Swahili word for lion is *simba*," Reggie was saying. She looked over at him. His eyes were hooded now against the sun and the pain. Against the exhaustion. His voice was soft. "What's lioness?"

"I don't know," she said. Then, afraid she had sounded curt, she added, "I'm sorry."

"Don't be sorry. It's just that your knowledge of things always surprises me."

"Why do you ask?"

"Because, Carmen, you're a lioness."

"I'm not. Katie—"

"No. You are. I say that with reverence and awe."

She smiled at him. At the compliment. She didn't think she deserved it and, when she felt her eyes welling up, looked away. The heat rising up from the dust made the great herd of zebras and wildebeest in the distance glisten; they grazed, the landscape slightly out of focus, the zebras' striping rippling in the incandescent air. A cinematographer or DP would either fix that or use that.

"What do you think? Are they Egyptian or lappet? The vultures?" he asked.

"I don't know that either."

"I think there are binoculars in the knapsack."

She didn't give a damn what the hell kind of vultures they were, but she didn't want to be contrary. Reggie was kind and courageous, and now he was curious. And so she went to the pack and retrieved them.

"I think they're Ruppell's," she told him, though she was only seeing them with her one good eye. "Ruppell's vulture."

He didn't say anything. She was sure he would tease her for knowing the species of vulture that was waiting for them to die. But it really wasn't all that difficult: the Ruppell's had a long white, almost swan-like neck and a white head. Muema had taught her that. He had taught the whole group that. Finally, after she had put the binoculars away, he murmured, *"Mbili."*

She worried that he was speaking nonsense. "What was that?" she asked.

"Mbili. It's the Swahili word for two. I was thinking of those

two critters who've landed. The pair that is already sidling up to the lunch counter."

She was relieved. He wasn't delirious. Just morbid.

When she'd been returning the binoculars to the knapsack, she noticed the aspirin and now she was torn. A part of her wanted to offer him some more, but another part of her feared overdosing him. He'd been popping them like M&M's, it seemed. Still, maybe that was a better way to end this. She just didn't know what it was like to die from an aspirin overdose. That might be even worse than what he was enduring now.

She'd managed to stop the bleeding in the night, but the bones in his forearm were gravel, and there was nothing to be done but douse the mangled flesh with eyewash, empty the tube of Germolene on it, and then wrap it in gauze and tape. Still, he'd lost so much blood. And a hyena bite? God, there was clearly going to be an infection, despite the antiseptic she had slathered on the wound like toothpaste.

It might very well be the infection that killed him before they both were eaten. She supposed that could happen before they died of hunger or thirst. She just didn't know.

Something spooked the vultures that had been sitting on the ground, and like two ballerinas they rose up and into the air. The birds flew across the sun, and when they were past it and she could watch them again, for a brief second one reminded her of a plane. An airplane.

God, imagine if an airplane spotted them and came to their rescue. Right now. Swooped down from that magnificent azure sky and scattered the zebras and wildebeest and those fucking vultures as it landed. And a pilot and a ranger raced over to them and carted them off to a hospital, where a doctor might not be able to repair Reggie's arm but could at least save his life.

Yes, that's what they needed. A goddamn airplane.

Which wasn't coming. Oh, they were out looking for them

by now—someone was—but two little people beneath a bao-bab? They were as obvious as a pair of dung beetles.

And that's when it dawned on her. She wasn't Margot in "The Short Happy Life of Francis Macomber." She had the wrong Hemingway story and the wrong woman. She was Helen from "The Snows of Kilimanjaro," watching as Harry went in and out of consciousness before dying, and she waited for the airplane that was never going to come.

.   .   .

Carmen watched Felix study the itinerary that Katie Barstow's travel agent had put together in consultation with some guide and outfitter—a hunter, really—named Charlie Patton. His eyes narrowed, and he ran his fingers over the map of the Serengeti she had placed on the kitchen table. Finally, he looked up at her and said, "God, we're going to be living in a Frankie Avalon movie."

"What?"

"*Guns of Africa*. Last year. That—"

"*Drums of Africa*," she said, correcting him. She was still in her nightgown, her hips against the kitchen counter. She reached for the percolator and poured herself a second cup of coffee. "And, no, I don't think this will be anything like that. I don't expect there will be slave traders."

"Is that what that movie was about? When I saw the preview with Avalon and the chimp, I just—"

"I told you: you'd like Frankie if you met him. He's a good sort."

"I just don't see why so many singers think they can act. I mean, I don't suppose I could write a history of the Civil War because I can write a screenplay. Totally different skill sets."

"Be nice. The world needs B movies. They keep a lot of people working." At the very last moment, she had said the word *people* instead of the word *us*. Thank God, she had caught herself. Felix would have heard *us* to mean *you*. *Him*. Quickly she continued, "I mean, did they even film that in Africa? I heard they used mostly stock footage of animals. This safari is a Katie Barstow production. I promise you, it will be nothing like that movie. A-plus fare all the way. Every facet."

He rolled his eyes and mimicked the line from the coming attraction that had been a running joke between them in the days after they'd seen the trailer. " 'When he kissed me, my whole world came alive.' Remember? I nearly spit my soda when Mariette Hartley had to say that. You know, don't you, that the writer behind that drivel also gave us *Reefer Madness* and—"

"The safari will be fun," she said.

"When I kiss you in Africa, will your whole world come alive?"

"Yes. I promise. My whole world will come alive."

"Seriously, do we have sex in tents?" He tried to look rakish, but the very fact that he had phrased it as a question made it sound only puerile.

"If we have sex, yes, it will be in a tent."

"If? We'll be gone a long time."

"Look at the itinerary. That hotel in Nairobi is pretty darn swank. We have a night there at the beginning and another one at the end."

"We'll be exhausted that first night. We will have just been on eleven flights."

"Are we really discussing when we're going to have sex next month? You're going on a safari, Felix! You're going for free! You're getting first-class accommodations—"

"Not first class on the flights from Paris to Nairobi."

"You are such a child sometimes," she told him, but she kept her voice playful.

"I guess." He folded the map once and then twice. It was a small map. "But if I really wanted to see lions, I'd just go to the zoo. And when you see lions at the zoo, you don't have to worry they're going to charge you and eat you."

"Oh, please. These days, a safari is like a long, elegant picnic. Nothing's going to eat you and no one's going to shoot you."

"You're sure?" He wasn't actually frightened. He just didn't want to go and was being obstinate and silly.

She put down her coffee and massaged his neck and his shoulders, kneading the muscles there. "I'm positive," she reassured him. "And when we get back to the hotel in Nairobi, you'll be so glad you went."

"And Peter Merrick will be there," he said, rolling his head, his voice mellowing. She knew, even without seeing, that his eyes were closed. "And Reggie Stout. And Katie. So, it won't be a total waste of time. Who knows? Maybe we can drum up some work. Or get a good story about us in the trades."

"Yes," she said sarcastically. "That's why we're going all the way to Africa. So the *Hollywood Reporter* or the *Los Angeles Times* will write about us."

"Well, if they do, it will sure as hell make it worthwhile. As long as we don't get eaten. Or shot. We wouldn't want the story to be about that."

"No," she agreed, leaning over and kissing the top of his head. "We wouldn't want that."

.   .   .

Had she really told Felix that no one was going to get eaten? No one was going to get shot? She had. God, she had. They'd really made jokes about such things.

She looked over at Reggie, and saw that his chin had fallen against his chest. She'd put his safari hat back on his head, despite the fact that a part of the brim had been eaten. They'd moved to the opposite side of the tree so the smell of the dead hyenas wasn't quite so pungent and they didn't have to watch the vultures pick their bodies apart. It seemed the jackals were keeping their distance from the carrion because of the proximity of the humans, but the vultures—five of them devouring the two hyenas—didn't seem to give a damn anymore, so long as the people remained still on the opposite side of the great baobab.

Just in case, on the off chance that there was a plane out there, she decided she had to start a fire. Otherwise, they were invisible from the air. Yes, a fire might alert their kidnappers, too, but she and Reggie were both dead if they didn't get help. She supposed a little plane could land easily here. They were west of the forests that climbed up toward the Great Rift. Far away there were hummocks, some the size of the studio warehouses back in Burbank, but the two of them were hunkered down amid a baobab and a couple of acacia trees. This earth? It really was flat. It was flat and thirsty.

It was noon now, and she had the rifle across her lap. They had no cartridges for the pistol. Reggie had apologized that he hadn't searched the wrecked Land Rover more thoroughly, but she'd reminded him that he'd salvaged it pretty damn well. She'd called him a pirate to try and make him laugh. A scavenger. He'd smiled and murmured that a peg leg and a hook for a hand were about what he had; he'd added that it was she, however, who'd earned the eye patch. That had been maybe an hour after dawn.

"I'm going to start a fire," she said to him. It was really just a way to see if he was awake. Even if he thought it a bad idea, he wouldn't stop her. Still, to do nothing was merely biding their time before the grim reaper—who usually wasted no time out here on the savanna, but was pitilessly slow moving now that they were wounded and sick—came for them. But he didn't say anything, and she found herself watching him carefully to be sure he was breathing. He was. Thank God. She didn't see any new blood discoloring the gauze on his arm.

She pushed herself to her feet and surveyed the grass. She wasn't sure how to build a fire. Two of the nights on the safari, the porters had pulled smudge pots from the lorries and used them instead of crafting a pyre from toothbrush trees, acacia, and strangle figs. But she didn't have a smudge pot. She didn't have kerosene. She had a lighter (two, as a matter of fact) and whatever brush she could find.

Which was when it hit her. Their baobab was dead. It was a considerable tree. If she could get it to ignite, it would burn like that fucking funeral boat at the end of *The Vikings*. The ship with the corpse of Kirk Douglas's character. Of course, that boat had been set ablaze by dozens of cliffside archers, and there'd been that gorgeous sail that caught fire. (Actually, she knew, it had been set ablaze by pyrotechnicians and a special-effects guru. But the archers had been a nice touch, what her father-in-law liked to call "a movie moment." Classic and magic.)

The gamble was that if no one spotted the fire, they'd both be spending the night here on the ground. In the open.

But this baobab was all fuel, if she could round up sufficient kindling.

She could. She would. She rose, and the vultures flew off. Not far. They never went far when she stood or moved suddenly. They landed about twenty yards away. She looked around and made a plan. She'd round up all the grass and brush she could rip from this arid soil, and then she and Reggie would move to the acacia in the distance and she would burn the baobab to the ground.

That assumed, of course, that Reggie could walk.

Or was even still alive.

CHAPTER TWENTY-SIX

Terrance Dutton

As many as three hundred Americans and Belgians are still held hostage at the Victoria Hotel in Stanleyville. The Simba leaders insist they are being treated well, but no one here has forgotten the cruelties inflicted on the nuns who were taken hostage only last month. Meanwhile, whites continue to flee the Eastern Congo, sometimes passing a gauntlet of Russian and even Cuban soldiers, who are aiding the rebels.

—*Los Angeles Times,* NOVEMBER 20, 1964

And now there are three of us, Terrance thought. Katie and Billy and me. David was dead and Margie was gone, likely dead too, and who the hell knew what had happened to everyone else. Billy had managed to share with him the news that the Russian captor calling himself Shepard was dead and the Americans in his care had disappeared. Rangers had found the Land Rover.

The fact that he had to withhold from Katie the reality that her husband was dead was easier than he had expected. It wasn't because he was so bloody talented. It was simply because they weren't supposed to speak—though they did occasionally whisper a word or two to each other, and their captors seemed willing to tolerate the occasional murmurs—and he was so beaten up that he wasn't sure what words would even sound like if he opened his mouth and attempted to speak above a murmur.

Also, his head hurt. His whole fucking body ached. And they all reeked. Their breath was toxic, and their clothing was wet with their sweat and, he supposed, some measure of urine and shit. He was seething.

They were back in the Land Rover and driving west. Southwest, he suspected. They were still in Maasai country, but he expected soon there would be signs of colonial civilization. They were on hard-packed dirt now: not pavement, but what was clearly a road that was used with some frequency. He knew roughly where in the Serengeti they were when they were abducted, and while the reserve was vast, it wasn't endless. Eventually they would reach either the Congo or whatever the hell was that secessionist part of the Congo. It began with a *K,* but that's all he could recall at the moment. In October, the rebels had taken a bunch of nuns hostage. He thought that had occurred in Stanleyville. But Stanleyville was impossibly far away: he knew that from the map that had hung behind glass in the lobby in the hotel in Nairobi. No, they weren't going to Stanleyville. Perhaps they weren't even going to the Congo. This was all conjecture.

He was in the third row, with the Russian who'd commandeered the name Glenn behind him. Billy and Katie were in the second row ahead of him. No one would tell them their destination, but he'd heard Katie whisper to her brother that she prayed it was the safe house with David and Margie. The idea that she could harbor such a hope broke his heart. The reality that they were siblings devastated him too, though he couldn't quite articulate why in his mind. Was it because their mother might lose both of her children? Perhaps. He supposed even the likes of Glenda Stepanov cared for her young. But there was more to it than that. It was because both siblings were fundamentally good people, despite their upbringing; nature had kicked the shit out of nurture in the Stepanov household.

He looked out the window and saw a body of water in the

distance, to the north. It looked substantial, and his first thought was that it was Lake Victoria. But he really had no idea. Before they left Nairobi, Charlie Patton had given them all crappy little black-and-white maps of the reserve, and the lake had been in the upper-left-hand corner. Still, the water could be anything. A wide river. A different lake. He noted there were neither buildings nor signs of mining operations.

Which was when the Land Rover bounced like a plane in an air pocket and he heard a pop and something metallic snapping, and the vehicle tilted and swerved. For a split second, he feared it was going to roll over. At first he thought it was a gunshot and, along with Katie and Billy, he ducked. But when the driver cursed and Glenn laughed at the panicked reaction of the three Americans, he realized it was something else. The vehicle slowed to a stop, half on and half off the hard-packed dirt track.

He looked up, and even though their abductors were speaking Russian, it was clear what had happened. They had a flat tire and something worse. He glanced out the back of the Land Rover at a deep fissure that ran across the road. The chasm had, he suspected, snapped the rear axle. Their driver got out and stood staring at the leaning vehicle with his hands on his hips.

Cooper, the one with the blue eyes who was in charge of this madness, was exasperated. He climbed from the front passenger seat and stood beside the driver. Then he said something to Glenn, and Glenn began to escort the Americans from the vehicle at gunpoint.

.   .   .

The five of them were drinking in the dusky light at the bar of the West Hollywood hotel where Eva Monley and Judy Caponigro were staying, the Chateau Marmont. Joining the two women, who had flown in from Nairobi only the day before, were Katie and David and Terrance. They were seated on stools

around a high-top table with a red candle in a hurricane glass
in the center, as well as an art deco ashtray with a naked water
nymph that seemed to have mistaken the tray for a pond.

Eva had just turned forty, and she'd been working as a location scout, script supervisor, and production manager on films
set in Africa for a decade and a half, including *King Solomon's
Mines* and *The African Queen.* Last year she'd shifted gears and
worked with Preminger on his epic *The Cardinal,* which was
set (it seemed) on every continent except Africa. Judy, a little
younger, was an actress who might have been a very big star—
Terrance knew that she was often compared to Gina Lollo-
brigida, and he saw it in her wonderful sultry eyes, and that
thick mane of (tonight) umber-colored hair—but after she went
to Kenya to film *The Missionaries,* her priorities changed. She
fell in love with Nairobi and put down roots there. Kept her
last name professionally, Caponigro, but married a Brit who had
acres and acres of coffee plants. She still worked, just not often
and not in the sorts of leading roles casting agents might have
expected of her once upon a time. It was rumored that both Eva
and Judy had been lovers of Robert Ruark, a big-game hunter
and novelist whose fame was so evident—at least in the minds of
his publishers—that some of his books used only his last name
on the front cover and spine, the type so elephantine it dwarfed
the titles. Katie Barstow had heard the two women were in
town at the behest of Preminger, who was contemplating a new
adaptation of Conrad's *Heart of Darkness.* She invited them for
drinks because next month was her honeymoon safari and she
thought it would be interesting to hear what Monley and Caponigro had to say about the "situation" right now in East Africa.
(*Situation* was the word that was sometimes used by the press, a
polite euphemism for upheaval and slaughter.)

Over the summer, Katie had told Terrance a little bit about
what David's father did: something heroic (or at least important)
with the OSS in World War II. Now he was with the Foreign

Service, whatever that was, and David's parents had moved to the capital. She'd said that David's father had expressed some reservations when David had outlined the safari itinerary, but he hadn't been sufficiently alarmed to encourage them to postpone the trip or change their plan. And, Terrance supposed, David's father would know. Nevertheless, Katie thought it would be worthwhile getting reconnaissance from two people who had spent serious time in East Africa.

"Kenya isn't the Congo," Judy was telling them. She pulled an olive from her martini and popped it into her mouth. "And neither is Tanganyika. Good Lord, the Serengeti is nothing like the Congo. Tanganyika is as safe as, I don't know, Canada. I've even flown in and out of that new airport in Kilimanjaro."

"My travel agent has us flying into Nairobi," Katie said. "He didn't trust that airport. I gather Pan Am doesn't either."

"It isn't L.A. International, but it was fine. I felt perfectly safe. Long paved runway, a tower, a decent bar. What more do you need?"

"But wasn't that the airport that a bunch of Tanganyika soldiers took over in January or February?" David asked. There was an eddy in his tone that left Terrance wondering if David knew something about the situation in East Africa that the others didn't. Something clandestine. "According to my father—"

"No," Judy corrected him. "That was Dar es Salaam. And it was January and it really wasn't a big deal. They wanted better pay, that's all. Nyerere—the new president—appealed to the British for some commandos, and it was over in hours. What does your father do?"

"He's a Washington, D.C., paper pusher. Government. Personnel. Nothing interesting."

"Well, Washington has a very jaded view of East Africa," Judy said. "I suppose people there see it all through the prism of the 'Soviet threat.'"

David seemed to take this in, stirring his gin and tonic with his pinky. He licked his finger and then pressed, "Okay, the Congo. What do you two know about the rebellion there? Those stories about what the Simbas did to the nuns were sickening."

"They should sicken you. They should sicken anyone," observed Eva.

"But not going to Kenya or the Serengeti because of the nightmare in Stanleyville would be like not going to Chicago because there's violence in Montreal," Judy reassured them.

"Or steering clear of Madrid because someone was kidnapped in Paris," added Eva.

"The Congo may get caught up in the Cold War, but I don't see Nyerere allowing that to happen in Tanganyika," Judy said.

Out of the corner of his eye, Terrance saw a woman pulling a Kodak with a black wrist strap from her purse and wondered if she'd take a photo of Katie. Of them. She'd need to attach a flashcube to the camera. She was with another woman and two other men, and he supposed they were tourists. "I hear the Soviets are back. I read in the paper they left a few years ago, but now they've returned," he said.

"David used the word *rebellion,* and I guess that's fine," Judy told them. "But it seems to me, it's more like a civil war."

"Judy's right," Eva agreed.

"And the Russians?" Terrance asked.

"They're there. But not in big numbers. And they're not what you'd expect."

"I've never met a Russian soldier," Terrance told Eva. "I have no expectations."

"Very sophisticated—the ones in the Congo. Cosmopolitan. At least that's what I understand. Advisers, mostly. More like spies, some of them. Not a lot of foot soldiers. Educated, erudite, multilingual."

"My father . . ." David began, and then he stopped. Terrance realized Katie's fiancé was a little drunk. Was he catching himself before saying something he shouldn't?

"Go on," said Judy.

"Nothing," he said. He motioned at his drink. "I forgot what I was going to say."

The woman with the camera found a flashcube in her bag and held it up for the others at her table as if it were a gold nugget she'd panned in a river. Terrance watched her stand and approach their high-top. They all stopped talking at her arrival. There was an awkward beat where no one said anything, and then the woman opened her mouth and a tornado of words emerged, one long, sweet run-on sentence that she delivered without, it seemed, ever inhaling for breath.

"My name is Fiona Furst and I am writhing in guilt—really, I can't believe I'm doing this—because I am interrupting you all, but, Miss Barstow, my family has seen most of your movies, I think, really, most of them, maybe all of them. And we are so happy you're going to be married, and you have no idea what it would mean to my daughters to have a photo of you, but I'd only take it if you said it was okay and you didn't mind." Terrance couldn't quite place her accent, despite the ample evidence she had offered, but something about it said Upper Midwest. He thought of his own family in Chicago.

Instantly, Katie said, "Of course. Would you like to be in it?"

Fiona Furst's eyes went wide, and for a second Terrance thought her knees were going to buckle. But then she nodded. "Oh, my God," she said, "oh, my God, yes, yes!" Her reaction sounded almost sexual, and Terrance had to look down at the burnished mahogany of the tabletop to keep a straight face. When he looked up, David was climbing carefully off the barstool and offering to take the picture of the woman and his fiancée. Fiona wasn't sure, it seemed, whether to lean into Katie, and so Katie leaned into her, and there was that smile and the flashcube went off, and David started to return the woman's camera. But Katie stilled his arm and said to Fiona, "You probably couldn't tell from where you were seated, but with me are Terrance Dutton and Judy Caponigro, who you've also seen in movies, I am quite sure, and Eva Monley, who's worked on some films I'd wager you loved a lot. Would you like a picture of all of us?"

Fiona stared around the table. "Oh," she said, "I didn't realize. I just saw you and that meant I didn't see anyone else. I'm so sorry. But, yes, I'd love—"

"Don't be sorry, please," Katie insisted. "Like I said, you didn't know. This is my fiancé, David Hill. Why don't you sit here, where David was sitting?"

"Perfect," said David when Fiona was settled, and then he snapped a second photo. Fiona thanked Katie profusely when she stood, clearly not wanting to overstay her welcome, but Katie told her it was nothing and thanked her, in turn, for watching her movies.

When the woman was back at her table, Eva said, "Katie, that was lovely of you. Very gracious."

Katie shrugged. "It took thirty seconds."

"God, you'll all have so much fun in Africa," Judy told them. "No interlopers. No one is going to want you to pose for pictures."

"No, we'll be the interlopers," said Katie. "We'll be the ones interrupting other animals while they're going about their lives."

David had finished his drink and crunched down hard on a remaining ice cube. "Just want to make sure, Eva. The Congo. In your opinion, could it have any effect on our trip?"

Judy sighed. "David, I have no idea what kinds of papers your father pushes or what he does in personnel. But it seems to me he has you all worked up over nothing. Stop focusing on the fighting in the Congo and start focusing instead on the image of a bunch of giraffes watching you light a cigarette. Or that moment when your guide smashes on the brakes of your Land Rover, because there in the tall grass is a lioness with a couple of her cubs. Or the idea of stopping at some overlook by a river because all of those things you thought were just gray boulders are, in fact, hippopotamuses. There's nothing like Africa. I don't miss America in the slightest when I'm there. The dirty martini at the Fairview in Nairobi is just this civilized"—and here she raised her glass—"but the next day, you can be staring at an elephant the size of the bungalow I have here at the Chateau. I love it."

"And the coffee plantation?" David asked.

Judy sat up straight on her stool and said in an accent that Terrance supposed was meant to sound Danish, "I had a farm in Africa."

Katie looked back and forth at everyone around the table, her face concerned. "Judy, did you and Blair sell the plantation?" Blair was her British husband.

Judy laughed. "No, of course not. I was trying—I guess rather badly—to mimic Isak Dinesen."

"That's the opening sentence of her memoir," Eva elaborated.

Katie looked embarrassed, and David kissed her on her cheek. "I'll get you a copy tomorrow. It'll be fun for you to read before we head out."

Eva clinked her glass against Judy's. "Your accent wasn't bad at all."

"Thank you."

"'Plantation,'" Terrance said, trying out the word as if he had never said it out loud before. But, of course, he had. As a child and a teenager. His great grandparents had been slaves on a . . . plantation.

"It's not like that," Judy said, as if she had read his mind. "Ours isn't, anyway."

"I'm sure it's not," Terrance agreed.

Eva nodded. "Terrance, I can't tell you what you will feel in Kenya or Tanganyika—as a Black man. It's not my place. And I only know you by reputation. But I am always happier there than I am in America. Just like Judy."

"Hear, hear," Judy said.

Terrance gazed for a moment into the flickering candle.

"There are parts of this country I will never set foot in again. Never," he told them. He said it calmly, wistfully. He wasn't angry; it was just a fact of his life. If anything, it made him sad.

"You have no idea the way people attacked Terrance after *Tender Madness*," Katie recalled ruefully.

"You, too," David reminded her. "It's not like that whole press junket was a picnic for you, either."

"No, it wasn't. But I experienced nothing compared to Terrance," Katie corrected him. "I know some people thought it wasn't a particularly savvy career move on my part, but no one threatened me or harassed me the way they did Terrance."

"And the kiss never even made it into the final print," Terrance said, and he shook his head.

"So, there was an actual kiss?" asked Eva.

"There was," Katie said. "There was a love scene."

"Well, of course they had to cut it. They would never have been allowed to show the film south of the Mason-Dixon Line if they'd kept the kiss in," Judy said. Then she turned her attention squarely on Terrance and said, "I'm sorry I used the word *plantation*. Next time, I'll use *farm*."

"No harm, no foul," he reassured her.

"East Africa has a long way to go in very many ways," Eva said. "But in some ways? America has a much longer road ahead—and the potholes are just as dangerous."

.   .   .

"Just a pothole," Katie was saying, as the three Americans stood in the short grass off the dirt track and one of the Russians crawled under the rear of the Land Rover. Terrance wondered if she, too, was recalling their drinks just about a month ago at the Chateau Marmont, the word *pothole* being the association in his mind.

Of course, that wasn't just a pothole that had nearly rolled the vehicle. That was a chasm across the road, and Terrance didn't suppose that the driver, even if he was an auto mechanic, was going to be able to repair the Land Rover. They had a spare tire, but they sure as hell didn't have a spare axle.

Suddenly Billy just sat down. Just collapsed where he was and put his forehead on his steepled knees. Katie knelt beside him and said his name and asked him if he was okay.

"I'm fine," he said. "I'm just tired. I just couldn't stand a second more."

Their guard, Glenn, gazed down at them but kept his rifle at his side. He didn't seem to care that Billy was sitting and Katie was kneeling, and so Terrance sat down, too. He was exhausted. He honestly had no idea whether he was in as bad shape as Billy, but it was a horse race. God, what the two of them must look like to Katie. And, still, she believed that her husband and her sister-in-law were alive.

And, just maybe, Margie really was. But Terrance doubted it.

He licked his lips. He was thirsty, but he didn't know how much water they had. Cooper had to realize that they weren't going anywhere and so whatever water remained, the six of them were going to have to ration.

Cooper wandered over to them, and he and Glenn shared a few words in Russian. Were they discussing the radio in the Land Rover? Terrance supposed it worked, but he had no idea whether it had the power to reach anyone who might help them. Besides, their peers, the pair who had taken Reggie and Felix and Carmen, had disappeared. No, that wasn't precisely right: from what Billy had heard, one was dead and one had disappeared— along with the other Americans. Or he was dead too, and the body was gone. Maybe they were all dead. The whole group.

Of course, there was also that lorry with the porters. Perhaps that was within radio range.

In the distance, he thought he saw a rhinoceros. There might even have been two. They were far enough away that they posed no danger, and Terrance didn't imagine that the Russians had any desire to poach one. Already their kidnapping had gone to hell. And they had no skinners or porters. He was trying to focus on the animals when he heard the fellow working beneath the Land Rover bellow, and Terrance's immediate reaction was that the vehicle had collapsed on the man's legs. That was what he had envisioned.

But it hadn't, and the guy was crawling out from beneath it now, cursing, his right hand on his left forearm, his eyes agog. And then, right behind him, coiling into an S the moment it emerged, came the snake. It paused, watching the humans and deciding whether fight or flight was in order. Terrance knew from the chevrons created by its scales that the snake was a puff adder—Juma had taught them that their first day, when he was going over the predators that were most likely to sneak up on them and kill them—and the son of a bitch who'd been bitten was probably going to be dead within minutes.

CHAPTER TWENTY-SEVEN

Katie Barstow

Dutton, like Poitier, is always a pot on simmer that any moment—with the flick of a wrist—can boil over. That's why I like to see him paired with Katie Barstow versus (for instance) Diahann Carroll, because it makes that Dutton edge even sharper. Suddenly, the movie says something about race, among the pivotal human stories on this continent since white people first arrived, bringing with them Africans in chains, even though there isn't a word in the script about the color of skin.

But it also makes Barstow sharper. Barstow has demonstrated in her best work that she is more than a pretty face: that her blood can run the thermostat from very, very hot to ice cold. My sense is that the real Katie Barstow has inside her as much venom as she has sugar—like the most interesting actors and actresses.

—Los Angeles Times, OCTOBER 15, 1962

The Russian's howls had become pitiable moans as Cooper used twine to wrap a tourniquet around his biceps. He was seated with his back against one of the vehicle's front tires, his legs stretched out before him. Cooper had ripped his shirt off him, and Katie could see clearly how the fellow's forearm had ballooned. Already the swelling was so great that she was reminded of that illustration of the cartoon snake that had eaten the elephant in *The Little Prince*.

The real snake was gone now, but she and Terrance and Billy had all stood. It was as if the savanna was radioactive and sitting on the ground increased one's exposure. Cooper had tried to shoot the adder with his pistol, but he'd missed and the snake had slithered into the brush. The creature's fangs had reminded Katie of a syringe. Scattered in the field around them were baboons, easily a couple of dozen, some watching the humans and some watching their children, and some skittering across the land in a game that Katie suspected might be something like tag. But maybe not. Maybe they were grubbing for seeds and roots. For rodents.

The victim abruptly turned his head away from Cooper and vomited into the dirt track, his whole body hiccuping violently. Katie was no expert on snake bites, but she was a good student and recalled what Juma had taught them that first day: swelling, vomiting, and then death. The bite was excruciating. The victim would succumb to anaphylactic shock, which—if it knocked the person unconscious—was arguably a humane response on the part of the body, because then you might black out before you died.

Katie looked at her brother and Terrance. They were watching the scene before them intently, and she knew what they were thinking. What they both were thinking. Once the guy who'd been bitten by the snake was dead, they'd be two on two. Three on two, if they included her. Right now, only Glenn was holding a gun, though it was some kind of automatic rifle or machine gun that could kill the three of them in seconds.

Cooper finished tying off the tourniquet and said something softly to his patient, an attempt to console or reassure him, when the man's chest convulsed upward and his arms, even the one with the tourniquet, flailed skyward. The spasm surprised Cooper so badly that he jerked back himself. The victim's eyes rolled up and his body started to loll to the side, toward the front of the Land Rover, but Cooper grabbed him before he could topple into the dust. Still, it didn't matter. It was clear. The adder's poison had done its work, and the Russian was gone, as dead as if he'd been shot by the elephant gun that had blown away half of Juma's head.

Which was when, as one, her brother and Terrance dove at Glenn, and so she threw herself at Cooper, who was still cradling the body of his dead comrade, and over her shoulder she heard the other Russian firing his automatic, but she didn't turn around. It wasn't that she was so focused on getting to Cooper before he could unholster his pistol. It was that she didn't dare. She just didn't dare.

. . .

A few days earlier, she had been sitting on the hood of the Land Rover, sipping from a canteen, the sun high overhead and the dust epoxied to her skin by her sweat. Charlie Patton was standing beside her, leaning against the vehicle, as the two of them watched a mother and child elephant amble into the distance. He had a double-barreled rifle in his arms, but no plans to use it. It was merely a precaution. The rest of the herd was strung out along a lengthy line heading south toward a river, and the sight of the two animals had her almost overwhelmed with happiness. Most of the men were lined up along the edge of the blankets where they had stopped for lunch, aiming their cameras at the pair. The group had just finished eating, and the porters were about to pack everything up when Benjamin Kikwete had spotted the elephants. There were probably twenty-five or thirty of them. It was clear they were going to pass within fifty yards of the humans, but it seemed evident that they didn't give a damn that a bunch of people had stopped to eat not far from what they viewed as their highway.

Which was when it clicked for Katie: this hadn't caught Patton off guard. It probably hadn't caught Benjamin off guard. She smiled at the old hunter.

"You're like a carnival barker," she said to him.

"A carnie? Are you really calling me a carnie?"

"I am."

"You grew up in New York City. You live in L.A. Have you ever even been to a carnival?"

"I have."

"Freak shows and all? Bearded ladies, dwarves, ponies the size of puppies?"

"I stuck with the Ferris wheel and the cotton candy and the ring toss, thank you very much."

"Ring toss? Pretty rigged game."

"It is."

"Now why would you suspect me of such tawdriness and manipulation? Do I look like a fraud?" Patton's skin was leather, and the lines around his lips grew deep when he grinned.

"You knew those elephants were coming. They use that trail often, don't they?" she replied. She knew she had busted him. He knew it, too.

"I *hoped* we might see some elephants. But I didn't know it. Big difference." He chuckled and then waved at the elephants with the back of his hand as they meandered across the savanna. "I'm no carnie. If I'm a showman, I'm . . ."

"Go on."

In a tone that balanced both sheepishness and pride, he said, "I'm Walt Disney."

"And this is Disneyland?"

He looked down at his boots. "No. I shouldn't have been so glib just now. This is most assuredly not Disneyland. This is a place where human beings, if they're not careful, are going to die."

"Then what did you mean? The scale of this world?"

He nodded. "Scale, yes. That's a good word for it. Maybe even the best word. There's nothing about this land that's as small as a carnival or as predictable as a carnival."

"Except those elephants. They were as predictable for you as clockwork."

"Not really. I have hunches where we'll see animals. I have

experience. My team"—and he motioned at Juma, who was about ten yards away, pointing at the great pachyderms and explaining something to Carmen and Felix—"teases me about my sixth sense. Maybe I have one. But if I do, it's only because I've been out here so many days and nights over so many years that I know what might happen. But I'm still just hoping to keep a lid on the chaos."

"Was it easier? In the old days? I imagine the groups were smaller when you were hunting."

"No. It was harder. I or someone in my care—a guest or a gun bearer—was more likely to wind up gored or maimed. Devoured. This is easier."

"But not as much fun for you? True? Not as manly?" She regretted the last question the moment the three words had escaped her lips. She had meant it to be flirtatious and light: she was teasing him. But it was a mistake, and for a split second she felt it was the sort of horrific and demeaning thing her mother might say. God, was she channeling Glenda Stepanov?

"Hanging around with Katie Barstow and Terrance Dutton and Carmen Tedesco? How could that not be fun?" he responded, and she thought she had dodged his wrath. She hadn't pressed a bruise, after all. Or he was just being gracious.

"You're a diplomat, Charlie," she said.

"Some mornings, I suppose, it isn't easy for any of us to look in the mirror. Imagine running a fancy-pants gallery in Beverly Hills when your old man fought the Nazis."

So, she had insulted him. There it was. Quickly she backtracked, a courtesy. "Seriously, we can't be easy to manage. I didn't mean anything by that remark. It was stupid. I'm sorry."

But Patton was a hunter, a creature who viewed himself as the very top of the food chain, even if his perch there depended upon a double-barreled .84-caliber rifle. He wasn't easily mollified. And now she had shown him her belly. "Nothing to apologize for," he said. "How is that gallery doing?"

"Thriving," she lied.

Without looking at her, his eyes lost to the shadow of the brim of his hat, he said, "You'll get an Oscar someday. You delivered those two syllables with utter conviction."

"You—"

"I just know you're footing the bill for this dance. That's all I know. And I, Miss Barstow"—and she understood that he had chosen the title because he wanted to denigrate her husband— "overstepped my bounds. Please forgive me." He doffed his safari hat to her and then called over to Benjamin to start rounding up the team. He (and once more Katie thought the words had been chosen for her benefit) wanted to "get this show on the road," a reference to carnivals and traveling road shows.

She felt bad about what she had said, but she was also miffed that Charlie would respond by demeaning David. And she felt something else, the sort of inchoate unease that often precedes a thunderstorm and one attributes merely to the idea that the air is charged. How much did Charlie Patton really know about the finances of David's gallery? And why? It wasn't as if the *Los Angeles Times* or *Curator* or *Galleria* had written about the place's struggles. Art galleries opened and failed all the time. David's hadn't been in the news. Had David been discussing his business travails here with Billy, his oldest friend, and Charlie had overheard something?

Yes, she thought, that had to be it.

The idea that he had failed to escape his worries, even here, dismayed her. She felt a stitch of sadness. And so when she climbed back into the Land Rover—the one that this time did not have Charlie Patton riding shotgun—she took David's hand and squeezed it, ever the faithful, dutiful, and loving wife.

.   .   .

Katie was aware that her fingers were in pain—she had tried to scratch at Cooper's face, to claw him—and somehow they had bent back. He had thrown her off him as if she were a kitten and pulled his pistol from his holster, and she put her arms across her face as she rolled in the dust because she knew he was about to shoot her, but then she heard that automatic again, and Cooper yelled, a thunderous roar. She looked up, and he was holding his right hand with his left, and she could see the blood waterfalling from his palm where once there had been fingers. He'd dropped his pistol, and she crabbed to the weapon and picked it up. She'd held pistols before on movie sets, but never one that was loaded. Not even one that was loaded with blanks. So, while the literal weight of the gun didn't surprise her, the idea that this was a revolver with bullets gave it a heavier, more ominous feel.

She turned around now and there was her brother, standing with the assault rifle, and in his swollen face and half-shut eyes she saw incredulity. Shock. Glenn, the Russian who'd been guarding them, was on the ground too, maybe nine or ten feet away, and he was dead. She could see the way a line of bullets had cut a swath like a bandoleer across his abdomen and chest, turning his khaki shirt red and creating a stream of blood from which a dung beetle was running away like a child from a tsunami. The man's eyes were still open, lifeless and glazed.

Billy ordered Cooper to sit down, but the Russian didn't seem to hear him: he was too focused on the obliteration of his right hand. And so Billy yelled louder this time, demanding he sit down now, and he fired the gun aimlessly, discharging a couple of bullets with the tiniest squeeze of the trigger, at least two of which punched holes in the side of the Land Rover. This time Cooper listened. He sat. And it was then that Katie saw Terrance. His body was half on and half off an anthill the size of a steamer trunk, his life seeping from him in bloody brooks running downhill into the grass from his side and his stomach. She scurried over to him and rolled him onto his back and rested his head in her lap and then, as she and her older brother surveyed the carnage around them—the dead and the dying, and more real blood than all the fake blood she'd ever seen on a set—she wept.

CHAPTER TWENTY-EIGHT

Carmen Tedesco

*"I think the animal I want to see most is the warthog. I once saw
a movie with a couple of baby warthogs playing in a little watering
hole, and they were like puppies," Carmen told us. Imagine: one
week you are Katie Barstow's maid of honor in Beverly Hills, and
the next you are on a safari in beautiful, magical Africa, watching
warthogs frolic in the Serengeti mud. Carmen Tedesco is one lucky
lady.*

—*The Hollywood Reporter,* OCTOBER 1964

The acacia offered as much shade as the baobab, and there were
no animals lounging beneath its canopy or perched like acrobats
upon its branches. The grass was cool, and it would be a fine spot
to wait and watch the baobab burn. She had no idea how long
the fire would last, but she had to hope it would send tendrils
of smoke into the sky for hours. Or that the fates were going to
smile on her now, and a search plane would be in the area at the
precise moment when she needed one most.

The walk here had tired her, which she supposed had mostly
to do with how little she'd eaten or drunk, how weak she was
from her wounds, and the stress from the likelihood that she was
going to die out here. After all, she hadn't walked very far: she
had always been able to see the baobab. But even the rifle felt
heavy on her shoulder or in her arms.

Now she started back, wondering how in the world she would be able to bring Reggie to the acacia. And then, if somehow she could accomplish that task, scavenge sufficient brush and grass to ignite the tree. It just didn't seem possible. And so she thought of that expression, one foot after the other, and told herself that, for now, she would make it back to the baobab and rest there for a few minutes. She could do that. She counted her breaths as she walked and tried to remain alert. She fantasized she was such a good shot that she could bring the rifle to her shoulder and shoot those fucking vultures that were waiting for Reggie—perhaps for Reggie and her both—to die. But that was childish. They were just being vultures, and if she were one of them, she'd probably be salivating over that pair of dying mammals, too. Hyenas and humans. What a feast.

When she reached the baobab, Reggie's chin was against his chest, his back against the trunk, his wrecked arm in his lap. She collapsed beside him and closed her eyes while she caught her breath. She was sweating monstrously.

"How do you feel, my friend?" she asked.

When he said nothing, she wanted to believe he was sleeping. She told herself she might hear a small whistle or snore. She wanted to postpone what she knew in her heart was the truth as long as possible.

"Good enough to fall asleep," she said. "That's something. You need your rest."

How long could she keep up the charade? Oh, until she died, too, she suspected. Until she was too weak to fight off the jackals or hyenas or leopards. The lions.

Maybe she should just put the barrel of the rifle into her mouth and make it quick. She'd been perusing the Hemingway African canon in her mind, so why not end it the way Papa himself had? Then there'd be no chance that she'd feel the pluck and yank as the Ruppell's ate the flesh from her face and her arms.

But, no. She didn't walk all the way to that acacia and back just to give up.

And maybe Reggie really was in a deep sleep. Dreaming of whatever it was that made him happy. At least she hoped they were happy dreams. Not dreams of Okinawa or the Serengeti. She knew that she herself had far more bad dreams than good ones. Dreams of anxiety and failure and postponement. If she lived, she'd have to talk to Billy Stepanov about that. What it meant that the nightmares outnumbered the pleasant dreams, and how that was the case for most people.

God, where was Billy right now? Billy and Margie and Katie and David and Terrance and Peter? Where was Charlie? Were all of them off the reserve and in some safe house somewhere? She supposed that wherever they were, it sure as hell wasn't cushy. It wasn't Katie's place in the hills outside L.A. with that scrumptious swimming pool.

But it also wasn't this.

Finally, she did what she had to do. She reached out her left hand and placed it against Reggie Stout's chest.

And felt nothing.

She ran her fingers up his shirt to his neck and felt the skin there. It was cold. So were his cheeks and his chin beneath his stubble.

She opened her eyes now and lifted his head off his chest. She kissed him. She kissed his dead and lifeless cheek.

"I love you, Reggie," she said. "I love you. We all did."

.   .   .

Carmen watched Reggie bring his chair from behind his desk and place it beside the chrome-and-glass coffee table in his office, opposite the teak couch with the long plaid cushion, on which, it was common knowledge, the publicist would catch forty winks after work before entertaining clients or a reporter at Revolution or Barry O's. His secretary had placed on the table glasses, a pitcher of water, and three cups of coffee. Katie had just returned from London and was talking about Michael Caine, and while Carmen knew there was nothing serious about her friend's infatuation with the young British heartthrob, she was glad that Katie was getting it out of her system here with Reggie Stout, and not when David was present.

"Do you know his real name?" Reggie asked, his tone professorial.

"I don't," said Carmen. "Is it as bad as Tedesco?"

Reggie smiled. "Your name is lovely."

"Hah! You can't imagine how many people have told me I should change it."

"Maurice Micklewhite," Reggie told them. "Maurice Joseph Micklewhite. Junior."

Katie nodded. "An old friend of his we met at the club—a childhood chum—called him Morey."

"How come you kept Tedesco professionally if you don't like it?" Reggie asked Carmen. "Felix is Hollywood royalty. When you married him, you could have become Carmen Demeter. The press would have eaten it up. Catnip."

"Well, it came up. Jean Cummings and I talked about it. But I decided that I already had my career and people knew me. They knew my name. Obviously, not as many as Katie, but enough. I think my parents were a little surprised. I mean, my legal name is Carmen Demeter, of course. My mom thinks it's very weird that I didn't start using that publicly."

Katie turned to her: "Does Felix have hurt feelings?"

"I don't think so."

"And Rex doesn't mind?"

"Rex would feel exploited if I started using the family coin like that. I think the old man feels exploited that his own son uses his name."

Reggie laughed. "That's the Rex I know."

"My parents understood completely why I changed my name," Katie said. "But it was still a source of . . ."

"A source of what?" Carmen pressed.

"A source of something. It was always one more source of"—and she paused as she searched for the right word—"tension between my parents and me. And, as you know, we had plenty already."

Reggie leaned toward them, his elbows on his knees. Carmen could feel his intensity. "Carmen, let me tell you something I once told Katie. Only you know you. Only you know what's inside you. There are no such things as mind readers, and we all have secrets. Oh, people think they know you, and they believe what they want. Look at the stuff *Movie Star Confidential* publishes. Look at the trash people read in the gossip columns. The faster your star shoots across the sky, the more people will want to see it collide with the atmosphere and burn to a billion cinders before it disappears into oblivion. There are people who love that sort of blaze. Watching someone flame out before their very eyes? It's timeless theater. And I don't want that ever to happen to you, Carmen. I don't want that ever to happen to either of you."

Carmen sipped her coffee. She supposed if anyone had secrets it was Reggie, and if anyone knew what it was like to have people both adore you and want to see you incinerated, it was Katie.

"Jean suggested that we bring a writer and a photographer on the safari—or at least a photographer—from one of the tabloids or magazines," Katie said. "Thank you for taking my side and vetoing the idea, Reggie."

He shrugged. "Jean is very, very smart, and it was a well-intentioned suggestion. But I just felt it crossed a line. We want our Hollywood stars to lead glamorous lives, but a little ostentatiousness goes a long way. It can be off-putting. The photos from the wedding will suffice."

"And I do want us to have our privacy. The trip is for my closest friends and family. That's all," Katie said. She patted Carmen's knee and squeezed it through her slacks. Then she turned back to Reggie and added, "Besides, you'll be there. No one's going to burn to a billion cinders or disappear into oblivion as long as you're around."

. . .

Carmen recalled that meeting in Reggie's office and thought once again of the movie *The Vikings* and the funeral pyre that consumed the Kirk Douglas character, and considered leaving Reggie's body right where it sat against the trunk of the baobab tree. She would surround it with kindling and brush, too, because that might be a more decent way to dispose of the corpse than allowing it to be devoured slowly by vultures or more quickly by jackals. But she wasn't sure that she could create a fire hot enough for cremation or (if she could) watch her friend burn, and so she dragged the body to the acacia. She held his good hand and his good wrist on his good arm, the one that had not been mauled by the hyena, and pulled him across the dust and the grass, around the anthills—and they really were hills here in Africa, she observed, they were like the stumps of great trees—and over animal scat. She kept the rifle slung over her shoulder. It took forty minutes, and she was not merely exhausted by the effort, she was in pain: her hands were blushing red, and the sunburn was starting to blister on her right forearm. She felt the eyes of myriad animals upon her, including the impalas that paused from their feeding, more curious about her than suspicious of her. When, at one point, she dropped Reggie to catch her breath and allow her back a respite, she had a staring contest with the antelope she supposed was the alpha male. The head of the herd. Or harem. That was what Muema had taught her you called a cluster of impalas. A harem. She lost the contest.

When she reached the acacia, she studied her sunburn, and she recalled the one that Felix had told her about soon after they met—the one he had gotten on his back after his sister, Olivia, had died in the car accident. The first time she had given Felix a back rub in bed, she had noticed the small scars that remained.

The sun was dead overhead now. She sat down beneath the acacia to rest and thought how easily she could fall asleep here. But she didn't dare. One foot in front of the other. She reached into Reggie's pants pocket for his wallet and took out all the paper money and traveler's checks that he had.

And then she trudged back to the baobab, trying to remain alert because now the impalas were gone and that might mean something. A predator was stalking them. She had gone no more than fifty yards when she saw the vultures lift off and glide over her head toward the acacia. Of course. They would feed on the dead publicist—a man who'd survived Okinawa, one of the most dangerous places on the planet, and Hollywood, one of the most toxic—while she was incinerating the tree that had saved her life last night.

At the baobab, she retrieved the pack with the antiseptic and the aspirin, and everything else that Reggie had salvaged from the wrecked Land Rover. She carried it thirty or so yards from the tree, what she supposed would be a safe distance from the baobab after she had turned it into a gigantic tiki torch. A flare. But she honestly had no idea what a safe distance was: the grass was dry. For all she knew, she'd scorch acres and acres of savanna and immolate herself. The fire might spread all the way to the acacia.

Still, this was her shot.

She looked at the ashes from the little fire that Reggie had started last night. She wanted something much, much bigger. She wanted a conflagration.

Shadows of more birds passing overhead dotted the savanna and there was a faint breeze now. She yanked up grass and foraged for twigs. She reached for the baobab's lower branches and tugged from the tree the ones that she could. She snapped the medium boughs into small ones. She peeled off some pieces of bark so small that probably they were worthless, and scraped off others that might help start the blaze. She made piles and teepees around the trunk. Then she looked at the paper and cardboard she had. It wasn't a lot: mostly bandages and gauze and the box that had held the Germolene tube, and the label on the bottle of Bayer aspirin. There was Reggie's money and his traveler's checks. It was why she had taken them. But it was all the paper she had been able to round up, and so it would have to do. She found nothing in the pack that might work as an accelerant.

She placed the papers and the bills in a ring beneath her mounds of grass and brush and twigs. Then she took the lighter and ran the flame along the bottom, walking stooped over in a circle around the base of the baobab.

It smoked and the paper blackened and curled, all of it more slowly than newspaper would: the cardboard was thick, the Band-Aids had a plastic coating, and money was, well, money. She had no idea why money burned slowly because she'd never tried to set fire to a bill before. But, as she'd feared, it sure as hell wasn't igniting.

Still, the whole circle was smoldering. And there was a breeze, she thought, and that was encouraging.

For a long moment, she held the lighter flame under a section that had a particularly high and airy patch of pulled grass, staring into it, and that was when she felt the gust on the back of her neck and the fire began to rise up along the circle of brush she had built around the baobab. She backed away and watched, barely daring to hope. But the lowest protrusions of bark and dangling, stalactite-like branches started to burn. In a moment, the flames were singeing the section of trunk where she and Reggie had fought off the hyenas and then licking the bottom of the thick and sturdy branch where she had spent the night.

She knew that fire climbed, and this blaze was definitely climbing.

She felt a ripple of pride, but also anxiety. Was this all that was going to happen? Was this it?

But then, with a burst so concussive that she fell back on the ground, the tree exploded into flame. It was an inferno, bright yellow at its base, the smoke belching into a tall column that curlicued high into the air before the wind currents propelled it south. It was all she could have hoped for, and now she stood and walked backward toward the acacia and Reggie and the vultures, never taking her eyes off the baobab. She was actually a little awed.

As she neared the tree, the birds scattered, settling to wait patiently no more than a few dozen yards away. She lowered herself into the dry grass. The vultures had started to pick at Reggie's face, and when she saw that parts of his cheeks were already gone, she looked away and vowed never to look back. She'd gaze instead at the baobab, her own burning bush, or she'd close her eyes, which she did.

Because her eyes had grown heavy in the heat. The sun was bright, even beneath the acacia, and it was easier to close them. She told herself that if she got her miracle—a plane saw the smoke or the fire and circled around to take a look—she would hear it.

Which she did.

She had lost track of time and honestly didn't know if it had been fifteen minutes or thirty. Perhaps it had been an hour.

The noise was a dull buzz at first that could have been an insect. But it grew into the rhythmic whirr of an engine, and so she opened her eyes and there it was. A plane. Mostly white, but some red striping on the tail and the fuselage. Maybe it was big enough for two people and maybe four. Perhaps even six. She had no idea. But it had a propeller at the nose and three land-ing wheels, and so she ran out into the open between the acacia and the baobab, which was almost burned out, and she shouted "Here!" and cried out for help, waving her arms, and then—and the sight caused her to howl in anguish in the blistering heat, "No, no, no!"—the plane continued to the south. It hadn't seen her. It was leaving.

But then it banked, dipping its left wing. It was circling back around, after all, and she collapsed onto her knees, sobbing, as the noise grew louder and the plane grew bigger as it descended. Then, with barely a bounce, it landed on the hard, flat grass between the burning baobab and the acacia and rolled to a stop.

CHAPTER TWENTY-NINE

Benjamin Kikwete

The Belgian paratroopers were dropped from American C-130 air-planes, and after securing the airfield at Stanleyville, battled their way to the Victoria Hotel. The house-to-house fighting against the Simba rebels was arduous and bloody, and as the Belgian soldiers neared the hotel, the rebel leaders marched their American and Belgian hostages into the streets and began to execute them.

—Los Angeles Times, NOVEMBER 25, 1964

The lorry stopped, and one of the Russians climbed from the front of the truck and peed into the nearby brush. It was mid-morning and the sun had burned off the morning fog, and the chill air of dawn was already a distant memory. They'd spent the night in the back of the vehicle, and Benjamin was surprised that he had nodded off for a couple of hours despite the way his hands were bound and the metal pressed hard against his spine no matter how he tried to position himself.

The Russian had left the door open, and Benjamin could hear the vehicle's radio. Not the walkie-talkie radios that the guides sometimes used to tell one another about a sighting or a road that had flooded out, but the radio that—depending upon the weather and where you were in the reserve—might pick up some music or news out of Nairobi or Arusha. The Russians were listening in this case to news, and discreetly Benjamin nudged Muema. He wanted him to hear this too. It was an

English-language station out of Kenya, and it sounded like the fighting in Stanleyville had escalated: Belgian soldiers were on the ground and there was fighting in the streets. But it was clear that the Simbas were losing.

In the distance, he heard an engine. Maybe more than one. The noise wasn't loud enough to drown out the truck radio, but it was real and the Russian who was guarding them stood up and squinted as he stared into the dust. The one who'd been relieving himself near the thorn brush zipped up, and Benjamin noticed that he switched off the safety of his assault rifle as he returned to the side of the lorry. The driver opened his door and stood on the step, his palms on the roof of the cab, and peered into the distance. Then he lifted one hand off the metal, which Benjamin knew was scorching, and used his fingers like a visor against the sun.

Approaching them were two vehicles, blurred by the waves of heat that rose up from the savanna like gauze.

"Rangers," Muema murmured. "Or soldiers."

The Russian who was returning from the brush started yelling at his comrades, and the driver responded with shouts of his own. The driver clearly didn't believe a truck full of hostages could outrun the jeeps, but the one in charge wanted them moving, and moving now. He jumped into the back with the captives, and the driver reluctantly ducked into the cab and slammed the door.

And they were off, racing down the dirt track road, going faster than they ever had, and the men in the back were jostled so badly that it crossed Benjamin's mind that some of them would be tossed accidentally over the side and, because their wrists were bound, perhaps break their necks when they landed hard on the ground. They passed a herd of buffaloes and a lone running ostrich—though it took them time to overtake the massive bird—but Benjamin kept looking back at the vehicles that were chasing them. The pair was gaining, narrowing the gap slowly but inexorably. And the Russians in the back with them could

see this, too. Eventually their pursuers would be within shooting range, and Benjamin knew who would fire first. The Russians were both at the lorry's back gate, their attention divided
between their hostages and the jeeps that were pursuing them.
They would have the first and the best shot. They might have
the only shots. Would those rangers or soldiers even fire at the
truck and risk injuring the hostages?

Nevertheless, those jeeps might represent rescue. Deliverance.

Assuming, Benjamin thought, that we survive the firefight.

.   .   .

Benjamin had been on a safari with Charlie Patton in which
one of the cooks was a Tutsi refugee from Rwanda. Easily 130,000
Tutsis had left Rwanda after the Hutu revolution of 1962. The
cook was in his early twenties, older than Benjamin, and he was
angry and intense and told Benjamin that he never expected to
return to his home country. In January 1964, however, Benjamin learned that the fellow did, in fact, go back. One time. He
saw the cook's name in the newspaper one morning in the lobby
of the Nairobi hotel before they all set out once again, as they
stood surrounded by the safari guests' suitcases and trunks and
valises. The cook had been among a group of a few hundred
men who'd crept across the border into Rwanda with bows and
arrows, and managed to seize considerably more deadly weapons
from a military outpost. They stole some vehicles and drove to
Kigali, the capital city, planning to incite a rebellion.

They didn't. Instead, almost every single one of them was
slaughtered, including the cook.

Muema and Charlie had read the same story and recognized
the name, too.

"He should have stayed here," Muema observed. "He should
have stayed with us."

"He was a good man and a good cook," Charlie agreed.

The Rwandan president, a Hutu, had used the "invasion"

to round up Tutsi terrorists and execute many of the remaining Tutsi political leaders.

"An African Bay of Pigs," Muema had called the attempted insurrection, and then explained to Benjamin what he had meant.

"In Tanganyika there are, what, a hundred tribes?" Charlie had asked the guide. It was a rhetorical question; he knew the answer.

"Closer to one hundred and twenty."

The hunter nodded. "And here in Kenya, there's another forty. But, somehow, you've all been spared the madness of Rwanda and the Congo," said Charlie.

"Why is that?" Benjamin asked.

Charlie was smoking a cigarette and stared for a moment at the black and white cylinder of ash at the tip, before tapping it into a standing ashtray. "Damned if I know. Might be as simple as the fact most everyone in Tanganyika speaks Swahili. So, you have that in common. But there's probably more to it. A lot more. Look at Ireland. The Catholics and the Protestants speak, more or less, the same language and read the same Bible, and still can't go very long without a pretty nasty brawl."

"As long as the Russians and Americans leave us alone, Tanganyika will be fine and Kenya will be fine," Muema said.

"Oh, they won't leave us alone," Charlie told him. "If the Americans are willing to go to the other side of the world to fuck around in Vietnam—and it seems that they are—and the Russians were willing to risk blowing up the planet over Cuba, I wouldn't suppose Africa is safe. They won't send whole armies. At least I don't think so. That's the good news. They'll send more advisers and more spies and more captains of industry. But the Congo or Kenya? Any place that has natural resources? This continent is like a wounded gazelle with hyenas on one side and jackals on the other."

Muema tossed the newspaper onto a high wooden table made of black wood with elephants carved into the edging. He smiled at Charlie and said to Benjamin, "I'm glad our work depends on zebras and wildebeest—a different kind of natural resource from coffee or gold."

"Or uranium," said Charlie.

"Right. Or uranium."

"Tell me something, Muema," Charlie asked.

Muema raised an eyebrow, waiting.

"Do you believe the stories of slave labor and illegal mining in the Congo?"

"I do. In the rebel provinces? Absolutely."

Charlie nodded. "Me too."

Two more of the safari's guests were coming down the stairs, sisters from Chicago whose family had something to do with beef. Their husbands were already outside on the street photographing the hotel facade for posterity.

Charlie sighed. "I've dealt with Russians and I've dealt with Americans," he went on. "I will admit to God and camp cook alike with the same candor: they all scare me a hell of a lot more than pissed-off rhinos and ornery lions."

"Why?" Benjamin asked. The two older men stared at him. Was the answer really so obvious that he should have known it?

"The rhinos know we're a threat, and the lions have learned we can be very risky prey," Muema said, with that lovely professorial lilt to this voice. "But to the Russians and Americans? We're just pawns on the chess board. Harmless and expendable."

.   .   .

One of the Russians worked his way through the hostages, up the center of the cargo bed of the rumbling lorry, and pounded on the roof of the cab. He barked something at the driver, and the truck squealed to a stop, kicking up dust and sending the hostages spilling into each other. The driver jumped out with a rifle and hopped into the back with his two comrades as the jeeps closed ground and then abruptly came to a halt too. They were, Benjamin guessed, no more than twenty-five meters away.

For a full minute, nobody moved and nobody said a word. The sun was blistering.

Eventually, a jeep door opened, and instantly one of the Russians unleashed a short volley of gunfire that punched holes in the metal and shattered the glass window. But whoever was inside was undaunted. He had a bullhorn and yelled from inside the vehicle that they needed to drop their weapons and surrender. The driver poked one of the young porters with the tip of his gun and ordered him to stand. Reluctantly, he did, the fear evident in the way his eyes were darting around him, and the Russian prodded him to the rear of the cargo bed so the men in the jeeps could see him.

"We have eleven more just like him!" the one who was in charge yelled back at the jeeps. Then, his own rifle slung over his shoulder, he took his pistol and shot the porter in the side of the head, pushing the body over the lorry's rear gate and onto the ground before the dead man's legs could collapse at the knees. "Back off now, or we'll kill another!" he shouted.

Benjamin wiped the sweat off his forehead. He was shaking, but it was rage, not fear. He hadn't known the porter before this safari, but they were roughly the same age. He'd grown up in Kenya and gotten the job with Charlie Patton because his grandfather and Juma were friends, and because he had astonishing eyesight. He was hoping to train someday to be a guide, too: to point out the tiniest of birds in the whistling thorns and the cheetah sitting in wait in the far distance.

When the jeeps remained where they were, when there was no sign of withdrawal, the Russian pointed at Muema. "Bring me the guide."

When Muema refused to stand, the guard grabbed him by the front of his shirt with his left hand, pulling him forward, and pressed the tip of the rifle against his chest. "Get up!"

Muema looked at Benjamin, his eyebrows raised in resignation, and nodded goodbye. Then he pressed his bound hands onto the floor of the cargo bay and struggled to his feet. Benjamin could see that the Russian was about to execute the guide, and that was too much for him. Muema was no pawn. And so *this* was the moment, it had without question arrived. Before the guard could shoot Muema, he threw himself into him, knocking both the captor and his captive onto the cargo bed. Benjamin's hands were bound at the wrists, but he used them like a club and brought them down as hard as he could on the Russian's neck.

"Not Muema!" he bellowed, and he was about to shout it again, when the drivers of both jeeps simultaneously gunned their engines and started toward them. The lorry driver, who had an assault rifle, started firing and managed to hit a front tire of one of the vehicles, and it skidded to a stop. But the other kept coming, even after the front windshield was obliterated, and then it was upon them, and all around Benjamin there was rifle fire.

And then he felt as if he had been hit in the upper back with a rock. It was like that time when he'd been a boy and he and some of his cousins were swimming in the river, and a few had been skimming stones. He'd emerged from underwater exactly when one of the rocks was careening along the surface—the cousin hadn't realized that Benjamin was about to pop up right there, that very spot—and the rock had hit him just below his shoulder blade. But then Benjamin saw the blood puddling beneath him, on the Russian's shirt and neck, and he knew. He knew. His blood was dripping from his own chest onto the man, and it was as this realization was dawning that he felt a deep and awful burning behind his ribs and suddenly it was hard to breathe. The Russian pushed him away, tossing him aside as if he were but a dead little dik-dik, and crawled to his knees, just behind the rear cargo door.

And then there was a pop and he toppled over beside Benjamin. Shot, too.

Their eyes met for the briefest of seconds, but then the Russian was gone.

Benjamin saw that Muema was looking down at him and the captives were all on their feet, and over the guide's shoulder he saw three Black soldiers climbing into the lorry and the two surviving Russians dropping their rifles and surrendering. Muema looked away from him, shouting at the soldiers that they'd hit one of the hostages, and he was furious, but then he turned back to Benjamin and Benjamin was grateful. He wanted to see Muema's face, those kind, penetrating eyes. The guide was speaking softly now, telling him that he was going to be okay, to stay strong, they'd send a plane for him. He tried to hang on to Muema's calm voice because it was reassuring and he was scared, so very, very scared. The guide was thanking him, and Benjamin wanted to tell him he was welcome but he had to do it, he had chosen his moment. But he couldn't speak. In the sky, which mostly was blue, he saw a trio of birds and a candelabra-shaped cloud that reminded him of the euphonium tree. Euphonium sap could blind you; it blistered the skin. And so the idea that the birds—he thought they were hoopoes, but it was all growing dim, or maybe he was squinting—were avoiding that cloud made all the sense in the world. Yes, he was squinting, he told himself. That was it. He should squint. You never stared into a sky so bright with sun. So, he gave in and closed his eyes completely, even if closing them meant, he had come to understand, that he was never going to tell his father he had met Terrance Dutton, and the great Black actor had wanted him—Benjamin!—to call him by his first name, and the regret was as deep and devastating as the physical pain. But the sun felt good on his face, and he listened to Muema until the voice was gone and the world was dark and he was no longer frightened at all.

CHAPTER THIRTY

Billy Stepanov

The majority of physicians and nurses in the study said they felt anxiety (64.2%), stress (72.5%), and depression (51.3%). William Stepanov, a West Hollywood–based psychologist who has doctors among his clients, said, "They all had parents who lived through the flu pandemic of 1918–1919 or were children themselves at the time. And so while 1957 might not have been as dire as its predecessor after the First World War, they knew this flu was killing tens of thousands of people in America. Some just wanted to curl up in bed or hide in a closet."

—The American Journal of Psychiatry, APRIL 1962

Cooper, the Russian, wasn't going to die. At least not right away. Maybe he would if they were out here for days—an infection, Billy supposed—but Katie had now finished wrapping his hand in all the gauze they had found in the Land Rover's medical kit, and the bleeding had stopped. But, hell, all three of them would die if they were out here a few days.

It was the damnedest thing, and Billy was trying hard to decide what he was feeling as he leaned against the grille of the Land Rover: part of him just wanted to shoot the bastard and be done with it. Throw the body beside his two dead comrades, which already were covered with insects, and let the animals here rip the flesh from the bones. But another part of him wanted Cooper alive because he just couldn't bear to see another corpse or, arguably, to shoulder another corpse on his conscience. He thought of the doctors and nurses who were part of his practice and had been on the front lines of the flu pandemic of 1957. He'd been interviewed by a young UCLA grad student who was among a group studying depression in ER doctors and nurses, because Billy had opened his practice that very year and was quoted in a *Los Angeles Times* article as saying that he was surprised by the disproportionately large number of doctors and nurses he had among his patients, and suggested the pandemic was among the reasons why. A third of his practice was made up of people who worked in the movies, but at least another third were people who worked in health care. The flu was not a pretty way to die. But then, there really weren't pretty ways to die, unless you were granted that rarest of miracles and died in your sleep. Usually, all you could hope for was fast. Fast and unexpected.

His father in that cab. His grandfathers' heart attacks: they'd both gone the same way.

David Hill. Terrance Dutton.

When Katie had stopped weeping over Terrance's body, he had dragged the dead actor into the vehicle and sat him upright in the second row, which at the moment was in the shade. It wouldn't be soon.

God, had he ever been around so much death? He thought of Reggie Stout. Now there was a guy who'd seen carnage. He thought of some of his clients, especially three who worked in hospitals and emergency rooms.

It had all happened so fast today. He and Terrance had rushed at Glenn, and the Russian had gotten off the single burst that had, essentially, unzipped the actor from the base of his neck to his navel. But he had only just barely had time to fire. Billy had reached him, and the attack had caught him so spectacularly unprepared that Billy had managed to get his hands on the assault rifle. He hadn't been able to wrest it from his captor's grasp, but at some point in the scuffle the barrel had wound up facing the sky and when it had gone off—when, Billy believed, he himself had squeezed the trigger—the sight had been just under the son of a bitch's chin. He honestly had no idea how many bullets had entered and exited the man's skull, but he had found bone fragments in even his front shirt pocket. They had rained on his face like hail. The firing was brief but booming, so loud that for a second or two he had thought he himself had been wounded. Afterward, he had wiped most of the dead man's blood and brains from his cheek and his chin with his shirttails, but pulpy remnants of the Russian still coated parts of his hair as if squeezed from a tube.

He hadn't told his sister yet that her husband was dead. That it might have been the very Russian whose hand she had bandaged and bound who had shot David. He hadn't told her that he'd concluded his own wife had likely perished too. If he could get a moment alone with the guy (no, he *would* get a moment alone with him), he would make it clear that he'd shoot him without hesitation if he ever offered Katie even the slightest hint that he'd murdered David. Billy feared, based on the way that Katie had collapsed upon the body of her friend, that the news her husband was gone as well might be too much for her. Yes, she had rallied: she seemed better now. Stunned, but not incapacitated. Mostly exhausted. But the fact they'd killed David just might put her over the edge.

He saw Katie was standing, leaving Cooper seated in the grass. She tucked into her belt one of the other Russians' pistols. Much to Billy's astonishment, a few dozen wildebeest appeared about a hundred yards away and were grazing rather placidly. They didn't seem to care that a few minutes ago their world had exploded with gunfire. His sister walked over to him slowly and stood beside him for a long moment, and the siblings watched the animals, though Billy kept glancing back at Cooper. Or whatever the fuck his name was.

"Well, this safari sure as hell went to pot," she said dryly. "Remind me never to use that travel agent again."

She had said it to elicit at least a small smile from him, and so he obliged. He wiped at the sweat that was dribbling down the temples on both sides of his skull. He understood why she was capable of making a joke, bad as it was: they were no longer in danger from their kidnappers. At least immediate danger. Imminent danger. He didn't know where the other Russians were, but they weren't here now, and so he felt as well his sister's relief.

"Can I ask you something?" he said.

"Of course."

"You and Terrance. Before David moved out to L.A. and you two reconnected, were you and Terrance ever lovers? I mean, I know you weren't publicly. But the two of you—"

"I know. There was a chemistry. Off-screen, too."

"But . . ."

"But we never wanted to screw up our friendship. And, in some ways, the fact there was always a slow burn between us made us even closer. And . . ." She gazed for a moment into the Land Rover.

"Go on."

"A romance? It would have cost him work. We all know that."

"You, too."

She turned away from the vehicle and slapped ferociously at a mosquito on her arm. Then she flicked the dead insect into the grass. "But it was mostly just the idea that we were better as friends."

"I'm really sorry, Katie," he mumbled.

"It's not your fault. If this nightmare is anyone's fault, it's mine. I'm the one who brought you all here."

"You know that's ridiculous. It's not your fault at all."

"We should have stayed in Paris. All of us. Just continued the party there."

He thought of the airport outside Paris where they had mustered, which immediately made him think of planes. God, if a fortune teller had told him two weeks ago how much death loomed in his life, he would have nodded and thought to himself, "Fucking Pan Am clipper crashing into the ocean." We know nothing of what's coming. Just . . . nothing.

"David wants giraffes at the ranch," she was saying. "I mean, not really. But I think they're his new favorite animal."

David wants . . .

The two words made him cringe. Present tense. He considered whether he was making a mistake not telling her the truth right now. Perhaps he was overestimating her fragility and he should just rip off the Band-Aid. But before he could decide, she was asking, "How long do you think it will be until someone finds us?"

He understood it was a rhetorical question. "You're supposing someone knows we're missing," he replied.

She motioned with her head toward Cooper. "I know they put in their ransom demands."

"How?"

"This morning he took that picture of me. The Polaroid. Someone's driving it to . . . wherever. He said that whoever he was dealing with was . . . he said the negotiations were getting contentious."

"Well, in that case, let's find out who knows we're out here."

"Think he'll tell us?"

"At this point? I don't see why he wouldn't."

Together they walked back to him. He was seated in the shade of their shadows, and Billy felt unexpectedly powerful as they stood over him. It was the combination of his height and the fact they both had guns.

"Your name isn't really Cooper," he began. "Obviously."

The fellow was sweating, and Billy couldn't decide whether it was more from the sun or the pain. There had been some aspirin in the medical kit and Katie had given him a couple tablets, but Billy assumed it barely took the edge off the agony that accompanied getting a sizable part of your hand shot away. Nevertheless, Billy didn't let down his guard: the guy was dangerous. How many stories had Charlie Patton told them about wounded animals charging well-armed humans the moment they relaxed?

"No," he said, and he winced. "Obviously."

"What is it really?"

"Does it matter?"

"It does."

He closed his eyes and shook his head. Billy had spent countless hours with patients, fossicking through their facial expressions to try to understand the depth of their emotional pain. This was physical pain. The aspirin hadn't done a damn thing. He considered not pressing, but then the fellow raised up his lids and there were those stunning blue eyes, and he said, "Colonel Viktor Procenko. But you're wrong, it doesn't matter. Either my boys get here first and they kill you. Or the rangers or soldiers get here first and they kill me."

"The rangers won't kill you. They'll arrest—"

"If they get here first, I'll make sure they kill me. Or you do. I'd rather die fast out here than rot in a jail in Dar es Salaam, waiting to be executed."

There it was, the universal: *die fast*. Live long. But die fast.

"They'd let you die? The Soviet Union?"

"They would deny their involvement in . . . this."

"Are you KGB and working with the Simbas?" Katie pressed. "Did you kidnap us for weapons?"

He nodded. "Money for weapons, to be precise. Though to most of the world, it just looked like an old-fashioned kidnapping where all that mattered was the money. A lot of money. Nine Americans from Hollywood, including the world's biggest movie star and the son of a CIA officer who works in MK-ULTRA? You have no idea how much more valuable your lives are than most people's. It's . . . it's shameful. But your value, Katie Stepanov? That was the point."

"Who did you ask?" Katie asked.

"For the money? Your lawyer. Your studio. And a third block

from the Kenyan government for their citizens. The money is—
or was—going to be delivered to Albertville."

"In the Congo?"

He nodded. "A cement factory. Where there was some fighting in August. And then the Simbas could buy what they needed
from the right brokers. The right arms dealers."

"If my husband has such value, why didn't you ask the
American government for the ransom?"

He rolled his eyes at her naivete. "Oh, we couldn't allow
the CIA to know what we know about your husband's father. If
they did? Overwhelming force, casualties be damned, to stop us
from bringing your David Hill to Moscow. He would have been
quite a prize. They would have killed him, if need be. Just like
they killed Frank Olson." He smirked. "The man who knew
too much. Wasn't that the name of a movie?" He asked the question playfully because he knew the answer. "Your father-in-law
was there, you know—when they tossed Frank Olson out the
window."

Billy had no idea who that was, but he could see on Katie's
face that she did. He started to ask, but Katie had a question.
"Did you read about my safari in the newspapers?" she asked. "Is
that where you got this idea? Or did Charlie Patton tell you we
were coming?"

Procenko grimaced again, but then offered the smallest of
smiles. "Charlie Patton was an idiot. He had nothing to do
with it."

"Then whose idea was it?"

He looked down at the ball of gauze on his hand, then up
into the sun. He seemed to be craving its warmth on his face.

"Whose idea was it?" she asked again, raising her voice for
the first time. "Tell me."

"It was my sister's. But it was one of you greedy Americans
with two faces who made it happen. One of your . . . guests. You
all think you're so much better than Russians. You're not. Your
corruption knows no bounds."

Billy's mind was making an inventory of the safari entourage as the guy spoke, and as if his mind were a roulette wheel with names instead of numbers, he knew instantly where the ball was going to land. If Procenko hadn't that moment revealed the source aloud, Billy might have told him to shut up, to not say another word, but it was too late.

"My sister is that renowned defector you all love so much in the United States. Nina Procenko."

"The artist? The one who had the painting in David's gallery?" said Katie.

Procenko nodded. "Small world, right? But really, it's not. The defection was faked. She does a lot of good work. And David? One assignment. And so easy to compromise as the son of a CIA officer. They had sex, you know. My sister and your husband. You weren't engaged yet. You were just starting to date. But that's where she got the idea to set him up. I haven't seen the pictures of him with our diner girl, and I don't need to. But they were enough. Because then you were engaged. At the beginning, Nina thought we'd only use him to get to his father and learn more about MK-ULTRA. But then we heard about this safari. And given how much money David owes everyone, it wasn't hard to convince him to help us with the kidnapping—after we showed him the photos. We even told him he'd get a cut of the ransom, because he didn't want to come to you, Katie Stepanov, with his hat in his hand. Not after he fucked our waitress. It was all very, very simple." He shrugged his shoulders. "Now, he wanted a safe kidnapping. A pretend kidnapping. A night. Two at most. Keep everyone comfortable. Nina and I said fine. Of course! But I don't pretend. I'm not an"—and he said the next word with robust condescension—"*actor*. I don't play games. He was never going home. How could he? He knew too much about Nina and me and the kidnapping. Besides, we wanted to bring him to Moscow. But he did something stupid."

"Tell me."

"He grabbed a gun. So, we killed him."

"You yourself?" asked Katie, her tone eerily monochromatic.

Procenko looked her right in the eye and said, "Me. Myself. I was the one who put the bullet in his head."

Which was when Billy's own sister saved Billy the guilt of carrying on his back for the rest of his life another dead man, and at point-blank range shot Viktor Procenko in the chest.

CHAPTER THIRTY-ONE

Carmen Tedesco

*Among the survivors of the ill-fated safari was Carmen Tedesco,
whose husband, screenwriter Felix Demeter—son of legendary
movie director Rex Demeter—died while struggling with one of the
Russian captors. "We were all out of our element," the actress said
from her hotel in Nairobi. "This wasn't a film set with blanks in the
guns or an Ernest Hemingway short story. And so what Felix did?
It was the bravest thing I've ever seen."*
—Los Angeles Times, NOVEMBER 26, 1964

She ran to the plane, her legs churning, and as the pilot climbed
out and she saw that he was white and he wasn't wearing a
uniform—khakis and a moss-colored shooting shirt, the quilted
pad against the right shoulder obvious even at a distance—the
idea crossed her mind that perhaps this wasn't part of a search and
rescue team, and he was among the group that had kidnapped
them. But then, right behind him, came two Black rangers in
their cocoa-colored uniforms, rifles slung over their shoulders,
and following them . . . Charlie Patton. At least she thought it
was Charlie. Perhaps she was mistaken. And so she slowed to a
jog, but they continued to sprint toward her, all four of them,
and when she saw it really was the hunter, she fell into his arms,
weeping because she wasn't going to die out here after all.

He patted her back as one of the rangers pulled a list from his front shirt pocket and asked Charlie, "You had three women on the safari. Is this one—"

"It's Carmen," Charlie told him. "It's Carmen Tedesco."

The rangers were roughly her age, though one, who was tall and heavyset and wearing a sunhat that looked a little small for him, was clearly more senior. He was holding the paper with Charlie Patton's manifest.

She pushed herself free of the hunter, sniffed, and still had to wipe her nose on her sleeve. "God. I thought . . ." *I thought I was going to die out here* was how she had planned to finish the sentence, but the words caught in her throat.

"You thought what?" Charlie asked.

She gathered herself and stood a little taller. "I must be pretty damn ripe," she said, trying to make a small joke.

"Your eye," he began, but she waved him off.

"It's not the eye itself. At least I don't think it is. It's just the swelling."

"Okay."

"I guess I should be relieved you're not with *Movie Star Confidential.*"

"For a lot of reasons," the hunter said. "But not because of your eye."

The shorter of the two rangers reminded them, "We have water in the plane. I'll get some." Then he jogged back to the aircraft.

The pilot had taken off his sunglasses and was surveying what was left of the baobab, his hands behind his back. The flames were dwindling now. "Nice work on the tree," he said. His accent was British. "At least I'm guessing it was you who turned it into a flare."

She nodded sheepishly.

"Carmen, this is Jack Chamberlin," said Charlie. "Jack, meet movie star Carmen Tedesco." The pilot gave her a small bow but kept his fingers entwined behind him.

"Are you alone out here?" Charlie asked.

She pointed at the acacia, where the vultures had returned to feast on Reggie Stout. "Reggie was with me," she said, and her voice cracked when she said the publicist's name.

The ranger took his rifle, planted the butt against his shoulder, and fired two quick shots in succession into the ground near the birds. They scattered instantly, flying up and around the acacia.

"When did he die?"

"A few hours ago. This morning."

"And you're sure he's dead?"

Jack Chamberlin, the pilot, brought his hands from behind his back, put on his sunglasses, and said, "Jesus Christ, Charlie, your eyesight isn't what it once was. The son of a bitch is half eaten. I think Carmen can be sure."

"What happened?"

The other ranger returned with a canteen of water and she drank so ravenously that she coughed up great swallows. She gave him back the canteen and bent over with her hands on her knees. "God, I'm a mess," she murmured. "I can't even drink like a human."

"Seriously, Carmen: what happened?"

And so she told him about how she and Reggie and Felix had managed to overwhelm their two captors—she told them how she had used her scarf to strangle one—but they'd crashed the Land Rover in the process, and Felix had been shot dead in the struggle for one of the rifles. She explained that her injuries were from the accident and she and Reggie had walked—limped, in Reggie's case—to their current location, trying to stay ahead of their kidnappers, and how they had fought off hyenas last night and the publicist had died in the morning from his wounds.

"Did he have a family?" asked the ranger with the manifest.

She told him he didn't, at least not a wife or any children. But then she added, a reflex of sorts, "We were his family. His actors and actresses. He would have done anything for us. And, in my case, he did."

The taller of the rangers nodded at the body beneath the acacia. "Let's go get him," he said, and the pilot and the second ranger trudged across the savanna to the tree.

"I thought you were probably dead," Carmen told Charlie. "I hoped you were with one of the other groups. But I feared they'd killed you when they came to the camp. The Russians."

He reached into his pants pocket and pulled out a pack of cigarettes and a lighter. He offered her one, but she passed. "Is there any food in the plane?" she asked.

"Some biscuits."

"I'd rather have that than a cigarette," she told him, and the two of them started toward the aircraft. He lit a cigarette for himself.

"Seriously, Charlie, how did you get away? What happened?" she asked.

They weren't looking at each other as they walked. They stared straight ahead at the red and white plane and the hills that rolled like waves in the distance. When Charlie began to speak, she wondered if he would have said something else if he'd had to look her in the eye. She guessed it would have been at least a slightly different story.

"I saw Viktor Procenko right away," he began, and he told her about their history together. "I'd heard a rumor he was working with the Simbas, and so I knew that whatever was about to happen . . . it would be nasty. I tried to get to my tent for my gun."

She didn't completely believe him: she had a feeling he'd run. But she walked and nodded and remained silent.

"But the shooting started, and someone was already in my tent. Or going into my tent. And so I laid low in the grass, watching and waiting for the right moment."

The right moment to flee, she thought. But thank God he had fled. She'd likely be dead before sunrise tomorrow if, in the end, Charlie Patton hadn't been a coward with a code of honor as brittle as carbon paper. So, she sure as hell wasn't going to call him out. "Thank God, you found that right moment," she said.

"I saw them taking you all away. It was heartbreaking. I knew Procenko could be very charming on the surface, but it was all part of his training. I mean, the man had a post for a while in Washington, D.C. He's a colonel. But he is merciless and despicable, and I'm going to guess KGB. So, I feared this wouldn't end well if I didn't get help."

"He didn't look for you? This Russian colonel?" The question had been instinctive, and she wished she hadn't said a word the moment she'd spoken.

"He did. They did . . ."

"And they didn't find you?"

They were at the plane now. "Let me help you in," he said. "It will be a toaster inside, but at least there will be some shade."

She took his hand and climbed the three steps, and then ducked through the snug door. There were six seats, including the pilot's, and she beelined to the side with the shade. She supposed one of the rangers would sit next to the remains of Reggie Stout. Charlie sat in one of the two front seats, both of which had a yoke. She wasn't going to repeat her question—*And they didn't find you?*—because she'd decided it was best to let it go. But he surprised her. He handed her a metal tin of biscuits with the logo of a roaring lion on the front and said, "They thought they did. They saw a leopard dragging away the remains of Peter Merrick. We were dressed alike."

"But—"

"But his head was gone. Mostly. They thought Merrick was already in one of the Land Rovers."

"My God, Peter. A leopard?"

"Yes."

The biscuits were animal crackers. Of course. She swallowed a lion, and suddenly her eyes were welling up again. Felix. Reggie. Now Peter.

"Any sign of the others?"

"Not yet," said Charlie. "But none of them have shown up yet in Albertville. That's where the ransom was supposed to be delivered."

"What does that mean?"

He shrugged. "It could mean a thousand things."

"But everyone else is alive, right? Katie and David and—"

"I don't know," he told her. "I hope so."

She nodded and made the mistake of glancing out the plane window. She saw the rangers and the pilot carrying Reggie's body: one had his legs and two had his arms and upper body. They were moving slowly in the heat. She looked away and finished off an elephant in a single bite, and then closed her eyes with her head in her hands.

Epilogue

Yes, I did go back to work. I was working again by the summer of 1965.

Scott Fitzgerald said there were no second acts, but I don't know if even he believed that. After all, he went to Hollywood, and there is nowhere else in the world where people dream quite so much. I loved my years on the sitcom, and I wouldn't have gotten the role if Rex hadn't cast me first in that movie about the college professor who had a ghost in her house. *Yardley.* That was the name of the ghost and, of course, the movie. That was one of the only comedies Rex ever made, and it wasn't very good. But it did get me cast in the TV series about the world's most inept hospital. I had a great time as Nurse Crocker. (General Mills was a sponsor, but Rachel Crocker was a character before the show had a single advertiser. It's one of those urban legends that my character was named after Betty Crocker as a wink to a corporation.)

Katie didn't do another film, as you know. I don't know what destroyed her more—and we talked about it, we really did—the way she felt responsible for so many people dying, or the way she felt David had betrayed her. She wasn't a recluse, but it was pretty rare for her to appear in the tabloids or fan magazines by, oh, 1970. When I would see her, she never said all that much. I'd do most of the talking. We'd sit around the pool at that really exquisite house of hers and drink this iced tea she loved that came in a jar. Some people thought she was medicated into a stupor or she was living out some strange Norma Desmond reenactment, but she wasn't. She was just the saddest person on the planet.

I mean, even sadder than Billy. Much sadder. At least he remarried. Katie never did and I never did.

For Billy, thank God, the third time really was the charm, although I think he and Margie would have been happy together for many, many years. And he had that bestseller, that self-help book. *The Soul in the Dark*. It was the perfect book for the early seventies, and it was so . . . so honest. So revealing. My God, for a month or two, people actually knew what the word *oubliette* meant. Telling everyone about that coat closet from his childhood? The way his parents treated him and Katie? Wrenching. And, let's face it, the book was the closest thing we'll ever have to a memoir of what happened in the Serengeti, even if it's not precisely about that. He did his homework, that's for sure. For years, the Johnson administration and then the Nixon administration covered up the Russian involvement. I read one book that claimed Nina Procenko was a double agent and worked both sides of the street, and another that said, yes, her defection was fake, but then we really did turn her. Either way, Billy worked hard to get the State Department clearances he needed, which seems insane when you think about what kind of book *The Soul in the Dark* was. But I think it was the first time that a lot of the real reasons for the safari nightmare were ever made public.

Still, it would be another forty years before we'd learn all that nastiness about MK-ULTRA. Do I have the name right? That crazy CIA plan to use LSD to brainwash people. "Mind control." The things that David's father did? The people he dosed and the people he tied up for days in the dark? When the writer of that book about it interviewed Katie, she told him the little that David had told her, but David Hill really didn't know anything. He was . . . he was a child.

Sometimes, I can't believe I'm the only one left. I think back on that night I spent in the baobab, and it's like I'm in a parable or a fairy tale. Some beautiful and complex Maasai fable about the woman who lived a very long time because she burned down the tree that saved her life. Or, perhaps, the tale of the woman who used a tree to save her life—twice. And then killed it.

I don't know.

As I recall, the tree was dead, which was the only reason I was able to set it on fire. At least I hope it was.

But I'm glad you asked. I have visions of the purple sky that night and when I am most fatigued they come to me, unbidden but not as unwelcome as you might suppose. I know there was all that talk about how we christened ourselves the lions of Hollywood, but I really do see myself in my mind as a lioness on that branch. (God, once upon a time they called Katie a lioness. Do you remember? Before he died, Reggie Stout called me that, and I almost wept.) Once more I am witness to that shooting star and I hear myself asking Reggie if he saw it too. Same with the azure sounds of the birds and the resolute snorting of the wildebeest. We all look forward— at least, I suppose, until you get to be my age—but how we see tomorrow is grounded so deeply in what we lived through just yesterday.

And it was only yesterday, wasn't it?

Wasn't it?

—CARMEN TEDESCO,
TRANSCRIPT OF THE LAST RECORDED INTERVIEW.
(THE FULL STORY RAN IN THE
Los Angeles Times, JUNE 21, 2022.)

ACKNOWLEDGMENTS

I went to the Serengeti to research this novel a few months before COVID-19 shut down the planet. I wrote most of this book while sheltering in place in 2020, the Year That Satan Spawned. Telling a story set well over a half century earlier helped keep me sane. But my memories of the Serengeti also encouraged me to remember that while the world in 2020 seemed awash in horror, there also remained great beauty on Earth. My gratitude to my safari guides is immense, because of their encyclopedic knowledge and their endless patience with my questions. (Also? Their humor when my questions would probe just how many ways there are to die in the Serengeti made the interviews as much fun as any I've ever conducted in my life.)

Many of the books that I read for research—though not all—were dated. That was by design, because this novel is set in 1964 and I wanted to immerse myself in that era. Those books included the following:

Charles A. Cabell III and David St. Clair, *Safari: Pan Am's Guide to Hunting with Gun and Camera Round the World*

Harold T. P. Hayes, *The Last Place on Earth*

Adam Hochschild, *Lesson from a Dark Time and Other Essays*

Stephen Kinzer, *Poisoner in Chief: Sidney Gottlieb and the
    CIA Search for Mind Control*
Martin Meredith, *The State of Africa: A History of the
    Continent Since Independence*
Rachel Love Nuwer, *Poached: Inside the Dark World of
    Wildlife Trafficking*
John Pearson, *Wildlife and Safari in Kenya*
Robert Ruark, *Uhuru*
Robert Ruark, *Use Enough Gun*

I also reread stories by Ernest Hemingway and novels by
Chinua Achebe, Joseph Conrad, and Barbara Kingsolver. I
perused copies of *Africana,* a magazine focused on safari tourism,
from the 1960s and early 1970s. I studied the ads as well as the
articles.

Jennifer DaPolito was among many people who gave me
time on their calendars to teach me about Tanzania today, but
she was especially generous, sharing with me articles and essays
and suggesting numerous books.

As always, I want to thank the extraordinary team at Dou-
bleday, Vintage, and Penguin Random House Audio, many of
whom are now some of my closest friends in the world: Kris-
ten Bearse, Jillian Briglia, Maria Carella, Alex Dos Santos,
Todd Doughty, Maris Dyer, John Fontana, Kelly Gildea, Elena
Hershey, Suzanne Herz, Judy Jacoby, Anna Kaufman, Ann
Kingman, Beth Lamb, Lindsay Mandel, James Meader, Nora
Reichard, Paige Smith, William Thomas, David Underwood,
LuAnn Walther, Lauren Weber, and Lori Zook.

I am so grateful to my agents: Deborah Schneider, Jane Gelf-
man, Cathy Gleason, and Penelope Burns at Gelfman/Schneider
ICM; to Brian Lipson at IPG; and to Miriam Feuerle and her
associates at the Lyceum Agency. I can't thank you all enough
for the myriad times you have walked me in off the ledge.

And, of course, there is Jenny Jackson, my brilliant editor
at Doubleday for nearly a decade and a half now, who is utterly

unflappable. Her editorial instincts are always spot-on and she will always fall on her sword for her authors. (She is also, you will see soon, a hell of a novelist in her own right.) This is our ninth book together, and she made each one so much better than it would have been without her counsel.

Finally, as always, I bow before the wisdom and insights of my lovely bride, Victoria Blewer, and our daughter, the always amazing Grace Experience. Victoria has been reading my work since we were eighteen years old, sometimes critiquing meticulously three or four drafts of a book. Grace has been weighing in on my work since she was in high school—and bringing many of my characters to life as one of the best audiobook narrators in the business. She has also become my go-to reader on my stage plays, candidly telling me what's working and what isn't.

I thank you all.

About the Author

CHRIS BOHJALIAN is the #1 *New York Times* bestselling author of twenty-three books, including *Hour of the Witch, The Red Lotus, Midwives,* and *The Flight Attendant,* which is an HBO Max series starring Kaley Cuoco. His other books include *The Guest Room; Close Your Eyes, Hold Hands; The Sandcastle Girls; Skeletons at the Feast;* and *The Double Bind.* His novels *Secrets of Eden, Midwives,* and *Past the Bleachers* were made into movies, and his work has been translated into more than thirty-five languages. His novels have been selections of Oprah's Book Club and the Barnes & Noble Book Club. He is also a playwright (*Wingspan* and *Midwives*). He lives in Vermont and can be found at chrisbohjalian.com or on Facebook, Instagram, Twitter, Litsy, and Goodreads, @chrisbohjalian.